HE'D WRING HER NECK, IF HE COULD JUST GET HIS HANDS ON HER . . .

Morgan could see Shannon moving about in the water. She had stripped off her outer garments and left them carelessly at the water's edge.

"Hawke! Morgan Hawke!" she called. "Come on in. It's just perfectly refreshing!" The thin silk of her petticoat clung to her, translucent in the moonlight. "Don't you want to swim? You look like you could use cooling off!"

Hawke pulled off his shirt. The water was cool as he entered it. He approached her, and his lips found their way to hers with an urgent hunger he had not intended. She swayed against him, her body trembling as her arms encircled his neck. In an easy sweep, he lifted her off her feet and carried her to the beach, cradling her head against his shoulder. His blood raced as she nuzzled her nose in his chest. He spread the voluminous skirt of her discarded gown with his foot and dropped to his knees, tenderly depositing her on it. He watched, mesmerized, as she untied the wet bow of her bodice and opened it. Her skin was white and smooth as the silken shift that soon lay tossed on the sand beside his own clothes.

His hands shook with passion as he explored the contours of her twisting body, skillfully torturing her senses to such a demanding height that she wrapped her arms abo~~~~ ~~~~~ ~~~~~ ~~~~~ ~~~~~ to her, groaning in g~~~~~ ~~~~~ ~~~~~ ~~~~~, sensually, he caresse~~~~ ~~~~~ ~~~~~ ~~~~~e writhed in abandon~~~~ ~~~~~ ~~~~~ ~~~~e ultimate crest of ecsta~~~~~

PIRATE'S WILD EMBRACE

LINDA WINDSOR

ZEBRA BOOKS
KENSINGTON PUBLISHING CORP.

ZEBRA BOOKS

are published by

Kensington Publishing Corp.
475 Park Avenue South
New York, NY 10016

First printing: February, 1990

Printed in the United States of America

Prologue

The Plunderer glided through the sea green waters of the Diego Suarez Bay. Its sleek black hull approached the crippled ship ahead slowly. Although the violent storm of the previous night had shredded her sails and broken the mainmast in half, her twenty guns jutting ominously from her sides caused the captain of the pirate vessel to temper his approach with caution. The East India merchant ships were formidable even when disabled.

Nick Brennan stood on the deck of the pirate ship and estimated the number of seamen topside of the *Lucinda*. He could see through his glass that they were armed and prepared to fight for the booty that made her ride low in the water. He knew that the only reason her fancy uniformed captain held his fire was the British flag flying high above the *Plunderer*'s mast.

He turned his gaze to his own crew. Outlandishly dressed in the costumes belonging to previous victims, they were a colorful and deadly lot. The most able fighters stood near the rail. Each fighter was backed by two men who provided loaded pistols when the ones strapped to their chest had been discharged. Their eyes gleamed with excitement awaiting the moment when the Union Jack above their heads would come down and the Jolly Roger would take its place.

Brennan turned grimly to his quartermaster. "Guns ready!" he called. The command echoed across the deck and down to the gunner below. "Let's show our colors then. Fire!"

The *Plunderer* shook under his feet with the roar of the first round as his men hauled down the British ensign and hoisted the infamous skull and cross-bones. A shout of approval filled the air as their seasoned gunner hit his mark with the canister, wreaking havoc on the merchantman's deck.

"Fire two!" Brennan called out. Another shot like the first and the boarding would be easier, he thought as he observed the uniformed bodies felled by the scattered musket balls fired into their midst. "All right, mates, swing about!" It was necessary to move the *Plunderer* out of range before the merchantman's guns could retaliate.

The pirate vessel swung easily away as the guns erupted from the side of the merchantman. Again Brennan's crew cheered as the shot went over the mainmast harmlessly. In a panic, the opposing gunner had fired on the crest of a swell. A second round quickly followed. Splinters exploded from the foredeck as one of the guns grazed its target. The other shot fell short, splashing into the narrowing span of water between the two ships.

"Close in, lads!" came the order as the roguish captain recognized his chance to board. The enemy's port guns exhausted, the *Plunderer* could breach the distance between them as they swung about and fired her readied starboard guns into the merchantman's gun decks before her gunners could reload. Her prey, disabled by the storm, could do nothing but wait.

Again he scanned the *Lucinda*'s decks with his glass. More men were coming topside to replace their fallen comrades. He turned to his quartermaster and sent orders to divide the fire—canister to the topside and ball to gun deck. As the mate turned to carry out his command, his eye caught a glimpse of rose near the gilded gallery aft of the disabled vessel.

A petite dark-haired woman clung tightly to a well-dressed gentleman's arm and looked in the direction of the pirate ship. Brennan saw the fear on her pale and lovely face. A smile tugged at the corner of his mouth at the prospect that presented itself. The journey to Tangiers to sell their booty promised to be entertaining and the wench would certainly bring a high price.

"Fire!" he bellowed, his giant frame braced for the recoil of the guns below deck. "Ready with the grapnels!"

His men swarmed to the side, armed and ready. Brennan drew his cutlass and rushed to the rail with them. Lines which flew across the water, caught and tightened as the pirates hauled the floating merchantman toward them. Fire from the pistols of the bloodied seamen met them as they swung across the rails and onto the splintered decks of the *Lucinda*. The two crews merged into a violent turmoil as the sound of gunshots and clashing steel filled the air.

Brennan jumped over the fallen body of the young sailor he'd just run through and slashed his way toward the uniformed officers on the deck above the gallery. Smoke drifted up from a hatchway and he cursed. The fight needed to be over quickly, before the fire reached the well-stocked magazine and they all were blown away.

A ball whizzed past his head and splintered a barrel

behind him. The red-haired captain drew his pistol and aimed it at the wide-eyed lieutenant standing by his captain on the deck above. Brennan fired with seemingly little effort and charged up the steps. Blood burst from the young man's chest and he fell lifeless at his superior's feet.

The mechantman's captain threw his discharged pistols to the side and drew his saber to meet the charging giant. It was evident he had no intention of giving in to the attackers. Surrender and possible quarter were out of the question. He met the pirate's charge with a thrust, stepping to the side to avoid his menacing cutlass. To his surprise, the big man twisted nimbly and pivoted to take the offensive again. The thrusts and parries served to warn each of the combatants that they were well matched.

A woman's scream from below broke Brennan's concentration as he ducked a wild slash from the tiring captain. He growled as the tip of the saber nicked his shoulder, ripping the voluminous white linen shirt. He roared as he thrust his cutlass forward, plunging it deep into the older captain's chest.

He watched as the well-dressed gentleman he'd seen earlier brandished a saber with polished form and deftly held off two of his crew. The rest of his crew was slowly but surely overtaking the remaining sailors. No more came up from below, fearing the grenades the pirates had dropped down the hatches to dissuade them.

"Jonathan!"

Again the woman's scream rang out, as the gentleman was overcome by numbers. Brennan snorted and jumped to the deck below. To his surprise, the woman, who had stood in the companionway while her escort fought valiantly to protect her, reached down and seized his discarded weapon. Taking his crew by surprise, she slashed at them wildly. He noticed for the first time the most incredible flashing blue eyes he'd ever seen.

"There now, missy. Me an' the boys, we ain't gonna 'urt you now," his first mate called out to the angered beauty, who had backed them into a semicircle around her.

"Stay back, lads!" Brennan warned, stepping into the small arena. He gazed at the petite figure before him in obvious admiration of her beauty and courage. "Now miss," he said softly, beneath the din of the ongoing fight, "give me your weapon and I promise no harm will come to ye."

"Get back!" she sobbed, hysteria mounting in her voice. She stepped toward him, swinging the saber with both hands. "Don't you come in here!"

Brennan looked past her at the half-opened door leading into the companionway to the cabins. Unconsciously, the woman followed his eyes and in that moment he leaped toward her and knocked the saber from her hand. Disarmed and surprised, she flew at him, raking his face with her nails and pummeling his broad chest. He fought to hold the twisting figure in his arms to the cheers of the men surrounding them when she suddenly jerked and stiffened, her wide blue eyes staring up blankly into his own.

He felt her body go limp against his chest. He moved his hand down her back and felt the sticky wetness of blood spreading through the rose silk. Gently, he lowered her to the deck as his crew watched in stunned silence. As he rose, his eyes narrowed in search of the murderer, but saw from the bewildered look on the men's faces that it was not one of them. A stray bullet had obviously sealed the lady's fate.

In a short time, resistance had ceased. Seeing the deck under control of his crew, Brennan turned his attention to the gallery of cabins. As he walked past the bodies of the young couple near the companionway, he felt a tightness in his chest and forced his attention toward the cabins the woman had fought so desperately to protect. What could have been worth such a lovely life, he wondered as he ducked his head and entered.

There were two main cabins on that level. Not knowing why, he chose the one on the right. As he opened the door, he kicked it back and stepped inside, cutlass drawn. He relaxed as he saw the room was deserted. A lady's cloak was thrown carelessly over the berth in the corner. He walked over and picked it up, astonished as his eyes came to rest on a sleeping child.

It was a small girl with dark hair like her mother's. She wore a pink silk dress that was shamed by the healthy pink glow of her cheeks where long dark lashes fanned on them in contrast. Brennan brushed the child's cheek with the back of his rough hand and she stirred.

"Capt'n, she's as loaded as any we've taken in a good while!"

Brennan glanced up to see his first mate burst into the room with a few men at his side. They stopped short at the sight of their captain hovering over the sleeping child on the bunk.

"Well I'll be!" the quartermaster exclaimed. "So that's why 'er mama was carryin' on so."

Brennan nodded and turned back as the little girl stretched lazily and opened wide blue eyes to stare at the big man standing over her. Instead of the fear he expected her to show, she smiled and reached for his hand. She grabbed a finger firmly and pulled it toward her with surprising strength. As the pirate jumped back startled, she laughed.

"Pa . . . pa!" she squealed, as the room erupted in laughter.

The red-faced captain turned to his men. "Get to the cargo, mates. We're losing valuable time!" he ordered. "Soon as we clear out, set fire to 'er. She's beyond use to us now." He paused as the child pulled herself awkwardly to her feet and reached for him with outstretched arms. "Well, get on with ye!" he ordered, as he picked up the child uneasily. "And see that the lady and gentleman are out of sight when we go topside."

Methodically, he began to search the cabin for valuables and any papers that might give him a clue to the child's identity. His woman in Nose' Be had just lost her baby to fever. It occurred to him that perhaps this lovely child playing quietly on the cabin floor might be what she needed. He glanced over at his charge in time to see the little girl pick up his cutlass by the handle and drag it in a swooping motion across the wooden planks.

He laughed as she pushed it headlong between his booted feet and squealed with delight. Then, realizing the danger, he placed a heavy foot on the blade. The child frowned as she tried to free her new-found toy. She pulled at the scabbard until she lost her grip and fell with a soft thump on her backside. Angrily, she looked up at the pirate captain and shrieked as if warning him. Then she pulled herself to her feet and tried again to remove the cutlass. Again she looked up at him and shrieked, stomping her foot in frustration.

At that moment, Brennan's eyes fell on a small metal box, partially hidden under the berth. He gave the child a quill pen for diversion and walked over to

11

investigate. The lock was no match for the steel blade of his dagger. Inside he found letters and papers of a legal nature, bearing seals. He managed to decipher the one on top, written on East India Company stationery.

"Dear Madame Devage," it began. "It is with regret that I have the duty to inform you of your father's death. It may comfort you to know that in his last days he forgave you for running off with that roguish Irishman. Indeed, he actually came to admire the fortitude and ambition your Jonathan has exhibited in his service with the East India Co. And, of course, he regretted most not having known his granddaughter. Shannon would be about three years of age, if my calculation is correct.

"Your father did not disinherit you as he threatened, but has left you his estate and his shares in the East India Co. He felt your husband would do well by your interests in the same. Therefore, it is my hope that the three of you will hasten to return to London as soon as you are able to make arrangements. Until such time, I shall continue to administer the estate as I see fit. God speed to you all. I remain your friend and uncle as always, Admiral Edward Bedlowe."

Brennan shook his head sadly at the thought of the young couple's end. Then he raised his eyes to meet the smiling blue ones of the little girl before him. At least he knew the name of their daughter. He could not have picked one himself that would suit her better. Shannon. Shannon Brennan, he mused. 'Twas a fine name for Brennan's daughter.

Chapter One

Shannon Brennan looked up sharply and nearly lost her grip on her bamboo fishing pole as the guns at the mouth of Brennan's Cove roared. Hurriedly she wound in her line. The chances were good that her father was coming into the protected harbor, the harbor that was haven to some of the most feared pirates to prey upon the Indian Ocean and the Mediterranean. She threw down the pole alongside scattered tackle and began to run up the narrow forest path that led to the point where the cannon were located. From that vantage she would be able to see the ship as the crew worked to bring her into the dock that was home to the *Plunderer*.

"Is it Papa?" she called out breathlessly as she clambered up the last length of path to the hilltop.

A swarthy-skinned watchman narrowed his eyes and then grinned a toothless smile of recognition. "It's not Brennan," he informed her as he turned to point toward the billowing sails approaching from the northwest of Nose' Be. "'Pears to be some fool set on gettin' 'imself blown from these waters!"

Shannon followed his gaze across the blue-green waters of the Diego Suarez Bay to the sleek sailing ship that approached. Behind her, a gunnery crew made its way toward the discharged cannon and began hastily to reload. She could not help but wonder at the audacity of the strange ship's captain to brave the well-armed entrance.

"Miss Shannon, you'd best get back to your papa's house 'fore there's trouble."

Shannon glanced over her shoulder at the guard. "I can look out for myself, Zeke," she answered, flashing a blue-eyed warning to her father's watchman. Whenever Nick Brennan was out of port, the remaining seamen protected her to the point of suffocation. "Besides, whoever he is, he's not showing any signs of hostility. And he's flying the filibuster."

Zeke spat and wiped his mouth with the sleeve of his tattered shirt. Although he'd made many a lucrative voyage with her father, he had nothing to show for it except the scars of battle, having spent his share of the booty at the tavern on women and drink. "Could be a trick, missy. Tho' if it is, he'll meet Davy Jones a'fore the sun sets this day. Ramon's out to meet 'im."

Again Shannon followed the sailor's gaze to the bay where another light but well-armed vessel came into view. She recognized the black hull of the *Dagger* slipping easily toward the intruder. "Aye," she agreed reluctantly. "His fate's sealed, if that be the case."

Ramon Gerarde was her father's best captain, second in skill and cunning only to Brennan himself. Tall and handsome, with the dark skin of his Creole ancestry, he was the bane of Shannon's life lately. His attentions became bolder and more unsettling with each passing day, in spite of her attempts to discourage them. His arrogance alone might blast the oncoming ship from the waters. Shannon smiled at the thought.

"Now look, will ya!" Zeke exclaimed, as the Jolly Roger was pulled down and a white flag of truce was hoisted in its place. "What are them blaggards up to?"

The group on the hilltop watched as the two ships pulled alongside each other. Words were obviously exchanged between the two captains, but they were lost on the observers. After a period of time elapsed, a longboat was put over from the stranger's vessel and was rowed to the side of the *Dagger*. A man climbed up the rope ladder tossed over the side and boarded the deck with ease. After the longboat returned to its own vessel, the *Dagger* swung about and proceeded to lead the other ship into Brennan's Cove.

"Let's go down to the docks to see what this is all about!" Shannon exclaimed excitedly. No one had ever entered the hidden cove on the small island of Nose' Be before. Few were aware of its exact location and those that did know of it, other than Brennan's own fleet captains, stayed clear.

"No ye don't, missy," Zeke replied. "There's still a chance of trouble an' Cap'n Nick 'll have our heads if one hair on your pretty head is harmed."

"But . . ."

"No buts, missy! To the house with ya a'fore I have to take ya there meself, slung over my back like a sack o' grain."

Shannon glared at the older man. Then with an emphatic stomp of her small foot, she turned and started back down the hill toward the house Nick Brennan claimed as his own. At eighteen, she was still treated like a child. It seemed everyone had authority over her when her father was out of port. Don't go to the village unescorted during the day.

15

Don't go at all at night! As if anyone would dare bother Brennan's daughter!

The house Nick Brennan had built halfway up the hilltop overlooked the village and the quay. It was a single story dwelling, only one room deep and four rooms wide with a thatched roof and a kitchen in the back. All the rooms opened on a veranda that afforded shade in the heat of the day. Wild flowers and vines grew in gay profusion around the dwelling and framed it in color against the rich green backdrop of the forest surrounding it.

The house was quiet when Shannon entered and made her way to her room. As she slammed the door she heard the housekeeper's voice calling from the back kitchen where the woman lived.

"Your papa, he come home?"

"No! It's a strange ship. Ramon's bringing it in."

"Doan you even think about goin' down der now, girl!"

Shannon grimaced. "The thought never crossed my mind," she called back, her voice rich with sarcasm. With that she threw herself down on the big brass bed her father had bought her in Tangiers and lay looking up at the ceiling. Suffocation! That's what it was. She knew they all meant well, but it was still suffocation—and it was becoming unbearable.

The dingy appearance of the tavern was no better inside than out, Morgan Hawke mused as he returned the suspicious gaze of the pirate captain seated across the plank table. He did not like the idea of leaving his first mate and crew under the guard of the vermin that inhabited the tiny harbor on Nose' Be, but he had been given little choice. He had to accompany his host ashore as hostage until his story could be verified or engage a formidable enemy in a battle where the odds were against him.

So he had agreed peacefully. There was too much time and effort spent to turn back, or to jeopardize his mission. He had the backing of his crew and the support of the royal navy. The monarch of England was always willing to sanction and support an attempt to bring the predators on her commerce to justice. And of course, there was the compelling lust for revenge that brought him to the infested nest of cutthroats and murderers—revenge for the death of his father.

It was nearly a year ago that he received the news of the tragedy. His father's ship had been overtaken, looted and apparently confiscated by a pirate ship called the *Plunderer*. The few crew members that survived by virtue of their surrender, told of how the older captain had fought valiantly to defend his ship. Wounded and weakened, he left the deck littered with the bodies of pirates before he was finally overcome. A huge red-maned captain by the name of Brennan spared the lives of the remaining crew and set them adrift in a longboat on the chance that another vessel might happen upon them and perhaps help them secure passage back to their native England.

Hawke tightened his grip on the handle of the tin mug of ale and raised it to his mouth. He barely controlled his anger at the thought of his father lying among bloodied corpses to be tossed over the side to a watery grave. It was too lowly a fate for Eric Hawke, Lord of Snowden—too horrid for the man who had through the years gained the love and respect of so many, particularly his son.

The captain of the *Dagger* toyed with a knife and grinned, his teeth flashing white against his dark Creole skin. "So you see, my friend, if the men with

17

Brennan do not recognize the *Sea Lady* from their days with the Brethren, you and your crew will suffer a terrible fate." His finger traced the finely honed edge of the knife.

"In the first place, Gerarde, I am not your friend. Secondly, my business is with Nick Brennan, not one of his underlings." Hawke pausd, the tug of a smile at the corner of his firm lips at the angry flush of his captor. "Thirdly, my story will be verified by your companions, so you can put to rest any bloodthirsty intentions you may have in the back of your mind."

Quickly, before the other man realized what he was about, Hawke reached across the table and snatched the dagger out of his hand. With a lightning flash, he sailed it over the table and smiled as it struck its intended destination, the dead center of a well-worn dart board mounted on the wall behind his startled companion.

Ramon jumped up from the table, nearly upsetting it. His fists clenched white as he leaned on them, glaring at Hawke. The few men in the tavern were silenced by the tension in the air. "You have made a grave mistake, Capitan Hawke," he hissed. His hand made its way slowly to one of the pistols on his belt.

Hawke was acutely aware that his own pistols tucked in his belt were useless to him, the other captain having disarmed them when he boarded the *Dagger*. "Don't be a fool, Gerarde," Hawke warned. "I have a well-armed ship that, although outnumbered, would do considerable damage to this hellhole before she was put to rest, and my crew has orders to do just that if they do not hear from me personally on a regular basis. Anyone approaching the *Sea Lady* without me will be blown out of the water, rest assured of that."

"It seems to me that the gentleman has you at a disadvantage, Ramon." The voice of the tavern-keeper rose above the tension. "And you well know that when our good captain returns, he'd have you strung up for any rash action that would bring damage to his castle, when a cool head could have prevented it."

The Creole stood up stiffly, never taking his icy stare from the Englishman's face. He was being tested and everyone in the room awaited his response. "For the time being, mon capitán, I will wait to deal you the justice you deserve. But you rest assured," he added emphatically, "it will be dealt!" Abruptly his manner changed and a wide smile crossed his face again. "But for now, I am your host." He clapped his hands loudly and called to the woman standing in the doorway that led to the kitchen in the back. "Carlota, show the captain to our finest room upstairs and, Mendez . . ." he said, nodding to one of the pirates at the bar, "see that he stays there to enjoy our hospitality."

Without a backward glance, he spun about and walked over to the target to retrieve his dagger. The weapon safely sheathed, he made his way toward the door and exited into the dirt street that separated the tavern from the warehouses on the docks.

"You're a lucky man, sir. You were this close to having a lead ball right between your eyes." The tavernkeeper held up his forefinger and thumb spaced barely apart to indicate how narrow Hawke's escape had been.

"Aye, sir, you're very likely correct!" Hawke agreed. "And thank you for your timely advice."

"Always glad to help a fellow Englishman."

The young captain regarded the man behind the bar. He was not a particularly big man but his stocky frame indicated he would be a worthy adversary in combat. His speech was definitely more refined than that of his comrades, and his jovial manner a marked improvement over his captain's.

"It seems your captain has a rather quick temper," Hawke remarked casually.

"He's not my captain," the round-faced man corrected curtly. "Nick Brennan is the only captain in this port. Ramon Gerarde is just a hotheaded fool we tolerate in Brennan's absence. Oh, he's good enough in the thick of a fight, but when a cool head is needed, his emotion overrides his intelligence. And his arrogance is only exceeded by his cruelty. As I said," he repeated grimly, "you're a lucky man."

"Well in view of that, I'll have another round to drink to my good fortune." As Hawke crossed the short distance to the bar, he noticed his guard move closer as though poised for any sudden action. "And one for my able guard as well, if you please," he added, smiling at the mustached Spaniard, dressed somewhat outlandishly in the attire of a Red Sea corsair.

"Now the liquor doesn't exactly come free here, even if you are a guest of this establishment."

Hawke reached into his pocket. He produced a gold coin which he tossed carelessly on the oak bar. 'I trust that this will cover my room and board for a night or so, Mister . . . ?"

"Cutchins," the tavernkeeper spoke up as he snatched the coin off the counter greedily. "Henry Cutchins is the name, Captain." He bit the coin suspiciously and turned his back to the makeshift bar to place it in a small box on a shelf behind it. "And this will provide you with the finest we have to offer, sir," he added quickly.

While Henry Cutchins set about drawing the ale,

Hawke became aware of a warmth pressing against his arm and turned to see the serving wench Ramon had summoned staring at the pocket from whence the coin had come. Caught unawares, she blushed only slightly before recovering with a seductive smile. She was attractive, Hawke mused, taking in her over-ripe bosom, barely contained in the once white peasant blouse that draped loosely over her smooth shoulders. And if he were not careful, she was likely to relieve him of whatever possessions he had on him, from his gold to the emptied pearl handled pistols his father had handed down to him from his own father.

"Madame, forgive me, but could I perhaps purchase a drink for you, as well?"

"Señor, I . . ."

"She's supposed to be working at the present, Captain, but you can buy her all you want when she's done after the evening clientele either leave or pass out," Cutchins informed him, ignoring the pout on Carlota's full rouged lips and the angry flash of her large brown eyes. He had dealt with women like Carlota for years and considered himself immune to their displays of charm and temper.

"And Ramon, he says you go to the room upstairs anyway," the man called Mendez spoke up. He took his tin mug and motioned toward a set of thick wooden steps. "You can finish yours in your room, señor."

"I will show him the way!"

Carlota pulled away from Hawke's arm with deliberate slowness and walked ahead of him toward the stairway. Her walk was as calculated as the provocative sway of her well-rounded hips from her narrow waist. When she reached the steps, she lifted her full red skirt well above her ankles to reveal shapely legs to the men that followed. Hoots from some of the men at the roughly made tables were ignored as she proceeded to the second floor.

The hallway was narrow and dimly lit. There were four board and batten doors on the right. It was at the third door that the woman stopped and lifted the latch to enter. Ushered forward by Mendez who was gaining more courage with each swallow of the strong brew, Hawke followed her into the room. The door slammed shut behind him and he heard a bolt slide into place.

The room was larger than he expected. Sparsely furnished, it boasted a wide bed with a thick stuffed mattress, a small washstand with a chipped porcelain bowl and pitcher, and a table by the window, obviously used for dining and as a desk as well, though Hawke doubted there were many in the pirate colony that were educated enough to use it for any purpose other than meals. Yet, he reminded himself, the innkeeper's speech was certainly that of an educated man.

"Are you not pleased, señor?" Carlota mistook the puzzled look on the lean, handsome face as one of displeasure.

"Indeed I am, madame. I am delighted with such adequate accommodations and more so at such lovely and gracious company." He bowed gallantly and raised his dark eyes to hers.

"Oh, señor!" Carlota giggled. "You are such as we have not seen here. Are you not perhaps a dishonored don or a bastard to the king of England?" she asked, widening her brown eyes becomingly with a practiced expertise, and closing the space between them to press her body next to his tall frame.

"I am a privateer. No more, no less," he answered, leaning down to brush his face against her thick black hair. She was heavily perfumed, to cover the

22

smell of sweat from her hard labors in the kitchen and lack of bathing. Yet the softness of her full body pressed against him began to arouse a passion suppressed by weeks at sea without feminine attentions. He put his arms about her waist and lowered his lips to her ear, teasing and blowing softly into it.

"But you are of noble background are you not?" she persisted, raising her face to search his eyes for the answer. She caught her breath as she gazed into passion's depths and was held mesmerized by the hypnotic glow.

"Many of the Brethren of the Coast were of nobility at one time. And like them, that time is in the past which I have left behind and to which I can never return. Any more questions, my bewitching love?" he asked.

Her head shook in denial as she pulled his fine linen shirt from his trousers, taking care not to dislodge the pistols tucked in his waistband, and raised it over his head. Her eyes roamed appreciatively over the tanned muscled chest all but covered with dark hair, as he carefully removed the weapons and placed them on the table between the bed and the window. Her hands began to shake as she fumbled with the laces of his trousers and lowered them. He sat back on the bed to allow her to remove them as well as his black polished boots. It was beyond her comprehension why she was trembling like a virgin before this man when she was about to do what she had done to support herself since she was but a child of fourteen.

Yet, he was different—decidedly so—from her Creole lover. Ramon desired her too, but he was rough and demanding. Many days she sported bruises from their nights of lovemaking, the results of his displeasure at something she may have said or done. For all the need she sensed in the man before her, she also sensed kindness, not the cruelty she had grown accustomed to from the only man ever to steal her heart and abuse it as his possession. Perhaps this one would serve to make her lover jealous so that he would cease his sudden infatuation with Brennan's daughter and devote himself to her again.

Sensing her apprehension, Hawke reached for her slender arms and pulled her in front of him gently. Then as she had done for him, he began to remove her clothes, his own desire mounting as her slender and beautiful body was revealed totally to him. He groaned as he pulled her back on the bed and felt the burning of her flesh against his. Slowly she began to move in a deliberately slow writhing manner, driving him insane with need.

She was a wildcat, the man thought afterward as she lay curled against him. He surveyed the damage done to the skin on his shoulders where her rough nails had raked red lines as they bit into him. So far his worst injury in the den of thieves had come from a hot and saucy tavern wench. He chuckled to himself, stirring the sleeping woman.

"Does my lovemaking amuse you, Capitán?" she asked sleepily. She stretched her arms above her head and yawned. "Por Dios!" she exclaimed suddenly as her eyes rested on the window which now permitted the last rays of the setting sun through its imperfect glass panes. Hurriedly she jumped out of the bed and began to dress. "I am to be working!" she explained, her voice revealing her distress.

Hawke watched her from the bed. "Look in my pocket over there," he instructed her, motioning toward his discarded clothing, "take whatever you feel will appease your employer for your lost time." He might as well give it to her to save her the trouble of stealing it.

After arranging her skirt, she removed the coins from his pocket eagerly. Her face brightened as she saw the generous amount it contained. "Oh, señor! I cannot take so much. Not even for me!" she stammered breathlessly.

Hawke laughed at the small drama being played to its fullest extent before him. "I insist, Carlota. Take it all. Give Cutchins whatever will keep him from giving you a hard time and you keep the rest. Buy something for yourself with it."

Carlota rushed over to the bed and gave him an overly enthusiastic kiss. *"Gracias, señor, muchas gracias!"* She glanced over her shoulder toward the door nervously. "I must go," she apologized, "but I promise I will be back after I am finished tonight. Then we will not have to worry about Cutchings, *querido,* for we will have all of the night, no?" Her eyes were bright and teasing.

"Then fly, lovely lady. I shall wait most anxiously for your return." He took her rough hand and brushed it lightly with his lips.

Carlota drew back her hand and stared at it in wonder. Then shaking herself, she turned and made her way to the door. She knocked gently and waited until Mendez unbolted it. As she passed through the door, she called out to him. *"Hasta la vista, querido."*

Then she was gone and the door was bolted once again. Hawke lay back upon the pillow, his hands folded behind his head. Hunger gnawed at his stomach as he recalled his last meal at noon that day. He wondered if Cutchings would remember to send something up to him. Yet, the hunger could not eliminate the druglike fatigue of his interlude with Carlota and closed his eyes to pass the time until the wench's return. Perhaps then there would be more time for his questions. Perhaps.

Chapter Two

The morning sun was barely peeking over the horizon when Shannon opened her eyes and stretched lazily. The birds chattered gaily from the treetops outside her open window and she could hear Marie moving about quietly as she often did in order to let her charge sleep late. No doubt the old Sakalavan slave woman, who had raised her since her mother's death when she was but five, had been up and about for at least an hour or so, as was her custom. The girl sometimes wondered when she did sleep.

Many times late at night she could hear the woman through the trees that separated their house from the small garden she had managed to clear and maintain in the dense growth, practicing her strange and occult religion. Once as a child, Shannon had sneaked out to observe the curious rituals, and had been so frightened by the scene that she had run back to the house to fetch her father to go help the woman, certain something terrible was the matter with her. From that point on, she was forbidden to speak to Marie of her nocturnal activities, and never was she to witness them again. Her father's decision needed no enforcement, for Shannon did not want to know more of the occult. She loved Marie dearly, and if there was something wrong or evil about her, she chose to ignore it.

But Marie was not in the garden last night. She sat in the parlor talking into the wee hours of the morning with Ramon Gerarde. Although Shannon did not like to eavesdrop on private conversations, she could not help herself, since she was the principal topic of the discussion. They were intent on planning her future with Ramon and it hurt the girl that her housekeeper would not acknowledge her dislike of the man and her determination not to marry him. For some reason Marie had decided it was time she married and had children. Ramon seemed to be the favorite over the others who frequented the cove.

He had come to see Shannon, but when Marie went to her bedroom to see if she had retired, the girl pretended to be asleep, hoping Ramon would go back down to the village. When he did not, Shannon had little choice but to listen to Marie give the man advice on how to win her affection. It had been a depressing conversation, until it turned to the captain of the strange ship that had been escorted into the cove. She could not wait to see this English dandy masquerading as a privateer from the West Indies.

She giggled as she swung her legs over the side of the bed. Nick Brennan would have him for breakfast if his story didn't prove true. She could imagine him, bedecked in ruffles and reeking of perfume, being set adrift in the middle of the Indian Ocean with his crew, while his ship remained in the hands of those he sought to deceive. She sobered thoughtfully. Perhaps, if she dressed quietly, she could slip out the door that led from her room to the veranda and make

27

her way to the tavern. She was sure that she could persuade Cudge to let her sneak a peek at the foppish fool Ramon had described so eloquently to Marie.

Careful not to make any noise, she pulled off the oversized cotton shirt she had confiscated from her father and tossed it carelessly on the bed. Although she had a huge mahogany wardrobe full of lovely dresses made by Marie, Shannon searched the bottom of the closet for her usual shirt and breeches. She would have to try to coax the housekeeper into helping her make another pair of the fawn colored pants. As she tied the laces about her small waist, she noticed the tightness across her buttocks; her once boyish figure rounding out. In a few moments she had her long dark hair brushed to a sheen and secured with a comb beneath a scarlet bandanna which she tied slightly to the side in the fashion of the seamen.

She listened carefully before opening the door and slipping outside. Halfway down the hill to the village, she stopped to pull on her leather boots, confident that Marie could not hear her footfall from that distance. As she sat on a log beside the dirt path that connected Brennan's castle and the village, she gazed curiously at the recently arrived vessel moored near the *Dagger*. She barely made out the name of the ship *Sea Lady* from the gold letters painted on her stern. Hardly a fit name for a fierce predator of the seas, she thought wryly.

The tavern was noisy when Shannon entered and made her way to the bar where Henry Cutchins was delivering brisk orders to the women in the back. She smiled and spoke to the hungry seamen, at ease among the men her father sailed with. She had known most of them since childhood. She had learned much as a result. She could handle a knife as well as most of them, and much to the tavernkeeper's

28

dismay, could curse equally well.

Henry Cutchings, or Cudge, as Shannon affectionately called him, had been her tutor since she was ten. Once a member of the clergy in Wales, he became involved in some scandal involving the daughter of a wealthy landowner and found himself on a prison ship bound for India. The ship ran up on the reefs of Madagascar during a storm and the survivors made their way to shore where they either joined the ranks of the pirate inhabitants or faced certain death at their hands.

It was on Madagascar that he met and joined Nick Brennan. Not being much of a fighting man, he chose to work ashore and built the tavern on the nearby island with Brennan as his partner. And Brennan, sensing a man of learning, engaged him to tutor his small daughter, socially as well as academically. The tutor and student became friends from the start in spite of his strict manner and intolerance for improper speech or social behavior on her part.

"Hey, you dimwitted lout. Got any of that garbage your help's burnin' in the back?" Shannon shouted loudly above the din of the rowdy diners.

"And who the hell . . ." the red-faced man broke off as he turned to deal with the offensive patron and recognized the girl. "Shannon! What takes you up and about this early in the day?" he asked, obviously pleased to see her.

Shannon leaned across the plank bar and lowered her voice in a conspiratorial fashion. "I hear you have a new guest upstairs under guard."

"Ah, the Englishman," Cutchins smiled eyeing the girl curiously.

"The very one. Do you think I could take look at him? After all, I ain't never seen a full-blooded real nobleman and . . ."

29

"Haven't," the tavernkeeper corrected.

"Well I haven't seen one either," she teased, wrinkling her small nose up in a face at the man.

"I think not, young lady. Best wait till your father's back, then you can see him. Can't have you getting hurt." The tavernkeeper turned as one of the serving women stood at the door and shouted a stream of curses in Spanish back at the kitchen. *"Basta, basta!"* he shouted.

"Please, Cudge. I just want to see him, and there's a guard at the door," Shannon pleaded, ignoring the outburst. "Maybe I could carry up some breakfast."

"I don't think so. . . . *Calmate!*" he shouted again to the angry woman. "Shannon, I'm very busy," he apologized, curtly dismissing her over his shoulder as he walked toward the door to the kitchen.

Shannon rushed around the corner of the bar and intercepted him. "I'll just drop the food off and come right straight back down, I promise. And I can take care of myself." Her hand went meaningfully to the small knife strapped to her slim waist.

Cutchins looked anxiously over her shoulders at the heated argument taking place in the back. "Oh, all right," he relented impatiently. "Carlota! Give that tray to Shannon. She'll take it up. You get out there and see to the men at the tables."

"Oh, thank you, Cudge!" Shannon hugged the stocky man impulsively and turned to take the tray the Spanish woman was carrying. She hesitated for a moment as the woman shot her a venomous look and thrust the tray at her roughly. Then with a shrug, she took it and walked past her toward the steps. She was unaware of the silent looks of admiration directed at her as she made her way upstairs, for the men kept their opinions to themselves. She was Brennan's daughter and respect demanded it of them.

The guard at the door was dozing when Shannon reached the top of the steps. She called out to him as she approached so as not to startle him and handed him one of the plates of hash and biscuits on the tray. He put it down by his bench seat and rose to open the door for her. His prisoner and the serving wench had kept him up most of the night and he was more than ready for Ramon to send someone to relieve him.

Shannon stepped through the door slowly and started slightly as she heard the bolt click into place behind her. The black-haired figure on the bed did not stir. One glance at the table, which held two empty liquor bottles and two mugs told her why. Suddenly the reason for Carlota's hostility struck her. She had mistakenly attributed it to the wench's jealousy over Ramon. The girl gave a quiet snort of disgust, as her eyes scanned the rumpled sheets where the sleeping man lay.

His face was buried in the pillows and sunbronzed shoulders showed above the sheets, his arms hidden under his head. She noticed his feet sticking out over the end of the bed. He certainly was a tall man, she thought, as she crossed the room quietly to place the tray on the table. She froze for a moment as she heard him catch his breath and move restlessly under the covers. As he settled peacefully again, she let out an unconscious sigh of relief. He was much bigger than she had pictured and something about the way he moved, even in sleep, made her wary.

She turned away from the bed to gather the empty bottles when her eyes fell on the pair of pearl-handled pistols. With an appreciation for firearms she had developed over the years, she reached across the table to admire one. They were among the fanciest pieces she had ever seen. The handles were inlaid with silver in intricate designs around the bold letter "H." They had been well cared for, she'd give the dandy that, she mused as she examined the sights, fixing it on an imaginary target outside.

Suddenly the breath was forced out of her as a powerful arm tightened about her small waist and another wrapped around her neck forcefully cutting off her air. She dropped the pistol to the floor and struggled frantically as she tried to reach for her dagger. The steel bands tightened and her head began to feel light. A small whimper escaped her as her knees started to buckle.

"All right, son. I'm going to let you loose slowly, but don't try to cry out for help or go for that knife, lest I be forced to break your thieving neck."

The deep voice penetrated her whirling consciousness and she ceased to struggle, weak from lack of air. The viselike grip that pinned her to the hard body behind her eased slightly and before she could gather her wits, she felt her dagger lifted from its sheath. Then there was nothing holding her. She stepped unsteadily away and turned to grasp the edge of the table for support.

"You bastard!" she rasped, her blue eyes flashing in indignant rage. "You damn near broke my bloody neck and I'm not so sure my ribs aren't broken!" she added, touching her rib cage tentatively.

"You're a girl!" The surprise on his roguishly handsome face was evident. Cobalt eyes raked over her figure boldly, resting on the deep vee of her loose fitting shirt that had pulled to the side in the struggle to reveal the swell of her breast. "I mean a woman," he corrected himself.

Shannon glanced down and quickly rearranged the shirt. One of her hands remained self-consciously at the neck, holding the vee together as she glanced back up at the man before her. Her color deepened as she realized for the first time that he was naked. For a moment she was stunned. She had not seen a man in the altogether since swimming as a small child with her father in the lagoon. And this Englishman had the body of the Greek gods she had read about in Cudge's classes.

"I take it I meet your approval?"

Quickly she bent over and picked up the discarded gun and turned her back to him to place it on the table beside its mate. "I . . . I was not trying to steal your gun," she stammered, ignoring the comment. "I was merely admiring it, when you so viciously attacked me." She kept her back to him, aware of his movement behind her. "I just brought your meal up, so if you'll kindly give me back my dagger, I'll . . ." She broke off as she felt his arms go about her again, gently but firmly. She heard her dagger hit the floor, carelessly tossed aside.

"And what do you serve with your meals, my fiery vixen," he whispered in her ear, his breath warm upon her skin.

"You common whoreson," she gasped, spinning in his arms to strike him. Before she could raise her fists she was crushed to him again and found herself being carried toward the bed. "I'll scream," she threatened, reluctant to do so. She had promised Cudge she'd not get in trouble—all she was going to do was put the food in the room and leave. Her breath caught in her throat as she felt herself falling ackward onto the bed, her attacker on top of her holding her down with his weight.

"Let's have a look at you, little one."

Shannon tried to push him off with both fists, but her hands were pinned between her body and his. He laughed and pulled off her bandanna, loosening the comb so that her hair spilled out upon the sheets. His

33

hands sifted through the satiny tresses and moved to scoop up her head as he lowered his mouth on hers harshly. She groaned in angry protest and clenched her teeth against his attack as she tried to turn her head to the side futilely. Her mind raced in desperation. She gave in for a moment and when he was certain of his conquest, she bit his lip, drawing blood.

"You little bitch!" he exclaimed, rising up on one arm and touching his lip with the opposite hand in surprise.

The break was all Shannon needed. She shoved him with all her strength and raised her knee up between his legs sharply. As he gasped in pain and doubled over, she rolled out from beneath him and scrambled to the floor in search of her weapon. She seized the dagger and sprang to her feet lightly, backing away as he came up from the bed, breathing harshly.

"Don't you ever try anything like that again, or I'll run you through," she threatened menacingly, her voice shaking in spite of her advantage.

"Who the hell are you?" His voice was forced as he met her angry gaze with an equally dark one.

Shannon ignored the question and pointed to her bandanna lying next to him on the bed. Slowly he reached for it and handed it to her, never taking his eyes from the shining blade of the dagger, glinting in the morning sunlight that shone through the window. She accepted it and shoved it in the waistband of her breeches. Then with a toss of her head to rid her face of the stray strands of hair that had fallen in her eyes, she backed toward the door and knocked lightly for it to be opened.

When Mendez opened the door, he stood aside in surprise at the disheveled appearance of the girl and glanced past her at the captain sitting on the edge of the bed dabbing his shirt to his bloodied lip. A smile crossed his face and he closed the door and rebolted it. As he opened his mouth to speak, a warning flash of blue eyes stopped him. He watched quietly as the girl sheathed her knife and tied the bandanna around her hair at the nape of her neck.

Shannon gave the guard a smile of gratitude for his silence and proceeded to the opposite end of the hall from the main steps where a narrow winding stairway emptied out into the yard behind the tavern between the main building and the out kitchen. She made her way straight through the small cluster of wood and mud structures to the path leading up to her house. It was the route least likely to lead to an encounter with Ramon or Cudge. Within a short time she was safe inside her room and Marie, now working out in the garden, had never missed her.

The rest of the morning passed without event. Shannon busied herself helping Marie weed the garden and clear more land in the dense thicket. She enjoyed working with the woman and tried to learn as much as she could about the different herbs grown there, as well as those that grew wild in the forest. Marie was well known about the island for her cures and concoctions. From her own experience, Shannon knew the virtues of this primitive medicine.

"You see dis, young ladee?" Marie called out to the girl, holding up a dirt-covered root she had just pulled near the base of a tall oak.

Shannon squinted her eyes in the bright sunlight and grinned impishly. "Whatever it is, I could eat a dozen of them about now. I'm famished."

Marie laughed as she wobbled over to her charge. Sweat was beaded on her black forehead and ran down to the bright bandanna tied around her head just over her eyes. She swung the full skirt of her shift back and forth to dispel some of the heat as she stopped before the girl. "Dis here is jus what you need, girl."

Shannon examined the yellow root she handed her. "What is it?" she asked curiously.

"Ah calls it love root. Maybe I feed you some so you treat dat han'some cap'n of your papa's better. Watch 'u tink?" She smiled, showing two yellowed teeth and dark gums.

"I think you should give it to Ramon and take him for yourself," Shannon remarked, arming herself for the direction the conversation was taking.

The black woman laughed slapping her rough hands on her heavy legs. "Doan you tink if dis ole woman wern' ole, she wouldn' tries it. He plenty good lookin' and bring you fancy tings!"

"Well, he shouldn't. He's wasting his time and money. Besides, Cudge says it's improper."

"Cudge say dis, Cudge say dat! Humph!" she snorted in disgust. "Dat book fool doan know nothin' less it in a book. Marie knows more what a young girl needs den he do, and what she know ain't in no damn 'me book!" the negress said emphatically. "Ah raise your mama, an' she was jus' like you—pretty and proud. Fust time ah see your papa ah tell 'er, dat da man fo' you, girl. An' your mama, she listen to ol' Marie 'cause she smart. An' your papa, he don't stand a chance 'cause she so beautiful, he have to have her."

Shannon's interest picked up at the mention of her mother who had died in childbirth with her newborn brother. She did not remember the woman very well except that she was sickly and very kind to her. She remembered she was petite and her coloring showed more of her Arab ancestry than of her African. She had been sister to the chief of the Sakalavas, the natives who inhabited the other side of the island. Her eyes reminded the little girl of a fawn's, large and brown with hints of gold flecks in them. Lillianne, her father called her, unable to pronounce either hers or Marie's native names.

"Do I look like her much? Except for my eyes and skin. I know I get that from papa," Shannon injected.

Marie sighed and put her thick arm around the girl's shoulders. "You as pretty as she ever was, girl. An dat why Ramon wants you so bad!"

"Oh!" Shannon exclaimed pulling away in exasperation. "And I don't suppose it would have anything to do with the fact that I'm Nick Brennan's daughter, or the power our marriage would give the rat?"

"You tink what you like, you do what I say!"

With that the housekeeper spun around with surprising speed for one her age and size and made her way back to the house. Shannon kicked the discarded root and ground it into the dirt with her boot, as infuriated with herself for even attempting to reason with the stubborn old negress as she was with the woman. She had never won an argument with her. Her own temper usually got the best of her and Marie's stubborn insistence would win out every time. All of Cudge's teachings were of no use against Marie.

A smile touched her full lips as she thought of the tavernkeeper. Where her father had not taken sides on the issue of Ramon's courtship, Cudge had sided solidly with Shannon. He made no pretense of liking Ramon Gerarde and thought him to be conceited and ambitious. And he made it clear that he did not think the man was good enough for Shannon. But then, he didn't think anyone in the cove was. "You're a very special young lady and have no business living in a godforsaken place like this," he had once told her. "And if you papa didn't love you so selfishly, he'd see that you left here." That was the only criticism of Nick Brennan she had ever heard from the tavernkeeper's lips—but his opinions about Marie were something else again. The two adversaries hated one another.

"It is good to see you smile, *querida*."

Startled out of her reverie, Shannon saw Ramon Gerarde leaning up against a tree watching her. His appraisal was as bold as the one she had received earlier and did little to improve her humor. "How long have you been there?" she asked suspiciously, wondering if he had overheard her conversation with Marie.

"But a few moments, *querida*." His smile was dashing, but it lacked warmth and sincerity. 'I thought perhaps you would like to walk with me for a while."

Shannon shrugged indifferently. "Why would I want to do that?"

Ramon crossed the ground between them with the grace of a jungle cat and put his hands on her shoulders. As he sensed her stiffen, he dropped them to his sides. He must be patient, he reminded himself; and that was most irritating considering the customary way women yielded to his charm. "I thought perhaps you would like to hear about the new capitán of the ship moored down by the *Dagger*. His presence here interests you, does it not?"

Shannon eyed him warily. She wondered if Mendez had told him of her meeting with the Englishman, realizing how incriminating the scene must have appeared. She really didn't care what her ardent suitor thought as much as she cared what Cudge or her father would think. She grimaced at the thought.

"It was foolish of you to go to see him alone and Mendez has regretted permitting you to enter at all." His stare was hard as he met her alarmed glance.

"What did you do to him?" she demanded. It dismayed her to think that the guard had possibly been punished for her own foolish action.

He waved his hand, dismissing her question. "It is of no concern. But I want to know what happened."

Shannon replied to his demand in kind. "It is of no concern." She turned her back and started toward the house when his hand latched onto her arm and spun her about so quickly she caught her boot on a vine and fell against him. "Let go of me, you bastard!" she hissed through clenched teeth as his fingers bit into the flesh of her arms. "You're hurting me."

"What happened?" he repeated. He shook her roughly, his patience exhausted.

"You're as bad as he is! Worse!" she spat. "At least he thought I was trying to steal his fancy guns."

Suddenly the Creole held her away from him and burst into laughter. Mendez had described the scene in detail. It seemed the Englishman had fared the worst for the encounter and that amused him. Where he had failed to best the arrogant captain, this mere slip of a girl had accomplished the feat as only a woman could do. He relaxed his grip in spite of the blue eyes attacking his own through black, thickly lashed lids. Instinctively, he managed to leap backward, avoiding the flashing blade of the girl's dagger as it swooped across the front of his shirt, its sharp tip ripping a gash in the red material. A curse escaped his thin lips as he stared at the girl in astonishment.

"Don't you ever try anything like that again, or I'll run you through!" Her voice rang with angry indignation as she repeated the warning for the second time in one day. "Men!" she shrieked furiously.

The roar of the cannon at the top of the hill distracted them both. Another ship was approaching the Nose' Be harbor. Ramon raised his hands declaring a nonverbal truce and started to run up the hill toward the lookout. Since the unusual arrival of the *Sea Lady* the day before, Shannon realized now was not the time to pursue the quarrel. The security of the cove could be at stake. She sheathed her weapon and followed in his footsteps, unable to keep up with his long easy strides as he lengthened the distance between them.

It was the *Plunderer*. She jumped excitedly from her vantage and waved the bright bandanna in greeting, certain her father was observing from the decks of his ship. He would be full of tales of his latest voyage to Tangiers and, of course, there would be presents. He never failed to bring her unusual gifts, much to her delight. But what mattered most is that they would have time together—his most cherished gift of all to her.

"It seems our capitán has met good fortune on his return voyage," Ramon commented as he pointed to the way the ship lay low in the water. "But it has apparently cost him."

Shannon sobered and walked over to the Creole. "What's wrong?" she asked worriedly. "Can you see him? Is he hurt?"

Ramon handed her the glass. "Your papa is fine. The *Plunderer* needs some repair," he explained.

Shannon thought she detected a note of disappointment in his voice and it was not about the ship.

40

Dismissing the notion, she searched the deck with the glass and saw the giant frame of the man she adored standing on the deck peering back at her with his own glass. Again she waved her bandanna with her free hand, and saw him return the gesture. As Ramon said, he looked fine. However, she did see the splintered rail and a gaping hole on the fore deck where a cannon ball apparently had hit its mark. She offered a silent prayer of thanks that the damage was no worse and that her father was returned safely home to her.

She was tempted to follow Ramon and the gunnery crew down to the docks to greet the homecoming crew, but knew that there would be much business to be attended to before Nick Brennan would have time for her, so she returned to the house. He would be home for supper and she would have a nice hot bath waiting for him as she often did. Then after he was refreshed and nourished with one of Marie's delicious meals, they would go back down to the tavern together for the homecoming celebration. And the more unobtrusive she could be as the night progressed the later she might be allowed to stay.

Chapter Three

Filling the large wooden tub in the fenced enclosure beind the house with cold water was no problem. Nick Brennan had ingeniously designed a string of wooden pipes from the nearby spring a bit farther uphill to permit its chilling flow to snake its way down to the enclosure and dump over it. A cork plug in the bottom made drainage equally easy, and usually there was enough water lying in the pipes heated by the sun to take the chill off. This time however, Shannon had used it for her own bath, so she had to heat the water in the kitchen to get the tub ready for her father.

Marie was in the kitchen, putting the finishing touches on a roast guinea for his homecoming meal. Since Shannon had informed her of Brennan's arrival the old woman had been in a dither, fussing and fretting so that everything would be just right. Shannon began to feel guilty for sulking in her room and pitched in to help. Marie allowed her to pick and clean vegetables from the garden while the fowl was prepared for the spit.

"Ahoy there! Anyone here?"

"Papa!" Shannon squealed in delight. She dropped

42

the empty bucket she'd used to carry the hot water in and ran into the house.

Nick Brennan waited for her in the parlor with open arms. His hair was touched with white throughout the thick red curls and lines showed in his face, etched by time and laughter; but his blue eyes, much younger than his forty-odd years of age, lit up as his lovely daughter, her long damp hair clinging closely to her oval face, bounded across the room and threw herself into his big arms. He picked her up and swung her around laughing loudly. It was only when he put her back down again that he sobered and whispered mischievously in her ear.

"You're a welcome sight for these old eyes, darlin', but ye'd be more than that to the gentleman puttin' me packages on the veranda."

Shannon looked at her father in bewilderment for a moment until it struck her that she still wore his big shirt. He sighed as he realized how soon he would lose her, even if it were to Ramon Gerarde. Although he sympathized with her feelings about the young man, he felt that she would in time come to see that he was the best match for her.

"Why such a long face, Papa?" Shannon asked with concern, dismissing the man on the veranda as she heard his retreating footsteps.

"Because, darlin', you're a grown woman, and a lovely one at that. And someday soon, ye'll be married off to another man and I'll . . ."

"Papa!" she chastised gently. "I'll never leave you. You're the kindest, bravest, gentlest man I've ever known. No one could fill your shoes . . . and I could not love a lesser man." She crossed the floor and hugged him affectionately.

"And you're as full of blarney as your old man!" Brennan teased, lightening the mood. "Now, hurry

43

up and open them packages. Me bath's gettin' cold."

Shannon glanced at the packages her father had apparently brought inside while she was dressing. Anxiously she picked one up and tore at the wrapping. She struggled to break the string and was reminded of the dagger she'd left on the dresser in her room.

"Here ye go, lass." Brennan offered his own knife.

"No thank you, Papa. I'd best get my own."

In a moment she was back and cutting the string away easily. She cried out in delight as the paper fell away to reveal a pair of fawn colored breeches and a voluminous linen blouse with full sleeves to go with it. Another package held a pair of new boots.

"Don't bother with the rest o' them. They're for the house," he explained. "The rest of yours is on the veranda."

Shannon ran excitedly to the door and rushed through it leaving it open for her father to follow. She held her hands to her face in awe as she spied the huge mahogany trunk polished to a sheen and trimmed in solid brass. She reached out and lifted the lid to reveal a rich satin lining.

"It's beautiful!" she whispered. A bulky package in the bottom caught her attention and she glanced up at her father in wonder. "More?" she asked. He nodded and she proceeded to open it.

Shannon was speechless when a mass of red taffeta unfolded to display a gown. It was Spanish in its design with a dropped waistline and full skirt doubly gathered in the back to form a fanlike train of red folds and black lace. Under the skirt were layers of gathered lace petticoats sewn in the garment. "I've never seen anything like it!" she exclaimed truthfully. She wondered where she might wear such a lovely dress, her new breeches and shirt much more serviceable. "I'll save it for a special occasion," she promised, tucking it carefully back into the trunk. After closing the heavy lid, she turned and hugged the giant man again. "Oh, thank you so very much, Papa!"

Supper was delicious as usual. Marie served the meal and after much insistence from Shannon and her father, sat down to join them. Brennan entertained them both with stories of his recent voyage and Shannon clung to every word, hardly touching her meal, as he described the port of Tangiers. She hoped that someday he would take her there. After the meal Marie opened the remaining packages and was as delighted with the various bolts of material and housewares as her charge had been with her gifts. Brennan, now scrubbed and dressed in clean clothing, relaxed for the first time in weeks enjoying the company of his small family, while the two females cleared the table and carried the dirty dishes back to the kitchen.

This last voyage seemed to have gone harder with him; and for the first time, he'd felt real fear when the cannon fire from his encounter with the merchantman splintered the deck near him, fatally wounding the helmsman standing at his side. Although the attack proved successful, he had been left shaken and in the remaining part of the voyage to Nose' Be, he began to reassess his life, many thoughts entering his mind where he had not let them trespass before. He grunted as Shannon reentered the small dining room, radiant and obviously anxious to accompany him to the tavern and dismissed the troubling thoughts for the time being.

The noise in the tavern made it difficult to hear as the captain of the *Sea Lady* strained to hear his first mate's account of the state of his ship and crew. Two of the seamen from the *Plunderer* who had sailed with the Brethren of the Coast in the Caribbean remembered the forty-gun vessel that once sailed with Henry Morgan's fleet of pirates before he fell into such grace with the king of England. They believed Hawke's explanation as to why Captain Jack Morrey no longer commanded the vessel. The life of a pirate was rarely a long one, and, often, when a captain was killed in a raid, one of the strongest of the crew succeeded him in command. That the news of her recent capture by the British navy had not reached the Red Sea Men proved to be to Hawke's advantage.

Michael Finney shook his head, giving up his attempt to give his captain the report and helped himself to a healthy swallow of grog. He wiped his hand across his thick blond mustache and licked it. "As fine a draft as I've ever tasted," he shouted to his companion.

Morgan Hawke laughed. "You say that every time you have a drink, Finney!" The big-hearted Irishman was not only his firstmate, but a lifelong friend. He had been a seaman on one of Lord Hawke's merchant ships when Morgan was cabin boy of twelve working his way up in his father's empire. It was Finney who introduced the youth to the wilder side of life, as he chose to call it, while Hawke's father saw to his education as the future lord of Snowden. "Take care that the brew doesn't outlast . . ."

"*Perdoname, querido,* but could I bring you more Madeira?" Carlota leaned over the dark-haired man intentionally brushing her bosom against his smoothly shaven face.

Hawke pushed away from the table and made room for the woman. She laughed as he pulled her down in his lap. "Finney," he called, trying to address his friend over her bustline, "this is Carlota. She works here and has made my stay thus far most enjoyable."

Michael Finney rose and bowed grandly. "Indeed it is a pleasure to meet such a beautiful creature such as yerself, miss."

Carlota laughed loudly and reached for the bowed head. A surprised Finney found his face buried in the ample bosom as she kissed him on the top of the head. "You are very good with the compliments, señor."

"And when ye tire of this youngster, ye might keep in mind that I'm very good at other things as well!" He winked wickedly at the woman.

Hawke squeezed the serving wench around the waist. "He's always after my women," he teased.

Carlota glanced toward the door where Ramon Gerarde sat at a large round table reserved for Nick Brennan's companions and smiled as she turned her face to her recent conquest, certain that the dark-complected pirate watched her. "How could I want anyone, *querido*, when I have, *como se dice*, had the better—best!" she corrected herself, before wrapping her arms around him and kissing him full on the mouth. She did not notice him wince, his lip still sore from his morning encounter with the tomboy.

A stir in the general noise of the tavern diverted Finney's attention from the amorous couple and he raised his eyes to see a giant of a man enter the room with a lovely young woman at his side. "Glory be to the saints," the firstmate exclaimed, his eyes fixed on Shannon as she casually glanced his way. "It's an angel come to this devil's den to save us all!"

Morgan Hawke extracted himself from Carlota's embrace and followed Finney's gaze. He stared in disbelief at Nick Brennan's companion. It couldn't be the little minx he'd tangled with that morning! He was suddenly aware of an icy blue glare from across the room that confirmed his suspicion. It seemed she hadn't told anyone of their encounter, he reflected, since it had not been mentioned by Brennan or Gerarde, and he wondered why.

Carlota jumped up from his lap suddenly, her cheeks flushed with anger. "She is a spoiled brat. A girl child not worth your trouble!" she warned through clenched teeth. "She steal my man. I would cut out her heart if I but could." With a swish of her skirt, the woman stomped away toward the door to the back.

"Well, *careedo*," Finney remarked, mimicking the Hispanic term of endearment, "I let ye out o' me sight for one night and see what a fine mess yer in."

Hawke ignored the jibe and nodded to Nick Brennan as the pirate motioned for him and Finney to join his table. "It seems we're to be entertained by Brennan himself tonight," he remarked to his friend as he rose from his seat.

Shannon stiffened as she saw the English captain and his burly blond companion approach her father's table. She glanced nervously at Ramon. He smiled at her and moved aside for her to sit beside him. For a moment she hesitated, but when she saw the stranger take a place beside her father, leaving her the choice of a seat next to him or the Creole, she chose what she thought to be the lesser of two evils and moved beside her would-be suitor.

"Morgan Hawke, I want ye to meet the pride o' this old heart, me daughter, Shannon."

Shannon forced a smile, but she maintained her icy stare; however, she was taken by surprise when the dark-haired man reached across the table and took her hand pressing it lightly to his lips. A becoming blush rose to her face as his deep blue eyes locked with hers. The color deepened as she remembered the last time she had seen him. Now he wore tailored tan breeches and a full-sleeved shirt open at the neck the same color as his tall black boots.

"It is an honor, Miss Brennan."

His smile told her he had read her thoughts and was thoroughly enjoying her discomfort. She wished she could slap it off his handsome face.

"And may I introduce my firstmate, Michael Finney."

Shannon, grateful for the diversion, grabbed the man's outstretched hand with both of hers and shook it enthusiastically. "Always glad to meet a fellow Irishman, Mr. Finney," she blurted out awkwardly.

"Michael, if it's not bein' too bold to ask, miss."

"Indeed not, Michael. And please call me Shannon." Realizing she still held his hand, she released it and dropped to her chair. It was going to be a long evening.

Shannon leaned back against the chair as her father ordered a light wine for her and became aware of Ramon's arm resting on it. She straightened and shot an irritated look his way.

Smiling, he leaned over and whispered in her ear. "I have saved you both a good deal of trouble with my silence. It seems, querida, it is the least you can do to permit me this small favor."

Shannon looked over at her father only to see him wink at her and turn back to his conversation with Morgan Hawke and Michael Finney. She sighed reluctantly and leaned back against the arm of her unwanted suitor. She was grateful for his silence, but she made up her mind, it would only buy him so much. The barmaid arrived with the drinks and

Shannon contented herself to sip wine, tolerating Ramon's attention.

There were several strangers among the celebrating pirates, apparently members of Morgan Hawke's crew. Nearby a group of seamen gathered around the dart board challenging each other's expertise. The more they drank the worse their aim became until some of darts strayed dangerously close to their fellow comrades. The competition was good-natured even when some of Hawke's crew became involved. Good grog had made them all the best of friends.

The serving wenches were kept busy by a demanding Henry Cutchins working behind the crowded plank bar. Occasionally, Shannon caught his disapproving look at Ramon's attentions, and shrugged her shoulders, helplessly returning his stare. Many of the women from the village were also participating in the homecoming gala, hoping to profit from the attentions of the rum-sodden sailors, now rich until their recently acquired riches ran out. Like most of the serving wenches, they were gaudily dressed and wore heavy make-up and perfume.

"Shannon! Shannon Brennan!"

Shannon saw Zeke standing unstably on a table in the center of the crowded room motioning for her to join him.

"We got us a bloke what thinks 'e's an expert with a blade. And I tole 'im, even our girls 're bedder'n 'e is." Zeke swayed precariously to one side and was righted by his comrades. "C'mon, gal. Show 'im yer stuff!" he shouted.

Shannon looked at her father anxiously and rose to her feet as he nodded, giving her his permission. She edged around the table and started toward the expectant group of competitors, when an unsteady sailor jumped to his feet in front of her to see the contest better and knocked her into Morgan Hawke's lap. She felt the familiar grasp of his strong arms as he broke her fall and held her steady. She glanced up, flustered at her predicament, to see amusement on his face. He made no attempt to help her. Unable to find her footing, she was grateful when Michael Finney stood up and pulled her to her feet.

When she reached the center of the cluster of men, she came to face her challenger. He was a stocky man with a scarred, roughshaven face and the way he looked at her made her involuntarily shiver. Zeke, now down from his lofty perch, slapped her heartily on the back, unaware of the undercurrent.

"Now lissen, gal," he said confidentially, putting his arm about her shoulders. "Me 'n da boys 'ere got us a little wager. You jus show 'im how ta throw a knife like we taught 'cha. Well go on!" the man encouraged.

Shannon eyed her competitor warily. "Perhaps we should let the gentleman go first, since he is our guest," she suggested politely.

The man flashed a snaggletoothed, tobacoo-stained grin at her. "Oh, naw, ladies first." It was obvious he thought the idea that she could be a serious threat to his wager a joke.

Shannon drew the dagger her father had given her from the leather sheath at her waist and balanced it lightly in her hand. The path to the target the men had drawn on the wall with charcoal was cleared. She was aware that all eyes were on her and it made her nervous. She stared at the target and then in a swift motion let the blade fly. It pierced the target just outside the center ring. She sighed and unconsciously hugged her shoulders, sensing the disappointment in Zeke and his friends.

The scar-faced man registered surprise at the

closeness of her throw, but covered it quickly. In an effort to show off he turned from her and threw his weapon simultaneously. The careless act cost him, for the knife landed squarely opposite Shannon's, equally distant from the center. His smug look faded.

The crowd of onlookers roared in approval and shouted for a rematch. Zeke rushed up to the target and withdrew the two knives to return them to their respective owners. Before Shannon could throw, Scarface shoved her rudely aside and positioned himself before the target, taking careful aim. His knife sailed through the air and struck in the center ring near its edge. The smug look returned to his face and he turned and motioned for the girl to throw.

This time Shannon took her time and breathed deeply to calm herself. She had done this dozens of times. All she had to do was concentrate. Mentally she shut out the noise as she balanced the dagger by its tip again, and eyed the target with steady blue eyes. With deliberate aim, she let the blade fly and squealed as it landed dead center of the target. As her supporters surrounded her, she caught the hostile glare of her opponent in the corner of her eye and it chilled her. This was definitely a man to cut a wide path around she decided as he disappeared into the crowd.

Fiddlers began to play a lively tune and before she could return to Brennan's table, Zeke grabbed her and swung her around on the floor. Shannon regained her balance quickly and laughed as she joined the overjoyed lookout in a jig. He moved his feet surprisingly fast for one who had consumed so much grog, while Shannon daintily lifted the hem of her skirt and matched him step for step. She could see however, that Zeke was quickly becoming winded. Before she could gracefully end their dance, she was swung about again. This time her partner was Michael Finney, who shouted a polite, "Might I?" to the grateful Zeke, as he let her go and put his hands on his hips to jig.

"Am I to have no rest?" she teased, again picking up her hem so that it did not trip her as she tried to keep up with the friendly Irishman.

"Not while Michael Finney has a breath!" he replied in kind.

When the fiddlers stopped, the partners were ready for a rest and refreshment. They made their way back to the table and dropped into their seats still laughing over their little contest of endurance.

"Well done, daughter!" Nick Brennan congratulated, as he lifted his glass in salute to her skill with the knife.

"Here, here!" came echoes of assent from around the table.

Shannon blushed modestly, uncomfortably aware of Morgan Hawke's intent study of her. She laughed nervously and grabbed Finney's arm. "I can only say I'm glad I was not challenged to out-dance this good man." Her good-natured remark was received with humor.

The attention was diverted from her momentarily as Alana brought two more rounds of drinks. Shannon, thirsty from her exercise, downed the first glass of wine greedily and reached for the second when she caught her father's disapproving glance. She put it back on the table guiltily, and returned to her engaging conversation with Michael Finney. Ramon was obviously annoyed with her, but as she slowly sneaked sips from her wine glass she began to care less and less.

Soon she found herself giggling, caught unaware by the liquor's heady effects, and leaned on the

Irishman's shoulder to hide her face from her father. Finney's stories were hilarious. She could see a mental picture of him and a young Morgan Hawke running half-dressed through a London alley after being caught with the innkeeper's daughters in a compromising situation by the girls' father.

The older man leaned over and whispered in her ear mischievously, "And we never did get our damned breeches back!"

"Oh!" Shannon shrieked hysterically, unable to take any more. She reached over and inadvertently took a huge gulp of Ramon's Madeira. Suddenly her eyes widened as she realized her mistake, and she coughed spasmodically as the heavy wine burned its way down her throat. She might have been discouraged by her father's stern look, but when she caught her breath, she met Morgan Hawke's eyes instead. Unable to control herself, she burst into another fit of giggles, as the mental picture paraded across her mind again, and sought the refuge of Finney's broad shoulders to smother them.

She started as Nick Brennan's chair skidded across the floor and looked up into the angry face of her father. Try as she might she could not straighten her expression, as she turned her own face up to him. She dared not try to speak. Strong arms lifted her lightly from the chair as if she were a feather and stood her on her feet.

"I think it's time ye said good night, Shannon."

It wasn't fair! How often had she seen Brennan boisterous and rowdy? It was another case of everyone else having a right that she didn't. However, Shannon knew her father was in no mood to argue. The prospect of having to go home sobered her slightly as Ramon Gerarde rose to his feet to relieve Brennan of his charge.

"I will walk her to the house," he announced, taking her arm possessively.

Shannon snatched her arm away and gave him a scornful look. Mustering what little dignity she could from the situation, she turned and politely kissed her father good night.

Before she could gather her wits, she was on the street with Ramon. Inside she could hear her father's boisterous laughter and she frowned. She had made a complete fool of herself. She allowed Ramon to put his arm about her shoulders without protest and leaned against him in defeat. They were back there laughing at her expense she thought miserably. A tear trickled down her cheek and she irritably wiped it away with the back of her hand.

"Querida," Ramon whispered gently, his annoyance apparently having passed, "what is it?" He stopped and lifted her chin with the crook of his finger.

"Oh Ramon," Shannon sniffed, dismayed that he had caught her crying. "I hate women that giggle, and I giggled!" A low chuckle escaped him, and Shannon glared at him indignantly. "I'm serious!"

"So am I." He caught her off guard as he swept her to him and kissed her slowly, tightening his grip as she started to struggle. He ignored her loud protest as he began to trace the graceful curve of her neck with his lips hungrily. Her struggles only heightened his growing passion. "Marry me, Shannon."

"No! I don't love you, Ramon, can't you understand that?" Her voice carried through the quiet outside and down to the village street below.

"But I can teach you to love me, querida. I can show you what it is like to be loved by a man . . ."

A sudden commotion from the tavern diverted his attention as Morgan Hawke emerged from the building trying to support a bellowing Michael Finney and steer him in the direction of the longboat from the *Sea Lady*. Shannon seized the opportunity and freed her right arm. With all her strength she clipped him under the chin with the heel of her hand. Caught off balance he stumbled backward to the sloping ground, striking his head on a stone.

The girl made a break for her house leaving the young man cursing and bleeding. She scrambled up the hillside, tripping on the hem of her dress and tearing the skirt at the waistband. She did not look behind her to see if she was being pursued.

Upon reaching the veranda, she bolted up the steps, holding her dirt-stained skirt above her knees and fled into the house to the safety of her bedroom. As she stood at the window overlooking the village path searching for any movement, her hand began to ache from the violent abuse. She pulled the ruined dress off and threw it on the floor, in an angry motion. Marie had thoughtfully filled the porcelain bowl and pitcher on the mahogany washstand, so Shannon seized a towel and began to wash her face and neck with the strong lye soap as if trying to scrub away Ramon's repulsive kisses.

In the moonlight shining through the side window, she caught a glimpse of her reflection in the oval mirror on the wall. She looked pale and exhausted. Tomorrow, she promised herself as she turned and fell across the brass bed, tomorrow she would put an end to this once and for all.

Chapter Four

Morgan Hawke stood at the rail of the *Sea Lady* and studied the familiar lines of the *Dagger* moored nearby. It was his father's ship. He was sure of it. The black paint served to change the color, but the figurehead was the same Grecian lady that graced the bow of every vessel in Lord Hawke's fleet. His father had commissioned an Italian sculptor to carve the figureheads that clearly set apart the ships of his company. Then they had been carefully painted. The lady on the hull of *Dagger* bore the same red hair and green eyes of her sisters.

His eyes narrowed in the sunlight and he ran his hand through his thick black hair. Gerarde. He wondered if the Creole had been the one who had killed his father instead of Nick Brennan. It would fit his character more so than Brennan's. Gerarde was a brooding sort, a loner driven by ruthless ambition. He'd seen the type many times, a breed bent on self-destruction. But Brennan was perplexing—a strange mixture of men in a giant frame.

"It's the lady all right."

Hawke turned to see his first mate standing beside him studying the figurehead on the *Dagger*. "Aye, we're in the right den of thieves," he mused aloud. "Is the longboat ready?" Brennan's loot from his last raid had been inventoried and the pirate leader insisted that he go over the ledgers at the warehouse with his daughter. The suggestion had come when their conversation was interrupted by a suddenly ill Michael Finney who insisted they go outside at once. Since there was little time to discuss the way the pirates divided the take, it seemed to be logical solution. The young captain turned to his mate curiously. "And how are you feeling this morning?"

Finney shrugged. "Fit as a fiddle. Why shouldn't I be?" Suddenly he grinned. "Ah, I take it you're referrin' to last night?"

"Exactly."

"Well now, it seemed to me that someone needed to see after that angel, considerin' the company she left with," the mate explained defensively as he met Hawke's admonishing look.

"Hah!" the man exclaimed, remembering his painful encounter with Shannon Brennan, "that little minx is perfectly capable of defending herself!"

"Minx is it! Well now if ye must know what a minx is, take a hard look at the one yer set on marryin'. That fair-haired mistress is a minx," Finney declared emphatically.

"Corrinne is . . . Corrinne," Hawke finished lamely, not wanting to get into a debate with his first mate over his betrothed.

She was a captivating beauty, blond-haired, green-eyed, and as delicate as the pale yellow roses he had given her when he left London to begin this mission of vengeance. She had cried softly as she stood in the doorway of her home, grief-stricken at their separation; yet, he somehow imagined that as his coach cleared the drive, she had blown her nose on her embroidered handkerchief and gone back inside to ready herself for the day's social schedule without so much as a backward glance. She was prone to theatrics and coyish games, but what woman wasn't when it came to getting her way. Not only was she charming and perhaps a bit more warm natured than a young woman of her station was expected to be, but her stepfather was a successful merchant. A merger of the two companies would likely result from the marriage, so the match was a good one.

And of course, there was the Lady Elaine's quiet, but stubborn insistence that her son give up his reckless life in the sea trade long enough to marry and provide Snowden with a future heir. She knew it would be too much to ask him to remain at the estate. He was too much her late husband's son to give up the call of the sea for a family life; and the estate was certainly self-sustaining under the management of their overseer. However, the grand dame longed for the sound of children playing in the great hall of the manor and perhaps the companionship of a new mistress of Snowden.

"Aye, Corrinne is a minx. Mark me words," the Irishman warned, refusing to drop the subject. He and the young woman had never liked each other. She dismissed him haughtily as beneath her station and contrived to use her feminine wiles to drive a wedge between the young captain and his long-time friend.

"We'd best be going." Hawke turned and walked toward the longboat bringing an end to the conversation and leaving his first mate little alternative but to follow. Corrinne was best left out of his mind at the present. It would take all his attention and effort to stay alive in this godforsaken place long enough to see justice delivered to the murderous brigands who harbored there.

Shannon had cried. It was something she had never done in front of her father, but he had never betrayed her before. Her fate was decided, her feelings neglected, and her heart was broken. Her throat constricted as if the blade of her dagger were lodged in it, cutting and making it impossible to swallow; her eyes blurred as she fought to focus on the entry she had just made. The ink smudged as she brushed away a tear that had fallen on the sheet in front of her.

One month. That's what Nick Brennan had give her to reconcile herself to her future with Ramon Gerarde. He hadn't even shown anger when she told him of the forced kisses, except to say that he would ask her fiance to exercise his patience a bit longer. Patience! The man did not know the meaning of the word. Angrily she threw the pen across the heavy table and pushed the book away.

"My, you're not in nearly as good humor as you were last night, Miss Brennan."

Shannon raised tear-reddened eyes to see the captain of the *Sea Lady* standing before her. "There's good reason for that, Captain Hawke. I'm not," she answered curtly. "So," she sniffed, "if you'll kindly study these numbers, you can easily see the way we handle things here." She turned the ledger around to allow him to see the columns of inventory. Her voice shook as she spoke in spite of her effort to appear businesslike. "Everything has been listed here. When the warehouse is full, Papa or one of his captains will take the goods to Tangiers. French merchants will purchase them and the gold will be brought back and divided like this." She tensed as Hawke leaned over the book and raised her face to his, his eyes searching the blue depths of her own.

"This can wait," he told her gently. He was intrigued as he watched a myriad of emotions swirling in the lucid pools. This was an entirely different side of her than the one he had witnessed dissuading the attentions of her ardent lover with a well-executed punch.

"No, we must put business ahead of everything." Her tone rang with sarcasm. "Everything," she echoed miserably. She ignored the urge to seek the comfort his eyes promised, and drew a long breath and concentrated on the ledger. "Let's get this over with, shall we?"

Shannon methodically began to describe the way the booty was divided. A quarter of the gold went to the captain, a quarter to the treasury used to arm and protect the cove, an eighth to the master, a sixteenth each to the helmsman and master at arms and the balance was divided equally among the members of the crew. If a ship was taken, the captain had the option of retaining it and selling his other ship, or selling the stolen ship. Usually he kept it if it was bigger and better armed than his own.

"That's how Ramon got the *Dagger*," she explained. "He was with Papa when they overtook it."

"Why didn't Brennan keep it?" Hawke asked, his eyes narrowing.

"Ramon led the attack. And Papa would never give up the *Plunderer*," she laughed bitterly. He would give up his own daughter, she thought, but not his ship. Tears sprang to her eyes again and she lowered her head to hide her face from the prying eyes of Morgan Hawke. She needed to get away before she made a fool of herself again. Desperation seized her as she rose from the chair. As she turned to escape, strong hands clamped down on her shoulders gently, but firmly, and held her in place. Tired of fighting, she found herself seeking the comfort of his arms as the dam of emotions gave way.

"I don't want to get married," she sobbed, "especially to Ramon! I won't be a brood sow for the likes of him!" Unable to stop the flood of words, she continued. "I have one month! That's all my loving father has given me to accept it. One month! And my feelings don't matter at all!" She clenched her fists and buried her face in his broad chest. "How could he do this to me! How?"

Her cheeks were hot and wet with tears as she pressed them against his chest exposed by the opening in his shirt and the sound of his heart was loud, yet somehow soothing. Without realizing it, she relaxed against him crying softly. She felt his lips caressing the top of her head and found it difficult to move—not because he held her captive by physical force, but by a force she failed to comprehend.

Suddenly she caught her breath and pulled away, confused at the new turn of emotion. She stared wide-eyed into a smoldering gaze that was both frightening and compelling. "I . . . I have to go," she blurted out awkwardly, as color rose to her cheeks. "We'll finish later."

"I think you should, querida." Ramon's voice cracked through the air like a whip. "Now!" he snapped.

Shannon gasped in shock as she saw the Creole standing in the doorway, his hand menacingly on the hilt of his cutlass. His face was white with rage and his black eyes glared maliciously past her at Morgan Hawke. She watched in disbelief as the two men moved with equal stealth, squaring off for the impending combat. Somehow she found her voice. "No!" she cried out, moving her small figure between them. "This is crazy!"

"Go home, Shannon," Ramon growled lowly, through clenched teeth. "I will deal with this in my own way."

"There is nothing to deal with!" she exclaimed emphatically.

"Nothing?" he spat as he pointed at Morgan Hawke. "This man cannot take my betrothed like some strumpet and go unpunished!"

"Strumpet! How dare you . . ." Shannon broke off as he pulled a familiar comb from his sash and tossed on the dirt floor at her feet.

"That is yours, is it not?" he demanded.

Shannon stared at the comb, at a loss for words, and shook her head in acknowledgment.

"It was found in his bed! Carlota discovered it." The scraping sound of his cutlass being drawn from its sheath shook the girl from her shock.

"Put that away, Ramon," she warned, her hand moving slowly to the hilt of her dagger. This was too much. She had suffered enough with his unwanted attentions, but his unfounded insult broke through her last emotional barrier.

"Shannon, you'd better go. One cannot reason with a fool." Hawke looked past her at Ramon, his eyes warily watching his challenger.

"I won't! He'll cut you to ribbons!" she swore under her breath at him. Suddenly she turned and sprang at the Creole in unbridled fury, swinging her dagger and cursing profusely, taking both men by surprise. Not daring to harm her and yet trying to protect himself from the sharp blade, Ramon parried her thrust with his cutlass and backed out of the warehouse into the sunlight. He halted with his back to a stack of barrels, and cursed as she nicked his arm drawing blood. Then with deliberate calculation, he thrust his weapon into the ground at her feet and ripped open his shirt, exposing his chest to her mercy.

Shannon held her dagger in check, its tip resting against his sweat-moistened skin, and stared in bewilderment. They had drawn the attention of many of the seamen on the docks and she was vaguely aware of their eyes on her, watching in anticipation. "Fight, damn you!" she screamed, almost blind with fury, as a smirk crossed her adversary's lips. He still did not take her seriously. He still mocked her with insult. She cursed vehemently and buried her dagger between his feet. Clenching her fists, she lunged forward wildly but halted in midair as Morgan Hawke caught her about the waist and pulled her back.

"You son of a bitch, let me go!" she gasped, the wind having been knocked out of her. Instinctively, she turned her curses on her new assailant as she struggled for release.

The thunderous sound of a pistol roared above cheers of the crowd bringing silence and a halt to the struggle. Nick Brennan stood a few yards away holding its mate, primed and ready for fire, and beside him was an armed Henry Cutchins. His giant frame cast a shadow between the Creole and the Englishman, still holding Shannon. His face was hard and muscles twitched in his cheeks betraying his black mood.

"Let the lass go." His voice was quiet and threatening like the distant warning of an impending storm.

"Papa . . ."

"Silence, lass!"

Shannon bit her lip apprehensively as she watched the big Irishman look from Morgan Hawke to

Ramon Gerarde, appraising the situation for himself.

"I'll see the two of you inside," he said at last. Without a backward glance, he led the way into the warehouse.

"But Papa . . ." Shannon broke off as her father swung around suddenly and pointed an angry finger at her. "You stay out here!" he commanded. As he went into the warehouse the two opponents followed him with Henry Cutchins at their heels.

Shannon ran over to the innkeeper. Perhaps he could explain for her. "Cudge . . ."

"Not now, Shannon." The tone in his voice dismayed her. He was disappointed in her. She had displayed every mode of behavior he had ever tried to dissuade. As he closed the door behind him, Shannon leaned against the side of the wood-framed building miserably.

"'Ere now, gal. Them too roosters 'll fight it out and it'll be done with."

Shannon looked up at Zeke and made an attempt to smile. "It's all so stupid. There's nothing to fight over. It's all a misunderstanding," she tried to explain.

"Well, it's either dat or Cap'n Nick'll 'ave 'em both whipped for fightin'."

Shannon let out a long breath, and hooked her thumbs in her breeches. Ramon deserved to be whipped, but Morgan Hawke had done nothing. If anyone else should be whipped for brawling, it should be she. Nick Brennan forbade public fighting in the cove. Disputes that required a violent settlement, were done in a controlled situation where innocent bystanders were not likely to get hurt and property was not likely to become damaged. Violators were whipped, regardless of who started it.

When the door finally opened and the men came out, Nick Brennan announced that a duel had been agreed to. The choice of weapons left to the Englishman, he opted for swords. A general murmur of assent echoed in the crowd. Everyone knew of Ramon Gerarde's prowess with the cutlass, and anticipated the stranger's inevitable defeat. Again Shannon tried to speak to her father, but was silenced by the threat to send her to the house if she tried to interfere again.

A large circle was drawn in the dirt as the boundary of combat. If either man stepped outside, he forfeited the duel and would make a public apology to his opponent. Yet, if they remained in the circle, it could become a fight to the death. Shannon bit her lips together in a thin line as she caught Morgan Hawke glancing her way and gave him an apologetic look with wide and apprehensive eyes. He regarded her coolly and turned to listen to Nick Brennan as he described the rules of the duel. She knew he blamed her and with every right.

As the duelists drew their weapons, silence fell over the crowd. Shannon winced at the first clash of steel, and rubbed her arms nervously. A movement to her right diverted her attention as Michael Finney took a place beside her watching his captain through narrowed eyes. A smile tugged at the corner of his mouth and Shannon looked back to see Morgan Hawke flourishing his saber to expertly parry Ramon's thrust. He circled the blade with his own and slung it outward with a fluid wrist motion, nearly disarming his opponent.

Ramon recovered his grip with the skill developed from years of combat and pressed in again. The crowd cheered as the tip of his cutlass lashed through the shoulder of Hawke's shirt with a clean ripping noise. Shannon paled as blood soaked the white linen and inadvertently grabbed Finney's arm. Ramon flashed a sinister smile of white teeth and pressed in again. He was playing with the Englishman, she thought apprehensively. He met Hawke's lunge and steel crossed and locked, bringing the duelists face to face. As they broke away, his leg shot out hooking behind Hawke's knee and bringing the captain down off balance. He raised his cutlass and plunged down at the Englishman's back.

Shannon caught her breath and held it as Morgan Hawke twisted away, Ramon's blade slicing through empty air. In one movement he was on his feet and slashing down on the extended cutlass, striking it near the hilt with such force that it flew from Ramon's hand to the dirt. As the pirate leaped to retrieve it, Hawke stepped on it with his booted foot and put his blade to the ear of the Creole. Ramon paled as sweat rolled down his forehead. Shannon noted quick exchange of glances between the captain and his first mate before he kicked the sword out of Ramon's reach and withdrew his weapon.

"I believe you owe the lady an apology," he prompted, as Ramon backed away slowly.

The Creole glared at him and then walked over to Shannon stiffly. She cringed inwardly at the hatred on his face as he spoke. "I am only sorry that I did not kill the bastard!" he growled lowly. He pushed past her and stalked off toward the tavern. Her knees felt as if they were going to give way, when her father grabbed her arm firmly. Summoning all her strength, she stood up and looked him squarely in the eye, tilting her chin defiantly. As she met his eyes, she thought for a moment they softened.

"Zeke," he called over his shoulder, never breaking his gaze, "see that this troublemaker stays out o' the village 'til further notice."

"Papa, if you'd only listen to me, I . . ."

"I've said what I have to say. Nothin's changed," he told her firmly. "Except," he added, watching

Morgan Hawke and Michael Finney make their way to the longboat tied up at the quay, "maybe ye'll have a choice of husbands." He scratched the stubble on his chin thoughtfully. "Maybe . . . Now get on with ye!"

Shannon's mouth gaped open in shock, but before she could reply, Brennan started for the tavern with a smiling Harry Cutchins on his heels. How could he! she thought incredulously as she started toward the path leading up the hill to the house. This was the most humiliating thing that had ever happened to her. What must Morgan Hawke think of her? All he had done was offer her comfort. Suddenly, he's forced into a duel over an honor he had not ruined in order to court a female who had nearly emasculated him over yet another misunderstanding! How could she ever face him again! The thought suddenly struck her as ironic. Thanks to her father, she would not have that to worry about for a while.

Shannon saw little of her father in the following week. He was seeing to the repairs on his ship and spending his nights at the tavern. Some fishermen from the village had reported the sighting of two of the English counterparts to Spain's Costas Guardas and a bomb ketch on the other side of Nose' Be patrolling the shore of the big red island of Madagascar. They had been first-rate ships bearing a hundred guns. Even the *Plunderer* could not hold its own against that firepower. So none of the pirate captains left the harbor, the decision to lie low having been agreed upon.

A full gun crew remained posted at the point overlooking the entrance to the cove instead of the usual lookout. Each ship in the harbor was fully provisioned and armed in case the small English fleet's presence was more than coincidence. Messengers had been sent to the chief of the Sakalavas to warn his tribesmen to watch for unusual activity on the other side of the island.

Yet Shannon was not alarmed. The Guardas Costas often sailed near Nose' Be, but the entrance to Brennan's Cove was hidden between the rocks and passage through the narrow channel lined with treacherous reefs discouraging those who did not know the harbor. And if they were lucky enough to get through, the guns high upon the embankment would blow them out of the water. Nick Brennan had chosen the tiny quay for that very reason.

A fish tugged at the end of her line snapping her out of her reverie. She hurriedly wound in the line and seized a small net to fetch her catch out of the water. The hem of her dress caught on her heel as she rose and she kicked at it irritably. Since her skirmish with Ramon, Brennan had forbidden her to wear her shirt and breeches. Her delay cost her her catch, as the fish dropped back into the water. She tossed the pole carelessly to the beach and began to pull the cumbersome garment over her head. Once it was off, she rolled it in a ball and threw it back from the water line.

It was intensely hot and humid, although the sun had not shown its face the whole day. Earlier that morning there had been a few threatening rumbles and a brief shower, but the ominous clouds never left the sky. Shedding her shift as well, Shannon waded into the cool water of the hidden lagoon. It was surrounded on three sidse by a thin strip of sand and protected by dense trees towering high enough to shelter its view from the lookout point over the cove. On the other side was a thick rocky wall that separated it from the bay, feeding the lagoon through an ancient lava tube. Shannon considered it to be her own private beach, her father having shown it to her as a child and she'd spent many lazy afternoons on its warm sandy shore.

As she dove under she realized her scarf still confined her hair. Breaking the water surface, she unfastened the scarf and threw it up on the beach playfully. As she splashed on her back into the water again the long tresses spread out about her neck and shoulders like a dark shining fan. She flipped over gracefully and dove, opening her eyes to peer through the crystal clear water at the brilliant display of color below. Small fish swam around the coral in fleeting schools, scampering away from her. A large white conch lay at the edge of the coral bed. After going up to take another breath of air, Shannon retrieved it. Marie would make a delicious soup from it if the shell were occupied.

She swam back toward the beach with her prize and rose as her feet touched the sandy bottom. Her hair clung to her back and chest covering her to her slender waist at the water line as she studied the ribbed pearly surface of the conch and put her ear to its opening, listening intently for the roar that had amused her often as a little girl. The silence indicated its occupancy, and she smiled triumphantly.

Suddenly, she was distracted by a movement on the beach as she spied Morgan Hawke examining the ball of her dress curiously. If he had seen her, he gave no indication. As cool as the water was she felt her bare skin burning with color as she eased back down into the water to seek cover. If she were quiet, he might leave.

That, however, was not to be the case she realized to her horror as he stripped off his shirt with a fluid motion of rippling muscles and tossed it on the beach next to the discarded dress. He was coming in, she thought in dismay, as she watched him pull off his boots and start toward the water.

"No!" she cried out, the alarm stopping him short

as he stared in her direction. "Please, I'm not decent," she explained as she dropped the conch and wrapped her arms across her chest, her face crimson.

"Shannon!" he exclaimed in mock surprise. "I wasn't aware the beach was occupied."

"Well it is, and I would appreciate it if you would kindly leave." She raised her voice on the last two words as he stepped in the water. He had her in an awkward position and was intent on playing it out to its fullest. Shannon moved backward toward the deeper water. "Please, don't come any farther," she pleaded in vain.

"Why shouldn't I? After all, fair is fair," Hawke teased, referring to their first meeting.

"If you've any shred of decency you'll turn your back and let met dress." Shannon was over her head, and treading water, as he continued toward her. "Damn you!" she cried out. "Go away!" Her heart pounded loudly in her chest as he plunged into the water and started toward her with long easy strokes. She swam frantically out of his path, cursing in gasping breaths, and was astonished when he passed her continuing toward the deeper end of the lagoon. Taking advantage of the opportunity, she made a bee line toward the shore and stopped in the shallows only long enough to see if she was being watched. She was reassured as she saw him dive under and darted to her clothes on the beach. Without taking time to dry, she donned her shift hurriedly.

"Come back in!" His deep voice carried across the water as he motioned for her to join him.

"No thank you!" She pouted peevishly and plopped unceremoniously down on the beach. He had given her a fright, and she didn't like bearing the brunt of his joke. She pulled her wet hair from inside her cotton shift and used her dress to dry it briskly. Watching him as he moved easily through the water,

71

she began to comb her hair with her fingers until it lay spread about her shoulders to finish drying. Absent-mindedly, she drew her legs up under the shift and brushed away the sand that clung to her feet. Then resting her elbows on her knees, she stared at the intruder as he emerged from the water carrying a conch shell.

"Here," he said his eyes dancing as he offered her the shellfish. "This could be the start of a promising meal."

"How long have you been here?" she asked, ignoring the gesture and wondering if the conch was more than a coincidence.

With a shrug, he tossed the conch on the beach beside her bag of tackle and settled down next to her. "Do you always swim like that?"

Shannon blushed in spite of her determination not to let him fluster her. "Very few know of this beach. And I . . ." she hesitated a moment. "What are you doing this far from the village anyway?" she demanded, taking the offensive. It was nearly a mile through the woods to her home and the quay was beyond that.

"Exploring, for lack of anything better to do. Every man in the port is restless for action of any kind at this point." He spread his shirt out on the sand and lay back on it, locking his hands behind his head and gazing up at the darkening sky. The taut muscles of his stomach contracted as he took a deep breath and exhaled slowly. "The sighting of those ships has made everyone a bit jumpy."

Shannon laughed nervously, averting her eyes from the narrow line of fine dark hair that trailed down from the mat on his chest to the narrow waistline of his breeches. "They can't do a thing, even if they knew where we were. Papa chose the cove for that very reason. The only way a ship can get in is through the channel, and it's well defended."

"But we can't get out either," he pointed out. He rolled over on his side and rose up on his arm, regarding her. She was like a beautiful wild creature with her damp hair unbound in waves around her bare shoulders. Impulsively, he reached out and caught his fingers in it.

Shannon drew away in surprise and yelped as he held her fast. She leaned over with her head tilted in his direction, trying to pry open his hand. "Let it go!" she demanded irritably. The loose shift hung away from her body as she faced him on her hands and knees innocently presenting a tantalizing view. Suddenly he dropped the lock of hair and looked away from her.

"I'm sorry," he apologized. "I had forgotten your aversion to the touch of a man."

Shannon was taken back. She had been so used to Ramon's stubborn persistence, that Hawke's consideration of her demand diffused her anger. Her voice softened as she reached out and touched his shoulder tentatively. "You don't understand, Hawke. It's not that I don't ever want a man to touch me, I . . . I just can't stand it to be Ramon . . . or you!" she added, quickly withdrawing her hand and leaning back on her knees in retreat as he turned to face her again, studying the struggle of emotion in her eyes.

She wondered why she felt urgent need to confide her innermost feelings to this man; or why she felt guilty for denying his touch. Her brow knitted as she continued. "You see, maybe someday I'll find someone I can love and respect, and when I do," she added thoughtfully, "I'll give myself to him on my terms." Her eyes earnestly searched his inscrutable ones for a sign of comprehension. In frustration, she exclaimed in a rush, "Well if I must be pawed and slobbered on, I'd rather it be by someone I love!"

His deep spontaneous laughter provoked her even further. Her blue eyes flashed in a rise of indignation and she tilted her chin stubbornly, refusing to bear the brunt of his humor again. She'd been foolish to confide in a man anyway.

Suddenly a brilliant flash of light illuminated the beach. It was followed by an immediate explosion of thunder. Shannon forgot her indignation for the moment as Morgan Hawke swore under his breath and rose hurriedly and pulled her to her feet.

"We'll have to make a run for it!"

Shannon froze as another flash of lightning struck in the trees between them and the village, and shook her head.

"No, follow me!"

Large raindrops began to fall as she scooped up her wrinkled dress and darted along the water's edge toward the rocky wall that separated the small lagoon from the bay on the other side. The incline was steep and slippery with moss and lichens, making her ascent difficult. Halfway up, Shannon pulled herself around a large boulder and led the way into the narrow opening of a cave concealed by it. Once inside, she leaned against the cool damp wall to catch her breath as Morgan Hawke entered brushing the raindrops off his bare shoulders and chest.

The cave had been her own secret. Not even Nick Brennan knew of the hidden access to the bay. She had discovered it while playing on the rocks and upon entering the cavern saw daylight filtering in from below. When she descended to a lower level, she found a low arch sculpted out of the rock over the years by the rising and falling tide. When the tide was high the opening was sealed by the water that filled the lower level of the cave. The rock enclosure served as a hideout for many hours of play.

"You are just full of surprises!" Morgan Hawke remarked, hardly believing his eyes as he looked around. The light coming in from the lower level of the cave outlined the form of a small native dug-out pulled up on the rock floor, leaning over on its side. "Yours?"

Shannon nodded as she wrung out the soaked hem of her shift. "I traded some jewelry with one of the Sakalavan villagers for it. Occasionally, I take it out in the bay through the arch down there." She pointed toward the opening.

"Doesn't your father worry about you going out alone in that thing?"

"He doesn't know," she answered with a grin, "and I never go out when he's in port." Sensing disapproval, she added, "Besides I always stick close to the shoreline."

The storm was fully under way now and the wind whipped through the rocks around the entrance making a whining noise, accompanied by the crashing booms of thunder and blazing lightning display. Shannon shivered involuntarily and shook out her damp gown which was considerably drier than her rain-soaked shift. She struggled with the garment halfway on as the skirt tangled in the neckline.

"Here, be still." Morgan Hawke stood behind her and unwound the hem. As it fell to hang its full length to the floor, he closed the hooks in the back, brushing her hair out of his way as it tangled in the fastens.

Shannon looked back over her shoulder patiently. Upon seeing her hair impeding his progress, she put her arms back under it and lifted the heavy tresses upward. She shivered again involuntarily, but this time it was not from the howling wind that drew the damp draft through the cavern, but by the touch of his hand at the nape of her slender neck.

"Are you cold?" he asked, placing both hands on her shoulders gently.

"No . . . Yes!" Shannon drew away from him disconcerted by her reaction. "I used to have an old blanket in the boat." She gave a grateful sigh of relief when she discovered the moth-eaten blanket in the bow under a fishing net. It was however, to her dismay crawling with large black bugs. Making a face, she held it out before her and walked back toward the opening where there was light. As she set about ridding the blanket of its inhabitants, she realized that it was a losing battle and tossed it back in the direction of the boat.

Hawke who had moved to sit down against the wall of the cave near the entrance watched her and weighed his words carefully before he spoke. He was slowly gaining her trust and did not want to jeopardize it. "Shannon, come sit here. I promise I won't bite," he added as he saw her stiffen warily. "I foolishly left my shirt on the beach and together we should sustain sufficient warmth to beat the chill till the worst is past."

Shannon's mind raced as she pondered his words and met his inviting gaze with uncertainty. As much as he had teased her, he had shown her a gentleman's respect. He had certainly had the opportunity to take advantage of her and he hadn't, she told herself. Giving in to an urge she did not fully recognize, she approached the man slowly. As she eased next to him, her body tense and unyielding, he put a strong arm about her shoulder and drew her under its warm protection.

The only sound that remained as the storm passed over was the brisk patter of raindrops as they splashed on the hard rocky surface, lulling and peaceful. Shannon yawned and gradually relaxed in spite of herself, leaning her head against the dark mat of hair on his chest. His heartbeat was like a rhythmic drum beating in harmony with the falling rain. The warmth of his body was inviting and as she closed her eyes she snuggled closer in the security of his embrace.

She had no idea how long she had been there, when the cry of the gulls shook her from her slumber. As she opened her eyes she saw Morgan Hawke's nodded head resting on his shoulder. Taking care not to awaken the man she studied the clean shaven face and square chin. He was almost too handsome, she thought as she put a finger in the distinct cleft and let it trail down over his adam's apple to the hollow in his throat. Asleep he did not frighten her, for she could not see the disturbing blue eyes that provoked feelings within her that she was not yet ready to acknowledge. His steady breathing encouraged her to continue her curious study. Her fingers lightly touched the healing red mark where Ramon's cutlass had slashed through his shirt. From there she moved to the coarse black curls that grew in swirls on the sunbronzed chest that was her pillow, tracing their abandoned pattern until it led down a narrow strip to his navel, just barely showing above the waist of his tan breeches.

Shannon froze suddenly as his stomach muscles contracted and a low chuckle emerged from deep within his chest. She started to scramble away but his arms tightened about her firmly, as he laughed.

"Surely you can't expect to tickle a man while he's innocently sleeping and escape unpunished?" His eyes were bright with mischief as they met Shannon's startled blue ones.

"You promised not to touch me," she reminded him, guilty color rising in her cheeks.

"I promised not to bite you," he corrected, as he drew her face to his and covered her mouth with his own, tasting the sweetness of her lips. As she gasped in protest, his tongue searched her mouth invoking a shudder of unwilling surrender. Her body yielded against the nagging objections of her mind as he moved his hands up the slender curve of her spine and locked his fingers in the silken hair. It was only when the salty taste of tears invaded his senses that he drew back to see her wet lashes fanned upon her rose soft cheeks and fought to control the rising passionate tide he had sworn to hold in check.

Shannon drew a shaky breath and her eyes fluttered open to see the fire she had ignited barely under control in the man before her and knew that a similar flame burned within her own traitorous body. She fought to gather her wits in the reprieve and pulled away unhampered this time. Her skirt encumbered her progress as she stumbled to her feet and backed away from the source of her inner turmoil. She felt cornered by wild and strange emotions and knew she had to escape. If she could get away from him, she could get away from them.

"Shannon," Hawke called softly, as he started to rise, "Don't run." He could see the wild and frightened look in her eyes. "Come here."

Panic seized her as he reached for her and she dashed out of the cave. She heard him call her name behind her as she half slid down the wet rocky slope to the beach and ran faster. The low hanging branches of the trees that lined the path to her house snapped back behind her as she pushed her way past them. She couldn't let him catch her. She had to get as far away from him as possible so that she could think clearly and reason things out—away from his touch, away from his warm embrace and away from the disturbing kisses that instilled an unfamiliar and reckless abandon.

Chapter Five

It was early morning when the slaver, captained by Gaston Labat, arrived in Brennan's Cove to the welcome of the guns at the point. The cannon fire was first met with alarm due to the sighting of the armed British vessels two weeks earlier, but a message was quickly sent from the point to assure the village that there was no threat. The Frenchman had been a friend of Nick Brennan's for many years although they plied different trades and the news he bore set the fire of action among the pirates. When he left Mangalore two of the Mogul's ships were being loaded heavily for their voyage to the Gulf of Aden ports. Based on their anticipated time of departure, they might be intercepted if some of Brennan's men could set sail within the week.

Morgan Hawke sat at the large table with Nick Brennan and the other captains gathered for the purpose of discussing the news and listened as the Frenchman described the luxurious cargo in detail to the seedy lot. Most of them were dressed in brocades of a European fashion—most likely having once belonged to ill-fated gentry that had become victims of bloodthirsty plunder—and some wore baggy Moorish costumes. Jewels and gold, however, with the exception of Brennan and his second in command, adorned them all, most likely a symbol of their success Hawke guessed.

"I have the *Dagger* ready to sail on the tide," Gerarde spoke up, the lust of greed bright in his eyes at the thought of taking the Mogul's ship. "Perhaps another vessel, for instance Señor Fletcher's might accompany . . ."

"Aye, at least two ships," Nick Brennan agreed as he leaned his rough-shaven chin on his hand, his blue eyes narrowed as he thought. "But not the *Dagger*. I want you to continue to see to the repair of the *Plunderer*. And of course, ye'll be wantin' to be here for your own weddin'. Even you're not so good as to scoot up to the Gulf, find them Indian ships and scoot back to marry me daughter in two weeks!"

Hawke forced himself to laugh in unison with the group as they offered their congratulations. He had been to the beach daily since he had last seen Shannon but she had not been there. He was genuinely concerned for her welfare at the hands of the dark-skinned captain and did not want to see her at his mercy. She was too spirited to submit to him and that would assuredly bring her to harm. Gerarde was the type who would be master if it killed her. The muscles tightened in Hawke's stomach at the thought of Ramon touching her smooth glowing skin and sampling the passion he had but tasted in the cavern.

"I think it would be best if we sent Fletcher and our new captain here," the red-haired leader was saying. "We've seen ye hold yer own in a fight, now it's time to see how ye fare on the sea."

Hawke straightened suddenly aware of all eyes on him. "Aye, I'll be most willing to set sail as soon as you give the word. My men are most eager for action after laying up for so long."

"Damn me, if 'e ain't eeloquent with them words," the man called Fletcher exclaimed, slapping him on the back heartily. "Maybe we'd best send ye ahead and let ye talk 'em outta their cargo!"

Again the table erupted in mirth, as Nick Brennan spoke up. "Day after tomorrow then. Sail with the mornin' tide. And the rest o' ye sit tight and enjoy the biggest celebration this cove'll ever see." He held up his mug in toast to his future son-in-law as he referred once more to the wedding. "That is, until I have my first grandson," he added with a mischievous wink.

Hawke was aware of Ramon's mocking appraisal as he pushed his chair from the table and rose with some of the other captains, the business of the meeting over. With a considerable effort, he ignored it and excused himself. He needed to get back to the *Sea Lady* and begin the preparations for the journey. It would do little good to involve himself any further with Shannon Brennan, and it would most certainly affect his mission. Yet, as he made his way to the door, he found it difficult to convince himself of that.

From the kitchen door, Shannon watched with a sinking heart as the captain of the *Sea Lady* exited, the books she was returning to the Cudge as an excuse to come to the tavern to see Hawke in her arms. Before she could retreat inconspicuously, Ramon spied her and rushed to greet her. She gave Ramon her hand and forcing a weak smile, permitted him to lead her over to her father's table. The men at the table made room for her readily as she took a seat between her father and Ramon. She never looked up as Morgan Hawke made his way past them and left the tavern.

Shannon had never liked Gaston Labat. She often wondered why her father maintained a friendship with a man who made a livelihood from a trade Brennan detested. She had persuaded her father to let her come to the tavern on the pretense of borrowing some books from the precious collection Henry Cutchins left in his private room in the rear of the tavern and now she regretted her impulsive attempt to see the English captain.

"You would like something to drink perhaps, Shannon?" Carlota smiled, her dark eyes flashing from Ramon to Shannon, belying her warm manner.

"No, thank you. I just had some lemonade with Cudge." Shannon returned the smile tersely. If Carlota wanted Ramon, she could damned well have him. But she'd seen the wench run out after Hawke, no doubt to some rendevous.

"So, mademoiselle, it seems that you are to marry this young rogue here. My congratulations!" Labot exclaimed, seizing her hand and kissing it enthusiastically. "And I had hoped when you grew up that it would be I who would win your heart."

Shannon could not help but smile at the expression of mock pain on the Frenchman's face, as she withdrew her hand. "I am sure that you have lady friends in every port who will try to help you overcome your disappointment."

"Alas, I must but let them try!"

"Why not stay for the weddin'?" Brennan spoke up as the idea struck him. "Them blacks'll keep their prisoners 'till ye get there to load 'em up."

"Or sell them to another trader before I can get there, mon ami," Labot pointed out. "But merci bien. My only regret is that I will not see this lovely creature gowned as a woman. I have yet to see you in anything but pants!" he teased.

Her father had relented to her pleas to wear her new breeches and shirt and she had donned them gratefully, relieved to be rid of the cumbersome dresses. "I find them much more practical than ruffles and petticoats, Monsieur Labot."

"But when we are married, you will find her in the finest gowns that can be had for I intend to dress her like the living doll that she is."

Shannon's face flushed with anger. It was enough that she tolerated Ramon's hand at the small of her back, but his insinuation that he would dictate her dress wore through her casual facade. She bit her lip in frustration, knowing that an angry outburst might force her to remain in isolation until the wedding.

"To the blushing bride!" Labot toasted, mistaking her anger for embarrassment.

As the men raised their glasses in unison, Shannon rose from the table to excuse herself. "You men must have a lot to talk about and I am sure my presence might inhibit your conversation. So if you'll be so kind as to excuse me," she smiled prettily, "I'll be taking my books and going home. I promised to help Marie with supper."

"I'll walk you there."

"No, Ramon. I insist you stay here and enjoy Monsieur Labot's company. It isn't often that you get a chance to do so." Much to the surprise of the young man, she pressed her hand down on his shoulder forcing him gently but firmly back to his seat and gave him an affectionate kiss on the cheek. She then leaned over and did the same to her father, winking as she met his questioning glance. "Good day, gentlemen."

As she made her way to the kitchen door she heard the Frenchman declaring how lucky Ramon Gerarde was to have won the daughter of Nick Brennan and it rankled her. Let them think what they may, she had not yet accepted their ultimatum. However, she must let them think they had until she had time to put together a plan to avoid the distasteful match—time that was quickly running out.

"And what are you up to, young lady?" Henry Cutchins followed her outside to the yard bordered by thatched roofed buildings with walls woven from banana leaves.

"I won't stand for the marriage," she told the only one who was on her side.

"I know that, dear girl, but how are you going to stop it? Lord knows, I've talked to that bullheaded father of yours 'till I'm blue in the face. He's got it in his thick skull that Gerarde is the best of the lot and that he'd never mistreat you as long as Nick Brennan draws breath."

"Cudge, I need to see Morgan Hawke," Shannon whispered urgently. "Papa will be at the tavern tonight with Labot, and Marie's been gathering roots and odd bits all morning, so I'm almost sure she'll be out back tonight."

The tavernkeeper smiled and shook his head. "I wondered how long it would be before you noticed a real man. What do you have in mind?"

"Cudge, I can't say until I talk to him. But you must get word to him to meet me at the house. My whole future depends on it. Please?"

"Well, if he stepped out and married you, it would certainly put Ramon out of the picture and after that little duel, I think your papa would accept him."

Shannon shook her head in agreement. If Cudge wanted to think that to be her plan, she would have to let him, for if he knew what she had in mind, he would not go along with it at all and she needed his help desperately.

"You two better come up with something soon though, because Carlota just told me that Hawke is sailing out with Fletcher day after tomorrow for the Gulf of Aden. Could be weeks before he gets back."

Shannon paled at the news. She had less time than she thought. "Then tell Hawke to meet me. My life depends on it." She choked on the words as she dropped the veneer of control and blinked her tear-glazed eyes. "Please, Cudge," she implored.

"What about Carlota?"

Shannon bit her lip and drew in a deep breath. "He's seeing her tonight?"

The tavernkeeper nodded, reluctant to further distress the girl, but not wanting to raise her hopes falsely. Carlota had informed him that she would be going to the *Sea Lady* to join the captain after she finished work at the tavern. "It'll be late though, after she's finished here."

"Then keep her as late as you can. He'll have to put off his evening entertainment until later," she added sarcastically. "Will you tell him?"

"I'll see that he gets the message . . . but I can't promise he'll come."

Shannon hugged the stocky man gratefully. Perhaps between his affection for her and the greed of the pirate in Morgan Hawke, she could find her way out of this damnable situation. She thanked him again and turned to make her way through the huts toward the path leading up to the house. She fought the strange pangs of jealousy as she thought of Carlota enjoying the comfort of Morgan Hawke's embrace. No doubt the wench knew how to make a man do what she wanted. For this one time, Shannon envied her knowledge. She picked up a stone and threw it down the slope toward the harbor in an effort to relieve her annoyance; the motion having been futile, she resumed her climb to the house, unaware that her progress was observed from the decks of the *Sea Lady* in the harbor below.

The moon hung over the harbor streaking the water's surface rippled by the easterly breeze from the bay. Its soft light broke through the shadows of the forest in scattered places where the trees were not quite so dense. The calls of the night creatures echoed throughout in a dissonant lullaby. Shannon sat on the veranda and leaned back against one of the posts listening for any sound that might signal someone's approach. She held a lilac bract of the fragrant boungainvillea that grew in abundance about the house and picked at it nervously. It was late and Morgan Hawke had not come.

Perhaps he did not consider her request worth giving up a few moments with Carlota. The intimacy of their relationship had been obvious. Shannon had seen that the wench gave him more reason to want to spend his time with her, as opposed to herself who trembled and ran like a frightened child from his advances. She threw the flower to the ground and rubbed her arms roughly. It was not her fear of him that made her flee, she admitted honestly, but fear of herself; fear that she was not in control of the situation. She had vainly fought for that control the afternoon in the cavern, but the unfamiliar responses aroused by his ardor too easily won out. Had he not stopped and given her the chance to regroup her thoughts . . .

"Shannon."

She started at the low sound of Morgan Hawke's voice and the gentle touch of his hand on her

86

shoulder and turned to face him, her eyes wide with astonishment. She leaned back against the post again and put her hand to her chest as if to hold back the pounding of the beating heart that threatened to burst through at any moment. With considerable effort she found her voice. "Damnation, Hawke, you scared the hell out of me!"

He chuckled and looked out at the golden moon just a day short of being full before raising his shoulders in an exaggerated shrug. "I come all the way up here to meet a lovely maid in the moonlight and this is the reception I get!"

"You're lucky you didn't get a knife in your ribs, sneaking up on a body like that!" Shannon retorted, color rising to her cheeks at his insinuation. "And as for moonlight romance, I'm sure you have all you can handle with Carlota. I sent for you to discuss a business proposition, if you're interested."

The smile faded from his lips as he studied her face intently. Shannon returned his study, refusing to be daunted by his unsettling gaze. As he motioned for her to continue and took a seat beside her on the plank floor of the porch, she relaxed and began.

"As you know, I'm to marry Ramon Gerarde in two weeks. The decision has been made for me and without regard for my feelings. But I will not go through with it." She emphasized each of the last words, through clenched teeth. "I have a plan. But it won't work without your help." She noted the arch of one dark eyebrow and continued. "I want you to let me stowaway on the *Sea Lady* when you leave for the Gulf of Aden."

"You what?" he exclaimed in surprise.

"I have some money. Some jewels actually, but . . ."

"Do you realize what you're asking me to do? Nick

Brennan and that hotheaded fiancé of yours would be in our wake before we ever cleared the bay!"

"Just take me to St. Mary's. I can get someone else to take me from there." Shannon leaned forward imploringly and took his arm. "It's only a little out of the way . . . or Socotra—that's right at the mouth of the gulf!" she added quickly, as she thought of the island southwest of Aden. "I could secure passage from there."

"To where, Shannon . . . where are you going?"

"Tangiers. And from there, Ireland maybe. I'm not sure," she admitted reluctantly. "But I have some jewels that would bring a fine price, if you'd only take just part of the way."

"That's a fairly desperate plan." His tone betrayed his opinion of her scheme.

Shannon straightened and tilted her small chin defiantly, in spite of the brilliant glaze in her eyes. "I am desperate . . . and if you will not help me then I will find some other way. But I am leaving this island." She watched him anxiously as he rose to his feet and came to lean over her, supporting his weight against the post. "What will you do once you reach your destination? How will you live?"

She bit her lip self-consciously and searched for an answer. All she had considered at this point was getting as far away from Nose' Be as she possibly could. "I . . . I'll worry about that when I get there," she answered lamely. "I'll have some money to last for a while." A telltale tear found its way down her cheek. She bowed her head and stared at his feet in an effort to keep him from seeing her weakening stance. With an effort to keep her voice steady, she asked, "Will you help me or not?"

"Shannon, look at me." It was a quiet command. He took her hands and pulled her to her feet. His hand curled under chin, and the other gently wiped away the dampness from her cheek. Her chin trembled as she fought to control her distress. His arms wrapped about her until she was pressed tightly to him, her face against his chest. She stiffened resisting the compelling closeness and the warmth stirring within as he nuzzled the top of her head. "I will not allow the wedding to take place. You have to trust me," he whispered lowly in her ear.

"Then you'll take me away from here?" she beseeched.

"I will not let you marry Ramon. You have my word as a gentleman."

A rush of joy overcame her and she reached up and hugged him, kissing him impulsively on the cheek. It was as though a heavy burden had been lifted from her shoulders. "I promise I'll pay you well. I'll give you the jewels now!" As she moved to pull away his arms tightened holding her close again, and bewildered she looked up at him.

"I only want this." He leaned down and caressed her lips slowly.

Shannon resisted as she thought of the last time she had seen him and pushed back sharply. "How could you do this?" she declared indignantly, as he stepped back in surprise. "Just how good is the word of a gentleman who kisses anything in a skirt, anytime?" And to think she had almost wanted his kiss.

Hawke regarded her, bemused by her sudden change, until the reason for her irksome behavior came to him. She'd witnessed Carlota's bold flirtations with him and was jealous! A smile tugged at the corner of his mouth as he spoke, reaching for her and pulling her against him again. "In the first place, I do not kiss any woman anytime. If you are referring to Carlota, it was she that was kissing me.

89

And as for the time, I prefer a quiet time like the present, in a secluded spot like this, and thirdly, you are not wearing a skirt."

This time his kiss was sensuously demanding and unrelenting as Shannon twisted in his grasp. "No, you bast . . ." she tried to protest, breaking off as he seized her shoulders and shook her roughly.

"Stop acting like a child, Shannon Brennan, and accept the fact that you are a woman! Not some wisp of a girl dressed in pants, spoiled and used to getting her own way. Damn you, you're impossible to deal with!"

Shannon stepped back as he raised his hands to his head and ran them over his dark hair in angry frustration. She met his blazing glare and caught her breath. The fire she saw there was something she was not quite prepared to face. "I . . . I never asked for your kisses Morgan Hawke!" Her words came out in a defensive rush.

"Asked? Hell, you frolic about half-naked, and experiment . . ."

"Experiment! Just what are you trying to say?" Shannon exploded, her own ire kindling. "All I did was ask you to give me passage away from here, for which . . ." she raised her voice as he started to speak, "I offered to reward you handsomely. And now . . . now I don't know what to do!" She kicked at his shin and pulled away as his grasp loosened. He grabbed at her again, but she avoided his clutch and ran into her room slamming her door and bolting it.

"Shannon!" He shook the door violently, and for a moment she thought the housing of the bolt was going to give way. "Come back out here and finish this!"

"Go away, Morgan Hawke! I was a fool to think I could trust you. You're no better than Ramon

Gerarde, just a little more polished."

Tears stung her face as she leaned against the door and listened as the sound of footsteps leaving the veranda echoed in the darkness outside. There was an ache in her breast that she could not fathom as she saw his retreating figure from the window moving down the path toward the village. If only he hadn't been so infuriating, shaking her like a child, questioning her like a child. And she admitted, she had driven him away with her childish outburst— away to Carlota.

Her heart froze as the image of his angry eyes flashed in her mind. If he had been willing to help her before, she was certain that her behavior had changed that. She groaned inwardly at her folly. The very stubbornness that she had cursed in her father had left her still in search of an escape from the island. Morgan Hawke was her only hope. No one else would defy Nick Brennan. No one, she thought as she lay back on the bed and stared at the moon outside the window. Closing her eyes and she buried her face in the pillow sobbing miserably at the twisted turn of fate.

The piercing scream that broke through the lonely stillness following their quarrel sent a chill up her spine as Shannon leapt from the bed in alarm. "Marie!" she cried out as she bolted through the door leading to the parlor. The sound of the housekeeper's voice had come from the garden. The furniture hampered her way in the darkness and she banged her knee sharply as she rushed to the back door. The scream rang out again, terrified and hysterical. It seemed to take ages to cross the small yard to the wild hedge that separated it from the garden. Shannon strained her eyes in the moonlight for Marie.

"Marie!" she called as she spied her crouched

figure and ran to her, forgetting her father's warning never to interfere with the nocturnal rituals of the African woman.

Marie's heavy body was oiled and as Shannon put her arms about the swaying moaning figure she realized that she wore only her ceremonial beads of animal teeth and bits of bone. The girl tried to lift her to her feet to no avail as Marie shrieked again.

"Marie! Stop it! It's me . . . Shannon!"

Her breath caught as the black woman moaned and lolled her head backward. Marie's eyes were rolled up under her eyelids so that only the whites showed. Frightened, Shannon grabbed her again and shook her roughly. "Marie, please stop it!" she begged, a sob rising to her throat.

"Fire!" the hysterical woman screamed, shaking uncontrollably, "I see fire!"

"Marie, there's no fire!" Shannon shouted. "You're safe! You're in the garden!"

"What the hell's going on?"

Shannon pivoted to see Morgan Hawke running toward them, his pistol drawn. "Something's wrong with Marie," she exclaimed breathlessly, her own eyes wide with fear. "She doesn't know where she is!"

"Here . . . let me help," he offered, as he bent over and wrapped his arms about the thick waist. "Where do you want her?" His voice strained as he lifted the moaning woman to her feet.

Shannon nodded toward the kitchen where the housekeeper slept and grabbed her dragging feet as Hawke struggled with her. As she stepped forward her foot slipped suddenly and she glanced down in horror to see that she had stepped on the entrails of one of Marie's sacrifices. She shrieked involuntarily and dropped the feet, shaking her foot and wiping it on the dirt. As she stooped to pick up her load again, she saw Morgan Hawke's admonishing glare and realized she had startled him. She gave him an apologetic look and concentrated on her job at hand.

The door to the kitchen was narrow and their passage through it with their heavy burden was laborious. It was difficult to get a good hold on the woman due to her sweaty, oiled skin. They made their way through the moonlit room to a cot on the opposite wall from the stone fireplace and deposited their charge as gently as they possibly could. Shannon pulled a woven blanket up over Marie to cover her nakedness, and leaned over her, holding her face to her own.

"Marie, this is Shannon. Please talk to me."

The moonlight glistened on the sweat of the woman's brow as she stared at the girl with large round eyes. Her eyelids fluttered and she shuddered violently. "There's gone be trouble," she whispered in a rasping voice that did not sound like her own, "and fire and death."

"She's obviously worked herself into some sort of frenzy," Hawke spoke up, placing a reassuring hand on Shannon's shoulder.

Marie jumped at the sound of his voice and began to wail incoherently.

Shannon pulled the woman's face to her breast in an attempt to soothe her. "Hush, Marie. It's only Captain Hawke. He's no threat to you. He's a friend." She felt Marie stiffen in her arms.

"De Engleeshman! Fire and trouble on de ships. Death!" Marie placed her hands on Shannon's shoulder and shook her hysterically. "Death!" she shrieked.

"Do you have any liquor? We need to get her calmed down."

Shannon nodded in answer to the man's question and motioned to a shelf over the table Marie used to prepare food on. "I think there's some brandy or wine up there." She continued to try to quiet the black woman while Hawke searched the shelf. He took down a likely looking bottle and pulled the cork. He made a face as he tasted it and crossed the room. "I suppose one might call it brandy," he remarked wryly as he handed it to the girl.

Shannon smiled briefly and turned to give Marie a sip of the liquor. Marie drank the brandy in loud gulps. To Shannon's surprise, the bottle was emptied when the rough black hands released it. She cradled Marie's sweat-dampened head and used the corner of the blanket to wipe her face. After a while, the trembling of the body on the cot subsided. When Shannon saw the wide eyes flutter and close, she carefully withdrew her arm and rose unsteadily to her feet.

She found her way through the dimly lit room to the door and discovered Morgan Hawke waiting outside. She reached out and took his hand, squeezing it warmly. "Thank you. I . . . I couldn't have possibly handled her alone."

"You look tired. Perhaps you had better get some rest yourself." His manner was cool and reserved.

"Hawke, Marie has a gift. She can see things before they happen." Shannon's brow knitted in worry as she reflected on the woman's words. "Perhaps you shouldn't go to the Gulf of Aden."

"Nonsense! I don't believe in voodoo or whatever it is that she practices," he retorted disdainfully. "And I find it hard to believe that you are taking her hysteria seriously."

"But what if she's right? What if your ship does catch fire during battle?" Shannon ignored his condescending manner as she sought to convey her concern.

Hawke regarded her for a moment in the pale moonlight and then lifted her hand from his arm firmly. "It's a risk we all take every time we go out," he said simply. "And now, if you will excuse me, I have to get to my ship." He bowed his head curtly and turned to walk around the house to the path leading to the village.

"Hawke!" Shannon called out his name impulsively and then looked away as she groped for words. As he turned and faced her, she relented, too tired to do battle again. "Never mind," she muttered. She was aware of his eyes on her as she made her way to the house. There was so much she wanted to say, and yet she could not bring herself to come out with the words, especially when he had behaved in such a cool manner. Her shoulders sagged in defeat as she entered the silent house and sought the solitude of her bedroom once more.

Chapter Six

Shannon sat in front of the mirror that hung over her dresser impatiently as Marie fussed over her hair. Had she known how long it was going to take, she would never have asked the housekeeper to help her. Although she wanted to make a special effort to look her best, she had not counted on the timely task of pinning the long dark tresses in large curls swept off her neck.

"Dere! You is gonna be the prettiest thing any of dem men has ever seen." Marie's hands rested on her shoulders as she looked into the mirror, proud of her accomplishment.

She had been late in waking that morning and was very much reserved, keeping to herself most of the day. Shannon had not broached the subject of the previous night's hysteria and Marie had not mentioned it. It was noticeable to the girl how strained and tired the woman's face looked. Now, however, her dark eyes were twinkling as if she had suddenly recovered from the fatigue.

"Dat Ramon, his eyes gonna pop right out when he see you in dis dress. Dis gonna be special night for you, girl." She squeezed Shannon warmly, and

Shannon thought for a moment she detected a misty glaze in her eyes. "Now stan' up and let's see you!"

Shannon rose from the table and straightened the full gathers of the Spanish gown her father had brought her from Tangiers. As she gazed at her reflection she barely recognized herself. The gown clung to her slender form tightly, dipping low in the front where the fullness of her bosom rose in provocative restraint, and plunging equally low in the back to the full gathers of ruffles and lace at the small of her back. The sleeves were long and close fitting, tapering down to her small wrists. The full skirt hanging from the dropped veed waistline swung as she moved in a graceful motion.

"Now put dis on your cheeks, make you rosy like a baby," Marie instructed, holding up a dish of crushed berries.

Shannon shook her head. "I don't think so, Marie. I look strange enough as it is. How about this?" She pinched her cheeks roughly causing the color to rise to the surface, and turned for inspection. "What do you think?"

"I tink your mama be proud to see you. Tonight you become a woman and ole Marie, she lose her baby girl."

"Oh, Marie. It's just another party and the only thing different about me is this dress and this coiffure you so artistically created!" Shannon hugged the woman affectionately.

"One ting!" Marie exclaimed as she remembered the special perfume she had extracted from the lavender in the garden. She pulled a vial from her apron and uncorked it. "You smell like the flowers and you twice as pretty!"

Shannon wrinkled her nose, but accepted the gift. Perhaps a little would not make her smell like the heavily perfumed harlots that frequented the tavern when Nick Brennan threw a party.

The occasion was twofold. It was a send-off for the two ships sailing for Aden the following morning, and it was a party to celebrate the formal announcement of her wedding to Ramon. The date was Saturday, two weeks away to the day. Brennan felt that since the crews of Hawke's and Fletcher's ships would miss the big celebration, that they might at least enjoy the preliminary one.

And so Shannon allowed Marie to think that she was dressing especially for her fiancé. However her true motive was different. She had tonight only to try to convince Morgan Hawke to help her and she was determined to use every feminine wile she would muster to do so.

The sound of Ramon's voice outside on the veranda shook her from her thoughts. Somehow she would have to get rid of him, in order to see Morgan Hawke, but her father had made it difficult. He insisted that Ramon escort her since the occasion was to announce their union. She scrambled down on the floor to search for the matching satin slippers as Marie went out to talk to Ramon.

Ramon was intently involved in a quiet conversation with Marie at the back door as Shannon stepped into the parlor. The rustle of her skirts diverted his attention and he straightened, staring at her in obvious admiration.

"Madre de Dios! You are a vision, Shannon." Crossing the room, he took her hand and kissed it. "I have never seen you so . . . so beautiful."

"What I tell you!" Marie laughed. "Now turn around and show him your dress. Go on!" the woman encouraged.

Shannon forced a smile and turned gracefully,

sweeping the gathered train in a circle with her arm.

"I have not ever seen such loveliness in a woman. I am your humble slave, Shannon Brennan. You have but to ask, and I will do whatever you desire." His dark eyes held hers for a moment and sent a chill up her spine as she recognized the hunger in their depths.

"Then I wish to go down to the tavern and sing and dance with Papa's men and just have a good time! Will you permit me to do that without your getting angry and spoiling my fun?" She raised a challenging eyebrow at the man to make good his words.

"But of course, you must. They all are but friends who wish us well. Our time together will come later." He placed his hand above the gathers on the back of her gown and escorted her to the door.

As Shannon expected, the path was difficult to maneuver in the dainty slippers and much to her chagrin, she had to depend on the strong arm of her escort for support. When they reached the tavern, she was relieved to find a seat at her father's table and slipped her feet out of the flimsy shoes for a few moments. "Damn me, lass, if I'd known ye'd look like that in that dress, I'd never have bought it for ye!" Nick Brennan exclaimed as he beheld the woman beside him. He winked mischievously. "Maybe ye should go put your breeches on after all!"

Shannon laughed and leaned against him affectionately. "I love you, Papa," she whispered lowly so that no one else could hear.

Brennan put his big arm about her shoulders and lowered his head to hers. "And I love you, too, lass. More than ye've been thinkin'. And whatever I've done, I've done because I thought it was best for ye. Just remember that."

Shannon nodded mutely and turned to accept the wine Ramon handed her. If she could contrive a way from the island, she would miss her father and Marie terribly; but, perhaps after she had been gone a while and they had accepted the fact that she was not going to marry Ramon, she could contact them and possibly come back. Her heart seemed to wretch as she realized the improbability of that.

The wine was only slightly sweet and Shannon sipped it frugally not caring to repeat her recklessness of the last night she had attended one of her father's parties. She had also made sure that she had eaten well before she left for the same reason. She needed all her wits to deal with Morgan Hawke. She glanced around the room again, wondering what she would do if he did not come.

The conversation turned inevitably to the prospective voyage to Aden as Captain Fletcher joined their company. There was speculation as to the ability of Morgan Hawke to follow through on the mission successfully, but Nick Brennan was most complimentary in his appraisal of the young man, much to Ramon's displeasure. He noted that the young man had not yet set aside his preparations for the early morning departure to join the celebration.

"He's a serious sort, that one. Not given as much to drinkin' and wenchin' as most I've sailed with. Includin' meself!" he added humorously.

"Papa!" Shannon chastised, hardly believing her father's uncharacteristic references. She realized to her amusement that Nick Brennan must have started his partying much earlier with some of his men.

"Well now, lass, it's time ye realized that all them nights I've been spendin' here at the tavern ain't exactly been to discuss them bloomin' books with our good tavernkeeper! A man has need of more pursuits than those of an intellectual nature!''

Shannon punched her father playfully on the arm and shook her head slightly embarrassed at his risqué banter. The fiddlers started to play as he laughed loudly and slapped her on the back, nearly causing her to spill her drink. Some of the men grabbed the nearest buxom wench they could find and started to swing them around recklessly to the music. Shannon glanced up to see Zeke unsteadily making his way toward their table and prepared for his proposal to dance, wondering if the man would last through the reel. It was annoying when he sought Ramon's permission to ask her, but as they made their way through the crowd, Shannon was at least grateful that her intended was more inclined to talk with the men than to dance.

She was breathless as she made her way down the line changing partners for each course of the dance. As she met her next burly partner she braced herself for the overzealous swing and squealed as in its midst he released her prematurely to move on, catching her off guard. She gasped as she lost her balance, but was caught firmly by the waist as her next partner came up behind her and spun her about to face him. Shannon met Morgan Hawke's appreciative gaze as she curtsied.

His hand rested in the small of her back and his warm touch on her bare skin exposed by the gown brought a becoming color to her face as he swung her around and promenaded to the end of the line of dancers. They followed the call to circle their neighbors and as they returned to each other the dance ended. For a brief moment Shannon was pulled against him and held before he bowed shortly and offered to lead her through the winded dancers to her father's table.

As they passed a boisterous Michael Finney, engaged in an obviously ribald story with some other of Morgan Hawke's crew, Shannon caught his eye and nodded in greeting. To her surprise, he rose and blew her a kiss with a grand sweep of his hand and winked. She felt a certain high at the reassuring touch of the captain and the congeniality of his first mate and returned the gesture with a flirtatious look. But it was short-lived as they reached Brennan's company and Ramon met them, removing Hawke's arm with a challenging glare and guiding her roughly back to her seat.

Shannon held her breath, fearing another outbreak of violence. Morgan Hawke, however, ignored the challenge and offered his hand to Ramon with a disarming smile. "My congratulations, Captain. It seems that of the two of us, you are the one who will win the most precious treasure of all."

Shannon's heart leapt to her throat as Ramon relaxed and accepted the compliment returning the handshake firmly. She could not believe her ears. Hawke had led her to believe he was against the wedding. The hurt knotted painfully in her chest as the blood drained from her face. She reached for the fresh glass of wine Ramon had put before her, making an effort to keep her hand from shaking. Leaning back against his arm, she sipped the warm liquid oblivious to its slightly bittersweet taste and watched in disappointment as Hawke spoke briefly to Brennan and returned to join his crew.

"For once the Englishman and I agree on something, querida. You are the most precious of all treasures to be had." Ramon leaned over and kissed her with rum moistened lips at the nape of her neck exposed by her upswept curls.

"Here now. There'll be time for that soon enough," Nick Brennan chided good-naturedly, blessing his captain with one of his hearty blows.

"I cannot help my ardor when in the presence of such loveliness."

Brennan guffawed and struck the young man again. "Haven't I been there meself!" Then turning to Shannon, he continued, "That's the kind of reaction a woman gets when she wears the likes o' that and looks as good as you do."

Shannon looked down at her glass and concentrated on swirling the amber liquid close to the rim without spilling it, before she finished it. A lot of good her appearance did if it could not entice the man of her choice, she thought sarcastically, ignoring the watchful gaze of her fiancé. She observed the captain of the *Sea Lady* across the crowded tables as he pulled Carlota down to his lap and laughed, his eyes dancing in amusement. Jealousy invaded her thoughts as the woman kissed him zealously and leaned her head on his shoulders.

Alana brought more refreshment to the table and Nick Brennan jumped to his feet to seize the woman familiarly. "A dance!" he shouted, his eyes searching the room for the Moorish pirate in Ramon's crew who played the eastern music to which Alana danced so artistically.

"Perdoname, querida," Ramon was saying, breaking her trancelike study, "but I have to go to the warehouse. Someone has seen some of the children from the village there and I am sure they are up to mischief." He kissed her again and Shannon could not bring herself to resist as he held her against him. When he released her, she swayed unsteadily and shook her head trying to clear her foggy state of mind. "I will be back, I promise," he whispered in

her ear.

Shannon acknowledged his remark and returned her attention to the captivating dance. The music had stepped up in pace and the crowd fell in clapping their hands and cheering as Alana's movements became more rapid and her body shook tempestuously. In the back of her mind emerged a nagging thought that she had to seek out Morgan Hawke while Ramon was gone and the crowd was occupied, but the dance was too captivating to break away.

"Now you try, Shannon." Alana leapt lightly to the floor and held out the bells to her. "Show your father what I have taught you."

Shannon shook her head suddenly aware that the attention had turned to her. "No, I can't!" she protested lamely. "I'll fall off the table!"

"Nonsense! I have seen you. Who would like to see Shannon dance?" she called out to the crowd which answered in enthusiastic assent.

"Go on now, lass. Show your young man what he's got to look forward to!" Brennan teased as she lifted her up to the table top as if she were light as a feather. "Where is Ramon, anyway?" he asked, suddenly missing the man.

"He left for a while . . . something about checking on some children playing around the warehouse." Shannon informed him as she permitted Alana to tie the bells to her hands.

"Now, watch me and do as I do, Shannon," she instructed. The musician started to play again at the clap of her hands and she placed them on her smooth flat stomach and motioned for the girl to do the same. "Now feel the muscles as you roll them slowly in and out until you feel them moving with the rhythm."

Shannon glanced down self-consciously and started to devote her attention to the steady beat, but the

104

encouraging cheers from her audience caused her to stop and attempt to get down, her face red with embarrassment.

Alana blocked her way and motioned for her to continue. "They only like what you do, little one."

"Perhaps you should let the child go to her papa!"

Shannon whipped her head around to see Carlota gloating from the door to the back kitchen and infused by the antagonism, nodded for Alana to continue. She held her hands flat against her abdomen and let the music infiltrate her body until they flowed as one. Her eyes closed shutting out all but slow sensuous beat. At Alana's command, she lifted her arms over her head and began to slap the bells with each fluid movement of her youthful torso. Her mind and body seemed to separate as the restrictions of her will succumbed to the passion of the dance that inflamed her. Her heart beat wildly and her breath was as rapid as the increasing tempo that drove her with unbidden abandon. The room was a haze of faces and the heat was overwhelming as she felt beads of sweat making its way down her spine in the hollow beneath her skirt. Suddenly she was seized roughly and she gasped as she was yanked through the air and landed against her father's chest with a forceful impact, imprisoned by his strong hands biting into her arms.

Nick Brennan shook her as his icy glare penetrated the giddiness and she roused to her senses. "I never want to see ye dance like that again, Shannon Brennan! Do ye understand?"

Shannon shook her head innocently, failing to comprehend the source of his fury. It was so terribly hot and all she could think of was getting out of the crowded room. The closeness was draining her.

"I'm leaving now, Papa," she spoke, not recognizing her own voice. "Tell Ramon, I'm not feeling well." She shrank under his penetrating gaze. "I'm sorry." She wasn't wholly sure why she should apologize, but the need for air overrode the need to fathom her father's anger.

She turned and ran out the door, seeking the cool air beneath the trees at the foot of the path leading to her house. Her body was clammy and as she leaned forward against a tree to support her shaking legs, she took in large gulps of air as if she were suffocating.

The movement of her head as she looked back at the rustling branches overhead was dizzying and as she drifted backward, a hard body blocked her fall. She made an exclamation of surprise and turned to see Morgan Hawke holding her upright. "H . . . Hawke!" Her mouth was dry as she focused on his face. "What's wrong with me?"

"I'm not really sure," he admitted, his face a mirror of concern. "Your father wants me to see you get home safely after your rather extraordinary performance."

"I need to sit down a moment," she informed him, ignoring his quizzical look. She needed to catch her breath and clear her head. The heat was still oppressive, but the giddiness was passing. If she could just cool off. "No, I don't want to sit down. I'm going swimming!"

Hawke tightened his grip as she attempted to break away. "I think not, young lady. I'm going to see you safely tucked in and then join my crew to return to the *Sea Lady*."

The *Sea Lady*. The name rang a familiar note in the back of her mind. "You're going to take me?" she asked in surprise. Then leaning up against him, she rested her chin on his chest and stared innocently up at him. "You are going to take me, aren't you," she stated with an impish grin.

"You are drunk."

Shannon grinned again and wrinkled her nose at him. "You are, aren't you?"

"I am going to take you home right now," Hawke answered firmly, evading the issue. He had to get back to his men. Tomorrow would demand his full energy and he had ordered that everyone get back to the ship early. Finney most likely would be waiting for him, his task of waylaying Ramon Gerarde most likely accomplished by now.

He and his first mate had noted the captain's barely controlled ardor and contrived to see that if Shannon left the tavern, that it would not be in his company. Her fiancé would have no idea who accosted him in the darkness and even if he suspected, it would do him no good. Hopefully, by the time the young man was discovered in the warehouse, they would be on their way to Aden and Shannon would be safely tucked in her own bed sleeping it off.

"No!" Before he realized what she was doing, she shoved at him sharply in the stomach, and knocked him over a fallen log lying at the foot of the path. "You stay there then, Morgan Hawke!" she called over her shoulder as she darted into the woods.

He tried to catch himself, but the log rolled and he lost his footing completely. His elbow painfully grazed a rock as he hit the rough ground. "Damn it, Shannon!" he cursed, "come back here!" He scrambled to his feet, as he saw her fleeing figure disappearing in the trees. There was no path that he could make out as he tried to follow. She was going to the beach, he was sure, but this was not a familiar way to him. He ought to let her go and leave her to her own devices, he thought angrily as a holly branch scraped his face, leaving a bloody scratch.

He stopped in a small clearing and peered ahead, listening. She had apparently gained enough of a lead that her running footsteps went undetected. He glanced up at the sky and determined the direction to proceed to the lagoon. As he stepped forward, his foot stepped on an inanimate object and he reached down to retrieve it. It was one of her red satin slippers. He cursed under his breath and tossed it aside as he pressed on. He'd wring her neck, if he could just get his hands on her, he vowed as briars caught his pant leg and pierced through painfully.

His lungs were threatening to burst when the forest ended at the edge of the sandy beach. He could see Shannon moving about in the water and lumbered over to where she had stripped off her outer garments and left them carelessly at the water's edge. His knees buckled in exhaustion as he dropped to the beach to recover his breath.

"Hawke! Morgan Hawke! Come on in. It's just perfectly refreshing!" Her voice was playful as she splashed about.

He moved toward the water on his knees and gasped as something sharp jabbed at his knee cap. Cursing, he fell back and felt in the sand for the offending object. His fingers sifted out a handful of hairpins entangled in scarlet ribbons. He swore vehemently and was about to throw them aside when he heard a giggle and looked up to see Shannon coming out of the water.

"What on earth are you carrying on about, Morgan Hawke?"

The thin silk of her petticoat clung to her, translucent in the moonlight. Its form-fitted bodice laced up the front with a narrow ribbon tied daintily in a small bow where the curves of her bosom met.

She ran forward and stopped in front of him, placing her hands on his shoulders and shaking her long wet hair so that the cool droplets of water showered him. "Don't you want to swim, since you're all hot and sweaty from your little run through the forest?" She laughed, delighted with the success of her ploy to get him down to the beach. "You look like you could use cooling off."

Her laughter turned to a scream as he growled and lunged forward snatching his arms behind her knees and throwing her to the ground. "You little minx, you're going to get what you've been asking for since the day I met you!"

He fell on top of her as she tried to scurry away from his furious attack. Her strength was surprising as she wriggled out of his grasp and crawled toward the water, nearly dragging him with her. He dug his knees in and yanked her ankles back toward him causing her to fall face down in the shallow water. The ensuing struggle as she fought for breath under water forced him to release her momentarily. As he pulled himself to his feet and leaned over, he was met with a face full of mud, and a stream of curses that would shame any man in his crew.

With an angry exclamation he started after her with a vengeance and attempted to wash away the clinging mud. The water around his waist slowed him down but his hand caught the hem of her shift as she lunged for the deeper water and dragged her backward, ripping it loudly as the thin material gave way.

"Damn it, Hawke!" She choked as she swallowed a mouthful of water and went under water.

This time he tightly pinned her flailing arms to her sides and started to drag her to the beach. She coughed spasmodically and writhed madly in his

109

unrelenting hold. A few gasping curses was all she could muster, winded by the struggle. His heart pounded from exertion as he dropped to the water's edge with his squiriming burden and maneuvered her across his lap. As his hand struck her rounded bottom, she screamed and kicked, helplessly pinned in his lap by his other arm. The silken material slid to the side to reveal her bare legs as she tried to dig into the sand with her knees.

Suddenly she collapsed across his lap, her struggles ceasing. Her face was buried in her folded arms as her body shook with soft recriminating sobs, disarming his angry frustration. Remorse mounting rapidly, he reached out and touched her shoulder gently. "Shannon . . ."

"D . . . don't touch m . . . me," she stammered between ragged breaths, as she rolled away and staggered to her feet. She was covered with sand, and trying unsuccessfully to hold her shredded shift together. "I ha . . . hate you, M . . . Morgan Hawke!"

He sighed heavily as he watched her wade into the water and attempt to wash away the abrasive sand from her body and hair. Realizing he was equally encrusted, he rose to his feet and pulled off his shirt. The water was cool as he entered it, but it burned the abrasions he incurred during his chase. He immersed his body and was soon free of the sand, as Shannon still battled with the long tangled tresses in teary frustration. Whether it was from the guilt he felt or the rising desire at the sight of her shapely form so scantily clad in the soft light of the moon, he was unable to resist the compelling urge to take her into his arms and soothe away the racking sobs that cut through his chest like a punishing blade.

He approached her as she leaned back and submerged her head in an effort to rid the thick locks of the worrisome sand and when she rose he met her, embracing her desperately and kissing away her tears. She made no attempt to dissuade him as his lips found their way to hers with an urgent hunger he had not intended. She swayed against him, her body trembling as her arms encircled his neck tentatively. His breathing was heavy as he lifted his lips from hers and recognized a fire to match that that burned within him in her bewildered, searching eyes.

In an easy sweep, he lifted her off her feet and carried her to the beach, cradling her head against his shoulder. His blood raced as she nuzzled her nose in his chest. He spread the voluminous skirt of her discarded gown with his foot and dropped to his knees, tenderly depositing her on it. He could not tear his eyes from the rapid rise and fall of her breasts beneath the strained laces, and was mesmerized as she untied the wet bow and opened the bodice. Her skin was white and smooth as the silken shift that soon lay tossed on the sand beside his own clothes.

His hands shook with the passion that promised ecstasy as he explored the contours of her twisting body, skillfully torturing her senses to such a demanding height that she wrapped her arms about his neck and pulled him to her urgently seeking fulfillment. His name echoed haltingly in his ear as she groaned in guileless anticipation. He took her quickly and held her to him as she cried out in pain at the sacrifice of her innocence. Then slowly, sensually, he caressed her with his lips until she writhed in abandon before joining her in the ultimate crest of passion's tide.

The call of an owl from within the depths of the forest caused him to start from the druglike aftermath of their lovemaking. He looked down in wonder at the sleeping girl snuggled against him and tightened his arms about her, not wanting to let the moment pass. Yet, as he checked the westerly progress of the moon, he remembered that Finney and his crew were waiting for him at the quay. Reluctantly, he leaned over and nuzzled Shannon's ear gently.

"Shannon, my love, wake up."

A soft moan escaped her lips and she buried her face in his shoulder.

"Shannon, we have to go now." He shook her lightly but she refused to be roused. He rose to his knees and pulled her to a sitting position, but her head rolled back limply, her hair spilling to the ground behind her. He tried in vain to wake her with growing concern, but the only rise he could muster was some incoherent mumbling.

Giving up, he lowered her back to the ground and dressed quickly. He had not intended to return to the *Sea Lady* this late, but he did not regret the circumstances that made him tardy. His gaze returned to Shannon's sleeping figure and again he felt the stir of passion. With considerable effort, he ignored it and contemplated the task of dressing the girl. She was apparently in a wine-induced slumber and without some cooperation, he was certain he would never get her in the gown. He pulled his damp shirt off and, after some difficulty, managed to stuff the limp figure in it.

The walk back to the house along the path seemed to take forever. As light as the girl was, his arms ached as he climbed the last stretch of path that led to the back yard of Brennan's house. He paused in the cover of the trees, wondering if anyone would be waiting and realizing the consequences. There was no sign of movement and from the noise that drifted up the hill from the tavern, he was certain that Nick Brennan was still partying heavily. He searched the windows of the small kitchen where the crazy housekeeper slept and, reassured by the stillness, proceeded cautiously around the house to the veranda.

Hawke tried to support some of Shannon's weight on his raised knee as he lifted the latch to her bedroom door. As the door swung open, creaking loudly in the deafening silence, he entered and waited for his eyes to adjust to the darkness. He made out the bed on the opposite wall and crossed the room. Carefully, he laid her on the mattress. He bent down and whispered in her ear. "I promise I'll take you from here, Shannon. As God is my witness, I'll be back for you." With that, he kissed her lightly on the temple and started toward the door. It creaked loudly again as he closed it behind him and walked across the plank floor to the center steps. As he stepped off the veranda, he heard the housekeeper's voice echoing from the back of the house.

"I tole you, Ramon. Ol' Marie's potion never fail." Her cackling laughter followed him as he made his way back to the quay.

Chapter Seven

The late morning storm passed over the cove and by mid-afternoon the sun peeked through the clouds and bathed the island in its warm drying rays. There was little activity at the quay, the outgoing ships having already sailed with the early tide, and those that had partied too heaviliy the night before gave in to the laziness of the afternoon and napped. At the far end of the harbor, some children played at the water's edge while their parents wrestled with repairing the nets strung out on a thin strip of beach. Gulls flew hungrily overhead searching for unwary fish near the water's surface, or waiting for the women at the tavern to throw out scraps in the back.

Shannon awakened to the sound of Marie humming quietly in the parlor. She winced as the sun's piercing rays slipped through a slit in the curtain the houskeeper had thoughtfully closed to permit her to sleep as long as possible. The dazzling light hurt her eyes and she raised her arm to cover her face. It felt like lead, she thought to herself, letting it rest there. As she slowly regained her senses, she began to realize the throbbing in the top of her head and tried to relax.

Her body felt damp and she tried to ease the coverlet off with her feet so as not to infuriate the misery in her head. It was so hot and the light breeze from the open window felt refreshing to her bare legs. It must be late in the afternoon, she thought, noting the sun was assaulting her from the rear window over her bed instead of the protected window over the veranda. Her stomach growled fitfully and she wondered if Marie had made any scones. Resolving to fight the drummers in her head rather than die there of starvation, she forced herself up on her elbow. Immediately she regretted her decision.

Moaning loudly, she buried her face in the pillow and fought a sudden rise of nausea. If she could just be still it would go away. Her hair clung damply to her face as she forced herself to lie back again on the pillow and breathe deeply and slowly. Her mouth was dry and she ran her tongue over her lips in a futile attempt to moisten them. She hurt too much to move when the door burst open and Marie entered the room carrying a tray.

"You feel pretty bad, sleep so late, eh?" she asked as she set down the tray on the dresser.

"I'm sick. My stomach is about to heave ho." Shannon groaned.

Marie brought a small cup with a steaming hot liquid in it and sat on the edge of the bed. "You drink dis and in a few minutes you be fine, girl."

Shannon carefully rose up on her elbow and leaned forward to sip the herbal tea. She had no doubt that it would work. Marie had nursed her since childhood with her strange mixtures and they always worked. An earthy scent assaulted her nose as she sipped the warm tea slowly. Her brow was damp and the concoction seemed to induce additional perspiration as she managed to drink it slowly. When she

115

finished, she dropped back against the pillows exhausted from the effort.

"I draw you a bath, girl. It's coolin' and now dat you done wid de sweatin', you be needin' it."

Shannon agreed and as the door closed behind the woman, she closed her eyes to regain enough strength to bathe. It seemed as though she had just drifted off when Marie appeared again to announce that the bath was ready. Shannon assured her that she would be right out and made a concentrated effort to rise. The pounding in her head had subsided to a faint ache and the nausea was all but gone as she walked over to her dresser and opened the top drawer to get her robe.

It was then that she noticed the wrinkled linen shirt she wore was not her father's. She glanced in the mirror and held it away from her. It was not quite as big, but swamped her small frame in folds of linen. Her eyes widened as the memory of the night before fought its way to the surface. She leaned on the edge of the dresser and lowered her head, shutting her eyes tightly as if trying to shut it out of her consciousness. It had to be a dream.

Suddenly she straightened in alarm and ran to the window overlooking the harbor below. She searched in vain for the tall mast of the *Sea Lady*. He had left her.

"No!" she screamed, hitting her fist against the cool plaster wall. She dropped to her knees and rested her head on the sill, moaning as the pain in her heart twisted more agonizingly than the ache in her head.

"Shannon!" Marie hustled into the room and ran to put her arms about the girl. "My girl, what wrong?" She pulled Shannon's hair back from her face and leaned over her to help the sobbing girl to her feet.

Shannon went into the comforting arms of her nurse and wept unashamed. The housekeeper held her tightly patting her on the back and shushing gently until the flood of tears ran out. When the girl finally pushed away, she could see the question in the woman's loving gaze.

"I loved him," Shannon explained in halting breaths. "And I let him . . . I . . . ." She bit her lip and shut her eyes to erase the most beautiful moment she had ever experienced.

"I know, girl. Ol' Marie, she understand. But not'ing change, Shannon Brennan. He still love you an' you be his bride soon."

"No, Marie, I won't be his bride. He's gone, and no other man could ever make me feel what I feel with him. Not Ramon, or anyone!"

Shannon broke away and threw herself on the bed, burying her face in the pillows with renewed sobs. She felt the bed sway as Marie sat beside her. Her hand was warm on her shoulder and her voice was stern.

"What you tell me, girl? Who you talk about if not Ramon?"

The girl rolled over and wiped her eyes with a sweep of the full sleeve and met Marie's shocked look. "Morgan Hawke," she answered defiantly. "I . . . I told you I'd never marry Ramon."

"De Engleeshman! Oh my girl, what have you done?" Marie shook her head in disbelief.

"I let him make love to me. I trusted him . . . and now he's left me to marry Ramon Gerarde!" Anger was gradually replacing the hurt, as she continued. "He promised to take me away so that I would not have to marry Ramon. The bastard lied!" Shannon punched the pillow repeatedly, wishing it were the handsome face with the dancing blue eyes. Suddenly she stopped and looked at Marie, surprised at her discovery. "No! He has helped me, in spite of his lies! I'm ruined. Now Ramon will not have me!"

"Girl, what happen to Ramon? Where he go that you spend the night with the Engleeshman?"

Shannon looked at her blankly and shrugged. It did not matter. Morgan Hawke had inadvertently helped her out after all.

"I tink you take your bath. Maybe tink about what you tell your papa."

Shannon paled at the mention of Nick Brennan. He would be furious . . . and when Morgan Hawke did return . . .

"You love dis Engleeshman?" Marie narrowed her eyes and studied her face closely.

"Yes, damn his lying soul!" Shannon swore, biting back the tears.

"Den your papa make him marry you! You be happy and dat what Marie want more den anyting." Marie hugged her affectionately. "An' you doan say anyting yet. Marie she take care of Papa Brennan."

Shannon barely heard her as the woman dragged herself off the bed and left the room. She rose from the bed and retrieved her robe from the open drawer. Marry Hawke! How could she even face him again. As much as she despised the way he had betrayed her, she wanted him in a way she would never have believed a day ago. He must think her another Carlota—another harlot to be toyed with. She couldn't let that happen, she told herself firmly as she made her way to the fenced-in enclosure in the back. She would fight the stirring memory of his touch and maintain a safe distance.

The cool bath fulfilled Marie's promise. When Shannon finished bathing and washing her hair, she was refreshed and much improved. She tossed

Hawke's shirt on the bed and donned her own shirt and breeches. Somehow she was going to survive this, she promised herself as she tied back her hair and picked up the sheathed knife on the dresser. She would not be forced to marry a man she loathed, nor would she have one she cared for forced to marry her. Hawke may have bought her enough time to come up with another solution and for now, that was enough.

She strapped the knife to her waist and entered the parlor. Marie had apparently gone to the kitchen, but on the table was a plate full of biscuits. Shannon picked up a couple and walked out the back door. As she devoured her late breakfast, she meandered down the path to the lagoon, her mind tumbling with possibilities.

She realized her mistake when she discovered the sand-covered swatch of scarlet on the beach. Memories flooded back to her, warm and beautiful. She dropped to her knees and picked up the crumpled gown. Clutching it to her chest, she stared blankly out at the water shimmering in the late afternoon sun. Her eyes were dry, her tears spent. It was inwardly that she wept. Amidst the turmoil of mixed emotions rose a fervent prayer for his safe return.

Three days passed and the nights were torturous. Shannon tossed restlessly in the humid darkness, haunted alternately by dreams of her sweet surrender to the English captain and nightmares of bloody duels between him and Ramon Gerarde. Gerarde had stormed up to the house while she was at the beach the day the *Sea Lady* departed for Aden and demanded to see her. Marie artfully deceived the captain into believing Shannon had been brought to her ill from the unexpected effects of wine and had been there since under the housekeeper's care.

He was infuriated and directed his abuse toward the woman, shaking her and cursing profusely in Spanish. Marie had reassured Shannon when she relayed the story, that she was immune to his outbursts, not understanding a word of the language. It seemed that his frustration of not being able to see his fiancée was compounded by the fact that he had spent the night in the warehouse bound and gagged and suffering from a blow on the back of the head that had left a rather tender lump. In short time, Marie had him on his way back to the village with a poultice for his aching head and a promise to send for him when Shannon would be well enough to see him.

Nick Brennan had come to the house as soon as he heard of Shannon's illness. By then the girl was home and easily confirmed Marie's story. She was so drained of emotion that it was not difficult at all to confine herself to her room and her pallor was genuinely convincing. Her father only stayed long enough to assure himself that her illness was nothing serious and left to see to his ship. Marie kept Shannon's confidence, explaining after Brennan left that the time to confront him was not right, and when it was, Shannon would not have to face her father alone.

The deafening silence of the forest around the small house awakened the girl from her uneasy sleep. The usual calls of the night creatures were unnaturally still. Shannon threw off the light coverlet and sat up on the edge of her bed listening to the eerie calm. The hair seemed to prickle at the nape of her neck and she briskly wiped it with her hand as if to suppress the reaction.

As she rose from the bed and placed her bare feet on the cool smooth floor, a scream broke the stillness. It came from the back. Not again, she thought miserably as she bolted to the door and charged into the dark parlor. As she made her way to the back door, she was seized by the waist and lifted off her feet. Too shocked to cry out, she twisted and pummeled blindly at her unseen assailant. Before she realized it, someone else grabbed her hands and pulled them behind her head causing her back to arch against them. She screamed in panic.

"There now," one of her assailants was saying, "just calm down. We're not here to hurt you."

Shannon's heart beat wildly as she ceased her struggles and felt their hold on her ease. She was about to react when the door burst open and two more men dragged a hysterical Marie into the room. The girl broke away from her captors and ran to the housekeeper. "Get your hands off of her!" she shouted, prying at their fingers grasped tightly around the old woman's heavy arms.

"Someone light a candle!"

Shannon took the frightened housekeeper in her arms and tried to comfort her as the men released her. She could hear the intruders rummaging about in the darkness. "Who are you?" she demanded, struggling to control her own fear.

"Marines of his majesty's navy, miss," one of them answered as he lit a candle and placed a blown glass globe over it.

Shannon's eyes darted from one white uniformed man to another, paling as she saw the shining pistols and sabers strapped to them menacingly. "What are you going to do?" she asked. Her voice betrayed her anxiety.

The young man who lit the candle gave her an appreciative smile as he noted her scant attire. "I told you, miss, we are not here to hurt you. Our orders are to protect you."

"From what?" She tried to draw the shirt down to cover her bare legs from the officer's eyes.

He ignored the question and turned to his men. "Fisher, you stay here with me. The rest of you go on with the others."

Others! Shannon watched as the armed men saluted smartly and left through the back door. The man called Fisher moved to it as if he read her thoughts and sought to block her escape. She could hear the sound of many footfalls moving through the trees and realized the number of these intruders was great. She had to get down to the village and warn the others, she thought desperately.

"Sir," she spoke up, addressing the young man who was apparently in charge, "if you would permit me, I would like to go to my room and put on some decent clothing." She could not help the color that erased her earlier pallor.

Again the young officer smiled, but in a most respectful tone answered, "Of course, miss. But I warn you, I will be just outside, should it cross your mind to slip out a window."

Shannon acknowledged the warning, and turned her attention to Marie, who by now was whimpering in her arms. "Would you like to come with me? I do not think they mean us harm."

"No, she stays here." The directive was firm.

"I'll be back out as soon as I've dressed," she assured the woman. She kissed Marie lightly on the cheek and rose to her feet. Self-consciously aware of the appreciative appraisal of her captors, she walked toward her bedroom door and entered. As she closed it behind her, she heard the parlor door to the veranda slam and knew the young officer was keeping his word. She saw his back at her bedroom window and rushed over to close the window and pull the curtain.

As she donned her shirt and breeches, she contemplated trying to slip out the back window, but dismissed the idea. Fisher would be watching the back yard, she was certain. As she pulled on her boots, she suddenly remembered the loose board under the chest at the foot of her bed. As a child she delighted in slipping out through the wide flooring and coming into the house to startle the busy housekeeper who thought her to be napping peacefully in her room.

The chest was heavy but it rested on a rug and slid easily and quietly away from the footrail of the brass bed. Shannon used the tip of her dagger to pry the board up and resheathed it at her waist after carefully laying the flooring aside. As she peered into the dark hole, she shuddered involuntarily, trying to conquer her fear of the crawling insects that surely dwelled under the house. A loud explosion over the harbor made her jump and she saw a brilliant flash of light through the curtains. Without another thought, she squeezed through the opening, scraping her body on the rough edges and tearing her shirt on a splinter that raked into her back.

She snaked her way to the side of the house and again used her dagger to cut through the vines that grew thickly between and around the stone pilasters that supported it. As she crawled stealthily into the cover of the trees, the harbor below erupted again with thunderous explosions and the very sky lit up as if the noonday sun had burst into showers of fiery sparks. She had to get to her father, she thought wildly as she increased the distance between her and her captors.

The unsuspecting lieutenant on the veranda

watched the powerful display of the bomb ketch that mercilessly bombarded the helpless pirate ships in the harbor. While he and the other marines had sneaked into the cove through a hidden cave and made their way up to disarm the cannon at the point above the protected harbor, the *Sea Lady* led the British armada through the treacherous channel and now the quay was under full attack. It was a spectacle to behold from his ideal vantage.

The lieutenant tore himself away from the fiery display and glanced at the curtained window of the bedroom where the lovely young woman he had been ordered to protect dressed quietly. He could see why the daring Lord Hawke had been so insistent that a small detail be assigned to see that she be spared. Indeed, she was lovely enough to stir the blood of the old admiral himself. The young man grinned and started to walk back to the parlor door to check on his charming captive. He was caught completely unaware as a hand clamped powerfully over his mouth and a penetrating blade severed his spinal cord bringing eternal darkness to his youthful eyes.

Fisher sat on a rough bench near the back door and called out to his superior suspiciously as he heard a slight scuffle on the veranda. He rose as silence answered his inquiry and looked at the trembling black woman huddled in the corner of the room. Ordering her to stay where she was, he crossed to the veranda door and cautiously looked outside. The porch was empty. Perhaps the lieutenant had circled the house to make sure everything was still under control. He paused as he passed the door leading to the girl's room and put his ear to it. Again silence.

He knocked politely and entered when he received no acknowledgment. The trunk sitting cocked in the middle of the floor drew his attention to the gap in the planking. So that's where he was, chasing after their pretty and apparently resourceful prisoner. He smiled. The lieutenant was probably embarrassed that his charge had escaped him and gone after her unannounced. Shaking his head, he stepped back into the parlor.

His eyes widened as he met the fierce gaze of a dark-skinned pirate, but before the shock could register, a pistol ball hit his chest, exploding and sending him reeling backward against the doorway. His body jerked involuntarily in the throes of impending death and his hand automatically reached for the pistol sheathed at his full girth; but, before he could grasp it, another shot rang out, and the bloody impact at his temple stilled him forever.

Morgan Hawke felt his pounding heart freeze as the sound of pistol shot met his ascent to the small house ahead. His legs carried him on, blind to the protest of the aching muscles. He prayed Shannon was safe as he staggered across the veranda, recklessly dismissing caution, and charged into her room. Dread seized him as he observed the empty room. A movement from the doorway brought his hand instinctively to his pistol, but he seemed to move in slow motion. Before he could assemble his wits, he felt the sharp tip of a cutlass at his throat and met the leering gaze of Ramon Gerarde.

"Throw the pistols to the floor, Capitán!" Gerarde's voice hissed the command.

Carefully Hawke complied, tossing the pearl-handled weapons at the Creole's feet.

"I have promised myself to enjoy such a moment as this, but I must admit, I did not expect it so soon."

"Where's Shannon?" Hawke asked, ignoring the painful prick of the blade as it cut just through the surface of his skin.

"It seems she has escaped your soldiers. But no matter. I will find her after I deal with you." Ramon moved cautiously to where the discarded weapons lay and picked up one, aiming it at Hawke's perspiration-soaked chest. Then deliberately, he pressed the Englishman against the wall with his blade. "How will you die, Morgan Hawke, by my blade, or by your own weapon?"

He laughed harshly and then wiped the crooked smile off his face. With a skillful slash of the cutlass he ripped the front of Hawke's shirt open exposing the muscled chest beneath. Then with a dangerously controlled touch, he began to slice a long shallow cut from the base of his victim's throat to his flat contracted stomach. Blood mixed with sweat as Hawke grimaced and watched the cruel blade poise above his navel and press in indenting the skin painfully.

"Damn it, Gerarde, be done with this insane game of yours and go find Shannon!" he cursed, raising his eyes to the man in challenge.

"To hell with the chaste little bitch! I intend to watch you sweat until you bleed to death." The blade pierced just a little deeper causing Hawke to gasp. "Or perhaps see the horror on your face as I disembowel you alive." His laughter was demented. "Or perhaps a gut shot would deliver the justice you deserve."

Hawke flinched as the sound of the hammer on the pistol drew back. He jerked his head back against the wall at the sound of the explosion. To his surprise, the plaster shattered next to his hand and the blade against his abdomen clattered loudly to the floor. He opened his eyes to see Ramon staring blankly in horror at him. Then stiffly, the dark-skinned pirate pitched forward and fell at his feet. A heavy meat cleaver protruded from his neck. Hawke looked past the dead man to see the black woman looking at his bloody chest.

"You go fine my girl!" she commanded, her eyes fierce with emotion. "She go to her papa!"

Hawke found the use of his legs again and accepted the other primed pistol the housekeeper handed him. He whispered a hoarse thanks and ran out of the house. He prayed his nightmarish delay with the Creole had not cost Shannon her life as he rushed down the hill toward the violent melee in the village below.

The village was in flames as men, women and children ran toward the forest in panic at the explosive onslaught of the bombs from the square-rigged ship in the harbor. Its cannons, mounted on a revolving platform on her bow, fired relentlessly while the accompanying ships blasted the cornered pirate ships with ball and canister. The dirt streets swarmed with uniformed soldiers incensed with the rage of the kill, and merciless slaughter prevailed. The few structures that were not ablaze were looted and the women who failed to make it to the protection of the forest were subjected to violent assault.

Perspiration from exertion and the intense heat of the fire beaded Shannon's face as she viewed the destruction in horror from the forest's edge. If she could sneak through the cluster of huts in the back of the tavern, she might make it through the structure which was not yet victim to the deadly missiles. From there, she could get to the dock where the *Plunderer* was tied. As she had made her way to the village she had seen her father's ship valiantly defending its position and holding off the British ship's attempt to board her. If she could get to him, she would try to convince him to seek the safety of the forest and retreat to her cavern until the raid was over. There was no way he could outlast the superior numbers and firepower.

She crouched down to avoid the flying musket balls and scurried to the back of the buildings. Hiding in a cluster of barrels, she watched as a group of soldiers raced by, headed in the direction of the warehouse. She caught her breath and made a dash toward the back door of the tavern. The sound of heavy footsteps behind her spurred her onward, but as she reached the wooden step, she was tackled around the knees and thrown forcefully to the ground. She was stunned by the impact, the wind having been knocked out of her and was vaguely aware that she was surrounded. She was roughly rolled over on her back to see the ugly blade of a bayonet plunging at her chest. She screamed and the blade halted abruptly in mid air.

"Blimey, it's a little girl!" one of the soldiers exclaimed in surprise.

"Not so little," another one remarked, reaching down and squeezing her breast painfully.

Shannon twisted her head and bit the hairy arm fiercely causing the man to draw back his hand and swear. However, she fell back as the bayonet pressed her to the ground again. His comrades laughed at the man who put the injury to his mouth and sucked the blood that oozed from it.

"Drag the viper behind them huts there, mates, and let's teach 'er some manners."

Shannon struggled helplessly as they grabbed her arms and legs and started off with her. Their hands were all over her, pinching and hurting and she screamed curses at them much to their amusement.

"Damn me, if we ain't got us a spitfire here!" one

of them laughed, as they pinned her to the ground. Her hair had come untied in her efforts to free herself and had wrapped about her face nearly blinding her. She felt rough hands tugging at her breeches and tried to kick at the man who kneeled over her breathing heavily. A missile landed in the woods beyond and exploded, lighting up the area.

"Hurry up, mate, fore we git our heads blown off."

"Let's see what you look like, darlin'." His hands stopped their prying at the laces on her breeches long enough to pull the damp locks of hair away from her face.

Shannon spat at him as he looked at her and moved his hands familiarly to her breasts. "Bastard!" she shrieked.

An explosion suddenly seemed to knock away the two men holding her hostage on her right, as a second one ripped away the two on her left. Shannon scrambled away from her captor, leaving him to face the pistol of Henry Cutchins, who stood holding the weapon at his forehead. At the tavernkeeper's feet were two discharged blunderbusses.

"Run, Shannon. Get away while you can!" Cudge shouted as his thumb released the hammer.

"Where's papa?" Shannon cried, as the weapon discharged, blowing away the face of her assailant.

"Forget him, Shannon. The *Plunderer*'s afire. Seek your own safety, girl." Cudge pushed the dead man to the side and took her arm pulling her toward the woods.

"No!" she shouted, breaking away.

She ignored Cudge's pleas as she dashed around the tavern toward the dock where the *Plunderer* moored. The ship was in flames as she reached the gangway and the water was full of fleeing crewmen.

"Your papa's hit, Shannon! For gawd's sake, get

away while ye can. She's gonna blow!'' one of the men warned her as she boarded the vessel.

Her eyes searched the bright deck frantically and she sobbed as she spied her father lying in a heap near the splintered rail. The heat from the flames burned her face as she ran to him and pulled his heavy shoulders to her chest. He was alive she thought gratefully as he moaned and rolled back his head. His eyelids fluttered open and he tried to speak.

"No, Papa! Save your strength. I'm going to get you off this ship," she sobbed, as she strained to move his heavy frame to the rail. If she could push him over the side and follow him into the water, he would be light enough to pull away from the ship.

His limp form was too heavy and he could not help her. As she struggled, he tried to dissuade her in a gargling voice. She refused to listen to him and pulled with all her strength. He cried out in agony, and she dropped to her knees beside him and saw for the first time the ragged splinter of decking that protruded from his stomach. She realized in horror that he was impaled on the deck.

"Shannon!"

She looked through her tears to see Morgan Hawke running toward them. "Hawke! For God's sake, please help me!'' Tears ran unashamedly down her cheeks as Hawke kneeled across from her by the dying body of the *Plunderer*'s captain and assessed the situation.

"Get her away before she blows, lad!'' Nick Brennan coughed, blood seeping from the side of his mouth. Then with surprising strength, he reached up and grasped the ragged edge of Hawke's shirt and pulled him down so that the young man could hear his weakening voice. "In the house . . . a journal . . . she's a lady, lad, as fine as any ye . . . ye have in them fancy courts.'' He gasped in pain, but held Hawke fast. "Take care o' her . . ." Brennan's body convulsed and Shannon screamed pushing the young man aside and hugging her father frantically to her.

Hawke tried to pull the sobbing girl away but she would not release her hold on the dead man. In desperation, he forced her back and slapped her sharply. She raised her tear-filled eyes to him in stunned confusion at first, and then he saw the blue pools ice over in spite of the flames reflecting in their depths. A look of pure hatred shot across the dead captain's body as she realized his involvement.

"Shannon . . ." he started, reading her thoughts. He jumped to his feet and stepped back as the girl snatched her dagger from her waist and sprang at him, its flashing blade sparkling in the fiery light. Her scream of fury was muffled as the deck behind them exploded with a force that threw her against him knocking them both over the rail. A searing pain invaded his shoulder as he fought to maintain consciousness in the cool water. He began a frenzied search for the girl and found her floating face down in the water a yard away. He pulled her head out of the water and gave a cry of relief as she coughed spasmodically spitting up water.

He started for the shoreline dragging his unconscious burden with him. His muscles seemed to tear with each stroke as he swam. Blackness hung over him threateningly, and in the background he could hear voices of encouragement that fortified his effort. As his knees raked the sandy ledge of the beach, he felt his burden lifted from him and tried to focus his eyes on the concerned face of Michael Finney. The mate's lips were moving but his voice was faint. He saw his helmsman holding Shannon's limp figure and closed his eyes in relief as his consciousness sought refuge from the torture in his shoulder in painless oblivion.

Chapter Eight

The nagging voices in the back of Shannon's mind kept calling to her trying to force her from her peaceful retreat. She moaned and tried her best to ignore them as she floated blissfully in darkness. Why wouldn't they leave her alone? Why did they insist on making her listen to them? They were the voices of strangers anyway, so why should she even try to shake herself from this dreamy world as they beckoned?

She resisted instinctively as she felt a tugging on her arm. The rough fabric of her blouse scraped her skin. Leave me alone, she cried out silently. There was something cool and wet on her forehead. A loud metallic clang made her jump. Her senses were awakening, she thought miserably, as her muscles began to ache dully. Those damned voices!

Heavy weights fell on her shoulders and legs. What were they trying to do to her, she wondered irritably? Someone was scrubbing her arm with a cold wet rag. Bleeding bowl. What sort of dish was that? Her eyelids felt as if they were sewn shut but she forced them open. Blue and white figures surrounded her, but she had trouble focusing. One man leaned over her and pulled her eyelid open with his thumb, staring at her curiously.

He was heavyset and a white mustache curled up on either side of his rather large porous nose. Shannon wrinkled her nose as his rancid breath assaulted her nostrils and turned her head away from him. Maybe he would go away. What did he want with her arm anyway?

"Now hold her still, men. I can't have her moving about when I make the cut."

Shannon spun her head back toward the intruder at the mention of the word "cut." Her eyes widened as she saw him brandish a peculiar looking assortment of oddly shaped blades that were somehow pinned together like a metal fan. Suddenly it dawned on her that for some reason he was going to use this strange weapon on her arm. She summoned her limbs from their sluggish sleep and began to struggle.

"Jehosephat! Hold her I say!"

"No!" Shannon screamed as the weights on her shoulders and legs increased, pinning her to the hard mattress under her. "Stop it!"

"Young lady, this will not hurt you," the older man told her gruffly, leaning carefully over her arm and peering at it through a spectacle. "Now hold the collecting dish under her arm right here," he directed a young man standing next to him.

Shannon felt the cold touch of metal under her arm and shrieked, resuming her struggles more intensely than ever. "You're not going to kill me, you bloodthirsty piece of dirt!" She continued with a full string of curses, as the man backed away, red-faced at her furious outburst.

Her wriggling managed to free one leg and she raised it suddenly and kicked, catching him full in the stomach. His assistants fell on her with renewed vigor and she fought helplessly under their weight and called for her father in a terrified voice. The surgeon, who dragged himself up from his undignified sprawl on the floor of the small cabin, shouted at her angrily and vowed to bleed her whether she liked it or not.

He broke off suddenly as the narrow door from the captain's cabin burst open and a pale-faced Morgan Hawke leaned heavily against the frame, supported by his first mate. Beads of perspiration covered his brow as he looked at Shannon's squirming figure barely held down by the physician's helpers and breathed a deep sigh of relief.

"What is wrong, sir?"

The flustered uniformed surgeon snorted indignantly. "I was about to bleed this young lady, and I use the term loosely, sir, when she suddenly turned into an expectorating wildcat!"

"Indeed? And to what purpose?" the young captain asked, meeting Shannon's imploring look.

"To restore her body humors, of course!"

Hawke chuckled and then winced as the action inflamed his wounded shoulder. "It appears to me, sir, with all due respect, that you have indeed restored a most grievous humor of animosity."

The man stiffened and jutted his angular chin out, ignoring the snickers of his men. "Well sir, if it is your opinion that this . . . lady has no need of my services, then I shall be most relieved to return to the Admiral's ship and quit her rather offensive company. Gentlemen?"

Shannon never took her eyes from her rescuer as the surgeon and his men vacated the cabin. He was deathly white in spite of his tanned skin, and his chest was covered with bandages. Her gaze fixed on the blood-soaked shoulder wrap, and she began to remember. Her father was dead. Morgan Hawke had led the murderous invasion. She recalled the sickening plunge of her dagger as she drove it into his body as if it had pierced her heart as well.

Her gaze hardened as she pulled herself up off the bunk. "You! You lying, murdering bastard!" she shouted, charging across the room.

Suddenly Michael Finney was between them, blocking her way. "Here now, lass. The cap'n saved your life and damned near died doin' it." He held her raised fists firmly as she collapsed against his chest, weak from her exertion.

"For what?" she wept bitterly, as he carried her back to the bunk and deposited her on it.

"It's none o' me business," came the grim reply.

Shannon looked past him at the empty doorway and raised her voice so that the man in the other cabin could not help but hear her. "You killed my father, Morgan Hawke, as sure as if you had personally thrust the splintered deck through him with your own hand! Do you hear me?" she sobbed wretchedly.

"I'm goin' back to me cabin now. But I'll say this. Don't ye try to harm 'im. As fond as I am of ye, that sufferin' young man in there is the son I never had, and I'd not like to have to deal with ye, if he was hurt anymore than he already is."

Shannon pulled the rough woolen blanket over her head to shut out the words and turned her back to the Irishman, her small form shaking miserably. She heard him sigh heavily and his footsteps echoed as he crossed the small distance to Morgan Hawke's cabin and closed the door behind him.

When she awoke again, the ship was rocking rhythmically with the tide. Her stomach protested loudly and she wondered how long it had been since she had last eaten. She moved to rise from the bunk, but her muscles ached unmercifully, forcing her to lie back and seek the respite of inactivity. She deduced that she was in one of the cabins in the gallery of the *Sea Lady*.

Perhaps she was a prisoner, she thought suddenly. With great resolve, she slid off the bunk and stumbled toward the wider door that likely opened on the companionway and tried it. It was not locked as she suspected, but a guard met her as she leaned against the wall for support and asked if she was all right. Shannon nodded mutely and closed the door. She groaned as her back slid down the wall beside it and settled on the floor, fatigued.

Dismayed at her weakness, she managed to crawl over to the other door that was unbolted from her side and reached up to try the latch. This one did not give way, apparently locked from the other side. She drew her aching knees up under her as she sat against the wall between the cabins and rested her head on them. The explosion must have knocked the strength out of her completely, she mused.

She lifted her head and glanced around her prison speculatively. A double casement window over-looked the stern of the ship, covered with thick drapes to block out the sun. Perhaps if she could regain her stamina, she might escape that way. She could slip out and swim to shore.

The door to her cabin opened and she turned to see Michael Finney enter, followed by a young boy carrying a tray. Upon seeing her sitting on the floor, he walked up to her and put his hands on his hips with an air of disapproval.

"And why might I ask, are ye sittin' there on the hard deck, when ye might have a more comfortable seat there on the bunk?"

Shannon smiled weakly. "I got down here and to tell the truth, it just wasn't worth the effort to climb back up."

"Humph! Yer as pigheaded as the cap'n!" he snorted, leaning over and pulling her to her feet. "This is twice in one day that I've put ye to bed and this time, I'm hopin' ye'll stay put."

To her surprise, instead of helping her over to the bunk, he shoved his broad shoulder into her stomach and heaved her over it like a sack of grain. She grunted as he deposited her unceremoniously on the mattress and glared up at him with indignation. She was about to express herself when she noticed the wide-eyed stare of the youth behind the mate and held her tongue.

"This Billy Randall. He's the finest cabin boy to be found on these seas and if you're good, he'll be more than glad to see to your needs. If you're not, ye'll be stuck with me!"

Shannon looked up sharply at the first mate's threat. There was a familiar twinkle in his eye and she genuinely smiled for the first time. There was something about this man that she was comfortable with. "I promise I'll behave . . . but please don't stay away." She took his rough hand impulsively and held it to her cheek.

Finney cleared his throat awkwardly and pointed to the cabin boy. "Billy here has some grub for ye. Mind ye, cook might not be as good as you're used to, but it's as fine as you'll find . . ."

"On these seas," Shannon teased. Her smile faded as she was reminded of Marie.

"What is it, lass?" Finney asked, noting the change.

"What happened to Marie?" Shannon's face betrayed her anxiety.

Finney wrinkled his brow and scratched his red head for a moment and then nodded as he figured out who the girl was asking for. "Ye mean that crazy voodoo woman that's been down here every day this week, threatening every man on our decks with magic curses if they would not let her see ye?"

Shannon closed her eyes and smiled in relief. "That's the one. Thank God she's all right! Can I see her?" She was certain that if anyone could help her, it would be Marie, the only person left from the world Morgan Hawke had destroyed.

"I imagine the cap'n will allow it, seein's how all the demons of hell will sail us to the bottom of the sea if he don't."

Billy's eyes grew wider at the mate's remark and Shannon laughed. "She's really harmless, Billy. I swear. Now how about some of that delicious smelling stew?"

The boy pinkened as Shannon winked at him and placed the tray across her lap nervously. Finney excused himself and the lad, promising that the youth would return for the dishes when she finished. After they left, she reflected on Finney's remark about Marie as she ate her food ravenously. Every day this week! She must have been unconscious for considerably more than the one night she had thought. No wonder they had sent for that bloodthirsty surgeon and his crew.

The rest of the day and the night that ensued was spent dozing off and on. Occasionally, Billy would check in on her to see if she needed anything, each time eyeing her warily as if he expected her to attack him in an escape attempt. There was a lot of movement and low voices coming from Morgan Hawke's cabin, but the thick door between them made it difficult to make out what exactly was going on. A dim light shone under the door into the wee hours of the morning and Shannon could not help but wonder just how badly the captain of the *Sea Lady* had been injured.

Marie was permitted to see her after being searched and interrogated by the captain and his first mate. Shannon heard her distinctive voice through the wall, but did not understand it any better than she had any of the other conversations. All she knew was that the housekeeper had been with Hawke a considerable length of time before she was at last admitted to Shannon's cabin.

The reunion was tearful, as Shannon clung to the woman who raised her. Marie stroked her hair and comforted the distraught girl as Billy and Finney brought in the heavy mahogany trunk Brennan had brought home from Tangiers and placed it against the bulkhead between the cabins. Their mission accomplished, they excused themselves and left the two women alone.

"Look at you, girl!" Marie exclaimed, standing back and taking in the sight of the child she raised. "You are a sight! Now where did dat boy git to?" With an air of authority, Marie went to the door and asked that Billy be sent to the cabin with some water for bathing.

Shannon glanced down at her stained shirt and then held out her tangled hair, staring at it as if for the first time. She was a sight. She had been too ill to notice and no one had tried to help her since Hawke had run off the doctor. Reminded of her first experience with a man of medicine, she relayed the story to Marie as the woman helped her to strip off her filthy clothing. Billy knocked on the door and was painfully uncomfortable as Shannon held the blanket over her to cover her nakedness, while he poured part of the warm contents of bucket into a pewter bowl on a rimmed shelf at the foot of the berth and set it with the remainder on the floor for later.

After he left, Marie began to scrub the girl roughly with a cloth she had taken from the trunk and some lye soap she had managed to scent with the flowers from her garden. Shannon winced as the water burned the abrasions on her back where she had crawled through the flooring in the house, but the bath was a welcome treat. They had to send for more water to wash her hair, and when the bath was finished, she lay back on the pillow too exhausted to dress.

"You jus' rest a minute, and I be back."

Shannon gladly obeyed and closed her eyes as the woman searched through the trunk and, finding what she wanted, left the room. True to her word, Marie returned with a steaming mug of herbal tea, laced with one of her own medicines. The girl sat up and leaned forward as the housekeeper propped up the pillow behind her back against the wall that was the headboard of the berth. She relaxed and held the blanket over her as Marie coaxed her into downing the hot bitter liquid.

"Dis de same ting what I give your Engleeshman. He weak too and be plenty sick if dat surgeon man has his way."

Shannon pushed the mug away. "He's not my Englishman."

Marie shrugged and placed the cup on the shelf. "Maybe not, but he almost die for you. And if he want to do dat, den ole Marie, she gonna make sure he be fit to do it."

Shannon was forced to listen as Marie told her of how Morgan Hawke had suffered at Ramon's cruel hand, demanding that the Creole finish him and go try to save her. She cringed at the detail and paled as Marie told her proudly how she finished the demented man.

"He a bastard man. And I tought he was de darkhair man I see for you.' The woman shook her head in disbelief. "Ol' Marie make big mistake, Shannon Brennan. Now doan you do same ting."

Shannon tried to swallow the blade in her throat. "I'm sorry, I cannot forgive him. He killed papa."

The housekeeper stepped up and shook her roughly. "De Engleeshman not kill Papa Brennan. Papa Brennan kill Papa Brennan. He been trying to kill himself all his life!"

Shannon frowned, confused by the woman's words.

"Papa Brennan a pirate, girl. A man dat live by vi'lence, die by vi'lence," she explained. "Your Hawke, he not dat way. I know dis here." She placed her fist over her heart. Her dark eyes noted the fatigue in Shannon's bewildered face and she clapped hands and changed the subject. "Now, I get help, and put clean linen on dis bed."

Shannon protested as Marie called for Michael Finney to help her over to the window seat in the stern of the cabin, so that she could change the sheets and blankets. She tried to argue that she needed to dress first, but the housekeeper told her when she put on clean nightclothes, she would wear them in a clean bed. When the task was done, the first mate cheerfully deposited the blanket-wrapped patient back on the bed and left her to Marie's ministrations.

Marie again dug through the trunk, and retrieved a lovely embroidered nightgown. It had a high banded collar and opened all the way down to her waist to facilitate putting it on. The front closed modestly with tiny pink bows. Large gathered sleeves hung

141

to her wrists, where they tied also with the same ribbon. The yoke boasted delicate pink flowers artistically appliqued by the patient hand of the woman. It hung just above her ankles and was as full about her figure as Nick Brennan's old shirt had been. By the time Marie finished combing her hair and twisting it in a long braid, the girl could barely hold her head up.

Shannon was asleep by the time the woman had straightened up the room and did not rouse when Marie kissed her on the forehead and left the cabin. She did not wake for the supper Billy brought in and left on the shelf, nor did she stir when Michael Finney knocked on the connecting door from the captain's cabin and opened it to check on her.

"Our angel's sleeping like a baby," he whispered to Morgan Hawke, who laboriously made his way to the door to gaze at the sleeping girl.

One arm rested in an arch over her head and the other lay on top of the blanket that covered her from the waist down. Her lashes were dark fans upon her cheeks and her lips formed an endearing pout as she breathed softly, her breast rising and falling gently under the chaste folds of her ribboned nightdress.

Finney glanced sharply at his captain as the man pulled inside his room and leaned back against the wall. His eyes were closed as he let his breath out slowly. After a moment, he motioned for the first mate to close the door and started across the room to his berth. As he settled uncomfortably on the mattress, he whispered sadly to himself, forgetting the presence of his friend. "Would God that she would stay that way."

It was nearly two weeks before the British ships

were ready to leave Nose' Be. Prisoners had been taken aboard the Admiral's ship to be returned to England for trial. The captains worked their crews diligently preparing for the voyage home. Provisions were taken from the warehouse which somehow escaped the devastating bombing of the raid. The pirates' booty was confiscated in the name of the King Charles of England and stowed in the holds of the victors' vessels.

The native inhabitants of the village returned from their forest hideouts and started to clear away the demolished huts, not much more than cinders, and to rebuild their homes. The tavern was operating, much to the delight of the off-duty marines, under the new management of some of the serving wenches. The women whose homes had been destroyed tempted the lusty seamen to help them in their spare time to clear away the debris and remodel the long warehouse into suitable lodging for them. While the work was under way, they stayed in the rooms above the tavern and entertained there.

Brennan's house had been left alone with the exception of the search and seizure led by the Admiral himself. Marie cooperated with the men, giving them any of Brennan's belongings they requested. She in turn was permitted to visit Shannon daily and was soon recognized as an authority to be dealt with by the marines who took her out to the *Sea Lady* at her will. Docking was impossible as the remains of the *Plunderer*'s wreckage lay under the water's surface, showing its charred hull only at the ebb of the tide.

Shannon sat on the window seat watching the longboat approaching with Marie in it. The woman was engaged in an apparently humorous conversation with the neatly uniformed men as sounds of laughter drifted toward the *Sea Lady*. The girl chuckled softly. It seemed that Marie had adjusted quite well to the sudden change at the cove and thoroughly enjoyed the position of importance that Morgan Hawke had granted her.

The girl stood up and leaned out the open window calling brightly to the housekeeper and waving a slender hand. She was clad in a simple cotton gown she had found in the trunk and its pink shade matched the color that was returning to her face. Shannon sat back as the woman in the boat returned her greeting and fingered the small locket at her throat thoughtfully. Now that she was much improved, perhaps she would be permitted to return home.

She had dismissed the idea that she was being held prisoner. Finney explained the guard posted at the door was there for her protection and safety until she was sufficiently recovered. And although he would not discuss the fleet's impending departure, he assured her that everything was being done with her welfare in mind. Why else would she be allowed visits by her nurse?

Shannon was truly grateful for that. As in the past, Marie had cared for her daily until, with the resilience of youth ,she recouped her strength. Now she was restless. She had been confined to the small cabin too long. She heard Morgan Hawke's voice on the deck above calling out to his crew authoritatively and realized that she was not the only one who had benefited from Marie's care.

Each day the woman spent almost as much time in his cabin as she had in Shannon's. When she had regained enough strength, Shannon tried listening at the door curiously, but the creaking sounds of the ship moving in the tide combined with their low voices made it impossible to determine the nature of

144

their conversation. Whatever they discussed they intended to keep to themselves for Marie never mentioned a word about her visit with Hawke except to give a report on his improvement.

Apparently foregoing her visit with Hawke, Marie was soon at the girl's cabin door. Shannon crossed the room in a rush and gave the woman an affectionate hug, delighted to have someone to talk to. As she stepped back she detected a trace of tears in the woman's eyes.

"Marie, what's the matter?" she asked anxiously.

"You wear de locket I put in de trunk for you." It was a statement and not the answer to the girl's question.

"Yes, I thought it was pretty." Shannon held it out and put her chin to her chest to examine the handsomely engraved coat of arms on the rich silver surface. "It's funny I've never seen it before."

"You keep it on. It belong to your mama, so your papa say. And he keep it to give you on your weddin' day."

Shannon closed her hand about the locket. "I will, Marie. I promise. I had no idea it was so special." She changed the subject abruptly. "Do you think you could ask Captain Hawke to let me go home now? I really am fine, and from the way things are looking in the harbor, the ships must be nearly ready to sail." Again she saw the tears. "Marie?" she said uneasily.

"Now you gonna be happy, girl. I know it here." The woman put her hands on her heart.

Shannon looked at the woman in disbelief. "What are you saying?"

"You go wid your Engleeshman back to Londun town. He take care of you better den old Marie kin." She touched Shannon's face with the palm of her hand tenderly. "Now doan mess dat pretty face up wid tears."

Shannon blinked and wiped her eyes with the back of her forearm. "Are you coming?" The very plan she had had to leave the island and those she loved was becoming a reality and unbearable.

Marie pulled her to her heavy bosom and wrapped her big arms around the girl. "Now what would ol' crazy voodoo woman do in Londun town?" she chided tenderly.

Shannon clung tightly to the woman as if to keep her from leaving her totally alone. Her father, Cudge . . . they were all gone. Marie was all she had. "I won't go without you!"

"Yes you will, girl. You can' stay here widdout your papa to protect you, and I can't leave."

"I won't go!" Shannon cried out defiantly. "I'll slip out the stern window and swim ashore. Then I'll hide where . . ." she hesitated, remembering that Morgan Hawke knew of the hidden cave, "well, I'll hide somewhere until they're gone. When do they plan to leave?"

"You do no such ting! You go! Marie gotta life to live now. Not takin' care of you!" Her voice shook the girl as sharply as her heavy hands.

Shannon could not understand the angry look in the woman's eyes. This was the woman who was more her mother than the one who gave her birth. "I d . . . don't believe you!"

The room rang with the slap of Marie's palm on Shannon's face. "Believe, girl. Marie know what best for both of us." The woman grabbed the stunned girl and hugged her tightly. Then releasing her as quickly, spun on her heel and left the room.

Shannon walked in a daze back to the window seat and sat down. Her mind raced as she idly fingered her braided hair. She watched the longboat, with a stoic Marie sitting quietly in the center, make its way to the shore and return without her. There was scuffling on the deck above as the command to hoist the anchor penetrated her thoughts.

Quickly, she ran to the chest Marie had brought her and rummaged through it for her shirt and breeches. Marie promised she would launder them, she thought frantically as she pulled the contents out and flung them aside. A knock on the door made her freeze for a moment before she found her voice and beckoned the visitor in. She did not want to give them reason to suspect her plan. She hastened to pick up the clothes and shoved them back in the trunk as Michael Finney entered the cabin followed by Billy Randall carrying a length of rope.

Shannon was wary as the first mate spoke. "Now lass, I've got an order to carry out and it's me hope that you'll be easy on me an' Billy here, and let us tie ye up so ye don't fall out the window there till we're well under way."

"Please don't do this, Michael," she implored in a small voice backing up to the window seat.

Sensing her ploy, Finney leaped toward her as she spun to throw herself through the opening and held her against the upholstered cushion. Instead of fighting, Shannon merely met his eyes with a recriminating look that shook him to the core. "The rope, Billy," he called over his shoulder.

Shannon permitted them to tie her wrists securely behind her, and as the mate put her in her berth, he apologized. "So help me, I'd not hurt ye for the world, lass."

"Please don't cry, Miss Shannon." Billy Randall leaned across the bunk and brushed away the frustrated tears.

Shannon's chin quivered as she gave the lad a weak smile. "You would think that I'd just run dry after a while, wouldn't you?"

The tiny harbor became a retreating speck in the

distance as Shannon sat up against the pillow cushioned wall on the berth and stared out the window at the only home she could remember. She winced as the prickly jute stuck her wrists where she had rubbed them raw trying to slip her hands through the snug loops Finney had tied. She felt like an animal trussed for the kill. Reluctantly resolved to her predicament, she relaxed against the pillows, rocked by the rolling motion of the *Sea Lady* as she ventured out on her first leg of the journey home.

The warm touch of a hand on her cheek made her start. Her eyes flew open to see Morgan Hawke standing over her with a knife. Instinctively she drew into the corner of the berth, as he read her thoughts and chuckled aloud. He was much recovered from the last time she had seen him. There was life in the cobalt eyes as they watched her instead of the dullness she had seen the day he had saved her from the bloody intentions of the Admiral's surgeon; and his tanned face had a reddish tint to it from the afternoon out on deck in the tropical sun.

"I am only going to cut your bonds, Shannon," he assured her. "Unlike some people we know, I am not free with the blade." He frowned as he noted the rope burn on her wrists. "Why do you have to fight everything?" he sighed in exasperation.

Shannon huddled against the side of the ship, refusing to look at him and held her tongue. She flinched as he ran his hand from her short gathered sleeve down her arm. She would not cry, she told herself firmly. She would not give him the satisfaction of knowing how much his betrayal had hurt her. And she would never give in to the flame he still could ignite by the tender sound of his voice and the touch of his hand.

She would hate him. She would groom the emotion carefully until she would not be able to stand his presence or his tormenting memory. And she would fight him any way she could; make him regret his ever having forced her to go with him.

"Shannon, I promised your father to take care of you," he was saying. "I couldn't leave you on the island to the scavengers that will pick the ruins."

"That promise. Was it before or after you planned to murder him?" Her voice shook in spite of her effort to sound defiant.

She felt the mattress sway as he sat down beside her and put his arms on her shoulders. Don't look at him, she warned herself, concentrating on the view from the portal over the berth.

"Shannon, I am sorry that it happened this way. I wanted to kill him when I sailed into Nose' Be. I wanted to destroy the man who killed my father. The *Dagger* was once my father's ship."

She leaned her chin against her arm resting on the rim of the open portal. So that was why. His possible reasons for the insane attack had racked her brain in her waking hours of confinement. "But I told you that day in the warehouse, Ramon led that raid. Papa stayed aboard the *Plunderer*. I . . . I'm sure of it. So he did not kill your father," she said dubiously.

"Nor did I kill yours."

No! He's twisting her words she thought desperately. He is so gifted in that respect. Like Fletcher said, he could talk a merchantman out of his wares. He lies and deceives. "You led a group of murderers into my home, my father was killed as a result, everything I know was destroyed. Now you have kidnapped me and are forcing me to go with you to your country under the pretense of a promise to a man you admit you vowed to destroy. And . . ." she said, silencing him as he started to protest, "you have kept me locked up in this cabin and bound like a slave."

"Shannon . . ."

"I hate you, Morgan Hawke, and I promise to have my own vengeance on your black soul!"

She winced as his hands tightened on her shoulder and pulled her around forcing her to look at the storm that brewed on his face. "Damn you, you're not listening to me! Shannon, your father was a pirate, a murderer, a thief, a vulture who preyed on innocent people. He and his kind had to be stopped."

"No!" she cried angrily, putting her hands to her ears to shut out the accusations. Nick Brennan was kind and loving. He pampered and spoiled her with fatherly affection. She would not ask about his business. She would not dwell on how he came by the treasures he brought in to the cove. She couldn't let herself think of the lives the plunder had cost—the blood that stained the hands that bounced her on his knee as a baby and swung her around happily as a young woman.

He pulled her hands away. "It's an ugly truth you have to grow up and face, Shannon."

Shannon glared at him icily. Her fists clenched as she lashed out at the one who made her see Nick Brennan as he was when he was away from her. "I hate you, you bastard!"

She lunged across the bunk at him and cried out as they tumbled to the floor of the cabin with a loud impact. As she recovered, she started to pummel his chest in her agonized fury, when she realized that he did not offer to protect himself. Instead he clenched his teeth and moaned involuntarily as the color drained from his face. Shannon stared numbly as blood soaked through the white shirt at his shoulder.

"Oh God!" she whimpered, forgetting her own rage and trying to pull him up. "Hawke!" She rose and hurried to the bunk to get a pillow. Upon returning, she leaned over and gently lifted his head, tucking the pillow under it. The blood! She had to stop the blood. She went to the chest and dug through it in a frenzy finally finding a dainty cotton shift to do the job. As she leaned over him, she carefully lifted the neck of his veed shirt up and slid the folded shift under it. His brow was damp with perspiration and she wiped it away with the hem of her gown and kissed his forehead tenderly.

She started as the door burst open and Michael Finney charged in the cabin stopping short at the sight of the girl leaning over his captain attentively. She swallowed hard as she glanced up at him, remembering his threat.

"I didn't mean to hurt him! I ... it was an accident. Please help me get him to the bunk."

Hawke was moving under her, attempting to rise up on his good arm. As Shannon straightened and tried to assist him, her ribboned braid fell in his face, annoying him. "Damn it, Finney, just don't stand with your mouth open!" he grunted irritably, flinging it to the side.

The first mate sprang into action and, with Shannon's help, lifted the disgruntled captain to his feet. As they started with him toward Shannon's berth, he pulled free of them. "I can make it on my own now," he announced, holding the bandage on his shoulder. "But I'll rest in my own bed."

Shannon's face reddened at the comment, and as the first mate followed his captain into the companionway, she slammed the door behind them. It was then she realized no one stood guard over her and she opened it again as the captain's door shut behind Hawke and Finney. She supposed they thought she could go nowhere in the middle of the Indian Ocean, and they were right. Damn them, she cursed inwardly as she slammed the door shaking the wall with a resounding protest.

Chapter Nine

The worst of the blustery winds were behind the *Sea Lady* as she made her way toward the rendezvous with the Admiral's ship at Cape Horn. The coastline was like a green ribbon separating the sea from the brilliant blue sky. The ship's sails billowed in the fresh breeze, straining the vibrating lines and keeping the crew busy as they carried out the order to lower them in preparation to anchor.

Shannon stood at the rail, oblivious to the action around her. She stared at the approaching land dreamily. The salt air dampened her unbound hair as it whipped around her face, tickling her nose. She reached down and held the skirt of her gown as it swelled with a playful gust. Gulls flew about the riggings and swooped down in front of her seeking more of the food scraps she had coaxed from the cook.

"I don't have any more!" she called out apologetically in response to their demanding cries.

For the most part of the four weeks since they had left Nose' Be, she had stayed below, only venturing out during the infrequent spells of calm. The crew remained distant with the exception of Billy, Finney, and the cook, who seemed to welcome her company and her help.

She enjoyed Billy's company in particular. One day he came in while she was reading one of the books Marie had packed in her trunk and was fascinated by the sketch of one of Homer's classical monsters. Shannon told him what the creature was and how it terrified the crew of Ulysses. The end result of the session was a promise to read the book to him whenever he had time off and teach him to read as well. It was a prospect that pleased both of them and a pleasant way to spend the long days of the voyage to England.

She also learned more about the cabin boy and his family. His mother ran a boarding house in London with his two sisters. His father had served on the merchant vessels of the Hawke family and, as soon as Billy came of age, he signed on with Morgan Hawke to pursue his own career at sea. He idolized the captain of the *Sea Lady* and aspired to captain his own vessel some day.

Shannon said nothing to tarnish the boy's opinion of the man, but, unlike Billy, who followed Hawke about like a second shadow, she avoided the captain's company. When she noticed him nearby on deck, she hastened below to her cabin. And when an invitation to dine with him was extended, she refused politely, preferring the safe solitude of her own room. To her relief, he respected the distance she put between them and devoted his efforts to the running of the ship through the unpredictable whims of the weather and seas west of the Cape.

As she made her way back to her cabin, she waved brightly to Michael Finney, who was engaged in conversation with the Master at Arms, a rather stocky fellow by the name of Pope, and started down the steps to the companionway below. She blinked as her eyes adjusted to the dim light from the brilliant afternoon sun and hesitated at the last tread for a moment.

"Fine afternoon, ain't it, missy?" The strange voice made her jump and she squinted to see a big sailor leaning against the bulkhead by her cabin door. "Ya ain't so high an' mighty now that the cap'n's taken ye down a peg and took away yer pig sticker."

"What do you want," Shannon demanded with a false bravado, recognizing the man she had beaten in the knife throw at the tavern.

"Nothin' what ain't due me."

"What do you want?" she repeated, inching along the wall as he moved toward her.

"Seems to me it's been cozy enough with you an' the cap'n down here . . . an' he ain't lost neary what I did on accounta you, missy." He put his arm over Shannon's head and leaned over, his face so close his rancid breath became suffocating. "An' everyone of us knows 'e's just brought ye along to keep 'is bed warm till we git to London. Then it's to the Tower ye'll go, quick as ye please."

"You son of a common—" Shannon was cut off as he pinched her lips together painfully with his fingers.

"Ye needn't git yer feathers ruffled, missy. I'm thinkin' it needn't be that way," he suggested meaningfully. "No, not at all, if yer nice enough to me as well."

Shannon brought her hand against the side of his face with a stinging blow and ducked under his arm to escape to her room. She tried to shove the door shut with her shoulder, but he was too quick and blocked her attempt with a powerful push. Just as he struck it, she jumped aside and watched as his momentum carried him into the room to sprawl on the floor. Quickly, she jumped over him and started out the companionway when she felt a tug on her skirt and heard the rip of material as he grabbed at it and tripped her.

Gasping to recover from her fall, Shannon tried to get up, but before she could move, he flung his body over hers. His rough hands pinned her shoulders to the deck as she screamed and tried to inch toward the steps. The pink sleeve of her garment tore as he tried to hold onto her and his ragged nails raked her skin.

Suddenly, a black-booted foot swung past her head and caught her assailant under the chin with a resounding crack. The man rolled off her and Shannon scrambled to the corner as Morgan Hawke followed the kick with another, catching him full in the ribs.

"It ain't me fault, cap'n, I swear it," Scarface called out in a terrified voice. "She led me on, sir, a swishin' her pink skirt up on deck and lookin' at me with them flirtin' eyes of 'ers." He tried to pull himself up the rail of the steps. "I couldn't 'elp meself, sir, bein' a man at sea with no female comfort. I swear—" He broke off and grunted as Hawke executed an angry punch to his midriff, bending him over. A swift upward lift of the knee caught the man's chin and threw him back against the step where he sprawled with a semi-conscious moan.

Michael Finney and a small group of men hurried down the companionway, stepping around the writhing man. Two of them hauled him to his feet to face the white heat of his captain's fury.

"Mister Pope, see that this man gets the lash for his apparent lack of self-control and his flagrant disregard for my orders!"

Shannon shivered involuntarily at the murderous

quality in Hawke's voice. She shrank against the wall when he spun about and fixed his angry glare on her.

"You!" he growled lowly. "You are confined to your cabin where you cannot excite this sort of behavior among my crew. Unless either Mr. Finney or myself escort you . . . do you understand that?" It was a challenge, not a question.

Shannon pulled her torn sleeve back up on her shoulder and drew herself to her full height. "You don't believe that bastard?" she exclaimed incredulously.

"You heard what I said."

"I did not do anything!" she protested hotly. "I was attacked!"

"If I catch you out of that room without proper escort I'll have you chained to your berth, do you understand that, Miss Brennan?" The muscles twitched in his jaw, clenched in rage.

Shannon's ire ignited at the threat. She stepped up furiously and slapped him full in the face. But before she could move, he returned the gesture in kind, sending her reeling against the wall. She raised her hand to her inflamed cheek in wide-eyed disbelief. Then with a ragged cry of hurt and anger, she fled into her cabin and slammed the door, leaving him to the anxious eyes of his men.

As the scuffling of the men returning topside faded, Shannon slid the bolt shut to the companionway and then did the same to the one adjoining the captain's chamber. Angrily she stomped her foot and knocked the pewter bowl across the room with a resounding clang. How could he believe that scum, she fumed. It was she that was trying to crawl away from him in a gown torn in his lusty attack. She ripped at the delicately sewn closures and peeled the pink dress over her hips, ignoring the shredding sounds of fabric that gave way to the violent treatment.

"Damn them all," she muttered, scooping it up and rolling it in a ball.

The stern windows crashed against the bulkhead on either side of them as she flung them open wildly. The glass rattled, threatening to shatter at the force of the impact. With a furious throw, she hurled the garment through the window and sank down on the window seat, her wrath and energy spent.

"Shannon!" The door from the companionway rattled at the captain's bellowing voice.

Shannon drew a pillow to her and held her breath, refusing to answer. She heard him curse and the sound of his booted footsteps faded as he quit the door. Suddenly the door from his cabin shook with violent pounding, its bolt holding securely.

"Shannon, open this door!"

"To hell with you," she muttered under her breath with a glance at the pink material floating on the water's surface in the wake of the vessel.

She jumped and clutched the pillow to her chest as a thunderous kick loosened a plank. Another forceful kick wrenched the screws that held the bolt from the facing and the door swung back, hitting the wall and bouncing back into the path of the charging captain. Shannon cried out as Morgan Hawke flung himself into the room.

"You little minx," he gasped, recovering his breath. "I ought to wring your tempting neck!" His look was murderous as he started for her, forcing her to retreat into the corner. With a threatening restraint, he pulled the casements shut and secured them with the latch before focusing his attention on her. "Why didn't you answer me?" he demanded, dragging her up by the shoulders so that his cobalt eyes burned into hers.

Shannon tried to answer, but the lump in her throat prevented the words from surfacing.

"I want your word of honor that you will not try to swim ashore. You do have some semblance of honor?"

"Not since I trusted you."

Her words hit their intended mark and his grip loosened from the blow. Yet there was no sense of triumph as she became acutely aware of his nearness and realized how vulnerable she was. She refused to let his gaze intimidate her and strove to return it with equal fierceness.

"Bitch . . ." he whispered under his breath. He grabbed her face and pulled it to his, punishing her lips with his own. His three-day growth of beard was abusive to her tender skin, burning and scratching unmercifully.

Her mind cried out for help as her senses sided with him. Hate, she thought desperately. She wanted to hate this man. He killed her father. She tried to conjure the burning deck of the *Plunderer* in her mind and the ploy worked. Her blood chilled as the scene she summoned filled her with horror.

"Cap'n, the Admiral's sendin' a signal . . ." Michael Finney's voice halted abruptly in the other cabin as he realized it was unoccupied.

Hawke released Shannon as the first mate stuck his head through the adjoining door. "Excuse me, sir," Finney apologized awkwardly upon finding them.

"I'll be right up, Mister Finney," Hawke told him, his eyes riveted to the revulsion on Shannon's face.

"Aye, sir." Noting the shattered bolt and splintered wood, the first mate shook his head grimly and left them to go topside.

"Don't ever lock me out again," Hawke warned evenly. "Ever."

Shannon sank to the cushion as he pivoted away and left her to the emotion that tore at her nerves viciously. From the turmoil rose the words of the sailor who had treated her. The Tower. Few of the men from Brennan's Cove had not heard of the nightmarish prison. No, she argued with herself. Morgan Hawke said he was going to take care of her . . . it couldn't mean that. She shivered uncertainly, shaken by the hostility she had just witnessed and buried her face in her folded arms, more frightened than ever at her unknown fate.

It was noon the following day when a longboat from the Admiral's ship pulled alongside the *Sea Lady*. An immaculately groomed messenger presented himself to Morgan Hawke in the captain's cabin and extended an invitation to dine with the superior officer. Shannon was also invited and, when Hawke objected, he was informed that the Admiral had specifically requested the girl's presence.

Shannon could not help but overhear the conversation through the broken door and wondered why the Admiral of the fleet wanted to see her. She had heard of interrogations by cruel naval officers who had captured pirates but convinced herself that this surely would not be the case. Perhaps if she made the right impression, he might overlook her connection with the pirates held prisoner on his ship and would treat her civilly.

She took the utmost care to dress for the occasion. There was a taffeta gown Marie had made for her wedding to Ramon in the huge trunk. Billy repeatedly heated an iron for her at the cook's hut and she spent the better part of the afternoon pressing out the wrinkles from the tight storage. Voluminous petticoats reinforced with whalebone made the draped skirt fall from her narrow waist in a bell-like fashion to the satin slippers on her feet. The pale lavender color brought out the contrast of her deep blue eyes. Adorning the scandalously cut neckline, she wore the silver necklace that had been her mother's. Aside from that, the only other frills she wore was a string of pearls which she wove into the braid that hung over her shoulder.

She was struggling with the last of the fastens of her gown, those she could not so easily reach, when Morgan Hawke knocked and entered the room unbidden. Shannon stared in spite of herself, for she had never seen him dressed in anything but the casual shirt and breeches he wore at sea. His broad shoulders were encased in a handsome jacket of the king's cloth, dark blue and tailored to the taper of his trim waist. Beneath it was a fine linen shirt, banded at the neck where an unadorned jabot hung in three neat folds. His breeches were of the same color as the jacket, stopping at the knee where white stockings proceeded down to polished leather buckled shoes.

"I see wearing clothes has the same effect on you as wearing nothing at all," he remarked dryly at her stunned appraisal. A smile stretched across his lips as her color deepened in reaction to his insinuation.

"I . . . I'm almost ready." Shannon turned her back to him to hide her fluster and attacked the awkwardly placed fastens once more.

"It appears you need assistance." Shannon froze as he crossed the distance between them and closed the hooks with ease. For a moment, his hands rested on her bare shoulders and then dropped as she jerked away. Bowing slightly, he motioned for her to precede him to the top deck.

Boarding the longboat in her gown was difficult, as Michael Finney handed her down to Hawke. The stiff petticoats rustled against the captain's face and, by the time she was seated beside him in the center of the craft, her face was crimson. The crew smothered their amusement with polite grins and devoted themselves to the task of rowing to the large hundred-gun ship that flew the flag of the Admiralty under the Union Jack. Her awkward climb to the deck was no more dignified than her previous descent, and it was in a somewhat flustered state that she was presented to Admiral Edward Bedlowe and his officers.

As she extended her hand graciously to the trim white-haired man and bestowed one of her most charming smiles, he cleared his throat and stared at her in amazement. There was an uncomfortable period of silence before he spoke.

"My dear Miss Brennan, I hope you will forgive me for my rude appraisal. Not only was my breath taken by your unrivaled beauty, but I thought for a moment that you were someone I knew a very long time ago."

"You are very kind, sir," Shannon replied modestly. She took his offered arm and accompanied him to the richly gilded gallery, ornately carved and decorated.

The room where they dined adjoined his private quarters. It was furnished with a large round table, bolted to the floor for stability in rough seas. A steward had set the table with linen and pewterware, accented by the fine crystal goblets engraved with the seal of the Crown. Shannon was seated between the Admiral and the commanding officer of his ship, Captain Wardlaw, while the others took their places about the table.

The meal was a luxury after weeks of salted ration. The cook on the *Sea Lady* was truly talented, but he did not have the fresh fare brought from the Dutch port to work with. There was roast of beef, rare and succulent in its own juices, scalloped oysters, wild rice with fresh sautéd vegetables, and several small loaves of fresh baked bread. The accompanying wine was a heavy Madeira, artfully bottled in the islands off the northwest coast of Africa.

"My dear lady, I do apologize for not having something of a lighter nature, but I must admit, it is a rare occasion that we have the opportunity to entertain feminine guests."

"The Madeira will be fine, Admiral," Shannon assured him. She raised her goblet and sipped daintily. The strong wine slipped down her throat, bringing tears to her eyes and she fought to keep from strangling at the shock. Across the table, she caught Morgan Hawke's amused smirk and flushed.

The Admiral asked the blessing and the men began to eat. Shannon glanced about nervously. Cudge had taught her table etiquette, but it had not been practiced in her home. She watched as the others chose their utensils and imitated them. As much as her stomach demanded that she try everything on the table at least once, she had read that proper ladies had delicate appetites. So she accepted modest portions and watched in dismay as the steward removed her plate at the end of the meal.

The officers discussed the impending resumption of their voyage. They had only assembled at Cape Horn to take on fresh water and a few supplies. Tomorrow they set sail for Isle de Los, a two-week voyage from the Horn where they would reprovision their ships for the last leg of the journey to England. The long-time base for slave trading was one of the few friendly harbors off the Portuguese-held coast of northwest Africa where English and French ships on their way to and from their trade with the East Indies could obtain fresh water and supplies to continue their long journeys.

"So, Lord Hawke, do you intend to keep the *Sea Lady* to replace your father's lost ship?" Captain Wardlaw asked, allowing the steward to refill his glass.

"That depends on the generosity of King Charles."

"Then you have a ship, sir! The King was overjoyed with your scheme to put an end to Brennan and his murderous lot," Wardlaw assured him.

"It's just a damned shame the ship you left with got away," another officer snorted in disgust. "But I suppose it was worth giving it up in order to catch the other vermin."

Shannon dropped her eyes to her lap uncomfortably at the harsh references to the people she'd grown up among. However, Admiral Bedlowe recognized the inconsiderate turn of the conversation and put an end to it.

"Gentlemen, I fear we have been remiss in our thought. We have a lady present who might not wish to endure the pursuit of this subject."

Shannon placed a grateful hand on the Admiral's arm and spoke, her voice husky with emotion. "Thank you, sir, for your consideration." Then, tactfully, she changed the subject. "Why are you calling Captain Hawke, Lord Hawke?" she asked, her eyes narrowing as she peered through the flickering candelabra at the man in question.

"For shame, Morgan Hawke! Have you sought to keep your identity from this lovely creature to some purpose?" the Admiral chided familiarly.

"No, sir. It seems the opportunity simply hasn't

presented itself. On the sea, I'm a captain. When in London or at Snowden, I assume the role of my family title."

"Snowden?" Shannon echoed, intrigued by this new revelation.

"A lovely place, dear," the Admiral informed her. "Young Hawke's father and I spent many a pleasant day hunting on the estate. Good days, they were," he reflected nostalgically.

"I see." Shannon looked over the rim of her glass at the captain, a spark of curiosity dancing in her eyes.

"My dear, would you think it impertinent of me to ask to see your locket?"

Shannon was shocked from her study, but nodded amiably. The steward assisted her with the delicate clasp and handed it to the elderly gentleman. "It was my mother's," she explained proudly.

"Who was your mother, Shannon?"

"A Sakalavan woman named Lillianne," she answered the man. "I really don't remember much about her . . . she died when I was only six. But she was very pretty and kind."

"Much like her daughter." The Admiral smiled and offered to replace the locket about her neck.

Again Shannon blushed at the compliment and turned her back to him to facilitate his task. Dessert was served and she found she simply could not resist the pudding covered in a heavy cream with fresh berries on top. By the time the meal was finished, she was blissfully contented and had to stifle a yawn as she tried to concentrate on the boring conversation. The evening had not been nearly as bad as she had feared, and she found she could not help but like the dear gentleman who commanded the small fleet. While his speech reminded her of Cudge when he was on good behavior, his carriage was truly that of

164

a gentleman.

As they bade goodbye and again began the climb down to the longboat, Shannon was relieved to be going back to the *Sea Lady*. Her eyelids were heavy from the effects of the strong Madeira and the strain of the evening. Her slipper caught on the rope ladder that hung down over the side of the ship and she fell backward, gasping as Morgan Hawke caught her in a swirl of taffeta and ruffles. Rearranging her gown from her unceremonious landing, she primly took her seat by the captain in a flush of humiliation. Farewells were made as the longboat started toward the vessel moored nearby, lighted with binnacles on its decks to welcome its strays home.

Chapter Ten

Morgan Hawke stood on the deck above the gallery and looked on as his crew manned the riggings overhead to reef the sails. The sky was a dismal gray and the air was heavy and still. There was sure to be a storm, he thought, checking the decks again to make sure everything had been battened down according to his orders. His eyes rested on the mid deck where some of his crew gathered to pass the time waiting out the calm. Their loud voices drifted up to him as they sang along with the live music one of them provided with a harmonica.

It was one of their more tasteful selections, for in their midst was Shannon Brennan, accompanied by Michael Finney. He watched her as she jumped to her feet lightly and pulled Billy Randall from his seat on the deck to coax the bashful lad into a jig. Her movements were as graceful as Billy's were awkward. They joined hands and spun each other around until they both collapsed in laughter on the deck. As she rose to her feet and straightened her blue dress, she saw that she was being observed and stiffened noticeably. In a short time, Michael Finney was seeing her back to her cabin.

The muscles of the captain's face tightened as she passed below him coolly without a glance. As warm and charming as she had been on the Admiral's ship—so much so that even the disgruntled surgeon had succumbed to her lovely smile—she remained determined to treat him with an icy disregard.

The night they returned from dining on Admiral Bedlowe's ship, Hawke had thought for a moment that she had relaxed in her stubborn will to vex him. She had rested her head on his shoulder as his men rowed back to the *Sea Lady* and closed her eyes peacefully. However, as soon as her feet were firmly planted on deck, she made straight for her cabin. By the time he saw to the duties of his ship and entered his own cabin, her lamp was out and no sound emerged from the adjoining room.

"The Admiral's still ahead of us there, but when she hits, we're likely to lose 'im," Michael Finney was saying, startling Hawke from his bemused reverie.

"Aye, most likely. How are things below?"

"Secured as tight as a tick. All's we have to do now is wait."

"Good! Then I think I'll get something to eat from the cook while I can. Perhaps you'd best do the same . . . and send Billy down with Shannon's supper."

The mate nodded and followed his captain down the steps to the main deck. It was damned eerie, this calm, he thought to himself. It made a man's hair stand up on the back of his neck. He glanced out at the small image in the distance that was their companion ship. Its tall masts were barren crosses against the horizon, waiting. Just like us all, he thought as he proceeded to carry out his captain's orders.

When the storm finally caught up with them, the

ship rolled so violently that Shannon had to make an effort to remain in her bunk. The heavy drapes swung from side to side, letting in the brilliant flashes of lightning. The rolls of thunder seemed to shake the very timbers of the vessel beneath her. Her oil lamp beat against the wall so many times that she was certain it would break, but the protective wire casing about the exterior cushioned the impact.

She had placed her empty supper dishes in the floor and wedged them with a cushion to keep them from rattling about the room. She regretted having eaten. Her stomach seemed to match the pitching motion of the ship, and the room seemed to close in on her in the flickering lamplight. Yet, she dared not open the portal covered with salt foam.

Unconsciously, she drew into a corner of the berth and pulled the woolen blanket up around her. The lonely silence of the gallery was unsettling. The door between the two cabins clattered against the wall as the wedge of cloth she used to keep it shut broke loose. Carefully sliding off the bunk, Shannon stumbled across the short span of decking as the ship rolled to the larboard and caught it. She grasped the jamb for support to keep from being pitched headlong into the dark and empty cabin of Morgan Hawke.

The captain had been up on deck with his crew riding out the heavy winds that tossed his ship about in the cruel waves like the paper ships Shannon sailed in the lagoon as a child. He had only come down long enough to don oilskins and to tell Shannon to secure anything that might move about the cabin.

She managed to slide her heavy trunk against the banging door and staggered back across the cabin to her bunk as the ship rolled back to the starboard side. Suddenly, the vessel seemed to shudder and lunge forward. A loud burst of thunder rattled the glass in the stern casements. Shannon screamed as the latch on the windows gave way to the onslaught of the gale and slammed against the bulkhead. The angry splash of the sea invaded the room in a heavy salt spray. Before she could reach the window, the ship rolled precariously over on its side and the heavy trunk slid away from the door, crashing into her berth. As the motion reversed and the trunk rolled back across the room, splintering the door, Shannon was thrown to the floor.

In a panic, she scrambled out of the cabin and into the companionway on her knees. Her sash caught under her knees and untied as she dragged herself up the narrow steps leading to the deck. The hatchway opened and she carefully hooked it against the wall so that it did not batter her as she sat on the top step and stared out into the torrential rain. She could see but a few yards of decking before the rest of the ship faded into the dark wet curtain that only allowed the faintest glimmer from a lantern swinging wildly from midship.

As she strained her eyes to catch any sign of movement that might allow her the comfort of knowing she was not alone, she made out a dark form tacking across the deck perilously. It was a small figure dwarfed in heavy oilskins. Shannon recognized Billy Randall just as he plummeted face down on the deck in front of her. He started to crawl in her direction when the ship rolled deeply to the larboard, taking him with it.

"Billy!" Shannon screamed, her voice drowned by another roll of thunder. She lunged forward and tried to catch his outstretched hands, but they were wet, and the motion of the ship slung him away from her. She watched in horror as his light form skidded across the rain-washed decking. His feet slipped through the space between the carved spindles of the rail. Frantically, the boy grabbed one of the rails with his hands and checked himself from going over the side. Shannon shouted his name again and started after him on her knees.

An angry wave lashed over the deck soaking her as she made her way to the rail where the cabin boy clung desperately for his life. The ship rolled again and she was thrown painfully against the section where Billy was being battered against the side of the ship. Shannon could hear his frenzied cries for help and she wriggled into a position that allowed her to reach him. She tried to get a firm grip on his clothing, but her hands slipped dangerously each time.

Suddenly, she remembered her sash. If she could secure him to the rail until someone discovered them, Billy might have a chance. Her fingers shook as she ripped it loose from the loops at her waist and doubled it over for strength.

"Hang on, Billy!" she shouted down to the terrified lad. "I'm going to tie you to the rails." She saw him nod and close his eyes as they were swamped by another swell. Shannon made two wraps about his wrist before tying the wet sash to the bottom of the heavy railing. Once he was secure, she tried again to reach through and pull him up by his slicker. The vessel lunged back and she held onto the rail to keep from being thrown to the opposite side of the ship as Billy's hand let go of the rail. "Billy!" she screamed, reaching for him again.

But the sash held. Her tears mingled with the pouring rain as she tried to haul the boy up, when suddenly she felt someone holding her firmly about the waist. Glancing over her shoulder, she saw Michael Finney's face under the heavy brim of the oilskin hood. Another member of the crew crouched down and together the men reached through the rail and dragged the flailing cabin boy back onto the deck. For a moment, they all lay, regaining their breath, before Finney cut Billy free of the cloth that had saved his life.

They climbed to their feet and made their way across the shifting deck to the main hatchway. Below the deck, the remainder of the crew rested in order to relieve their comrades topside on the next shift. Upon seeing Shannon and Billy, the cook poured fresh coffee into some tin mugs and handed it to them. Some of the others rustled up some blankets and soon the two drenched companions were huddled together sipping the warm and bitter brew.

Shannon's hands shook so much, she had to make a concentrated effort to keep from spilling the beverage. Her heart seemed to quiver in her chest under the strain. When she relinquished the empty mug, she tugged her blanket over her head and retreated meekly from the company.

"Every man topside!" came a loud command bellowed from the main hatch. Morgan Hawke dropped from the upper deck, his feet hardly touching a step in his hurried descent. His face was white as he frantically looked at the startled men. "The girl's gone," he explained hoarsely.

"She's here, sir!" Michael Finney spoke up, pointing to the woolen bundle where a large pair of blue eyes peered out in alarm.

Before Finney could say another word, Hawke pushed past him and stared incredulously at Shannon. "I told you not to leave your cabin!" His voice shook as he pulled her to her feet.

"Sir, she . . ."

"Silence, Mr. Finney!" the captain commanded abruptly. He held her arms so tightly in his fists that they went numb. "By God, I warned you what would happen if you left the cabin unescorted."

"She saved Billy's life, sir!" Finney blurted out, risking the captain's ire.

Her nerves raw and reason fleeing at the insanity of it all, Shannon stiffened, blue eyes flashing. "You wouldn't dare!" she spat defiantly.

The pressure on her arms lightened as Hawke glanced over at the sleeping figure of the cabin boy and back to Shannon, disconcerted. "Don't push me, Shannon." He had died a thousand deaths in the time it took him to get from her cabin to his men. Even now he shook with the sick fear he felt at the thought of her going over the side. "I gave you an order . . . if you had some reason . . ."

"I don't need a reason to disobey you, Morgan Hawke!" Shannon shrieked, her voice bordering hysteria. "You're too pigheaded a fool to captain a dingy, let alone this vessel. You're not my captain! You're nothing but a sneaking, cold-blooded murderer and you can't make me do anything," she shouted, jabbing at his chest sharply with her finger. Her body began to shake with rebellious rage. "You can't . . . do you hear me?" she challenged. Blindly, she kicked at him, only to be released so suddenly, she stumbled backward to the deck, her feet entangled in the blanket.

There was an ominous silence that deafened the storm outside before the white-faced captain spoke. "Mr. Pope, when the gale is spent, see that she's chained to her berth."

"Captain!" Michael Finney protested.

"Mr. Finney, when I want your opinion, I'll ask for it!" he snapped, unable to tear his gaze from the spitting eyes that goaded him beyond rational thought.

"Bastard!" Shannon snarled through clenched

teeth, refusing to back down. For a moment, the captain looked as if he would strike her and she stuck out her chin defiantly.

"Cap'n, the helmsman needs to see ye right away!"

The voice shouting above the din of the storm forced an end to the battle of wills. Breaking away, Hawke strode over to the steps and up the hatch as quickly as he'd descended. As his feet disappeared, Shannon sank to her knees and curled up beside Billy, her face ashen. She had gone too far this time and it was too late to back down. If only he hadn't been so condemning because she broke one of his divinely inspired rules, she thought miserably. But she'd been so frightened. Only she hadn't told him that, her conscience reminded her. Perhaps she'd been too quick to condemn, as well. She closed her eyes, sinking into despair. Now it was too late.

The storm ran into the following day before the gale force winds dwindled so that they could be harnessed by the sheets of canvas to carry them to Isle de Los. A light drizzle remained of the torrential downpour that flooded the decks. The patter of the droplets against the side of the ship and the gentle roll of the calmed swells were a welcome relief in spite of Shannon's imprisonment in her cabin.

Mr. Pope carried out his orders diligently, allowing her time to bathe and don clean dry clothing before doing so. He'd had to use manacles about her ankles to secure her, for her wrists were too small for the chains meant for strapping men. It was attached to the berth, leaving her enough room to move in a semicircle about the cabin. A length of cloth had been wrapped about her leg first, so that the heavy metal would not rub her skin raw as the ropes had done earlier.

Billy Randall took his meal with her that evening. Feeling partially responsible for her confinement, the cabin boy was trying to make up for the long day of inactivity that was only briefly interrupted by walk with the first mate. His shoulder was sprained from his near-fatal fall during the storm, and he favored it as he placed a plate in front of her.

"I hear the cap'n's not really going to keep you in chains very long," he told her brightly, trying to bring a smile to the sullen face that stared blankly out the portal.

"Maybe I should stay here. After the rope and chain, I fear the lash may be my next peril under Captain Morgan Hawke's protection," she finished bitterly.

"Miss Shannon, the cap'n would never do that to you! I know it."

Shannon turned to see earnest brown eyes protesting her affront to their idol and smiled sympathetically. "You're very young, Billy. Sometimes there's a side of people that you can't see, they hide it so well. Morgan Hawke can be as cruel as Satan when he chooses."

Billy tensed. "You don't really mean that. If you and him would just talk to each other instead of stewin' over your differences, things would be a lot different."

"Who told you that?" Shannon was certain the boy did not make that observation on his own.

"I heard the men talkin'," he answered smugly.

"And what else did the men say?" she asked, perturbed at being the subject of the crew's speculation.

"They say it's your own fault that you're in chains. That the cap'n wouldn't have done it, if you'd just said you was sorry. You made him do this."

Shannon looked away and swallowed dryly. "Well, they're probably right, Billy," she admitted. How many times had she condemned herself in the past hours for the same thing, she wondered. "I have this damnable temper . . . and when I get around Morgan Hawke, it just seems to take over. That man can get me so worked up, I could just . . . well, I just don't know what I could do," she finished lamely.

Encouraged by her admission, Billy continued. "You know what else they say?" He took a bite of a biscuit and sopped some of the gravy from the hash up with it. "They say you work the cap'n up too. That he fancies you . . . and I think they're right."

"Why?" Shannon was intrigued by the chance that perhaps the crew's suspicion might be true.

"'Cause he ain't never been so grumpy before you came on board. He usually is a lot of fun to sail with. Now he's mad all the time."

"Billy," Shannon denounced scornfully. "That is hardly a sign of infatuation." For just a moment, she'd hoped for more. Her suppressed emotions sank back into submission in disappointment.

"Like a trussed-up rooster in a hen house, they say."

Shannon cleared her throat awkwardly as the meaning sank in. It was apparent that the lad was innocent of the implication as he watched her expectantly for a positive reception. "Do you want my biscuit? I really can't finish all this." It was time to change the subject she decided, disconcerted by Billy's gossip.

When they'd finished their meal, Shannon asked Billy to get the book she'd been reading aloud and they both settled in for an evening with Homer. She loved the way the boy's eyes sparkled with excitement and tried to read the parts in different voices with feeling. He grinned wickedly as she read to him about the sirens that lured the sailors up on the rocks with their haunting voices.

"What's so funny about that?" she asked curiously.

"Those men were in danger."

"Well, I was thinkin' maybe we should tie the captain to the mast so's he'll behave when you go up on deck."

"Billy Randall! You devil!" Shannon chastised, unsuccessfully smothering her amusement. "I think you've heard enough!"

"Awww!"

"We'll do this again tomorrow, although if you compare me to the Cyclops, I shall not read another word!" she threatened mischievously.

An impish grin still on his face. Billy took the tray and left her to prepare for bed. The chain dragged awkwardly at her feet, but Shannon managed to wash and don her nightdress with relative ease. As she climbed into her bunk, she blew out the lamp hanging over it. To her surprise, the moon was shining through the portal for the first time since they had left the Cape. She studied the clearing sky from her pillow, Billy's innocent account of the men's speculation dwelling heavily on her mind.

Slumber brought an onslaught of disjointed dreams. She whispered Morgan's name as he held her close on the deserted beach of Nose' Be and kissed her in passionate abandon. She tried to tell him of the feelings she had for him, but the words would not come. Dreamily she opened her eyes as she lay in his warm embrace, but, instead of her lover, she saw the death-like face of her father.

"Papa!" she cried out in horror as blood trickled out the side of his gaping mouth and his blank stare fixed on her. She reached for him frantically, but was roughly pulled away as he collapsed on the burning deck in a crumpled heap.

"We got us a little wildcat, mates!"

The uniformed men who had taken her eyed her hungrily. Fire from the explosions all around them

176

leapt from their eyes. Their hands were all over her, pinching and prodding. Perspiration dampened her brow as she struggled helplessly in their grasp. She prayed she'd swoon to escape, but the blessed darkness only teased her, leaving her victim to the lusty attack. Sobbing hysterically, she cried for her father again, but he could not come.

"Shannon!"

Morgan Hawke shook the moaning girl and pulled her upright on the berth. He had just fallen into bed in a state of exhaustion from days with no more than short intervals of rest when he heard her incoherent mumblings and checked on her. She fought weakly and cried for help as he tried shake her from her nightmares.

"Wake up, love. It's only dream!"

He caught her face between his hands and shook her until her eyes fluttered open. In the pale moonlight shining through the portal, he witnessed the terror in them.

"Nothing is going to happen to you, Shannon. You're dreaming," he assured her gently.

"H . . . Hawke?" Her voice trembled as she reached out and touched his beard-roughened face.

Disbelief showed in her eyes as she stared at him, ragged breaths tearing at her breast as it rose and fell beneath the chaste folds of her gown. Stray wisps of hair curled about her face in sleep disarray, clinging to the dampness. A flicker of recognition registered on her face and she collapsed against him, hugging him tightly.

"I . . . I'm so s . . . sorry!" Her tears burned his skin as she placed her hot cheek against his bare chest. "I was s . . . so frightened. The windows broke open and everything was crashing around the room."

"Shannon . . ." he began, hardly daring to trust

his ears. He shifted on the edge of the mattress and her grasp tightened.

"No! Don't leave me!" She was nearly hysterical, her nails digging into his back in her desperation.

"My love, I have no intention of leaving you," he whispered solemnly, his heart swelling with compassion and unprecedented joy.

Gently he removed her hands and eased her back against the pillows. The protest of his aching muscles, tortured by fighting the tempestuous storm, were ignored as he slid his arms beneath her and lifted her to him tenderly. There was more room in his own berth and moving her there seemed more prudent under the unexpected, but decidedly welcome turn of events.

The sound of heavy metal clanging to the deck made him start and he cursed his stubborn folly as he saw the end of the chain fastened at the end of the berth. His Master at Arms had the key and Hawke dared not risk losing the moment to seek out the man to release her. With a resigned sigh, he sat down on the mattress, his precious burden cradled in his arms, and settled against the bulkhead with the pillows to his back.

Her sobs subsided as he stroked the silken softness of her hair. He loosened the thin material of her gown where it clung to her back, wondering at the irony. The voyage had been a nightmare since they'd left Nose' Be and it had taken one to end it. The girl in his arms snuggled closer and he tucked a sheet about her shoulders tenderly. In a short while, her breathing was soft and regular against his chest. Not wanting to disturb her, he tried to make himself comfortable against the hard bulkhead, resting his head in the corner until fatigue claimed him in spite of the discomfort and he slept contentedly.

Chapter Eleven

Isle de Los was a bustling little port where European ships sought respite from their long journeys to and from the East Indies. There was plenty of good fresh water and merchants who profited from the sale of provisions needed to restock the holds for the remainder of the voyages. Ships flying the assorted flags of their respective countries crowded the harbor and a constant traffic of longboats moved to and fro from the docks where only a few vessels could tie up at one time to load their purchases.

It was sunset when Shannon peered anxiously through the window at the longboat making its way from the shore and sank back against the cushion in disappointment as she realized that Morgan Hawke was not one of its passengers. He had gone ashore to make arrangements for provisioning the *Sea Lady* and promised to be back in time to dine with her. She studied the row of buildings along the two docks where a small fleet of French merchantmen were tied and wondered if the man who had held her so tenderly that morning was in one of them.

She was shocked at first as she realized her pillow

was moving under her but when she opened her eyes and saw that it was a flat stomach rising and falling with the slow breathing of slumber, she remembered the nightmare and the gentle way Morgan Hawke had rescued her from the anguished sleep. The girl smiled as she recalled his tall frame sprawled against the bulkhead of her berth, his head jammed awkwardly in one corner and his legs hanging loosely over the side. One of his arms rested on her shoulder and as she raised her head he stirred only slightly in his exhausted sleep.

It was then for the first time that she saw the thin white lines of Ramon Gerarde's torture and recalled Marie's vivid account. The angry red scar on his shoulder inflicted by her own blade brought tears to her eyes as she recognized how close she had come to killing the man she loved. She raised up her knees and kissed the healing wound. Her braid dragged across his chest and he started. His eyes flew open to meet hers and for a moment neither of them moved. Then she was in his arms returning his kisses through tears of joy, until Michael Finney interrupted them with news of their arrival at Isle de Los.

She rose from the window seat and entered the captain's cabin where she had taken great pains to set the small table for their meal. The cook was preparing a fresh roast duckling he had managed to secure during his morning visit to the market place. It smelled delicious as it baked on top of the stove, but Shannon was so excited she hardly noticed the stirring of her appetite.

She wanted the evening to be special. Billy had helped her press the dress she had worn to Admiral Bedlowe's dinner party and promised to bring their meal to the cabin as soon as he saw the captain had returned. Now as she examined her reflection in the small mirror on the wall, she wondered if he would think she had overdressed for the occasion. She frowned prettily and straightened the bow that held her hair off her face.

A sudden noise came from her room and she hurried over to the adjoining door thinking that her captain was entering there from the companionway. As she rushed into her cabin, she froze at the sight of a familiar figure climbing in through the stern window.

"Captain Fletcher!" she gasped in astonishment.

Two more armed pirates followed the man over the window seat as he straightened and stared at Shannon, his hand drawing his cutlass from its sheath at his full waist. The girl backed against the wall, as he stepped toward her.

"No need to fear, Miss Shannon. Me an' the boys have come to rescue ye."

She felt as her knees would give way, as four more men came in through the window. There was only a skeleton crew on deck, most of the men having gone ashore to enjoy the hospitality of the taverns. If Hawke returned, he would not stand a chance against so many.

"Oh thank God, Captain," she exclaimed as she crossed the room and threw her arms about him convincingly. "I have been so frightened."

"'Ere now, Miss Shannon. Ye should have known as long as a friend o' your papa's lived that e'd not let 'is cap'n's own daughter be took by the likes of these chaps." He held his weapon to the side and locked his fingers in her hair.

"But Captain, we must leave quickly before we're found out!" She pushed away from him and gave him

181

an imploring look. "I fear your men may be outnumbered."

"I don't think so, miss. We been watchin' all day and most of 'em seem to be ashore. So ye take your time and git what ye want to bring. As pretty as ye are in that fancy dress, it's yer shirt and breeches ye'll be needin' now."

Shannon swallowed hard. She had to get them to leave before Hawke returned. "All right," she agreed reluctantly. "If you and your men would kindly retreat to the longboat, I'll change into something more appropriate." She smiled modestly at the swarthy man.

"All right you men, into the other room and give the laidee 'er privacy."

To Shannon's horror they went into Hawke's cabin and left the door ajar. She could hear them as they quietly ransacked the contents. Her heart in her throat, she fell upon the chest and searched for something less bulky to wear. Marie had not packed her shirt and breeches. She found a plain yellow dress and shook it out as the sound of footsteps echoed in the companionway. She rose in panic and rushed to the door as Morgan Hawke entered his cabin. He looked at her in surprise as the heavy hilt of Fletcher's cutlass caught him across the back of the neck and he pitched forward stunned.

One of the pirates kicked him viciously in the ribs and he bent double in a state of semiconsciousness. Shannon stared horrified and a cry escaped her as he was kicked again in the side of his face and rolled over on his back.

"'Ere now, Miss Shannon. Yer papa never wanted ye to see the likes o' this, so ye'd best go back to yer cabin and change like I told ye while we finish this deceitful beggar off."

"No!" Shannon exclaimed, as the eyes of the pirates fixed on her warily. She cleared her throat and prayed for the courage she needed. "I want to see him swing from a yardarm. T'would serve him right to suffer the same fate our comrades will face when the Admiral's ship reaches England." Her eyes flashed wickedly as she stared at the drawn figure on the floor. "I say we tie him up and take him with us." For emphasis, she walked across the deck to the fallen man and kicked him in the ribs. "You bastard!" she growled, cringing as Hawke's eyes flew open in pained bewilderment at her change in humor.

The evil laugh from Captain Fletcher caused her blood to chill as she prayed inwardly that Morgan Hawke could forgive her. "Damned if ye ain't the very likes of your papa, gal! Well, ye heard the laidee. Truss 'im up and dump 'im in the longboat. He'll live longer and be the worse for it."

A knock on the door made the pirates start and they stealthily braced for action as Fletcher pulled the door to the cabin open and yanked in a startled Billy Randall. The boy came flying in the room, spilling the contents of their supper on the floor by his fallen captain.

"Slit the whelp's throat and let's be gone!" Fletcher commanded closing the door to the companionway behind him.

Shannon ran between Billy alnd the men who were about to carry out his orders. "Not this one!" she warned, pulling the boy behind her skirt and turning to the pirate captain to explain. "Sir, he is the only one who has been kind to me. I'll not have him harmed."

Fletcher's eyes narrowed in scrutiny.

"I beg of you. I have been tied and chained at the hands of that bastard," she said pointing to the still

Morgan Hawke, "but Billy has done his best to see to my comfort . . . he's just a small boy!" She leaned over and stretched out her hand to the pirate captain, pleading with her eyes, acutely aware of his bold appraisal of the low drape of her neckline.

"All right then, miss," he relented, showing her a full display of tobacco-stained teeth before he turned to his crew. "Tie 'im up and gag 'im so's 'e don't raise any attention to us."

"Wait!" Shannon held her breath as Fletcher spun and faced her again, his patience obviously flagging. "I need his clothes," she explained meekly. Billy was close to her size and if she were to be of any help to Morgan Hawke later, she would not need to be encumbered by a skirt. "Strip him, if you will men, and toss his clothes through the door to my cabin while I undress." With a rustle of taffeta, she swung around and exited.

"Where is your ship?" she called through the door as she stepped out of the lavender dress and tossed it on the berth.

"The other side o' the island. Been waitin' 'ere nearly two weeks . . . Damn ye boy, if ye try that again, the laidee ain't gonna be able to save yer ungrateful neck!"

Shannon closed her eyes. Billy, please don't antagonize them. She heard the door creak open and saw Fletcher's arm extended into the room holding Billy's shirt and trousers in his hand. She took them and donned them quickly. When she stepped back into Hawke's cabin, she met the hostile glare of the cabin boy, clad only in his underclothing, and turned away.

"I'm ready," she announced, "with the exception of one thing."

She went over to Hawke's desk and rummaged

184

through the drawers until she found what she was seeking. Her dagger. She smiled slyly as she strapped it to her waist and spoke to the stirring figure tied up on the floor. "This time, captain, I shall finish the task of avenging my father's death."

"All right, let's move out."

At Fletcher's command, the men pulled Hawke roughly to his feet and dragged him into Shannon's cabin. She winced as they tossed him unceremoniously through the window to their comrades below. Fletcher handed her down to the longboat and dropped agilely beside her as she took a seat. The darkness covered them as they shoved away silently, but Shannon could feel the angry look of betrayal coming from the bow of the boat where Morgan Hawke lay bound and gagged.

They moved steadily toward the outer edge of the development where dense trees thinned down to a thicket of rushes. The boat parted the rushes and its veed hull scraped the muddy bottom. Some of the men jumped out into the shallow water and pushed the vessel farther up on the beach. Shannon was handed out to Fletcher who carried her gallantly to dry land and let her down to the ground slowly so that her body rubbed against him in her descent. She ignored the leer of the pirate captain and glanced back to see their prisoner hauled over the side of the craft and half-dragged through the water to join them.

"Now we're gonna put up in an abandoned hut we found back in the woods 'ere for tonight afore makin' the rest o' the way at first light. Me boys'll be waitin' for us then," Fletcher told her, putting his jacketed arm about her waist as he guided her toward the thicket.

The trees loomed ominously above and the

branches rustled as the small group passed under them. Shannon drew back as a sticky web tangled in her face and hair, but felt the pressure of Fletcher's hand in the small of her back and pushed on. Hawke had recovered somewhat from the abuse on the ship and walked on his own stumbling only when shoved roughly. She could not bring herself to look at him, but felt his eyes burning into her back as they moved along.

The hut was a low-thatched roofed dwelling, much like those in Nose' Be. The pirates built a small campfire confident that they had not been followed. It was likely that no one would discover the captain missing or Billy Randall until morning when the crew's hangovers were subsiding from celebrating their first night ashore. By that time the abductors would be on Fletcher's ship and bound for Cape Horn.

The men secured Hawke to a tree and turned their attentions to a case of rum one of them had stolen from the village and stowed in the longboat before their visit to the *Sea Lady*. Fletcher offered the privacy of the hut to Shannon which she gratefully accepted, glad to be free of the bold looks of the men. She touched the small dagger and wondered how she could possibly get herself and Morgan Hawke out of this dangerous situation.

She sat in the darkness of the hut and watched through the narrow doorway as the men huddled in a close group about the firelight and imbibed heavily. From time to time, they would glance her way and she shuddered fearing their thoughts. She noted the woven walls about the stick frame construction of the building. Perhaps after they settled down under the effects of the liquor, she might be able to cut her way out the back and sneak around the campsite to cut Hawke free.

Her thoughts were interrupted as the light from the fire was shut out by the looming figure of Captain Fletcher in the doorway of the hut. She could smell the stench of the rum mixed with the putrid odor of his unwashed person as he peered in the darkness seeking to make her out.

"Be ye asleep, missy?" he asked as his eyes adjusted and found her.

"No sir. I'm afraid I've been too frightened of our possible discovery to rest. Are you sure we'll make it to your ship . . . that Hawke's men won't follow?"

"Now ye needn't be concernin' yer pretty little 'ead about such things while yours truly is about to protect ye," he assured her as he crossed the dirt floor and slid down the wall to a seat beside her. The flimsy construction shook and settled as he did. "Ye know, I'm thinkin' the honorable Cap'n Hawke is gonna regret yer savin' his neck."

Shannon stiffened involuntarily. "I do hope he will, sir," she said softly, putting her hand on his arm. "I have suffered much at his hand. But tell me, sir, how did you find us?"

"Not a great deal of deduction to figger it out. When I saw the *Sea Laidee* fall back after we left for Aiden, I got to thinkin' somethin' might be amiss . . . specially with them English warships bein' seen earlier. So I gave 'em a bit o' slack and turned about to follow 'em." He shook his head and belched loudly. "Aagh! The whole bloomin' 'arbor was lit up by the time I got within sight of it. So me and the lads sailed straight for the Horn. We waited a bit and when ye didn't show we headed for Isle de Los, sure that ye'd be puttin' in 'ere, it bein' one of the only friendly 'arbors what them damned Por'gese don't own."

"But we did put in at the Horn," Shannon told him.

"I wasn't sure. Ye must have stayed at the cove a bit

longer than I wagered.''

"Indeed. The captain needed to recover from the dagger wound I put in his shoulder the night I found my dying father impaled on a splintered deck. Dear God, it was a nightmare.''

Fletcher was quiet and the girl wondered for a moment if he saw through her. "Ye know I been thinkin','' he said, swilling another drink from the bottle and wiping the back of his hand across his mouth. "I know it be too soon after Ramon and all, but . . . well maybe . . .''

Shannon squeezed his arm and smiled in the dim light cast by the fire outside. "I fear it is too soon at this time, my dear captain, but if I understand you correctly, I would be most honored to consider you as a partner . . . in every way, sir.'' She drew back as he moved toward her and held up her hand. "But please, sir, I shall need time.''

"O' course, dear laidee.'' He grunted as he rose to his feet and offered her his hand. "But I would consider it an honor for ye to sit with me for a bit and perhaps share a dram or two of rum with me an' the boys.''

Reluctantly Shannon accepted the offer. If she remained in the hut, the captain was likely to stay with her and the more he consumed of the rum, the less chance she stood of holding him off. As they joined the group, the man shouted loudly at the men.

"Stand up, ye filthy louts. Me future bride is joinin' us fer a drink an' I'm thinkin' we should start off with a toast.'' He raised his bottle over his head. "To Shannon Brennan, the finest, most loveliest female pirate what could sail the seven seas.''

The sailors readily lifted their arms in salute and offered congratulations to their proud captain. Shannon accepted a small drink from Fletcher and coughed as the raw liquor gagged her. The captain laughed boisterously and seized her in a bear hug as she fought for her breath. "Now I kin see right now, missy, ye gotta lot to learn about the fine art of drinkin' . . . and me men here are experts." Suddenly he stopped laughing as he peered past her at the man tied to the tree just outside their cozy circle. "I don't believe the good cap'n has toasted me bride-to-be."

He released the girl and swaggered across the campsite where Morgan Hawke met him with a fierce look. "What's the matter, cap'n? Can't ye stand the idea of us takin' back what's rightfully ours?" He unexpectedly lifted his boot sharply under Hawke's chin and kicked his head back against the tree. "Ye ain't exactly been kind to the laidee so she says." His fist exploded against his victim's face bursting Hawke's lip and he laughed as the blood ran down the side of the young captain's face. Sadistically, he reached out and smeared it on Hawke's forehead.

Shannon held her breath, helpless to stop the brutal abuse. If Fletcher kept this up Morgan Hawke would not be able to escape.

"Now drink to the ladiee and then apologize to 'er good 'n proper like!"

Fletcher grabbed Hawke's hair pulling his head back and poured the fiery liquor over his mouth. "Drink damn ye!" he ordered, jerking the man's head so that the skin was stretched tight on his throat. The run ran down his neck mixed with the blood.

"Go to hell," came a gargled curse as Hawke spit the run at him.

The pirate captain seemed to erupt in fury as he threw aside his empty bottle, smashing it against a tree and swung back at the bound man with both fists clenched together. As the blow struck, Hawke's head whipped to the side and Shannon felt the color drain from her face when she saw the ugly gash the pirate's ring made across the firm jaw she had caressed so tenderly a few short hours ago. As he was struck again, she cried out and ran toward the cover of the trees. Leaning against the rough bark, she wretched violently.

She was shaking when she felt the rough hands of Hawke's assailant pull her upright. He turned her to see the deathlike pallor in her face and squinted at her.

"The b . . . blood," she gasped. "I could see my father . . . all over again. I'm sorry."

She bowed her head and swayed toward the dubious man. Disarmed, he caught her and picked her off her feet. Although she was light, he staggered a bit as he made his way toward the door of the hut. As he reached the opening he put her down, holding her about the waist so that her body was rubbed against his paunch and scrutinized her face in the flickering firelight.

"It's me that ought to be sorry, Miss Shannon," the man apologized to her surprise. "I wasn't thinkin' about what ye must have seen durin' the blaggard's raid. Maybe ye just better rest a while. Me 'n the boys 'ere 'll put off our fun for a bit."

Shannon breathed a sigh of genuine relief. "Thank you, dear captain." She was taken aback when his thick wet lips suddenly claimed her mouth in a brief kiss.

"Hawke!" he shouted, never taking his eyes from hers, "I think the laidee and I'll be wed right under yer swingin' corpse."

Shannon lowered her face to the man's sweat-drenched chest to hide her horrified expression. Fletcher mistook the gesture as another spell of weakness and insisted she go into the hut and rest while he and the men finished off the rest of the rum.

190

As he retreated through the doorway, she put her hand to her mouth to hold back the sob that rose in her throat and found her way to the back of the musty smelling structure to wait for any chance to escape. When the men would lean across the circle to talk to each other, she could glimpse the bowed head of Morgan Hawke and see the stains of blood crusting on his white shirt in the dim glow of the fire.

It was well into the night when the men quieted and by the time the fire died down, they were asleep. The whole time they laughed and slurred stories to one another, she had been cutting through the thin wall of the hut so that a slit, large enough for her to squeeze through, remained. She glanced at the still campsite once more and then squeezed through the opening and melted into the forest.

She circled wide around the encampment, trying ever so delicately to walk on the forest floor without a sound to alert the abductors. She could see the back of the *Sea Lady*'s captain through the trees and crouched down low as she approached him. Her heart seemed to beat so loudly that she feared it would stir the drunken pirates as she came up behind Hawke. His head jerked slightly as she warned him lowly in his ear not to make any sound. Her dagger sawed at the thick ropes that held him captive and it seemed an eternity before it cut through.

He struggled to his feet with her help and nodded toward the direction they should make their escape. Cautiously they picked their way through the trees and Shannon held her breath with each step. The stillness of the night was loud in her ears as the distance between them and the pirates lengthened, but it soon broke with the loud explosion of a pistol shot. Hawke pushed her forward and stumbled after her as the ball crashed into a tree nearby.

The forest behind them seemed to burst into action all at once as the pirates, alerted to their escape, started after them. The crashing sounds of their footsteps spurred her on until she glanced over her shoulder to see Morgan Hawke stumble to his knees. She ran back to him and tried to help him to his feet.

"Get out of here," he ordered breathlessly, jerking his arm from her grasp.

"I'm not leaving you," she informed him stubbornly, grabbing his arm again.

A shot hit the tree beside her splintering the bark and showering them with bits of wood. Hawke lunged at her pulling her to the ground and covering her with his body. Crushed beneath his weight and winded from their run, she fought for air, as the heavy booted steps of the pirates caught up with them. She raised her eyes at the stocky figure standing before them with pistols drawn and squealed in recognition.

"Michael!"

The Irishman aimed past them and discharged one of his weapons. A corresponding cry rang out as the ball found its mark. "This way mates!" he shouted out and the trees came alive with armed men. "I'd suggest ye stay here with the lass, cap'n," he called over his shoulder as he leaped over them and charged into the pirates' fire to their backs.

Hawke maneuvered Shannon around the base of a large tree so that it blocked them from the gunfire. He collapsed against it weakly and held the girl to him. There was shouting as Finney's men met the pirates hand to hand and the sound of metal clashing frantically rang out in the violent darkness. Shannon huddled as close to Hawke as she could and strained to see if she could make out any identities of the mingling crews.

The cold touch of metal on her face made her freeze. Without moving she cut her eyes sideways to see the cruel face of Captain Fletcher in the moonlight that filtered through the branches of the trees. Hawke stiffened as the man spoke lowly.

"Well now, ain't this cozy?" He reached down and yanked Shannon to her feet. She yelped in pain as his fingers bit into her arm. Hawke was motionless as he saw the blade of the man's cutlass at Shannon's white throat. "Thought ye'd pull one over on me with them helpless blue eyes, didn't ye missy?" he was saying as he backed away. "What say ye just watch while I blow yer lover's 'ansome face off with me pistol 'ere."

Shannon felt his hand moving to his waist to withdraw the weapon sandwiched between them. His other hand still held the flat edge of the blade to her throat. She wriggled as much as she dared in protest, hoping that the struggle would hide the motion of her hand drawing her dagger from its sheath. She grasped the hilt tightly as the pirate aimed the pistol at the rigid Hawke. Then with a fervent prayer, she pretended to swoon and fell against the pirate.

Fletcher dropped the cutlass as he instinctively grabbed at her waist to catch her. His pistol arm waived for an instant and Morgan Hawke sprang at him knocking it aside and crushing Shannon and the man to the ground. He shoved her roughly aside and struck the startled pirate full in the face with a vengeance. The pirate twisted wirily and threw the young man off. His foot thrust into Hawke's injured ribs and the captain crumpled in agony as his assailant scrambled to his feet. Hawke tried to pull himself up on a tree, but Fletcher booted him again in the face and he sprawled on his back with a sickening

193

thud. The pirate reached for his fallen pistol to finish his victim. As he straightened, he gasped in amazement as the blade of Shannon's dagger buried in his chest.

Shannon stared in terror as the man raised the gun slowly and aimed it at her. As he walked toward her, his bulging eyes glared at her face and she backed against the tree terrified and defenseless. He was but a few feet from her when his pistol hand began to shake and his face contorted convulsively. She closed her eyes and screamed as the shot rang out. Then realizing the ball had missed her, she forced them open to see the dead pirate stretched out at her feet with Morgan Hawke's prone form wrapped about his knees from the desperate tackle.

She dropped down beside him and broke his grip on the dead man. As he rolled over on his back, his breathing was labored. She bent over him and tried to soak up the blood that oozed from the contusions on his face with the hem of her borrowed shirt. "Morgan Hawke," she warned in a trembling voice, "don't you die on me!"

A forced chuckle emerged from deep in his muscled chest. "I wouldn't think of it."

"Hawke!" She wanted to strike him and hug him in relief at the same time. However, she resisted both urges and as he attempted to rise and let him use her shoulder for support, all too aware of the discomfort he experienced. She was certain his ribs were fractured from the vicious kicks of the pirates and felt remorse that she had added to the injury. He leaned against a tree and searched the dimly lit forest for familiar figures.

"The bastards must be retreating," he mused aloud. "Now hand me his gun. We'd best reload in case some of his friends happen upon us before my

194

men regroup."

Shannon obeyed and fetched the horns and leather pouch that contained the balls and patches as well. A shudder of revulsion shook her as she saw pirate's face in its death stare and she turned her back to the still figure to assist Morgan Hawke with the loading. He motioned toward the cutlass and after some difficulty, she untied the sheath and brought it and the weapon to him.

"What about your dagger?" he asked, as he wrapped the cutlass's sheath about his waist and returned the weapon to its home.

"I don't want it." She paled at the thought of removing it from the dead man. "I . . . I never killed anyone before," she explained looking up into his questioning eyes. When he offered his arms she went into them gladly and rested her head on his chest. "And I never meant to hurt you. I was crazed by all that was happening that night . . . and I tried not to kick you too hard . . ."

"Let us say you were convincing."

Shannon groaned miserably. "Can you forgive me?" she asked, searching his face in the moonlight for an answer.

"Can you forgive me?"

She nodded solemnly as his meaning registered, her eyes locking with his. They both had been forced to do things they regretted. And there was no way Shannon could hate the man who, even now, stirred her as he held her in his arms.

"We got some of 'em, cap'n, but the rest got away." Michael Finney stopped in his tracks at the sight of the upturned body with the hilt of a dagger protruding from its back. "Fletcher," he muttered in disgust. Reaching down, he withdrew Shannon's dagger and wiped it on his pant leg.

"Throw it away, Finney."

The first mate glanced up at his captain in bewilderment.

"Just toss it in the trees and let's get back to the ship."

It seemed to Shannon to take forever for the crew to regroup. When the last of them straggled in with their bound prisoners, they formed an irregular line to return to the settlement. Hawke managed to walk on his own, but Shannon knew he was in pain by his strained expression. By the time they reached the longboats, he was visibly drained. She was grateful when, at last, she and Michael Finney helped him into his bunk aboard the *Sea Lady* for the rest he so badly needed.

As they stripped off his blood-crusted shirt, Finney cursed under his breath upon seeing the red and purple coloring of his battered ribs. Hawke's face was badly bruised and cut as well, one eye no more than a swollen slit. Tears glazed Shannon's eyes as she touched it ever so gently and offered a silent prayer that he'd never again suffer because of her. The first mate eased the captain against the pillows that she'd fluffed and put behind him and then left to find some bandages to wrap his chest.

With Billy Randall's assistance, Shannon bathed the wounds as best she could, wincing herself each time her patient caught his breath. Billy told them of how, after they'd left with the pirates, the cook had become anxious that he'd not returned with the dirty dishes and came to look for him. Upon discovering what had happened, he alerted the crew. A few men went ashore to round up as many of the *Sea Lady*'s men as could be found for a rescue party and proceeded based on the information Billy had overheard the pirate tell Shannon. The cabin boy ended his account with his disappointment about being sent back to the ship to miss the action and an apology to Shannon for thinking the worst of her.

"I should have known you'd never do anything like that," he told her as he wrung a wet cloth out and handed it to her.

"You have to admit, Billy, she's quite a convincing actress," Hawke remarked drowsily.

"Yeah, and she looks better in my shirt and breeches than I do." The cabin boy yelped as Shannon tossed the wet towel back at him playfully.

"Billy Randall!" she chastised, her face pinkening.

"It seems you have more than one admirer, Miss Brennan." Hawke circled her hips with his arm and pulled her closer. The sudden motion caused him to grimace at the painful cost of his impulsive action.

"Morgan Hawke, you're too ill for such antics!" she chided, removing his arm resolutely and returning it to his side.

"Maybe we should tie him to the mast."

Shannon spun at the mischievous suggestion and pointed to the cabin door in exasperation. "Out!" she ordered.

"Tie me to the mast?"

"Out!" she insisted, ignoring Hawke's confusion.

The cabin boy shrugged at his captain and with a snicker headed for the door. As he left, Michael Finney returned with the bandages. Shannon leaned over the injured man and locked her arms under his to hold him upright as Finney worked with him. She was acutely aware of his warmth as their bodies pressed for a moment and her face became scarlet as she met Hawke's intense searching gaze. Self-consciously, she looked away and loosened her grip.

Finney wrapped his rib cage tightly until the captain was covered from the dark mat of hair spanning his chest to his midriff. Then he eased the patient back against the pillows once more.

"Ye should sleep like a baby now that you're bundled up nice and tight there. Speakin' of which," he added turning to Shannon, "it's time ye went to your own cabin and got some shut-eye as well, lass."

"I think you're right," she agreed with a tired smile. She could not help but wonder what they would have done without this kind and loyal friend. So moved, she hugged the big Irishman and whispered affectionately, "Thank you so much, Michael." Before the first mate could muster a response, she hastily gave the captain a goodnight peck on the cheek. With a shy, "Goodnight, Hawke," she retreated to her room.

As the door closed behind her, she heard the captain call out after her, "My name is Morgan, Shannon."

Smiling as she unlaced her breeches to undress for bed, she answered huskily, "Goodnight . . . Morgan."

Later as she sat on the edge of the mattress unsnarling the tangled tresses that had come unbound during their adventure, she realized she was totally spent. She saw the light go off in the next cabin and heard the first mate closing the door to the companionway as she worked her hair into a braid and tied it with a pink ribbon that matched her nightdress. In darkness, she snuggled under a light blanket and closed her eyes, but her mind wandered to the man in the next cabin. Smiling sleepily, she whispered softly to herself in experimentation, "Morgan . . ."

Chapter Twelve

"Well sir, as best I can figure it, that storm blew the Admiral's ships past here. They're most likely safely moored in the Madeiras or maybe the Canaries. But no one has seen 'em here."

Michael Finney perched casually on the edge of Morgan Hawke's desk reporting his find to his captain. The younger man sat up on a stack of pillows and listened with keen interest.

"And we're to tie up tomorrow to restock our holds?" Hawke asked, still trying to get his days sorted out after the two days he'd spent recovering his strength in sleep.

"Aye. That done, I'd think we'd best be shovin' off. No sense in waitin' for Bedlowe if he is behind us."

Finney was restless. In the darkness of the trees he and his men had not been able to capture all of Fletcher's men. Although he did not think they'd be fools enough to try anything else, he saw no need to tempt fate.

"Well, I've been cooped up here long enough, that's for sure." Hawke threw the blanket off his legs and swung them over the side, grimacing as his ribs protested.

"Whoa there, sir!" Finney exclaimed, crossing the room quickly in case he needed assistance. "Ye promised Shannon to stay put till the end of the week."

"I have recovered faster than I thought, thanks to her . . . irresistible care." He smiled wryly. "But if I have to drink any more of that herbal mixture old Marie sent with her, I shall truly be ill. What I wouldn't give for a good mug of cook's coffee!"

As if on cue, the latch lifted and the door to the cabin opened. Shannon squeezed through sideways as Michael Finney hastened to hold the door for her. She smiled prettily at the first mate and walked to the table under the starboard portal to deposit the supper tray.

"Morgan Hawke! What are you doing up?" she demanded as she turned to see her patient standing at the foot of his berth.

"About to get dressed so that I may take my meal at the table instead of in bed like a damned invalid." His tone reinforced his stubborn stance.

Shannon set her mouth in an equally determined fashion. The swelling had gone down after hours of soaking with a cool wet cloth but his face was still a discolored blue, mottled with the yellowish tint of a healing bruise. She watched as he walked carefully to the trunk where his clothing was stored, favoring his injuries. She marched over to him and took his arm firmly.

"I have taken great care to see you this well, Morgan Hawke, and I'll not allow you to set yourself back. Now, please . . . get back in that bed!"

"I'd best be gettin' topside. Me an' the boys were goin' to go ashore." Finney winked at Shannon and nodded to his captain before he started for the door.

"Hold up, Mr. Finney," Hawke commanded. "I'd

appreciate your staying here for a moment in case I need assistance. As for you, Shannon," he said taking her hand off his arm firmly, "you can either stay here while I strip off this damned nightshirt and see me as we first met, or you can go to your cabin until I am ready to receive you for supper. It's up to you."

"You promised," she pouted obstinately, blushing at his reference.

"Mr. Finney . . ." He started to pull up the hem of his shirt.

"You pigheaded fool!" she called over her shoulder as she retreated hastily to her cabin.

The adjoining door to the cabin bounced open as she slammed it and she made an exclamation of frustration as she slammed it again, holding it firmly in place this time by leaning against it. It would serve him right to hurt himself, she thought angrily. The amused chuckle of the Irishman from the other room only served to incense her further. Damn the ungrateful beggar, she cursed inwardly. She should simply stay in her own cabin and refuse to dine with him.

Her curiosity began to stir when a considerable amount of time elapsed and she could hear the door to Hawke's cabin opening and closing. The voices of the Irishman and she thought that of Billy Randall were too low to make out. There was some shuffling of furniture and finally the distinct sound of a bolt sliding into place. Shannon put her ear to the door and called out to the captain.

"Hawke?"

Silence answered her.

"Are you decent?" she saked, perturbed at the apparent game he was playing with her. "I'm coming in!" she warned before opening the door slowly.

The drapes had been drawn to shut out the last rays of the brilliant sunset and the room was aglow with the soft light of the candles placed on the dining table which was set for two in the center of the room. A wine bottle sat next to two crystal goblets and in the center was a covered platter surrounded by smaller covered dishes.

She jumped as she realized her host was leaning against the wall behind her. "Hawke!" she accused, "you startled me."

To her relief he was fully dressed in a black shirt that laced up the front and tan breeches. She noted just the tip of the white bandages showing at the base of the veed neck as he approached her. "Will you join me, my lady?"

"I shouldn't," she chided, as he bowed shortly and motioned her to her seat.

"But you will?"

Shannon grinned sheepishly. "You make it very difficult to refuse you when you've gone to such ends to prepare such a lovely surprise. I'd be honored, sir."

He held her chair for her as she took her place and then opened the bottle of wine. "It's not quite as heavy as the Madeira," he told her as he filled the glasses with the golden liquid. As he took his seat, he lifted his glass for a toast. "To our remaining voyage . . . may it be as enjoyable as our previous journey has been hellish."

Shannon put her glass to his and laughed lightly. "Hear, hear!" she agreed. The wine was a fruity vintage, just slightly sweet.

"Now for cook's surprise," he told her lifting the lid from the large platter in the center.

"He found another duck!" Shannon exclaimed delightedly.

"With all the trimmings," Hawke added, as he

removed the other covers.

"No wonder he was so jittery when I went in the hut to get your supper . . . the rascal was up to something then. And I thought the hash smelled too good to be hash." She looked over the rim of her glass at him suspiciously. "How long have you been in on this?"

"I have to admit, not until the men already had the scheme cooked up, if you'll pardon my expression."

Shannon giggled and put her glass down to serve the delicious fare.

"Oh no, dear lady. You sit and drink," Hawke said, rising to his feet. "I will be steward as well as host for you tonight."

Shannon started to protest, but accepted her offered glass of wine and gave in as he firmly pushed her back in her seat. Everything was as good as it smelled and she ate heartily, forgetting her previous resolve to have a lady's delicate appetite. Hawke told her of his plans for leaving Isle de Los as soon as they had reprovisioned the ship. He hoped to be in London by late fall and get the *Sea Lady* outfitted again to sail for his company to the East Indies before the winter freeze.

"I can't imagine a river frozen," Shannon remarked dreamily. "Especially so hard that you can walk on it and not drown."

"There is so much that I want to show you, Shannon Brennan." His eyes met hers and she blushed in the warmth of his gaze.

"What about the theatre?" she asked, trying to ignore the undercurrent. "I would love to see one of the plays I've read about. It must be exciting!"

"Definitely!" He refilled her glass and settled back in his chair to watch the way the candle light danced in her eyes.

"And fairs?" she asked, sipping the delicious nectar. "I would so love to go to a fair and eat a tart from a pieman."

"And balls, and the court . . ."

Shannon sobered suddenly. "The King's court?" He nodded, amused at her childlike excitement. "You know the King of England . . . personally?"

"I do know His Royal Majesty, Charles II. We have hunted on Snowden on many frosty morns."

Shannon sat back somewhat stunned as she recalled the title that had been used in addressing the man she dined with. "I forgot you're a lord!" She frowned and sipped her drink.

"We do not carry the plague, Shannon," Hawke teased, lifting her chin so her eyes met his.

"But you are so ordinary!"

"Hah! I'm not sure that is an intended compliment, my lady."

"Oh, I meant no offense!" she added quickly. "I just meant . . ." She sighed deeply at a loss for words. "You must think me terribly dimwitted."

"Dimwitted? Never!" he denied emphatically. "I find you fascinating, refreshing, unpredictable, never boring . . . should I continue?"

Whether cheeks burned from the wine or the blood that rushed to her face, Shannon could not tell. The candlelight, the wine, the cozy meal with this gentleman were suddenly overwhelming. She pushed away from the table awkwardly.

"It's very late. I think I had better retire to my cabin," she said in a flustered rush.

"Shannon . . ." Hawke rose to his feet to block her path.

Her nerves screamed at his touch on her shoulders. "Don't stop me, Hawke!" she warned in a shaking voice, frightened by her vulnerability.

He saw the fear mounting in her wide eyes and dropped his arms to his side, as she rushed past him to the refuge of her cabin.

Once inside the door, Shannon wedged it with a towel and breathed deeply to calm her riotous emotions. One side of her conscience called her a fool for running from something she had ached for, while the other congratulated her for escaping in time. She stumbled slightly from the heady effects of the wine and shook out the nightdress that lay on top of her trunk. She washed mechanically, her mind absorbed with the confounding feelings that tore at her unmercifully. The ritual of dressing and braiding her hair done, she climbed in her bunk and blew out the light.

The creaking of the ship only added to the edge of her nerves as she stared at the ceiling. In the other room, she heard the scrape of Hawke's chair and his footsteps as he crossed the room to his own bunk. His movements were quiet and soon she saw the light go out through the cracks around the doorway. The rustle of the window latches echoed in the stern bulkhead as he opened one of the windows. A loud crash brought her out of the bunk with a start. She cried out his name as she tore open the door sending the wedge to the floor and searched the moonlit room for his figure.

She rushed over to his bent figure and grabbed him by the shoulders to help him up.

"Are you hurt?" she asked anxiously, trying to see his face in the semi-darkness.

"No! I stubbed my toe on this damned chair that I left in the middle of the damned floor!" he cursed in aggravation. "And when I kicked the damned thing . . ."

He broke off as Shannon giggled in relief. His

fierce brow relaxed as he beheld the laughing vision in white and he forgot his angry frustration. Compulsively his hands found her small waist in the voluminous folds of the nightdress and he drew her to him seeking her lips with his own.

"Don't leave me, Shannon," he whispered hoarsely, as she pushed back against his shoulders and stared wildly up at him. Her body was warm and inviting beneath the thin material and his hands roamed up and down her back, refusing to release their possession.

Shannon froze as the voices within her argued. She wanted to run but her feet would not carry her. His hands set her skin aflame and she was hypnotized as she watched them unbraid her hair and spread it about her shoulders like a silken cape. Then one by one they untied the pink bows that held the front of her gown.

"I have wanted to do this since I first saw them." His confession made her look up in trance-like wonder as he slid the gown off her shoulders and let it drop to the deck in a circle about her feet. He showed no sign of pain as he lifted her up and carried her over to his bed to lay her on the pillows. His fingers ran through her hair and he stared in awe at the beauty bathed in the light that filtered in through the open window. Her eyes would not leave his as he stripped and joined her.

The voices of protest faded altogether as he teased her inflamed body with his lips and tongue alternately. When his mouth covered hers, she returned his kiss wantonly, moved by an instinct as primitive as time. His body moved gently above her own and she trembled, recalling their first blissfully painful union. Her apprehension was short-lived and soon she grabbed at his buttocks and pulled him to her desperately, demanding that he satisfy the fire he fanned within her. Her senses exploded with ecstasy and she cried out in release as he drove her to the mattress beneath them. When she opened her eyes, he gazed at her tenderly and leaned down to caress her lips with his own.

She rested her head on his shoulder contentedly as he lay down beside her. This had to be the love that Marie promised her. It was right, just as the old woman had said. Shannon knew it in her heart; and this was the man to whom she entrusted it. She smiled as she felt his gentle stroke on her hair and wriggled closer.

"Morgan?" She had to make an attempt to call him by his given name after calling him by the other for so long.

"Hmm?" he murmured as he nuzzled her forehead.

"I . . . I love you." There! She said it at last! Her heart leaped for joy as he lifted her face to his and embraced her again passionately.

When he released her, he whispered lowly in her ear, "I fear the feeling is mutual, Shannon Brennan."

The tender words echoed in her mind as she slept in his arms and when the brilliant rays of the morning sun filled the room and nudged her from her contented sleep, she turned to seek out the man who uttered them and found a pillow tucked under her back instead. Somewhat disoriented, she opened her eyes and saw that she was still in the captain's cabin.

Shannon swung her legs over the side of the berth lazily and sat up. The dirty dishes were still on the table and his overturned chair lay sprawled on the floor next to her crumpled gown. As she slid to her bare feet on the cool deck, she pulled a sheet off the berth and wrapped it about her before crossing to

207

retrieve her nightdress. She was about to pick it up when the door burst open and she started, clutching the sheet tightly to her chest.

"Did you sleep well?" Morgan Hawke asked wickedly, as he entered the cabin and closed the door behind him.

"As well as you did," she responded tartly, as she blushed and glanced away self-consciously. She presented a fetching picture with her disheveled hair in wild array about her bare shoulders.

He laughed as he crossed over to her and took her in his arms. "I am bewitched," he whispered, kissing her briefly. "I came to my cabin to fetch my purse so that I might go ashore and finish my business with the local merchants and find a saucy wench clad only in a sheet, tempting me from my duty as captain of this vessel."

Shannon snickered as he nibbled at her neck teasing and tickling her. "Hawke, stop it!" She lowered her chin to her chest to protect herself and tried to thwart his playful attack by pushing her hands against his chest.

"And I'll take my sheet!"

"No!" she shrieked as he yanked it away. She darted past him and scrambled up on the berth drawing the blanket about her modestly.

"That, dear lady, is exactly where I want you."

Shannon's heart beat with excitement as he pushed her back against the mattress and hovered over her, his eyes reflecting his hunger for her. Tenderly, she reached up to put her hands on his face and drew it to hers. She covered it with tiny kisses until her lips reached his. Then timidly she tasted them until they overtook hers with passion.

It took another round of knocking before the couple recognized the unwelcome intrusion. Hawke swore under his breath and broke away from her reluctantly. "What do you want, Finney?" he demanded irritably.

"Well sir, ye told me to let ye know when the longboat was ready," came the disgruntled voice from the other side of the door. "And beggin' yer pardon sir, but the longboat is ready!"

Shannon pursed her lips at the sharp look on her lover's face. "You've hurt his feelings," she teased, running a finger down the hollow of his throat.

"I'll be right up, Mr. Finney!" Hawke called out, ignoring the jibe. Then turning back to the girl, he promised, "I will return as soon as I finish up with my business."

"Do you have to go?" Shannon pouted prettily, her eyes full of mischief.

"That is not fair, young lady," he said, pointing an accusing finger at her. "And I promise I shall administer a delightfully wicked punishment when I return."

Shannon threw a pillow at his retreating back and ducked as he caught it and returned it from the door.

"You had better get dressed before Billy comes in with your noon meal. I told him to let you sleep this morning and leave last night's dishes till noon."

Shannon hugged the pillow for a moment and then hopped out of the bunk to heed Hawke's warning. She scooped up her gown and went into her own cabin to bathe and dress for the day. She hummed merrily as she performed the ritual and wondered that she could be so intoxicatingly happy. She was tying her hair up on the back of her head with a yellow ribbon that matched her gown when Billy Randall arrived with their meal.

She greeted him enthusiastically and chattered brightly about the wonderful meal the cook prepared

209

the night before and the exciting places Morgan Hawke promised to show her when they reached England. As she spoke she could not help but notice that the boy did not share her zeal and, finally, she pushed her plate away and asked him in concern what was wrong.

"Nothin'," came the sullen reply, as he gathered the empty plates and returned them to the tray.

Shannon frowned, certain he was not telling her the truth. Whatever was wrong, he seemed determined to keep it to himself. Her face lit up as she thought of an idea to cheer him.

"Billy, you have been so helpful to me when I was down," she began hesitantly, "and I was wondering . . . is Michael . . . Mr. Finney topside?"

"I guess so," he answered, wondering what she was getting at.

"Well, I have been cooped up in this stuffy old cabin and I thought that maybe, if Mr. Finney thinks it would be all right, you and I could walk topside for a while and perhaps spend the afternoon together. Maybe fish over the side?"

The cabin boy shrugged. "If you want," he replied, a spark of excitement in his eyes betraying his indifference.

"Then you wouldn't mind if I asked him?"

Billy shook his head and started for the door with the tray. "I'll send him down when I take this back to the cook," he called over his shoulder as he shut the door behind him.

Michael Finney laughed and shook his head when Shannon told him of her plan to cheer the lad. "He's just moontruck. He'll get over it soon enough," the first mate assured her. "But if ye want to go topside, I see no problem with ye goin' with the lad. He's a fine boy . . . keeps the crew up half the night with them crazy stories ye been readin' 'im about some fool named Ulysses chasing about the seven seas after monsters."

Shannon grinned and hugged the snorting Irishman affectionately. "Thank you again, Michael."

The man slapped his cap on his head and turned to leave when he glanced at the open door to Hawke's cabin and paused. For a moment he acted as if he wanted to say something else, but then he proceeded on to the companionway. Again he paused outside the door and stuck his head back inside. "Good luck, lass!" he told her with a wink of a blue eye. He tipped his cap and then shut the door.

The ploy was a success. Soon Shannon and Billy were laughing as they held their lines over the side opposite the dock where the *Sea Lady* was tied. She and the cabin boy exchanged stories and watched the dockmen and the crew filling the holds of the ship for their remaining journey home.

"What are you going to do when you get home, Billy?" Shannon asked as she dangled her legs between the rails over the side carelessly. She had pulled her dress up between them in a trouser-like fashion and exposed them to the basking warmth of the sun.

"Probably go home for a few days till one of the cap'n's ships head out again. I got one!" he exclaimed excitedly as his line tugged.

"Hold on, I'll get the net!"

Shannon drew back her legs and scrambled to her feet to help the boy haul in the silvery catch thrashing desperately on the end of his line. She sprawled on her stomach as she held the net over the side and attempted to scoop the fish up with it. It was just beyond her reach and she wriggled out a bit farther so that her shoulders hung precariously over the water.

"Got it!" she gasped, trying to squirm back to firmer decking without dropping their prize.

"Got you!"

She squealed in surprise as the captain of the *Sea Lady* hauled her backward by the ankles and nearly lost the fish, net and all. Billy hurried to take them from her as she rolled over and stared up at her rescuer. "Back so soon?" she asked, shielding her eyes from the sun. She took his offered arm and allowed him to pull her to her feet.

He put his arms about her and looked down at her in amusement. "You are providing quite a distraction, dear lady. The other ships are short of dockmen to load their holds. Most of them are out here."

"We were only fishing," she replied innocently. "Show the captain our catch, Billy."

Billy held up a bucket with their haul, grinning proudly. "Enough for your supper tonight, sir."

"So I see," Hawke commented. "You two have really been busy. But I am afraid we'll not be here for supper tonight," he apologized. "I need to take Miss Shannon ashore to outfit her for the remainder of the trip."

"What?" Shannon could hardly believe her ears.

"I've taken the liberty of engaging a room for you at the inn. I thought you might like to have your feet on shore for a short while before we set sail again," he explained, "and there is a seamstress who has some warmer clothing in her shop that you might be needing as we get closer to London."

"Oh, Hawke!" She threw her arms about his neck and kissed him enthusiastically. Suddenly she thought of the cabin boy and turned to face him. "Billy . . ."

"It's all right, Miss Shannon. We got enough here for me 'n the cook and what few of the boys'll be

212

stayin' aboard, this bein' our last night here," he assured her, forcing a smile.

"I'm sorry about that, too, Billy," Hawke told him, placing a hand on his shoulder. "But I understand from Mr. Finney that it's your night off duty and if that's the case, you'll be going in town with the men tonight."

Billy's eyes widened in astonishment. "Me?"

"You're one of the crew, aren't you?"

"Yeah, but . . ."

"Well I was no more than your age when Michael Finney first took me ashore with the men," Hawke confided, "so unless you have your heart set on fish . . ."

The boy whooped and tossed the fish over the side. "To hell with the fish . . . 'scuse me, Miss Shannon," he said in a rush. With another whoop, he skipped off in the direction of the cook's hut, leaving the smiling couple looking after him.

"'Twas my sentiment exactly," Hawke whispered as Shannon leaned her head against him and watched the cabin boy disappear below deck.

Chapter Thirteen

The main street of the settlement was lined on both sides with warehouses interspersed with offices and shops. Some were painted the pastels of the French and others were the weathered color of once-painted white. At an intersection of a narrow lane stood a rather large two-story structure with an inviting painted sign hanging over its entrance that boasted food and lodging. A walk made of planks nailed on two main runners provided a dry passage to and from the establishment when the rainy season made the streets impassable without bogging down in mire.

Inside the double French doors that opened on to the boardwalk was a hall with a wide stairway to the second floor and to its right was the dining area, furnished with an odd assortment of English and French furniture. Here some of the wealthier travelers, either going to or returning from the East Indies and the Orient, sought respite from the rocking confines of their ships for the few days it took to reprovision. The fresh fare and wide beds in the rooms above were welcome luxuries from weeks of sea travel.

Shannon sipped a glass of wine and stared in

fascination as a group of apparently well-to-do travelers impatiently waited while the servants put several smaller tables together to accommodate them. There were two women with them, a mother and daughter by their resemblance, elegantly attired in shimmering silks and bedecked in obviously expensive jewels. Their hair was powdered and fashioned in upswept curls, topped with wide decorated hats covered with the same silk as their gowns.

The men who accompanied the women were dressed quite as elegantly and wore powdered wigs that struck Shannon as ridiculous. Furthermore, the way they catered to the whims of their feminine company made them appear even more the fools. One of them glanced in the direction of the table she and Morgan Hawke occupied and she looked away quickly and smothered a snicker in her napkin as she pretended to blot the wine from her lips. She met Hawke's questioning glance.

"That man has a beauty mark stuck on his cheek!" she whispered in obvious amusement.

"That, Shannon, is quite the fashion," he informed her, the corner of his mouth twitching to show he shared her opinion. "You're not eating very much," he pointed out, changing the subject.

Shannon looked down at the half-eaten fillet of veal that had been ordered for her and shook her head apologetically. "I just can't eat, Hawke. I'm too excited."

When they left the ship, the captain had taken her to a small shop crowded with bolts of material and piles of clothing the proprietress had taken in trade for other goods. Apparently, many of the ladies traveling to a warmer climate simply traded in their heavier clothing for the lovely summer colors of the simple gowns the seamstress sewed so skillfully. Since her patrons were not likely to have enough time for her to make their garments from scratch, the illustrious woman had several basic items made that could be altered up or down a size in a matter of a few hours.

To Shannon's embarrassment, the robust woman stripped her down to her thin shift and proceeded to measure her while the captain of the *Sea Lady* watched with interest. Not having much choice and assuming that that was how things were done, the girl simply stared at the scrap covered floor until the seamstress was satisfied that she had the figures necessary to fit the girl properly. Shannon was grateful when the woman led Hawke into another room to discuss the selection and arrangements and permitted her to dress in privacy.

"Did Madame Blanchot think she would be able to have my things by the time we sail tomorrow?"

"She promised," Hawke assured her as he placed his hand over her small one. "If you are through with your plate, perhaps we should retire to our room."

Shannon glanced up sharply at the mention of the shared occupancy. Her coloring betrayed the still modest nature of her new relationship with the man across from her.

Hawke smiled, sensing her discomfort, and stood to pull out her chair. As she rose, he whispered in her ear, "I promise, I won't bite."

"I've heard that before," she retorted wryly.

His arm was about her small waist as he guided her toward the doorway to the main hall. Shannon could not resist another sideways glance at the noble party and was surprised to see the gentleman with the beauty mark rising and waving at them.

"Lord Hawke! I say there!"

Morgan Hawke squeezed Shannon's waist and stared at the man blankly. It was not until he joined

216

them that Shannon saw the glimmer of recognition in her companion's eyes.

"My dear young man, you cannot imagine my surprise when Elissa pointed you out to me!"

The gentleman extended his hand and seized Hawke's enthusiastically.

"Sir William, I am equally astonished," the captain replied, looking past the man and nodding to the two ladies. "I gather you and your family are on your way to India again?"

"Indeed, sir. Do come over and join us . . . and of course your lady friend," he added, raising a quizzical brow as he took Shannon's hand.

Shannon permitted the man to kiss her hand as Hawke introduced her to Sir William Wolsey and resisted the urge to wipe it on her dress. "Delighted to make your acquaintance, sir."

"I insist you join us, both of you!"

"I appreciate your invitation, Sir William, but we will be leaving tomorrow and Miss Brennan is quite exhausted."

Shannon gave Hawke a questioning glance. Whoever these people were, he did not want to linger in their company. Yet she was intrigued and smiled prettily at the young man. "I do think I could manage for you to at least speak to the rest of Sir William's party, my lord." She held her tongue in her cheek as she spoke.

Reluctantly, Hawke allowed the man to escort Shannon over to the table, where the other two gentlemen rose as introductions were made. Each one took her hand in turn as the older gentleman had done. The girl tried hard not to stare as she realized that the men wore as much makeup as the women. It was only when she recognized that she was the topic of conversation that she focused on the rather dour face of the older woman.

"Lord Hawke, where did you meet such a lovely young lady, when you left London a year ago to search out and put an end to a murderous lot of pirates?"

Shannon could sense his uneasiness and spoke up.

"I met Lord Hawke on the island of Nose' Be. He was gracious enough to let me secure passage on his ship back to England."

"Nose' Be?" the woman echoed unfamiliarly.

"Well what about the pirates, sir. Did you find the beggars or not?" Sir William interjected.

"I would say that it was the pirates who found him, father. What happened to that handsome face?" The pale-featured lady glanced coyly up at Hawke.

"Elissa!" the young woman's mother chastised.

"I fear Elissa is right." Hawke smiled at the young woman and Shannon could not help the sudden sting of jealousy. The exchange of glances between the two led her to believe that Elissa knew Morgan Hawke quite well. "I have had a recent encounter with the last of them, and they are presently imprisoned on the Spanish vessel moored in the harbor."

"Damned good work! Damned good, sir!" Sir William exclaimed, slapping him on the back.

"Everyone misses you in London, Morgan... particularly our mutual friends." Catlike eyes peered out from under heavy lashes as Elissa Wolsey watched him.

"Well then, my homecoming should be a joyous one, Miss Wolsey," Hawke answered crisply. "Good people, I am delighted to see you all, but we have a long day ahead of us tomorrow."

The gentlemen rose again and bade them good evening and the ladies smiled graciously as Hawke kissed their hands. As he again guided Shannon to the door, she could hear the murmur of their voices and was certain that she and the captain were the subject of the discussion. She wondered if the guarded conversation could have been because of her and frowned.

They were Hawke's peers. She was a mixed breed of Irish and Sakalavan descent. Although she had her father's coloring, her blood was not the blue blood of nobility.

Her thoughts were distracted as Morgan Hawke opened the door to their room and she saw a richly carved mahogany bed draped with finely woven netting in the center of the large room. She froze for a moment disconcerted by the meeting with the Wolsey party and suddenly realized what they must be thinking of her. His hand was at her back gently encouraging her forward. When she spun and faced him, her eyes were glazed with tears.

"They think I'm your whore!"

"I love you, Shannon Brennan. To hell with them."

The sincerity in his eyes touched her and the tears she held back fell on her sun-pinkened cheeks. Suddenly she needed him, his arms about her, protecting her from her own fears. She clung to him as he coaxed her into the dimly lit room and closed the door behind them.

"I want you to forget those people," he told her gently. "There are more like that in London and we will face them together. But there are good people, too, Shannon. The Admiral's family, my own family . . ."

Shannon drew away and sniffed, raising her eyes to his. "Your family?"

"My mother will adore you. And I shall have to

fight off my cousins to keep you for my own," he teased, twitching her nose playfully.

"Your mother? I can hardly picture you with a mother."

"Do you think I am the devil's spawn?"

Shannon laughed and shook her head. "I only meant that you are so . . . independent. And my idea of a mother is one who rules her house firmly, but gently and . . . Tell me about her!"

"Shannon," he said taking her by the shoulders, "I will have weeks to tell you about my mother, but the water in that tub is cooling by the minute, and the servants, no matter how well paid, will think hard of us if they have to empty it and refill it again." He turned her toward the right side of the room where an exquisitely ornate bath tub stood.

Shannon had never seen anything like it and ran over to touch the smooth porcelain, warm from the water inside. Beside it was a small brandy table set with a bottle of wine and two glasses. Towels lay neatly folded on brass rings that hung on either side of the long fixture and served as handles for carrying it from room to room. She peered through the scented water and made out the shape of a plug near the bottom for draining it.

"My lady, permit me to assist you." She stiffened as she felt his hands working at the fastens on her gown.

"Am I being seduced?" she asked pointedly, her skin warming to his touch.

He chuckled lowly. "I do hope so, madame."

Shannon turned and shook her head. "No . . . I have loved you, but I cannot allow you to bathe me."

"I am only returning the favors you gave me when I was injured," he answered with mock innocence.

Her pulse was racing. "I did not bathe you altogether, Hawke . . ."

"Morgan," he corrected, lowering his lips to hers and taking her in his arms. He delighted in her modesty, her innocence, and his desire flamed when he felt her response as her body molded to his.

Shannon hardly felt her clothes falling away, and his lips were still on hers when he picked her up and lowered her into the scented water. She leaned against the slanted back while he pinned her braid in a crown on her head and reveled in the first full bath she had had since leaving the cove. The sound of a cork popping caused her to start, but she kept her eyes shut as he filled the glasses. Her muscles relaxed and her forehead misted with fine perspiration from the warmth of the water.

"I think I shall sleep here tonight, Morgan. You can have the bed," she murmured dreamily.

"Then I shall sleep with you, lovely lady!"

She gave a cry of alarm as he joined her, and drew her legs up to her knees in mortification. "You're wicked!" she accused him, her eyes wide in disbelief.

"Intensely so," he assured her. "Now come here." He held the soap up and crooked his finger.

"You are the devil's spawn!" She remained obstinately at her end, drawing her feet closer to her as their toes touched.

"Then I will come to you," he informed her, pushing himself up on his knees and leaning toward her.

She turned away from the hard-muscled body, now free of the bandages, and pulled herself up on the high back of the tub to escape, but his hands pulled her back against him. Her skin slid against his as she struggled, splashing the water over the side, and she caught her breath at the erotic reaction she felt despite her panic. He held her tightly and teased her ear with his tongue until she was still.

His fingers began to knead the muscles in her shoulders methodically and when he shifted to lean against the high back, she sat obediently in front of him as he alternately massaged her back and lathered it. When he drew her against him, her breasts were taut in anticipation. Her breath was rapid as his hands worked the suds in sensual caresses until she moaned in pleasure. She called his name in a frenzy as she rolled over so that she pressed him against the slant of the tub and sought his lips hungrily.

"It's my turn, my love," he groaned, as she slid down his body and kissed his chest.

She met his heated gaze and understood his need. Hypnotically she took the soap and began to rub it in circles until his chest was nearly white with suds. She drew designs with her finger, teasing until he stopped her and slowly moved her hand lower. Her hand trembled and she dropped the soap as she felt his throbbing desire.

He splashed water on his upper torso to rinse and rose to get out of the tub. Then with tormenting slowness he cupped water in his hands and washed away the remaining soap from her body before lifting her from the water and setting her lightly on her feet. The toweling played riot with her senses and when he finally lowered her to the cool mattress, she burned for him as never before.

Her aggressive response only heightened his ardor and he rolled over her, pulling her on top. Shannon lost her consciousness in a wild storm of passion as her body writhed and gyrated above him. Her braid fell down to her breasts as she rolled her head and contracted the firm muscles of her abdomen. His hands were on her hips holding her to him and she felt him arch his back as her mind reeled in the rapture of their satisfaction; and when she began to grasp reality, she collapsed against him weakly.

As she lay there she heard the tumultuous thunder of his heart gradually slowing and closed her eyes. The rise and fall of his chest lured her into the slumber of fulfillment. The lamplight continued to flicker until it burned out and left the couple to spend the rest of the night in darkness as they lay entangled in love's embrace.

Morning found Shannon back at the dress shop where Madame Blanchot presented a small stack of miscellaneous garments for her to try on. Morgan Hawke left her to the seamstress's care and promised to return for her as soon as he finished some business with the French merchant who owned the warehouse across the dirt street. The woman fussed over the fit of a traveling dress made of heavy dark blue fabric. It was actually a two-piece garment consisting of a full skirt and matching over-jacket tailored to fit snugly at the waist and slashed at the round of her hips. The lapel was the same black as the contrasting material of the jags on her jacket.

"It's very lovely," Shannon commented as she stared at her reflection in the full length mirror that hung on the scant bit of wall that was not piled high with materials and pattern books.

"You do more for it than the dear lady who traded it for one of my cotton gowns," the woman commented, pinching a slight excess of material at the girl's waist. "She had just had the dress made when she discovered that she was with child. So she only wore it one time."

"I am pleased with the fit, Madame Blanchot," Shannon informed the woman, wincing as her waist was caught between the woman's critical fingers. The heavy material was causing the girl to swelter in the tropical heat and she wondered how cold it would get that she would need such a garment.

"Humph!" came the disgruntled reply. "But if you are satisfied . . ."

"I am," Shannon replied a bit too enthusiastically. "Must I try on everything?"

"But of course!" the woman exclaimed. "I cannot have anyone wearing something purchased from my shop that does not fit them to my satisfaction."

"Very well, madame," Shannon relented. If this kept up she would be ready to jump over the rail to get cooled off. "How much will all of these things cost?" she asked curiously.

"Not so much for you to be concerned about. Your handsome captain is taking care of it."

Shannon frowned, uneasy with the arrangment. She could not accept such a gift. It was one thing to permit Morgan Hawke to treat her to supper and a romantic evening, but to purchase her clothing was too much. She set her mouth firmly. She would not be kept by him. He had her heart, but she had her pride.

"Madame Blanchot, I insist you tell me how much these things will cost the captain. I have every intention of reimbursing him and I need to know."

"Mademoiselle, from the way he looks at you, you have already paid him well enough. Pooh!" the woman dismissed the idea with a wave of her hand, "Do not worry. Let him spoil you while he still has the interest to do so."

Shannon paled at the woman's careless insinuation. She loved Morgan Hawke and he said he loved her. Somehow she could not conceive that that could change. The rattle of the latch announced the entrance of more patrons and the seamstress excused herself to go to the front of the shop. Shannon hardly heard her, but promised to wait until she returned to finish the final fitting.

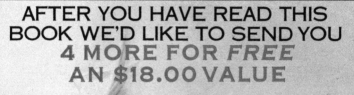

MORE PASSION AND ADVENTURE AWAIT... YOUR TRIP TO A BIG ADVENTUROUS WORLD BEGINS WHEN YOU ACCEPT YOUR FIRST 4 NOVELS ABSOLUTELY *FREE* (AN $18.00 VALUE)

Accept your Free gift and start to experience more of the passion and adventure you like in a historical romance novel. Each Zebra novel is filled with proud men, spirited women and tempestuous love that you'll remember long after you turn the last page.

Zebra Historical Romances are the finest novels of their kind. They are written by authors who really know how to weave tales of romance and adventure in the historical settings you love. You'll feel like you've actually gone back in time with the thrilling stories that each Zebra novel offers.

GET YOUR FREE GIFT WITH THE START OF YOUR HOME SUBSCRIPTION

Our readers tell us that these books sell out very fast in book stores and often they miss the newest titles. So Zebra has made arrangements for you to receive the four newest novels published each month.

You'll be guaranteed that you'll never miss a title, and home delivery is so convenient. And to show you just how easy it is to get Zebra Historical Romances, we'll send you your first 4 books absolutely FREE! Our gift to you just for trying our home subscription service.

BIG SAVINGS AND FREE HOME DELIVERY

Each month, you'll receive the four newest titles as soon as they are published. You'll probably receive them even before the bookstores do. What's more, you may preview these exciting novels free for 10 days. If you like them as much as we think you will, just pay the low preferred subscriber's price of just $3.75 each. *You'll save $3.00 each month off the publisher's price.* AND, your savings are even greater because there are never any shipping, handling or other hidden charges—FREE Home Delivery. Of course you can return any shipment within 10 days for full credit, no questions asked. There is no minimum number of books you must buy.

4 FREE BOOKS

TO GET YOUR 4 FREE BOOKS WORTH $18.00 — MAIL IN THE FREE BOOK CERTIFICATE T O D A Y

Fill in the Free Book Certificate below, and we'll send your FREE BOOKS to you as soon as we receive it.

If the certificate is missing below, write to: Zebra Home Subscription Service, Inc., P.O. Box 5214, 120 Brighton Road, Clifton, New Jersey 07015-5214.

FREE BOOK CERTIFICATE

4 FREE BOOKS

ZEBRA HOME SUBSCRIPTION SERVICE, INC.

YES! Please start my subscription to Zebra Historical Romances and send me my first 4 books absolutely FREE. I understand that each month I may preview four new Zebra Historical Romances free for 10 days. If I'm not satisfied with them, I may return the four books within 10 days and owe nothing. Otherwise, I will pay the low preferred subscriber's price of just $3.75 each; a total of $15.00, *a savings off the publisher's price of $3.00.* I may return any shipment and I may cancel this subscription at any time. There is no obligation to buy any shipment and there are no shipping, handling or other hidden charges. Regardless of what I decide, the four free books are mine to keep.

NAME

ADDRESS _____ APT _____

CITY _____ STATE _____ ZIP _____

( )
TELEPHONE

SIGNATURE _____ (if under 18, parent or guardian must sign)

GET
FOUR
FREE
BOOKS
(AN $18.00 VALUE)

AFFIX
STAMP
HERE

In a moment Madame Blanchot returned and hurriedly rushed Shannon through the remainder of the garments. The girl was most delighted with a pair of woolen breeches or galligaskins as the seamstress called them.

"You can wear them well with the jacket for riding or under your skirt for extra warmth. It gets devilishly cold with the wind whipping your skirt up on the deck of a ship in the Channel."

"They are a bit itchy," Shannon noted, as she pulled them off and handed them to the woman.

It seemed the seamstress had an answer to every objection. With a sweep of her round arm, she pulled out a thin pair of silken breeches and handed them to her. "This will most assuredly help you, ma-demoiselle. Many ladies have the same irritation."

Shannon laughed as she examined the delicate liner. The woman had sewn little embroidered flowers and vines about the hem which ended above the knee and a pink braided drawstring pulled in at the waist to hold them daintily but securely in place.

The French woman was pleased with Shannon's reaction and instructed her to dress while she wrapped the purchases out front. Shannon stepped into her taffeta gown and struggled with the back fastens as she listened to the conversation between the proprietress and two Englishwomen whose voices could only be those of Lady Elissa Wolsey and her mother. Shannon took as long as she could to finish dressing and attempted to smooth her wrinkled skirt before going to the front of the shop.

"Why Miss Brennan what a surprise!" Elissa Wolsey exclaimed as she took obvious note of Shannon's dress. "I take it you rested well?" she asked.

"Very well, thank you, Lady Elissa. I was just

purchasing some heavier clothing for my first visit to England. I fear I do not know quite what to expect when I reach there."

"Indeed!" The haughtiness of the young woman's smile was annoying and Shannon could not help but bristle behind her forced smile.

"Have you family there, dear?" Lady Wolsey asked curiously.

"No, milady. I left my family on Nose' Be. My father . . ."

"Her father asked me to take her to London as my ward," Morgan Hawke injected, surprising them all at his quiet entry into the shop. "It was his dying wish that she be taken to a more civilized society."

"Oh my dear, I am most sorry," Lady Wolsey apologized, giving the girl a polite embrace.

"But you are most fortunate to have Lord Hawke as your guardian," Lady Elissa assured her dryly, repeating her mother's gesture of sympathy. "Was your father a planter?"

"No, he was a pirate," Shannon retorted hotly to the condescending tone of the tawny-haired woman. "A murdering thief, true, but as dear to me as your own father is to you." Her eyes flashed, defying the astonished young woman to reply.

"Shannon . . ." Hawke began.

"My lord, I am grateful for your consideration of my feelings, but I do not need your protection," she warned him. "I am what I am, and . . ." she said, turning to Elissa Wolsey, "sadly, she is what she is."

Shannon held her chin up as she pushed past them and stepped out into the street. She did not heed Morgan Hawke's call to wait, but proceeded blindly toward the busy docks. She had no trouble finding the *Sea Lady*'s berth and paid no attention to the glances of admiration as she passed the dockmen in

226

her determined path to the gangway. She was nearly running as she touched the deck and hurried to the security of her cabin below.

Her hands fumbled with the hasp on the mahogany trunk. As the lid hit the bulkhead behind it, she dug down through the few precious belongings Marie had packed for her until she spied the satin pouch that contained her jewels. She considered them too gaudy to wear, but they would provide her with enough money to live on until she could find a way to support herself. She spilled the assortment of precious gems on her berth and picked up a diamond brooch set in gold. Guilt shook her momentarily as she reflected on the fate of its owner, but she pushed it from her mind. This was now. There was little she could do to change what had already happened.

She carefully put the remaining jewels back in the pouch and returned it to the bottom of the chest. Footsteps were clambering down the steps of the companionway as she entered Hawke's cabin and placed the brooch on his desk. When the door to the room burst open, Shannon straightened and met Hawke's angry look evenly. His eyes traveled briefly to the jewel and returned to her.

"I am sorry if I embarrassed you in front of your peers, Hawke," she began, breaking the uncomfortable silence, "but I am not sorry for what I said." She held her ground stubbornly as he approached her.

"I thought you showed a great deal of restraint, considering the temper I have witnessed from time to time. And you certainly put Lady Elissa in her place very politely." He smiled as he raised her chin and studied her as if he saw something new for the first time.

"And you're not angry?" she asked warily.

His expression changed. "Yes, I am angry," he

227

admonished. "I am angry that you left alone and would not give me time to settle with Madame Blanchot. Your bullheadedness is going to lead you to harm, Shannon Brennan." He shook her shoulders in gentle emphasis.

"I arrived here safely, Morgan Hawke . . . I am not as defenseless as you would have me be!" She pushed his hands off her shoulders irritably. "And I'll not be treated like a kept woman!"

"What?" He was obviously confounded by her words.

She seized the brooch from the desktop and pressed it in his hand. "I will pay for my own clothes!"

His face darkened as he stared at the jewel. Suddenly he threw it through the open door to her cabin and turned to her ominously. The muscles in his jaw clenched as he spoke. "I will buy you what I will, when I will, Shannon. And you had better learn to accept that."

"Very well, then. Buy what you will, when you will. But I will not wear them. And you had better learn, Sir, almighty Lord Hawke, that title or no, you are but a man and have no right to dictate to me. I will do as I please, not as you please! Come ahead," she dared him as he stepped toward her, "You are stronger and can overpower me, and you know I could hurt you if I chose," she pointed out, her voice rising as she referred to their first meeting, "But I do not want to hurt you, nor will I change my mind."

For a second, Shannon thought he would strike her. His face was almost purple with frustrated rage and she resisted the urge to shrink away from his nearness. A brisk knock cut through the air like a knife as Michael Finney announced from the companionway that the crew was ready to shove off.

Hawke spun on his heel and strode over to the door. When he jerked it open, an astonished first mate stood there with his hand raised to knock again. Angrily, the captain pushed past the startled Irishman and slammed the door behind him.

Shannon had barely had time to collect her wits when she heard someone fumbling with the latch in her own cabin. She hurried to answer the door and saw what appeared to be Billy Randall struggling under a pile of precariously stacked packages. She took some off the top as the boy stumbled over to her berth and deposited them. As he straightened, she noticed his uncharacteristic pallor.

"Billy, are you ill?" she asked in concern as she placed her palm on her forehead. It was clammy and cool to the touch.

"Naw," he denied sheepishly. "I just ain't real well."

"Then perhaps you had better lie down here for a while. I'll tell the captain . . ."

"No!" he warned her in alarm. "I'm s'posed to feel like this . . . and the men'll call me a baby if I give in."

"I see," Shannon replied, recalling that the young man had gone into the tavern with the first mate and the crew the night before. "Do you feel as if you're going to lose your breakfast?"

The boy nodded and sighed miserably. "And I couldn't even eat any."

"Well then, go fetch me some hot water. I'd like to have some tea."

She winked at him in a conspiratory fashion and put her arm about his shoulder as he dragged his feet toward the door. As soon as he was on his way, she returned to the trunk to find the small pouch of Marie's tea. By the time Billy returned, she had moved the packages to Hawke's berth and had the tea measured out for the hot mugs.

She supervised the lad as he sipped the tea obediently. There was water in the bowl and while he determined whether or not he chose to survive this new ordeal, she bathed his forehead and neck in the cool water. Then methodically, she massaged his tousled head, as she had seen Marie do to her suffering father, and instructed him to relax against her and close his eyes. By the time she finished, the lad's eyes were a bit brighter and he assured her that although his head still ached, he was certain now that it was not fatal. When he was ready to leave, she made him promise to escort her on deck as soon as he finished with his chores.

The favorable wind rapidly put Isle de Los behind them. The late afternoon sun beat down on the gently rolling decks of the *Sea Lady*, while her white sails billowed above and strained the halyards. Shannon had changed into one of her cotton dresses and laughed as the salt water sprayed her wind-tossed hair. Billy Randall greeted the playful offense of the waves with a shout and rubbed the refreshing droplets on his cherub-like face. The bow rose and fell gracefully over the swells as it cut its path toward cooler waters.

Shannon dropped unceremoniously down beside the cabin boy and crossed her legs under her skirt to brace herself against the motion of the vessel. There was a certain fascination in watching the blue-green waves move peacefully along and then splash against the ship's hull transforming into dancing white foam until it dissolved again behind them. A restlessness like that of the sea itself seemed to fill her very being and she breathed deeply of the salt air. Had she been a boy, Nick Brennan would never have kept her ashore. She began to understand the call that beckoned men and boys alike to this life.

It was nearly sundown when Billy accompanied her back to her cabin and left her at the open stern window to observe the brilliant display of colors in the western sky. Occasionally she could hear the deep voice of the captain from the decks above her and it blended with the faint cries of the gulls and the hushing sound of the wake as it folded behind the ship. She catnapped dreamily with her head resting on her folded arms until Billy arrived in the next cabin and began to set the table for her and the captain.

She quietly asked Billy to bring her meal to her own cabin and when he left, she shoved the heavy trunk in front of the adjoining door. Morgan Hawke would dine alone and sleep with his damned packages, she thought as the tranquillity of her afternoon wore off and she resumed her stand against the captain of the *Sea Lady*. Her meal was tempting, but her appetite failed her as she picked at it with little interest. When Billy returned for her plate, he noted the position of the trunk and remarked innocently that that was most likely why the captain took his supper with the crew.

"I sure hope I never fall in love, if it's goin' to be like this," he mumbled in disgust. "Too fickle for me."

Shannon's mouth hung open in surprise at the youth's parting observation. What could he possibly know, she thought indignantly. He had not seen Morgan Hawke's barely restrained fury. She looked at the trunk again. Well, it certainly would not stop him if the bolt didn't, she admitted to herself. She felt ridiculous as she pushed the heavy piece of furniture back to its original place. She did not want him kept from her, but she would not give in where the clothes were concerned, she decided.

She was wide awake in her bunk, when she heard the door to the captain's cabin open and close quietly. The cracks around the adjoining door filtered light into her cabin as he hung up the lamp. Her heart skipped as she heard muffled curses and the sharp rattling of paper and she closed her eyes as the door opened between the cabins. Sensing his nearness, she held her breath. Perhaps he would see that she was sleeping and leave her be.

"Move over." It was a quiet and startling command.

Her eyes flew open. "What?"

"I said move over." He shoved her over against the bulkhead and proceeded to slip under the blanket beside her. She was completely taken off guard as he propped his head on his arm and looked down at her bewildered face. The firm line of his jaw twitched in the moonlight. "It seems my bed is covered with packages that are absolutely worthless to me," he informed her. "Now, I will keep an account of the trouble and expense you cost me and will collect payment when you are settled and satisfied in London. Will that appease your sense of independence, Shannon Brennan?"

She answered with a kiss and fell into his waiting arms readily. "I love you, Morgan. I . . ." His lips were on hers and whatever she had to say escaped her as she gave in to the rising need of the man she loved.

Chapter Fourteen

The weeks that followed passed quickly. When the *Sea Lady* braved the late autumn winds of the Straits of Dover and maneuvered into the Thames, it was a blustery day, one of the first since the departure from Isle de Los. As Shannon stood on the deck next to Morgan Hawke, she thanked Madame Blanchot silently for her foresight as her skirt furled upward and the brisk air whipped about her breeches. It would be late afternoon the following day before they would tie up at Billingsgate, Hawke had informed her, however, she was far too excited to remain below when the ship entered the great river that led to London.

She walked over to the rail and watched as they met a tall ship on its way from the great port. It rode low in the water, obviously provisioned for a long journey of equitable trade. As the men on its decks scurried about, a few waved in her direction and she returned the friendly gesture. She smiled and leaned backward as she felt the captain's hands encircle her waist, enjoying the warmth of his hard body against hers.

"Flirting already, and you haven't even reached

the city!" he accused her good-naturedly.

She pulled his arms tighter about her. "I would not flirt with anyone but you, sir, and you well know it." As he turned her, she looked up at the ruggedly handsome face, now completely free of the ugly bruises, and grinned wickedly. "How much longer will it be before it will snow?"

"Weeks, my love. Why?" he asked, brushing a stray wisp of hair from her face.

"When it does," she whispered, lowering her voice for him only, "I want you to make love to me in it!"

He leaned his head back and laughed as his hold tightened about her. She squealed in delight as he lifted her off her slippered feet and spun her around. "I am not so sure that you know what you are asking! That, my lady, is the warmest cold request that I have ever had made of me."

"Then I shall have to think of ways to entice you so that you may withstand the cold." Her eyes danced with mischief.

"Then I shall have to teach you." He held her closely and lowered his lips to hers oblivious to the grins of his men.

The latter half of the journey had been a pleasant one. The captain escorted his lady on deck frequently and they all enjoyed her lilting voice when they gathered about in the evenings to pass the time. The stars shone overhead and only the quiet lapping of the waves and the straining of the halyards could be heard above the harmonicas. While they would be glad to put in at London, they would miss the small family atmosphere.

The night was a restless one. Most of the men were on deck under the light of the binnacle lamps and even after they sang their last songs together and the musician put away his instrument, small groups milled about watching the dark shoreline. After she and Hawke retired to his cabin, Shannon perched on the window seat and stared out the open windows at the full moon reflecting on the waters behind them and the shadows of scattered homes that dotted the continuous rolling land to either side of them.

"They must be palaces," she sighed aloud, as Hawke shut the light and joined her. "They are so huge!"

"Some are. When we get to Isle of Dogs tomorrow you shall see the new palace under construction for His Royal Majesty."

"Is London full of palaces?" she asked innocently. "Do you live in a palace?"

He chuckled as he pulled her on his lap and cradled her lovingly. "No and no," he whispered, blowing gently into her ear. "London is a cluster of assorted buildings, some are palatial and others are built together like your village on Nose' Be."

"And what about Snowden. Is that in London?" She was keenly interested in the estate he promised to show her.

"Snowden is an estate which has a manor house on a hill overlooking a beautiful tree-lined pond that provides an excellent place to ice skate in the winter."

"Is that half a castle?"

His amusement embarrassed her, and she glanced back out the window again, realizing her own ignorance. There was so much to learn, in spite of all she had read in Cudge's books.

"In a manner of speaking, I would suppose it might be called that," he admitted, turning her face to him. "I am not laughing at you, my love. I take such delight in your innocence and look forward to showing you all the things you ask about."

"Will you be courting me?"

"What?"

"I mean when I find a house and get settled, are you going to court me?" She had worked a plan out with Billy Randall that his mother might need help at her inn and in exchange for room and board until she found a place of her own, she would work for the woman.

Hawke tensed sensing an impending controversy and chose his words carefully. "Of course I will court you . . . but it is my hope that you will stay at my home until such time as you decide exactly what it is that you are going to do."

Shannon considered his offer thoughtfully and leaned against him. "Is there work to be had at Snowden? I would not accept charity . . ."

"My mother is always in need of someone to help if you insist on this stubborn idea that you need to pay me!" he exclaimed in exasperation. There was so much he wanted to say to her but he could not in clear conscience until he cleared up things in London.

Shannon smiled in satisfaction and rose from his lap. "Then I would love to stay at Snowden! And I promise that I will do anything your mother might need me to do."

"And what of her son?" He seized her suddenly and carried her over to his berth. "What of my needs?"

Shannon laughed and pulled him down with her as he deposited her on the mattress. "He'll have to wait until it snows."

"Vixen!" he snarled, burying his face in her bosom and tickling her until she begged for mercy, which he dealt with great tenderness.

Later, as she listened to his soft breathing and rested her head on the strong arm that enveloped her shoulders, her thoughts tumbled in confusion. She wanted to be with him forever. She loved him more than life. Yet a nagging fear kept surfacing. How could an English lord marry a woman of mixed race and no more dowry than a small pouch of jewels. What sort of disgrace would she bring to his noble family. She recalled the haughty regard of the Wolseys.

She closed her eyes to prevent the tears that welled in them from falling down her wind-burned cheeks. How naive she was to think they could live happily ever after! Madame Blanchot had seen it and treated it so lightly. No matter how Morgan Hawke loved her, she could not continue this wonderful relationship without marriage; and she would not shame him with such an ignoble match.

"Oh, Morgan," she whispered, turning to embrace him desperately. He sighed in his sleep and pulled her to him instinctively, smothering her face in his chest. His leg curled over her as he wrapped her in his embrace, unaware that it would be the last time. He did not notice the dampness of her cheeks as she quietly cried herself to sleep over her decision to leave him.

Billy brought their noonday meal to them on the upper deck of the gallery so that Shannon did not miss any of the sights as the *Sea Lady* passed the Isle of Dogs where Charles II was rebuilding the old Tudor palace. She ignored the chafing wind that played havoc with the tresses tied at her neck with a black ribbon. Her eyes were as deep blue as the heavy gown she wore, but telltale circles betrayed her fitful night's slumber. She barely touched the salt pork and gravy and when she finished, she tossed most of it over the side to the gulls.

"Are you ill, Shannon?"

She turned from the rail to see Morgan Hawke studying her face in concern. Forcing a smile, she shook her head. "I didn't sleep well," she admitted lamely, not wanting to confront him with her decision until they were ready to leave the ship. She had already asked Billy to take her to his mother's home and made him swear not to reveal her plan to anyone until she had the chance to talk to the captain.

She pressed her back to the man as he showed her various points of interest as if trying to absorb enough of his warmth to last her through the lonely nights she had ahead of her. The skyline of red tiles was broken by sharp steeples and swelling domes. The infamous Tower loomed ahead, once gleaming white as green growth from the dampness crept up its walls. St. Paul's Cathedral was imposing with its lead-covered spire soaring high above all the others with an eagle and gilded cross.

The sea of masts seemed to part for the homecoming vessel and Shannon stared in awe at the London Bridge. It was a chain of great stone arches where small crafts of all types passed through with ease. Near its center was a drawbridge, but Hawke informed her that they would tie up at Billingsgate before they reached it. To Shannon's surprise, the bridge was covered with houses several stories in height and clustered together so that it appeared to be a small city stretched across the river.

As the *Sea Lady* maneuvered toward its intended dock, Michael Finney called out to them from the rail. "The Admiral's ship, sir!"

They followed the direction of his gaze to see the royal ship with its brilliant banners waving in the breezes moored next to the cobbled embankment lined with warehouses. The docks were swarming with curious people interested in the incoming vessel and the sounds of more than one language drifted up to the girl. As the crew scurried about on the deck, following Hawke's crisp orders, she noted the arrival of two coaches at the dock's end and saw a group of well-dressed people making their way through the babbling crowd.

She recognized the sprightly uniformed figure in the front as Admiral Edward Bedlowe and groaned inwardly. There would be no time to talk to Hawke as she had planned. The gangway dropped loudly to the dock and in a short time the group seemed to swarm on the deck, surrounding Morgan Hawke. Shannon hung back, suddenly frightened by the overwhelming reception below. She would have retreated to her cabin, but for Hawke breaking away from the congratulatory group and escorting her to their midst.

"My dear, Miss Brennan, I am most delighted to see you again." Admiral Bedlowe exclaimed taking her hand and kissing it enthusiastically. "Now, I have someone who has been waiting to meet you! May I present my wife, Harriet."

The man stood aside and Shannon extended her hand to the plump lady he introduced. Mrs. Bedlowe's face paled for just a second and Shannon took her arm in alarm. "Are you ill, madame?"

"Oh, my dear!" the woman cried, holding her arm tightly so that her gloved fingers bit into her flesh. Tears sprang to her eyes and Shannon glanced over at Morgan Hawke disconcerted.

"You must forgive my wife, Miss Brennan, but as I told you, you bear a remarkable resemblance to someone very dear to us . . . and for a good reason." The elder gentleman's eyes twinkled as he put his arm about her shoulder. "This is hardly the place to discuss such a matter, but I fear we cannot wait."

"What is the problem, Admiral?" Hawke asked,

239

his face mirroring his concern.

"Lord Hawke, this lovely girl is my late niece's daughter!" Mrs. Bedlowe injected, throwing her arms about Shannon and hugging the astonished girl.

"Hawke . . ." Shannon started, giving him a pleading look.

"I have it all in your father's . . . Nick Brennan's papers," Bedlowe explained. "He wrote how he took you as a baby from a merchantman bound for England. And that necklace proves it even further."

Shannon disengaged herself from the woman's arms and drew back in disbelief. Her hand went to her necklace defensively. "I . . . I knew my mother. She was Sakalavan."

"Nick Brennan's woman was Sakalavan, but your mother was Jennifer Devage," Bedlowe told her kindly. "Dear girl, we practically raised your mother. And after I saw you and recognized the coat of arms engraved on your necklace, I knew it had to be more than coincidence. I pored over your father's papers to no avail, until I discovered a false bottom in his trunk, and there, dear girl, was the proof I needed."

"Shannon dear, I pray you will come home with us," Mrs. Bedlowe implored, her gray eyes still misting.

Shannon shook her head in confusion. "I . . . I am not sure . . . I . . ."

"Morgan! Morgan darling!"

Shannon broke off as a beautiful fair-haired woman rushed across the deck and threw her arms about Morgan Hawke, kissing his face and neck repeatedly as tears of joy fell on her too-rosy cheeks. She forgot the issue of the moment as she watched him place his hands on her tiny waist and push her away. His face was as crimson as the woman's cheeks when she cast a sideways glance at Shannon with cool green eyes and then fluttered them up at him again.

"Is that the pirate wench we've heard so much about?" she asked in a kittenish voice.

Hawke cleared his throat uncomfortably as Shannon tilted her head waiting expectantly. "Corrinne Devage, this is Shannon . . ." He stopped, glancing at the Admiral and raised a questioning brow. Upon seeing the man shake his head slightly, he continued, "Shannon, this is Corrinne."

The woman smiled sweetly, extending a gloved hand. "I am Morgan's fiancée, and am most anxious to hear of your trip."

Shannon shook her hand and looked past the woman at Morgan Hawke. Her face paled under the natural rose of her cheeks. "Pleased to make your acquaintance," she answered numbly. Her knees felt as if they might buckle at any moment, but she took a deep breath and turned to Mrs. Bedlowe who was still staring at her in wonder. "Mrs. Bedlowe, I am ready to leave with you, if you can have someone bring along my trunk. It's already packed."

"Why is she going with you, Aunt Harriet?" Corrinne asked curiously.

"Corrinne dear, we shall explain everything at our dinner party tonight," the elder woman told her, taking Shannon's arm and squeezing it. "I want to get Shannon home so that she might rest till then."

Morgan Hawke crossed over to Shannon. "Shannon, I need to talk to you a moment." There was an edge of desperation in his voice.

"I think not, my lord. I am sure that you and your fiancée have much to discuss after so long a separation and I am anxious to accompany these kind people. Perhaps later." Shannon held her head high, her eyes daring him to stop her.

"Morgan darling, can't you see the girl is exhausted," Corrinne chided, placing a possessive hand on his arm, "and we have so much lost time to make up for."

"We will see you at dinner then this evening?" Admiral Bedlowe extended his hand which Hawke accepted politely, his eyes following Shannon as she made her way down the gangway with Harriet Bedlowe.

"Of course, sir. I'll bring Shannon's things as well."

"Very well then. Until later," he called back over his shoulder as he hurried to catch up with his wife and her new charge.

A coachman waited at the end of the dock and helped Shannon into the vehicle. The seat was tufted leather and hard, but it was a refuge for a while. A wave of nausea rose in the back of her throat and she held her face to the window for air. Harriet Bedlowe seemed to sense her illness, though not the nature, and sat beside her patting her hand affectionately. There was much to see and Shannon could not help her fascination as the coach made its slow progress toward the Strand.

The narrow streets were paved with cobblestone and down the center were gutters which, by the smell, she deduced to be sewers. Buildings were clustered on both sides of the street, most of them stone or brick at least on the first floor. Their second stories almost touched, having been constructed to hang over the street and almost blocked out the sun in some places. People chattered away, some in a friendly manner and others shouting in languages foreign to her ears.

Mrs. Bedlowe pointed out a grand building of Italian architecture situated on the river as Whitehall

Palace and on the other side of the street was the Banqueting Hall where public feasts and celebrations were held. Sedans carrying the wealthy citizens of London moved slowly among other coaches along this route and Shannon leaned out of the window curiously to get a good look at the strange vehicle carried by two men with the elegantly wigged lady inside. A well-dressed gentleman accompanied her and they chatted gaily as she fluttered a painted fan in front of her face.

"I fear I have never seen anything quite like this!" Shannon sighed, as she sat back against the seat.

"Dear niece, it is our fervent hope that we might help you to adjust to this new life. When Edward arrived with the news that you were alive and well, I simply could not believe it until I saw you this day."

Shannon endured another hug and the woman's heavy perfume caused the bile to rise again. She leaned her head to the window again and gasped for air. "I am not feeling well. I am sorry," she apologized, wiping her damp brow with the palm of her hand. "Maybe instead of mal de mer, I suffer from the opposite."

"That's not so preposterous as it sounds, Shannon!" the Admiral assured her. "I've seen it happen to sailors more than once. It takes time to develop one's sea legs, and I suppose it takes time to develop land legs as well."

Shannon smiled and sought the air again.

"I don't think it's a thing that won't be cured with a little nap and freshening up. You did ask someone to bring her things along, Edward?"

"Lord Hawke said he would see them delivered when he came for diner."

Shannon rested her head against the high back and prayed that the swaying journey of the coach would soon come to an end. She listened only halfway to the chatter that Harriet Bedlowe ran on about her alleged family, her mind on the green-eyed beauty who claimed Morgan Hawke as her fiancé. Corrinne Devage. The name was the same as the family they professed to be her own.

"Mrs. Bedlowe . . ." she started.

"Aunt Harriet, dear. It would mean so much to me if you would indulge me that small request."

"Aunt Harriet, is Corrinne Devage in my mother's family? If that is my family name," she added doubtfully.

"It is, Shannon Devage. There is no doubt. And I am sure your father will be not only astounded but delighted that you survived that terrible voyage that claimed the life of your dear mother."

"My father?" The situation was becoming more involved by the moment.

"Jonathan Devage! And Corrinne is your sister."

"Stepsister, dear," Harriet Bedlowe reminded the gentleman. "When Jonathan returned from India without you and your mother, it was assumed that you both had perished in that horrible pirate attack. He remarried a few years later to a wealthy widow who had a seven-year-old daughter. So Corrinne is about your age," she explained to the bewildered girl.

The coach stopped with a sudden jerk and Shannon caught herself before she was thrown forward to the floor. She looked out the window as the coach resumed a slower pace along a tree- and shrub-lined drive toward one of the grandest homes she had yet seen. It was three stories high and constructed of white stone with tall Gothic columns in the front. A rather handsome young man stood on the front steps watching the coach approach and gingerly climbed down them to meet it as it came to a stop in front of him.

"Mother, I was just going out and thought—" he broke off as he stuck his head through the door and saw Shannon. "My word, who have we here?"

Admiral Bedlowe tapped the side of the carriage doorway with his walking stick to force the smiling face out of the way and exited. "If you had come home last evening instead of gallivanting about town, you might know young man!" he chastised gruffly.

Shannon took the Admiral's extended hand and stepped out of the coach in awe of the structure and hardly noticed the appreciative stare of the younger gentleman.

"Shannon, this degenerate is my son, Brian Bedlowe," the Admiral informed her as he assisted his wife to the ground.

"You are cousins, dear," Mrs. Bedlowe said warmly.

"I am enchanted."

Shannon was shaken from her fascination when Brian Bedlowe grabbed her hand and touched it to his lips, holding it for a moment until he had her full attention. Her eyes widened as she realized she had missed his name.

"Brian," he prompted, his brown eyes dancing as she pinkened in embarrassment.

"Shannon will be staying with us for a while, Brian. Isn't that simply wonderful?" His mother squeezed her arm again.

"Indeed so," he exclaimed, taking her other arm and walking her up the steps. "Where are you from, lovely cousin?"

"I'm beginning to wonder," Shannon replied, as the door was opened by a uniformed doorman in a dark green velvet jacket. "Oh my!" A large marbled hallway with a grand stairway leading to the second floor lay before her. It was lined with several white classical figures and beautiful murals. "It's a palace!" she whispered, as she looked around her.

"Hardly," Brian Bedlowe laughed, "but it will do."

"Shannon dear, allow me to show you to your room. You are pale as a ghost and I fear you'll be too ill for our dinner party."

"Dinner party?" Brian questioned as his mother took Shannon from his arm and started toward the shining white steps with a dark green runner up the center.

"You're on your way out, young man," his father reminded him. "If you can't stay home to welcome your own father, I don't suppose you'd be interested in the little family reunion we have planned this evening."

"Father, will you please tell me what this is all about?"

Shannon could hear the Admiral baiting his son as she and Harriet Bedlowe made their way up the winding steps to another hall. It was lined with doors on both sides and frescoes decorated the ceiling lighted by small ornate lamps that hung at intervals down the corridor. Shannon was shown a room on the right and she gasped when her aunt opened the door to reveal a spacious boudoir. It was lavishly decorated in burgundy velvet with imported oriental rugs scattered about richly carved furnishings. The canopied bed had fancy turned posts and the carvings were similar on all of the cherry pieces.

"Now you just rest a while, dear. I'll send Frannie up with some water to wash your face so you can freshen up and . . . oh, you cannot imagine how happy I am." The woman's eyes glazed again and she wiped them briskly and smiled. "I have to warn you, I am such a fuss-budget."

Shannon walked over to her and hugged her in genuine affection. "I fear that I need just such a person right now, Mrs. . . . Aunt Harriet. Thank you so much."

When the woman had gone, Shannon walked over to the window and opened the bottom shutters. The view overlooked the river and the most beautiful gardens and ponds filled with ducks and geese. At the edge of the terraced gardens was a small dock and beyond that the Thames. As she sat on the velvet cushioned windowseat, and stared out at the tall masts of a ship forging its way up the river, the maid came in and filled the pitcher with warm water. She pointed out the clean towels to Shannon that hung on the washstand and with a curtsy left the girl alone.

Shannon stripped off her jacket and loosened the neck of the shirt underneath. As she washed her face, she caught a glimpse of her reflection in the mirror and tears came to her eyes. Her hair was disheveled by the wind and her face was as ruddy as the men's who sailed with her up the Thames. How could she have believed the lies of the captain who had taken her love so carelessly. She had just been a substitute for the living porcelain doll that was his fiancée.

A silver hairbrush and comb lay on a beautifully etched tray and Shannon did her best to unsnarl her hair, inflicting pain as she pulled the comb through it unmercifully, as if to punish herself for her foolish relationship with a man she had known to be a liar, a betrayer of trust. Her heart ached but as she stared at her tear-stained face, her eyes hardened icily.

You are a survivor, Shannon Brennan, she told herself. This Jonathan Devage may have sired you, but you are Brennan's daughter. You have your pride. Let Lord Hawke have his delicate doll, for he'll not get the chance to hurt you again. Sheath your heart in ice and close your ears to his sweet lies forever.

She closed the shutters against the afternoon sun and reclined against the stack of pillows piled on the bed. Her heart was heavy, burdened with betrayal, but her mind took reprieve in her resolve to shut out the man she had loved. There was a new family to face and a new life to begin and neither of them concerned Lord Morgan Hawke. The golden clock on the mantel of the marble fireplace in the corner of the room ticked in the silence until she closed her eyes and rested peacefully.

It was dark when Harriet Bedlowe entered the room with a lighted lamp and shook her gently to awaken her.

"I've let you sleep as long as I could, dear. Lord Hawke is here with your trunk. I'll have the servants bring it up immediately while you gather your wits." She stopped and looked at Shannon curiously. "He wants to talk with you before the other guests arrive. I told him I would tell you, so that you might want to hurry up and get dressed."

Shannon nodded mutely as the woman left and waited for her trunk to be brought up to the room. Morgan Hawke could wait forever before she would speak to him alone, she vowed. When the trunk arrived, she dug through its contents and saw nothing that would be suitable to dine with the guests of these wealthy people. Her taffeta gown would require hours of pressing, she thought as she shook it out and laid it across the bed.

Suddenly she turned to face the full-length mirror mounted in a free-standing cherry frame and touched the open collar of her blouse, her mind racing. The pirate wench, Corrinne Devage had called her. Well, if they expect a pirate wench, a pirate wench they shall have. She unfastened her skirt and let it drop in a crumpled circle about her feet along with its supporting petticoats. Her puke, or blue-black galligaskins remained, neatly fastened at her trim waist. From the knees down, she wore netherstocks of white jersey and small black leather slippers with round onyx buttons for decoration.

She brushed her hair forward, holding her head down so that it hung down to her knees in the front and then straightened, tossing it back in shining disarray. Her pink cheeks were a startling contrast to her bright blue eyes, flickering icily in the lamplight. As an added touch, she unlaced the front of her blouse a bit more in the open style of her previous compatriots. Her hand touched the silver necklace, which sparkled between the rounding curves of her breasts and she prayed for the fortitude to see the evening out.

She waited, toying nervously with the gathered lace at her wrists and twisting the voluminous sleeves of her blouse about her slender arm until she heard footsteps approaching her door. A polite knock echoed in the room and a man's voice called from the corridor.

"Shannon, it's Brian. The guests are here and anxiously waiting to meet you."

She crossed the room and opened the door. Her voice was husky as she spoke to the startled young man who stared at her incredulously. "I thought you were going out for the evening."

A dashing smile crossed his lips and he winked at her. "I did not want to miss the excitement when my darling cousin finds out her inheritance will have to be shared by her . . . most beautiful sister."

"Brian," she said, hesitantly placing her hand on his arm, "I am frightened."

"Milady pirate," he answered, covering her hand with his own, "I shall be ever at your side. In fact, had I known Hawke was going after pirates of this sort, I would have signed up with him from the start."

Shannon could not help but laugh at her new cousin. "You are going to enjoy this, aren't you?"

He leaned over and gave her a cousinly peck on the cheek. "Immensely," he whispered wickedly.

The company was in the parlor sharing a drink before supper when Brian escorted Shannon into the room. There was a deafening silence, before Morgan Hawke rose to his feet leading the other gentlemen to follow. His eyes met hers briefly and she coldly turned from them to fix her gaze on the distinguished gentleman beside Admiral Bedlowe. He was a well-built man about the age of Nick Brennan and his black hair was salted with white at the temples. The man stared at her suspiciously through dark eyes, before softening his facial expression.

"I cannot believe my eyes," he said at last. "You are your mother's image!"

Shannon tightened her grip on Brian's arm and felt his hand rest on her waist reasuringly. "Pardon me, sir, I mean no disrespect to my gracious hosts or to you and your family, but I have yet to see the proof."

"Oh dear God, I hope it's all a terrible misunderstanding!" Corrinne leaned against Morgan Hawke's arm as if she would swoon.

Shannon regarded her dispassionately. "So do I."

"No! Don't say that, dear. Come here, I must show you something."

Mrs. Bedlowe, recovered from her initial shock at

Shannon's appearance, led the group into her private parlor. There was a small fire in the fireplace and a large rocker surrounded by baskets holding sewing notions. But above the gilded mantel was the portrait of a young woman about Shannon's age wearing a low-cut white gown and no other adornment except a white rose in her dark hair, piled high on her head in loose curls. Her complexion was the color of the palest rose and her eyes were like shining sapphires in a china setting.

"That, Shannon dear, is your mother," the woman informed the astonished girl.

"Dearest cousin," Brian whispered lowly in her ear, "but for the gown, it is you."

"My Jennie was as wild and unpredictable as you apparently are," Jonathan Devage told her.

"How can you talk about 'my Jennie' when mother is hardly cold in her grave." Corrinne's voice bordered hysteria as she glared at Shannon maliciously. "My mother has been his faithful wife all these years, while yours was only his long enough to bear you and give you up to a gang of murdering animals who raised you in their own ways!"

"Corrinne!" Hawke shook the sobbing woman and she collapsed against him, clinging to him tightly. "Please take me home, Morgan. I simply cannot bear this . . . this farce!"

"Perhaps, Lord Hawke, if you could calm your fiancée, we'll return to the parlor." That the Admiral was disgusted with the woman's theatrics was evident.

As they left the couple to the privacy of the room, Jonathan Devage tried to apologize for his daughter's behavior. "Her dear mother was buried only last week, and this has only added to the trauma she has had to suffer. I am sure she will soon come to cherish you as her sister." He embraced Shannon and the girl could not help but stiffen.

"Sir, I am truly sorry for your recent loss. It seems we have similar needs. I need time as well to accept all this. You are a stranger to me. I will need time to get to know you and I am sure that you will require the same."

The announcement for dinner came as a relief. Shannon was gratefully seated between Brian and her father, while the host and hostess sat on either end of the elegant banquet table. The places reserved for Morgan Hawke and his fiancée were filled by the time the first course of stuffed shellfish was served.

Each time the butler would pass with the wine bottle, Brian would have his glass refilled and top off Shannon's in spite of her protests. Once Shannon caught a reproving glance from Harriet Bedlowe directed at her mischievous son, who managed to keep Shannon on the verge of giggles during the entire meal. That Brian did not like his cousin who sat primly across from him in a velvet gown of emerald to match her eyes was quite obvious; and it was equally obvious that Morgan Hawke did not approve of Brian.

Shannon was actually beginning to enjoy herself when the meal ended in a delicious dessert of apple pie. It was agreed by all parties concerned that it would be best for Shannon to remain with the Bedlowes for a while, until such time as she felt comfortable in moving into the Devage home in Westminster. When it came time for the guests to depart, Morgan Hawke insisted that Corrinne accompany her father home as he had pressing business to discuss with the Admiral. After another round of tears and a pouting farewell kiss, the Devages left.

Shannon quickly excused herself and rushed up

the steps to avoid a confrontation. After studying the long row of doors in bewilderment, she chose one that might be her own and found to her chagrin that it was not. She cursed under her breath, and backed out of the dark room into her cousin.

"If you really want to go in there, be my guest. It's my room!" He leaned over her and grinned. "Your room is the second door from the end."

Shannon smiled back. "Thank you, cousin."

She ducked under his arm and headed toward her door. When she reached it, he was on her heels. "What now?" she asked as he planted his hand on the wall above her head again.

"Your presence is requested by his lordship downstairs."

Shannon slumped against the doorjamb and shook her head. "Tell him I'm too exhausted. I really am tired," she added defensively, as he raised a quizzical brow.

"Very well, then. Sleep well." He gave her an impetuous kiss on the forehead, and started down the corridor toward the stairs. "Oh, and cousin . . ." he began, as he paused at the head of the stairwell, "welcome to the family!"

Shannon smiled as he winked and disappeared down the stairway. Once inside her room, she walked over to the window and opened the shutter. The river glittered like a wide silver ribbon in the moonlight. There was much to occupy her mind as she disrobed and prepared for bed. The bed had been turned back, and a small fire was going in the fireplace, so that when she blew out the lamp, the flickering glow of the flames danced on the walls. A tender memory surfaced as she lay dwarfed in the huge bed alone and her hard veneer cracked in the desolate silence of the night.

Chapter Fifteen

The dress shop in Southwark was humming with the chatter of patrons and seamstresses that worked under the supervision of the slender russet-haired proprietress who looked over Shannon's shoulder from time to time as the girl studied the worn pages of Taylor's "The Needles Excellency." Shannon was looking for something specific—a gown that resembled the one her mother wore in the portrait. She had studied the portrait every day in the week since she had been with the Bedlowes and wondered if she could ever imitate Jennifer Devage's ethereal beauty that entranced each beholder. Although she would not admit it to herself, she longed for Morgan Hawke to look at her in the way that he had stood transfixed before the portrait the night of their arrival.

She found what she sought at last and pointed to the sketch, gaining an approving nod from the master seamstress. As she had with each of the other selections, the woman immediately selected a bolt from the mountains of materials that were neatly categorized along the walls of the selection room and presented it to the girl. It was the white brocade, heavy enough for the cool weather that chilled the city's streets and smogged the air with the soot of the sea coal fires.

"And you must have a hooded cloak to match, trimmed like so, in white fox or ermine. Like this one." The woman pointed a graceful finger at a voluminous garment that fastened its loose hood at the neckline with a braided loop over a large button. "Mother of pearl buttons are what we shall use, one functional and one to match opposite it."

Shannon glanced at her aunt hesitantly. "It must be very expensive. And I already have a cloak."

"Dear Shannon, it is not every day that one is presented to the King. And you must adapt to the idea that you are a very wealthy young woman."

Shannon nodded, torn between her desire to look her best for the feast honoring Lord Hawke's successful mission in His Majesty's service and her remorse over inheriting her grandfather's fortunes out from under her father and stepsister.

She heard the whole story of her family from her aunt and uncle. How the rebellious and willful Jennifer Sterling had met Jonathan Devage and after a discreet and brief courtship, presented him to her father to ask his blessing on their engagement. Sir Robert vehemently refused and threatened to disown her if she went ahead with the reckless marriage. So, madly in love, the couple defied Sir Robert Sterling's will and left London together for India where the brash young Irishman hoped to seek his fortune with the East India Company.

Shannon read the faded letters written in an elegant script imploring her aunt to use her sisterly persuasion on Sir Robert to change his mind, but the stubborn man was too smitten with his daughter's betrayal to relent. The girl's heart ached sympathetically as she read her mother's pained words. It was evident that Jennifer's heart has been broken.

Her mother's spirits brightened as the girl read on with the news of the impending birth of their first child. Her parents were overjoyed when Shannon was born and detailed reports of her playful antics were sent with regularity to Harriet Bedlowe who, in turn, insisted her brother listen to them. It was only when he became infirm with consumption that he began to weaken. By the time he realized his desire to see and hold his granddaughter, it was too late.

His letter asking Jennifer to come home and bring her family was followed very shortly by Edward Bedlowe's letter, informing the young mother of her father's death. In the remaining time he had, Sir Robert had instructed his solicitors to change his will so that Jennifer and her daughter would inherit his estate in Westminster and his shares in the East India Company. While he had kept a keen eye on Jonathan's exceptional progress with the company, he still did not want the man to receive the benefit of the Sterling fortune, except to manage it under the critical eye of appointed solicitors.

It was here that Shannon's story was supplemented by the journals of the father she knew, Nick Brennan. In a large scrawl difficult to read, he briefly wrote how he saved a small lass from the burning merchantman and took her home to his native wife, Lillianne. Succeeding entries brought tears to Shannon's eyes as she read for herself the joy that she brought her foster parents as well. The entries also served another purpose, for they revealed to others who read them the side of the pirate Brennan who had loved and raised her as a daughter.

Jonathan Devage returned to England without his wife and daughter who had fallen victim to the murderous pirate attack, barely recovered from the same. He had been wounded on deck when an explosion threw him over the burning ship's rail. Another ship found him floating half-conscious on a charred piece of wreckage with nothing to show of his past but the water-soaked letters from England tucked inside his tattered jacket.

There being no provision in the will in the event of Jennifer and Shannon's demise, he claimed the inheritance as the shattered widower and gradually began to rebuild his life. In time, society accepted the handsome and wealthy prospect for a husband and a few years later, he married a widow with a seven-year-old daughter. While the Devages understandably did not develop a closeness with Jennifer's remaining family, they prospered well in the social circles of the city.

As soon as Shannon realized the implication of her late grandfather's will, she insisted that the solicitors continue to allow her father and stepsister to live in the same lifestyle as before. There was enough wealth for them all. Still, each time she spent money, she felt guilty, as if she were taking it from her father's pocket.

"So, it is agreed then?" the proprietress asked, glancing at each of the women in turn.

Shannon nodded. "How long will it take before the clothes will be finished?"

"My niece has just arrived from the tropics and has hardly any winter clothing at all," Mrs. Bedlowe explained sweetly. "And the banquet will be upon us in only three weeks!"

The shopkeeper smiled at Shannon as she put the pattern book back in its place on a wide shelf above a row of fabric bolts. "I will have six of my best seamstresses start immediately. The white gown will take precedence."

"Mrs. Benson, there is no other seamstress in London as far as I am concerned," Harriet Bedlowe assured the woman gratefully. "I would have no other, Shannon."

"You are most kind to rush so for us. Thank you so much." Shannon extended her hand and shook the woman's.

"You just keep that lovely figure and try to be more patient in the fittings. That is all I ask."

Shannon grinned sheepishly. The morning had been trying and she was about to scream by the time the women finished taking her measurements for every type of garment imaginable. "I promise I will try."

Her stomach was growling by the time the Bedlowe coach picked them up to carry them to the Tabard where they were to meet Brian for the noonday meal. While her aunt was going to visit a sick friend for the afternoon, Brian had offered to take Shannon riding for the first time. It was something she looked forward to with anticipation and trepidation. She was determined to master the art that appeared so easy from the seat of their coach as she watched equestrians pick their way through the streets.

Her aunt's perfume filled the coach as it pulled up in front of the popular tavern and when it stopped Shannon hurried out of the vehicle before the flustered coachman could assist her. She felt clammy as she leaned on the back of the coach and breathed deeply to settle her queasy stomach. She chastised herself for skipping her breakfast and assured her concerned aunt as the woman was helped out of the carriage that she was fine.

She started to join her when a young boy gazing into the windows of the shops on the opposite side of the street caught her eye. His tousled brown hair looked familiar and without thinking she stepped out from the back of the coach and lifting her skirt as she jumped the slow moving gutter, called out Billy Randall's name. She had no idea where the racing wagon came from as she heard her aunt scream her name above the din of the busy street. Thunderous hooves bore down on her and her feet refused to move as she turned to see the charging snorting beasts.

Suddenly her arm was nearly wrenched from her shoulder and she was dragged out of the way. She fell against her rescuer and the impact sent the two of them sprawling on the cobblestones. She lay still for a moment trying to regain the strength that had drained from her in that horrendous moment when she saw her danger, when she heard Brian Bedlowe's voice under her.

"A little further, dear cousin, and not even the horses would step on us!" He wrinkled his nose at the stench from the gutter only a few feet away from them and handed her to the pale-faced coachman who ran to assist them.

Harriet Bedlowe raced over to her with surprising speed and hugged her, pinching her arms to assure herself that her niece was not hurt. As Shannon brushed off her skirt, she apologized. "I should have looked before I pulled that little stunt."

"That driver did not even try to stop, Master Brian. I could have sworn he sped up!" the indignant coachman blurted out as he brushed off Brian's well-tailored jacket. Its tawny color was becoming to him and he looked much improved since breakfast when he had shown up at the long dining table deathly pale and suffering from too long at a local gambling house.

"That does not surprise me, Charles, the rogues

that these market men can be. Are you sure you're all right?" He straightened the blue bonnet that his aunt had purchased for Shannon earlier that day. "Very pretty!"

The crowd that had gathered dispersed upon seeing that no one was injured, and the threesome made their way into the tavern. Aunt Harriet seemed more in need of the calming effects of the wine they ordered with their meal, than Shannon, who chose a delightful new drink the Bedlowes introduced her to instead—chocolate.

Shannon ate her salad as Brian relayed an account of a disagreement that had developed at the gambling house the night before. It seemed the quarrel was to be settled in a duel and he was disappointed that he had not been chosen as the second for his friend. His mother predictably was appalled at the idea and admonished him gently.

That Brian was his mother's son was evident. He loved the arts and architecture and frequented the homes and offices of those with similar interests. He confided that he hoped to go to Italy to study there, but he was reluctant to press the issue with his father. The Admiral was not as proud of Brian as the young man so fervently desired, but was disgusted with his interests. He wanted Brian to follow in the footsteps of all the Bedlowe men and take to the sea. The sad part was, Brian held to his interests with the same determination as his father held to his—so much like the elder gentleman and yet so different.

When their meal was finished, Brian assisted his mother into the coach concerned for her state of distress over the near accident. "Are you sure you are up to seeing Lady Flemington?"

As the woman settled on the seat, she patted his hand. "Nonsense! You two children go on. I'm fine," she assured him. "And you listen well to Brian, dear. He's an excellent horseman."

Shannon blew her a parting kiss as the coach pulled off. As Brian offered her his arm, she glanced up at him. "Now what?" she asked excitedly.

"You have a choice . . . to the park by coach or sedan chair."

Shannon had no trouble in deciding on the coach over the queer looking human drawn vehicle without wheels. As they had walked a bit farther along the street looking for a vacant one, she observed the various assortment of people around them. There were beggars, adult and child, peddlers selling their wares and their wealthier counterparts, the merchants who stood in the doorways of their shops, and patrons of all classes milling in front of the display windows.

Brian finally secured a coach and helped her inside. The clip-clopping of the horses' hooves on the cobblestones mingled with the general music of the street as Shannon sat back against the tall back of the seat and continued to watch in interest as the scenery passed by. Her eyes were bright and the sunlight danced in them as her cousin observed her unnoticed. She spotted a lady daintily perched atop a noble-looking steed as they neared the park and turned to Brian with a frown.

"Must I sit half-cocked on the beast?" she asked anxiously.

"Well, the sidesaddle is designed so that lady might ride in her gown," he explained matter-of-factly.

"But I dressed so I might ride astride." To his astonishment she unfastened her skirt and shoved it down over her hips along with its supporting petticoats, revealing her blue-black galligaskins.

261

"What are you doing?" Brian exclaimed incredulously as she stepped out of her crumpled garments.

"I thought I'd ride in my breeches. That way I won't have to bother with my skirts hanging up and I'll be able to stay on the horse better if I ride astride." Her voice trailed off as she saw his rising color and realized her ignorance. "I've embarrassed you!"

"Well, let's say I was not quite prepared . . . Shannon," he told her, smothering a grin, "don't ever, ever do that in front of any other gentleman, lest you wind up ravaged for your boldness."

Her chin quivered as she looked out the window. "I would never intentionally do anything to embarrass you or your family." Her face was now the same shade as her cousin's.

He crossed the coach and sat beside her. His arm went about her shoulder reassuringly and he lifted her chin so that her face looked up at his. "I am hardly the best example of propriety—as my father will be quick to point out, dear cousin, but I promise that I shall endeavor in any way that I can to help you along so that you will avoid doing just that. However," he added seriously, "there is little you could do that we would not still cherish that impetuous innocent nature of yours that has enchanted all of us." He kissed her tenderly before she realized what he was about.

Collecting her wits, she pushed him back and withdrew as far away as the wall of the coach would permit. Her voice was firm as she spoke. "Don't ever do that again, Brian. You have been very kind to me and I am fond of you . . . but my heart is not free to any man," she warned him. "So it must be my friendship or nothing at all."

He raised his hands in surrender and returned to his seat on the opposite side of the coach.

"Friendship it shall be then," he agreed, with a devilishly handsome smile. "Now put your skirt back on. Ladies are more formal in the city, save those becoming breeches for country sport."

When they arrived at the stables, Shannon waited while Brian made the necessary arrangements for their mounts. The Thames was a flurry of activity with vessels loaded with produce and wherries transporting citizens to and from various points of the city. An ornately gilded barge was of particular interest as its lord and lady sat on high-backed chairs near the center of the craft and enjoyed the music provided by a violinist. Its notes were melodious as it drifted her way in the breeze.

She was startled by the long whinny of the shining salt and pepper mare that Brian led to her.

"This is Sarah. Sarah, Shannon." With a wink, he handed her a small cut of tobacco and motioned toward the dark-eyed animal. "Hold your hand flat and give her a treat," he encouraged.

Shannon obeyed and marveled at how soft the horse's nose was as it greedily lapped up the tobacco.

"Now she loves you . . . at least as long as you have something for her," Brian teased. "Ready to mount?"

Shannon gave Sarah another fleeting study and then nodded. Her heart was pounding as the stable boy took the reins and Brian lifted her up on the horse's back. He helped her settle her leg in the hook of the sidesaddle and checked the tack to make sure everything was secure. Then leaving her to the care of the stablehand, he walked back into the stable and returned mounted on a sleek chestnut stallion which picked its white-stockinged feet up proudly as he approached her.

"Sarah is a follower, so you need not fear that she'll run off with you," he told her as the boy handed her the reins to her horse. "Now simply lean the reins in the direction you wish to turn and coax her a bit. If you need to stop, pull them toward you. And we'll walk first," he finished, passing her and taking the lead.

Shannon tensed as the large muscles of the beast moved under her and her free hand clutched the rim of the saddle until her knuckles were white. As Sarah fell in behind the chestnut and Shannon realized that she was not going to fall, she began to relax her grip, but only slightly. Brian watched her patiently as she trudged along behind him and gave her words of encouragement.

By the time they had made their third sweep about the horse trail that led them down by the river, Shannon was much more at ease. Brian called a warning for her to hold on, and urged the stallion to a trot. Sarah, not to be left behind, jumped ahead to follow and Shannon gasped, resuming her death grip on the saddle while the reins hung limply on Sarah's dark-maned neck.

The jolting was most uncomfortable and she tried to follow Brian's advice and move with the animal with little success. Shannon met every one of Sarah's ups with an equally hard down, and could not coordinate their efforts until Brian moved to a faster gait. At that point, Shannon and Sarah seem to realign their movements and the ride became more enjoyable. When they reached the stables again, Shannon was laughing as Sarah pulled up alongside the chestnut and she cast a disappointed look at her cousin as he dismounted.

"Must we quit?" she asked, unaware of the disarming pout she gave him. Curls fell in shining disorder about her shoulders having worked loose from the confines of her combs and bonnet. "Maybe we could ride home instead of taking a coach. Are we near there?"

"I don't . . ." He stopped and eyed her thoughtfully. "Well, if we take it slow," he warned her.

Shannon held her mount's reins and waited patiently while Brian paid the stablemaster and tipped him heavily to permit them to take the horses to their homes and have them returned to the stables later by servants.

The ride was actually not that long. Shannon swayed with the movement of the animal beneath her and Sarah was most cooperative moving in and about pedestrians along the tree-lined way. When they maneuvered the mounts into the stone drive leading up to the white mansion, she was quite at home. Mischievously, she cast a sly look at Brian and clicked her tongue, egging Sarah ahead of the chestnut. Responding to the challenge, her cousin easily outdistanced her. She squealed as her bonnet flew off and tumbled to the ground and reined in Sarah so sharply that when the horse halted in immediate obedience, Shannon nearly lost her seat. She struggled to keep from pitching over Sarah's dark mane and pushed herself upright against the animal's damp neck.

Brian swung the chestnut about and upon assessing the situation, rode back toward the fallen bonnet. With flourish he leaned over deeply and scooped up the hat with his free hand. Shannon, now recovered, clapped at his display of horsemanship and permitted him to replace the bonnet on her head gallantly. He smoothed back her tousled locks and tied the ribbon under her chin to secure it once more. Side by side, they finished their ride up to the wide steps where a visiting coach stood.

Brian dismounted easily and handed his reins to a

servant who appeared from around the side of the house. He grinned as he approached the mare and extended his arms up to Shannon. "That is all for today, young lady. You need much more experience before you're ready to race."

Shannon made a face at him and unhooked her leg from the side saddle. She gasped as she slid off Sarah's back too quickly and grabbed at Brian in brief panic. His arms were strong as he caught her and lowered her to her feet.

"My legs feel funny," she confided, as he released her.

"Young man, I hardly think Shannon is experienced enough to be gallivanting about London with you on horseback!"

The couple glanced up at the main entrance in surprise to see Admiral Bedlowe and Morgan Hawke standing on the landing.

"Sir, it was my idea," Shannon burst out defensively, trying to avoid a confrontation between Brian and his father. "I begged him to let me ride Sarah home. And I never fell off . . . not even once!" she added proudly, too high from her equestrian experience to permit the frown on Morgan Hawke's face to inhibit her.

"She really has an excellent seat for a beginner!" Brian chimed in, sharing her good humor. "Lord Hawke . . ." He extended his hand in greeting to the man who accepted it with cool politeness.

Shannon approached her uncle and grasped his arm, her blue eyes shining as she summoned her most charming smile. "I do hope you'll permit me to ride every day with Brian." Her knees were a bit unsteady and she tightened her grip momentarily till she regained her composure. "I guess I have to develop my horse legs as well as my seat," she laughed.

"Humph!" The elder gentleman exclaimed unsuccessfully attempting to hide his amusement at her blunt comment. "Let's get inside where these aching bones can seek the comfort of a warm fire," he suggested, changing the subject.

As the group moved into the grand hallway, Brian patted Hawke on the back and mouthed the words so that Shannon, attentive at his father's side ahead of them could not hear. "She's a delight!"

As they entered the gentleman's parlor, the Admiral offered brandy to everyone. The man-servant poured four glasses of the liquor, and Shannon chattered excitedly about the day elaborating on Brian's gallant rescue in front of the Tabard. She took the offered glass and stopped long enough to take a small sip. It burned her throat, and she tried to clear it quietly. Its warming nature was welcome as she suddenly realized how chilly it had been outside.

"Charles told us he thought the rascal meant to run her down," her uncle was saying to Brian as if to solicit his son's opinion.

Brian leaned back against the settee and shook his head. "I really can't say. I was too busy trying to reach Shannon before the damned horses did.'

"Don't you think that's a bit far-fetched, uncle?" Shannon asked doubtfully. "I mean I did act rather impulsively. I thought I saw Billy Randall," she explained to Morgan Hawke. "I really had hoped to see him."

"Perhaps I can take you to his mother's boarding house for a visit." Hawke had been uncharacteristically quiet until now and Shannon suddenly recognized she had fallen into his plans. "That is, if you are rested enough from our grueling voyage to manage the visit." The challenging look in the steel blue eyes made her shift uncomfortably next to Brian.

He was more than aware of her ploys to avoid his company. Each time he tried to see her, she was either still sleeping in, napping in the afternoon, retired early or simply out with her aunt.

"Well, I must check with Aunt Harriet first. I am not sure exactly what schedule she has in mind for me," she replied evasively.

"Perhaps you might give up your afternoon ride tomorrow to go. I must leave for Snowden day after tomorrow." He had trapped her by her own admission.

Admiral Bedlowe cleared his throat and motioned for his son to follow his example as he rose from his chair. "Since you two need to work this out, I think Brian and I had better go check on Harriet. She was quite upset by the morning's accident and will be relieved to know you have not had any more adventures and are safely home."

Shannon fought the urge to seize Brian's wrist as he rose and set the empty brandy glass on the table. Her eyes expressed her panic and he hesitated momentarily before deciding to leave her to Morgan Hawke's company. She paled as the folding doors to the parlor were closed to allow them privacy.

"I understand why you have been avoiding me, Shannon," Morgan Hawke told her as he crossed the room to her.

She finished off the last of her drink and put her glass beside Brian's with a shaking hand. "If you do, sir, then why do you waste your time talking to me. There is little you can say to make up for your deceit." Her voice was surprisingly strong.

"Shannon . . ."

She drew away from his touch and flashed a defiant

look of anger. "Touch me again, and I shall break off the stem of that glass and do my utmost to finish the job I started on my father's ship."

"Shannon, you must listen to me. Corrinne and I were engaged before I met you . . ."

"Damn you, Morgan Hawke! You took my innocence, you let me think you loved me, all the while promised to that whining bitch? By God, would that I could cut your heart out, but I would be hard-pressed to find it!"

"I did not want to tell you about Corrinne until I had the chance to . . ."

"To seduce me . . . to . . . to use me to satisfy your rutting needs?" Her eyes hardened as she stood to face him squarely. "Well sir, do not think that you are the only one capable of deceit." Her mind raced as the lies fell into place. "Carlota got her money from you the same way I got my passage to England. It's a pity your brains lie in your breeches or you might have seen what a lovestruck fool you were."

"I don't believe you, Shannon. You are a poor liar." He grabbed her shoulders and yanked her in his arms, punishing her lips for the cruel words they spoke. His fingers locked in her hair and he groaned at the taste of her. He would not relent until her struggles ceased. Then slowly he lifted his lips from hers and gazed into blue ice that chilled him to his soul.

"If you are quite through, I should like to go wash the animal sweat from my person. Dinner will be served shortly." Her words were low and filled with venom.

His mind recoiled from the impact of her words and wounded pride smothered his desperation for her understanding and surfaced in its cornered fury. He stiffened and dropped his arms to his side

269

appraising her with barely restrained hostility.

"Madame, compared to you, Corrinne is a saint. You are your father's daughter . . . a slayer in your own right with a tongue as sharp and vicious as your own blade. That the angel in your aunt's portrait could have spawned you is indeed a blasphemy."

Shannon unleashed her pent-up emotion and the sound of her hand striking his face cracked in the tense silence of the room. He made no effort to stop her as she whirled away from him to hide her tears and pushed through the folding doors to flee to her room.

She nearly knocked Brian over as she climbed the stairs, snapping at him to release her when he tried to steady her. He stood at the rail stunned as her petite figure dashed down the hall and retreated behind the heavy oak door of her room. Assuming that Morgan Hawke had created this sudden change in humor, he started to resume his descent to confront the man, when Hawke stormed out of the parlor. His face was like a thundercloud as he strode to the door and let himself out, closing it with a resounding crash.

The young man let his breath out slowly. Perhaps it was just as well . . . To have crossed Morgan Hawke in his departing mood would have been folly. The Lord of Snowden was a formidable opponent in any field. Brian was intrigued with the strained relationship between his cousin and the Lord of Snowden. That he had sensed hostility, nay jealousy in the daring Morgan Hawke was certain. He smiled to himself as he went into the parlor and poured another brandy. Somehow the prospect of thwarting the man whom his father so often threw in his face as an example to follow pleased him almost as much as the means to accomplish such a feat—developing a closer relationship with his most beguiling cousin.

Chapter Sixteen

The day Morgan Hawke left for Snowden, Shannon had not yet left the seclusion of her room. She declined to take meals with the rest of the family and spent her time reading over the faded letters and journals of her past and crying herself into fitful sleep. Her sudden depression concerned her new family and her aunt was beside herself with worry.

"Dear, if you do not eat more than a morsel or two I fear you shall become ill." Her aunt's eyes were full of dismay as she surveyed the picked-over plate of food on the tray the maid had brought up to her. "You are so pale from being shut up in here . . . I . . . please go with Brian this afternoon. The air at the park will do you good."

Shannon raised her gaze dully to the kind woman standing over her and forced a smile. "I don't feel like riding. I'm still sore from the last time."

"But of course you are, dear. That is normal when one doesn't ride often. I fear I should be crippled if I tried it at my age, but when I was your age I cut a fine figure on horse, if I do say so myself." Aunt Harriet looked off dreamily as she reminisced. "As a matter of fact, I met your Uncle Edward in the same park. He was quite a dashing fellow in his white uniform."

Shannon half-listened as she rose and crossed to the window to stare out at the river. Perhaps her aunt was right about fresh air, she mused, but she would take it in the gardens behind the mansion where she could be alone. The thought of having to socialize, to put up a bright front was overwhelming. There was too much hurt to hide right now. She glanced around as she felt her aunt's hand on her shoulder.

"Dear, if you would like to talk sometime, please know I would gladly listen."

Shannon realized as she looked into the woman's eyes that her aunt was as agonized as she was. Impulsively the girl turned and hugged the woman affectionately. Shannon's voice trembled as she spoke. "If my mother had lived, I know she would have been as kind and understanding as you are, Aunt Harriet."

It seemed natural for Shannon to release her misery on the soft and comforting shoulders of the sweet woman who held her and wept also because she had finally reached the terrified child within the young woman who tried to be so brave in her new role in life. Her husband had told her of the bloody invasion, how Shannon had nearly been killed herself trying to save the dying man she thought to be her father.

That he had allowed her to travel unchaperoned with Lord Hawke was a mistake that would have been rectified once he discovered her true identity, but his ship was separated from the *Sea Lady* and they missed their rendezvous at Isle de Los. Feminine intuition told her that there were deep reasons for her niece's sudden compliance to go to a strange home with her and her husband and avoid the man who had rescued her from such a horrible existence. Perhaps in time, the girl would share her heavy burden with her, but for now she needed comfort.

Shannon drew away, her tears exhausted. She could not cause this dear woman any more alarm than she already had. "Aunt Harriet, I promise I will go out with Brian tomorrow afternoon. Today I think I will just stroll around the lovely gardens in the back. I haven't taken time to see them except from this window."

"And you'll join us for supper this evening?" her aunt asked hopefully.

"I promise."

After another hug, her aunt left Shannon to dress. As she bathed and slipped on one of her new gowns that had been hurriedly put together for her by the women at the dress shop, she began to feel guilty about the way she had stayed secluded in her room. Whatever she felt, she must consider the feelings of these kind and wonderful people.

The dark gold hue of her dress matched the leaves that fell listlessly to the grounds as she strolled along a neatly trimmed path lined with brilliant beds of fall flowers. About her shoulders was draped a woolen shawl her aunt had loaned her, as her cloak was still too heavy for the afternoons warmed by the sun. She noticed a gardener working on a bed at the opposite side of the gardens and thought nostalgically of Marie, for they both worked with the same diligence.

When she reached the edge of one of the perfectly rectangular ponds, she was spotted by the tame ducks who swam toward her expectantly for a treat. She smiled as she reached in the pocket sewn in a slash at the side of her heavy skirt and withdrew bits of stale bread the women in the kitchen had given her when she stopped by there on her way out. As they quacked and waddled about her skirt demandingly, another memory of her voyage on the *Sea Lady* surfaced. Would she never be free of the ship and its captain, she wondered miserably.

The ducks followed her a short distance toward the river before they realized that she had no more food for them and returned to their ponds in a disorganized babble. The closer she got to the small dock, the cooler the breeze seemed to be from the moving water and she pulled her shawl tighter. When she reached the end of the pier, she sat on the edge with her feet hanging over the side and stared at her reflection in the water.

She did favor her mother, she thought indignantly, in spite of what Morgan Hawke had said. More than ever she wanted to be like her. She wanted to show the man that she could be an angelic lady like her mother. She wanted to make him regret his cruel words and the feast at the Banqueting Hall would be the perfect time to do so as she had been told he would present her to the King.

The unexpected appearance of Brian's reflection beside hers made her start. He leaned down quickly and seized her waist as she moved toward the water. Upon realizing she was not going to slide off the edge he released her. "You must wait until a storm before you can fish with your bare hands," he teased. "New gown?"

"Yes. Mrs. Benson delivered it this morning. She's really been anxious to please."

"And well she should. Mother and her friends support the woman!" Brian snorted indignantly. "But she's done a lovely job. Stand up, turn around." He helped Shannon to her feet and she turned obediently. "It is almost as lovely as you are, cousin,"

"Thank you," Shannon replied modestly. "Brian, do you think I look like my mother . . . I mean really like her."

"Of course, it's uncanny! It's all anyone who has seen you talks about," he informed her. "Of course, none of us have had the pleasure of your company

274

since your visit with Lord Hawke."

"I wasn't really fishing with my bare hands," Shannon retorted avoiding the subject. "Although it's something I do enjoy . . . with a line," she added quickly.

"Well, when there's been a heavy storm the river becomes so muddy one can scoop haddock from the bridge and docks with bare hands." He resigned himself to follow her suit. "Can you do that in Nose' Be?"

Shannon was incredulous as she shook her head. "You're teasing me," she accused.

"Indeed not. I assure you that when we have a downpour over a period of time, you can fish with your hands and I will show you personally when that happens again. Mud is washed from the banks into the Thames and fish swim to the surface and call out for you to pick them up for dinner."

Shannon laughed at her cousin. It was the first time she had been amused since their enjoyable afternoon. "You are good for me," she told him, sobering suddenly. "I enjoy your company."

"Well then, the next time you lock yourself away, you must keep me with you to lift your spirits." He grinned wickedly and put his forehead against hers, awaiting her reply.

"You are also outrageously silly." Shannon pushed him back and started for the house. When he caught up with her, she linked her arm in his. "Brian," she began hesitantly, "will you teach me how to dance the sort of dances they dance at balls and feasts?"

"The allemande? The minuet? Dear cousin, I shall be delighted. Although, I must admit, I am frightfully poor at the curtsy."

"Brian!" Shannon exclaimed in amusement. "Have you ever entertained a serious thought in mind?" She stopped short as he stepped in her path.

His eyes were intent on her own as he spoke.

"Most definitely, dear Shannon." He smiled and looked away briefly. "Although I must admit, I seldom get credit for them. Now," he sighed, switching back to the original subject, "we must engage mother on the harpsichord and if we can, we'll start your first lessons right after supper." He twitched her nose playfully and with his arm about her waist, walked her back to the house.

The evening of the feast at the Banquet Hall was upon them and Shannon was a bundle of nervous energy as Brian helped her from the Bedlowe coach in front of the stately building designed by Inigo Jokes, the son of a poor Welsh cloth-maker who studied in Italy and brought that classical influence into play at Whitehall. Brian pointed out the civilized facade with straight skylines and rows of pilasters. He was enamored with the symmetry of the windows, but Shannon hardly heard him as she looked with apprehension at the multi-storied building that towered above the surrounding structures.

Each evening the family gathered in the music room of the Bedlowe home and instructed the girl in the art of dance as well as the etiquette required in the presence of His Majesty, Charles II. The role playing proved an entertaining amusement and even the staid Admiral joined in the fun. Brian proved to be a hilarious version of the King, donning his father's wig and a beauty patch from his mother which he insisted on wearing on the tip of his nose. Shannon had teased that if the King appeared as ridiculous she would be hard-pressed to keep from laughing at his appearance.

Yet, now as Brian escorted her up the carpeted steps to the main entrance where uniformed sentries and doormen awaited, she feared she would most likely swoon at the King's feet rather than find amusement in his dress. The heavy satin-lined cloak blocked the cold night air and when they stepped inside, she was reluctant to part with it, wishing instead that she could shrink away within its folds. There was a blast of trumpets as the party ahead of them was announced.

She allowed a servant to remove her cloak and stood patiently before a mirror while another fussed to restore her hair to its order where the furred hood had mussed it. The hairdresser rearranged the large dark curls that had fallen out of place, taking care to adjust the pearled combs that adorned it just so. Another maidservant added a touch of color to her cheeks, Shannon's natural coloring having paled under her stress, and was about to administer to her lips as well, but the girl refused. She had nearly bitten them bloody as it was. She was certain her knees were wobbling noticeably as she and her aunt joined the men to be announced to the roomful of guests and His Majesty Charles II.

Lord Morgan Hawke of Snowden sat at His Majesty's left with the Lady Elaine between him and his King and his fiancée and her father on the opposite side. He was engaged in conversation with the jubilant monarch when the trumpeters interrupted them.

"Master Brian Bedlowe of Kenton Place and Lady Shannon Devage of Sterling Court."

He was speechless as Brian Bedlowe escorted the vision of loveliness down the long length of scarlet carpet that ended at the King's table. Her gown was fitted to her to show the fullness of her bosom within modest limitations and her waist inspired him to want to see if his hands would indeed encircle it. The white brocade shimmered in the lights of the chandeliers in startling contrast to her dark hair that beckoned to be pulled down about her bared shoulders edged by a strip of white fur that decorated the plunging neckline and belled sleeves. A pearl choker adorned the graceful curve of her neck and he ached to bury his face there hungrily.

The clearing of the royal throat reminded him of his duty and broke the hypnotic trance. He moved around the edge of the table and met the couple halfway down the length of the hall. He offered Shannon his arm and she placed a trembling hand on it as she met his gaze with wide eyes glazed with anxiety. It reminded him of her wild and frightened look the day he had kissed her in the hidden cave and he wondered that she might break away and flee the room. They left Brian behind to be seated by a servant and approached the standing figure of the royal monarch of England.

"There is nothing to be frightened of," he assured her, placing his hand over hers. It was warm in contrast to her cold one.

Shannon could not respond. She stared ahead at the stately figure and was grateful for the support of Hawke's arm. King Charles II was richly dressed in a gold brocade long jacket, velvet breeches and silk netherstocks. He wore a great black wig of falling curls and gold rings adorned almost every finger on both hands. He seemed to loom ahead of them and when she heard Morgan Hawke present her, she lowered her eyes to his buckled shoes and curtsied as she had been tutored. She inadvertently held Hawke's hand in a deathgrip and did not release it until the hand of the King of England claimed her other.

"We are pleased to meet the granddaughter of our late and most loyal subject, Sir Robert Sterling." Charles brought her to her feet and placed her hand on his arm to escort her to her honored seat at the right of his.

"It is an honor, your majesty." She repeated automatically the practiced words. Her eyes darted to the side seeking out Brian's approving look and returned them to the King.

When they reached his chair, Charles stopped to introduce her to the gracious lady seated next to him. She was taller than Shannon and slender with black hair touched only slightly by gray. Her dark blue eyes met Shannon's and before the King spoke, Shannon knew the woman to be Morgan Hawke's mother.

"Lady Shannon, please meet Lady Elaine Hawke of Snowden."

As Shannon curtsied the woman brought her to her feet and bestowed a gentle kiss on her forehead. "My Morgan has told me of your beauty, but he could not do you justice, dear child. I am delighted to meet you at last."

A sharp intake of breath diverted her attention momentarily as Corrinne swelled with indignation, but Shannon smiled under the warm gaze of the woman and spoke.

"You are very kind, milady."

"Gads, a maiden's blush is as refreshing as a good liquor and we are privileged to have both!" Charles exclaimed, raising his glass to Shannon. "Milady, we welcome you to this Court."

Glasses throughout the hall were raised to Shannon and she was comforted by Brian's enthusiastic cheer from the other end of the King's table. Charles showed her to the seat beside him and clapped his hands to alert the many servants to begin serving the meal. Her aunt and uncle spoke briefly to the King and he heartily congratulated the Admiral on his part in the capture of the pirates from Nose' Be. Shannon sat quietly at his side so torn with mixed emotions that when the sumptuous meal was placed before them, she could hardly eat.

Brian was very attentive and coaxed her through, seeing that her wine glass did not empty and by the time the King signaled for the musicians to begin their music she was giggling merrily at his various quips about the staunch lords and ladies about the room. It was not until she felt the presence of the royal hand on hers, that the nervous tension consumed her again.

"We would be pleased to dance with you, Lady Shannon."

Shannon froze as the King awaited her acceptance and felt her color drain from her face. Brian had warned her that she would be expected to dance with Charles and had taught her the intricate steps of the minuet so that she moved gracefully without thinking, but face to face with the King she fought the panic that showed in her eyes.

"Your Highness, my cousin is overwhelmed by your attention. It is not her intention to insult you." Brian nudged her gently as he smiled at the quizzical face of the monarch.

Charles rose from his seat and pulled Shannon to her feet. As he placed his hand in the small of her back he leaned over and whispered in her ear. "Are you so frightened of us that you cannot speak?"

"Sir, I have only just learned this dance and am frightened of stepping on both of you," she replied lowly, crying out in dismay as she realized her blunder.

The loud laughter of the King drew great attention as he led Shannon to the center of the hall. At his nod the musicians started the number again. Shannon curtsied to his bow, too horrified by her slip of the tongue to meet his gaze.

"Milady, we assure you if you should place a light

foot upon ours, we would hardly notice and it would not be the first affront to our feet."

As he took her hand and walked gracefully together, Shannon chanced a look in his direction and was grateful for the royal pardon he blessed her with both in word and with his eyes. She returned his smile with a genuine one of relief and followed his lead with ease, her anxiety disarmed by the royal charm. Other dancers followed the monarch into the center of the hall and soon the room was graced with a brilliant display of moving color.

As was his royal duty, Charles II moved on to converse and dance with the ladies of the court and left Shannon to the comfortable company of Brian Bedlowe, who introduced her to innumerable people until their faces all began to look alike. From time to time Shannon caught glimpses of Lord Hawke dancing with his beautiful fiancée.

Corrinne's swaying skirt of the palest pink was matched by tiny bows placed in her upswept blond curls. The decolletage of the gown drew much attention to her powdered breasts bound tightly and supported by a corset. She stared up dreamily at the handsome lord dressed in a royal blue doublet and matching pants as he walked her through the stately dance and Shannon's heart wretched painfully.

"Lady Shannon, are you feeling ill?"

Shannon turned from the dancers to face Lady Elaine and shook her head. "I think the excitement of my first ball is taking its toll on me, milady."

"It all must be so new and strange to you after living on that island most of your life. I should love to hear of it."

Talking to Lady Elaine Hawke came as easily as the wine that Brian occasionally handed her. As opposed to most of the people who inquired about her previous home, she did not seem interested in

Shannon's background for the purpose of criticism, but because she was genuinely interested. She asked the girl about Marie and her father, remarking that they had done well in bringing up such a charming and intelligent young woman so far removed from civilized society.

"I do want to personally invite you to our Christmas ball. We usually have our friends and neighbors stay for the week before the holiday to hunt and spend time together. It's quite a good time really and I would love to show you Snowden." The sincerity in her voice touched Shannon. "Of course you'll accompany your family. Harriet and Edward have always attended."

"I would be delighted," Shannon replied, reluctant to turn the gracious lady down.

"Good! I know we shall be such good friends," she said, hugging Shannon unexpectedly. "Morgan has told me so many wonderful things about you."

The music changed and before she could recover from the surprising comment, Brian wrapped his arms about her waist from behind and claimed her for the dance. As he swept her through those who were retreating from the dance floor, they met Morgan Hawke and Corrinne. Shannon looked past them, ignoring the venomous look from her stepsister but she could not help but overhear her words.

"She has the nerve to imitate us when everyone here knows what she really is."

"Don't pay any attention to her, Shannon," Brian warned her as he placed his hand on her waist and raised her other. He pulled her to him and winked to rally her spirits. "The woman is plainly jealous . . . insanely so, I would say."

But she has him, Shannon thought miserably and said with a sigh, "I hardly think so."

"Shannon darling, open your eyes! No man here

who can still breathe can take his eyes off of you. I thought Charles himself would devour you instead of his meal." He lowered his voice as he swung her about gallantly to the allemande. "Both of him!"

Shannon could not help but laugh in spite of her indignation. "He told you!"

"His Royal Highness is enchanted as anyone who knows you must be. He was charmed by your ready wit."

The dance ended and Harriet Bedlowe insisted on showing her niece off to a group of her friends while Brian sought more refreshments. Shannon was cordial as she responded to their questions about her life as a pirate's daughter, but she could see they clearly pitied her unfortunate upbringing and it irritated her. She needed no pity, nor was she ashamed of her past.

"Shannon dear, do come over here for a moment." Lady Elaine beckoned her over to where she stood with her son. The two of them together were a regal pair and the resemblance was unmistakable. "I've told Morgan that you have agreed to come to Snowden and he for some reason finds it difficult to believe. I thought perhaps if he heard it from your own lips . . ."

Shannon met his inscrutable gaze and raised her eyes to him demurely. "I was always taught to listen to my parents."

"Milady, where you are concerned I do not know what to believe."

"Morgan Hawke! If the lady should refuse you right now, I should not blame her," his mother chastised indignantly.

"Lady Elaine, I still hold to my acceptance of your invitation. I would enjoy visiting you at your home," Shannon assured her, pleased at the surprised look she invoked in Hawke's face.

He took her hand and raised it to his lips bringing an abrupt end to her satisfaction. "Since you are predisposed to acceptance, I would be honored to dance this selection with you, milady."

Before she could answer his hands were on her back directing her toward the milling couples who waited for the musicians to start another allemande. His closeness as he held her to him was disturbing and her body reveled in the familiarity. Her knees weakened and he nearly carried her as he swung her around causing the room to spin dizzily. She kept her silence, hoping that the dance would go on so that she could have his strong arms about her for the rest of the evening. This was borrowed time, she told herself as she closed her eyes and swayed against him, not noticing that he was moving her through a side door to a long corridor.

When the music faded, she opened her eyes to the dimly lit hallway and her heart leapt as he lowered his lips on hers longingly. She could not bring herself to struggle as her senses demanded the satisfaction so long denied them in the lonely bed of her boudoir. This was what she wanted. She wanted him to desire her, to hunger for her as she did for him.

"Morgan . . ." she moaned softly as she leaned against one of the classic columns and felt its coolness against her burning skin.

"Damn you, Shannon," he cursed as he drew away from her, his voice ragged with passion. "I want you as I have never wanted another."

He seized her roughly and his lips hurt her mouth. It was a sweet pain, and she parted her lips, inviting him to forget the infliction of punishment and taste of her. His hands pushed the fur-trimmed neckline of her gown completely off her shoulders and his kisses burned her neck and bosom. Borrowed time kept echoing in the back of her mind as he dragged her

284

deeper into the shadows of the deserted hallway.

"Morgan? Morgan, where are you?" Corrinne's voice filled the empty corridor as he pushed away from Shannon and put his finger to her lips. "Morgan, the King is looking for you."

He straightened and in the glow from a far-off lantern, Shannon saw the accusation in his eyes and drew back against the column in disbelief. Temptress, they shouted mutely. She shook her head in denial as he wiped his hands on his hips as if to remove any trace of her and left her alone in the darkness to join his fiancée.

Sinking to the floor in desolation, she leaned her head back against the pillar and cried silently. The desire that he awakened in her tortured her body and her weakness for him tortured her mind. She cursed him for saving her life so that she would know this terrible pain of love and betrayal.

When her eyes were dry and her emotions spent, she slowly rose to her feet and attempted to rearange her gown. A numbness set in as she made her way down the length of the corridor avoiding the lights to hide her swollen eyes. Perhaps if she could find her way to the main entrance a servant might fetch her cloak and hail a coach to take her home. Her second thought reminded her that she had no purse and dashed the idea of a quiet retreat.

Left with little alternative, Shannon found a deserted corner near the entry and sank onto a settee richly upholstered in red velvet that stood in front of a window dressed in the same fashion. She parted the drapes and stared out at the London street lined with coaches waiting to carry the jubilant guests home. There appeared to be a slight mist surrounding them like the fog that sometimes hung over the lagoon, but it was a chilling sight and Shannon rubbed her arms under the voluminous sleeves of her gown and shuddered.

"I thought you might still be here." The voice of her stepsister was colder than the fog outside.

Shannon closed her eyes not wanting another confrontation and ignored her, keeping her back to the woman as she pretended to study the street.

"You needn't think that I did not see Morgan sweep you away from the others. He has had eyes for no other this night, and I resent that, sister." The tremor in Corrinne's voice made Shannon look her way. Tears welled in the green eyes as they made their ugly accusation. "Is there nothing left of mine that does not belong to you?"

Shannon was overcome with remorse as she realized that she was not the only one who suffered because of the Lord of Snowden. "I want nothing of him, Corrinne. I detest his touch," she lied.

"You seemed hungry enough for it to throw yourself at him as he held you. I hardly saw protest when he took you away from the others!" the woman said vindictively. "Well, I won't let you take him, Lady Shannon." She spoke Shannon's name as if it were a curse. "I will ruin your prim facade of innocence."

Shannon gasped as Corrinne tore the satin rose from her own shoulders and pulled the draped sleeve off to reveal her white skin. "What are you doing?" she exclaimed in horror.

Corrinne raked her own exposed body with her nails so that red welt appeared and then shrieked, and flew at Shannon shaking her wildly.

Shannon grabbed at her wrists and held the long nails at bay as she forced her deranged stepsister to her knees in self defense. "You're mad!" she grunted as the woman spat at her.

She glanced up as the commotion drew attention from the archway to the main hall. Corrinne began to cry for help and struggled desperately. Horrified, Shannon released her and backed against the wall as her stepsister collapsed in sobs on the plush carpet. It was a nightmare she thought incredulously as Morgan Hawke burst through the gathering on-lookers and stared first at her and then at Corrinne.

"That pirate wench attacked me!" Corrinne sobbed reaching out and grabbing Hawke's leg.

"She's lying!" Shannon exclaimed, imploring him to believe her with her eyes.

Morgan Hawke never took his eyes from Shannon as he reached down and helped Corrinne to her feet.

"I never touched her, except to hold her wrists . . ."

"Then how do you explain my torn gown and this!" Corrinne jerked her finger at the angry welts on her porcelain skin. "You're a murdering bitch who seeks to steal everything I have."

The familiar flash in Shannon's eyes warned Hawke. He stepped between the two women as Shannon sprang at Corrinne and caught her clenched fists. Shannon fought fiercely as he held her subdued. "Let me go, you bastard!" she cursed, trying to kick him through the volumes of petticoats.

"Shannon!" His voice thundered with reproval as he managed with some difficulty to hold the girl.

"If that she bitch insists that I am a murderous pirate, by God, I'll oblige her!"

"Shannon!" Brian Bedlowe pushed his way through the small cluster and stopped short as he saw the small figure in white fighting and kicking at the Lord of Snowden while the disheveled Corrinne stood behind him pale as a ghost.

Shannon ceased to struggle as she saw a friendly face and pulled away from Hawke to run to her cousin. She buried her face in his chest as his arms went about her. "She's lying," Shannon mumbled into the heavy cloth of his jacket, refusing to let anyone see the hurt on her face. "Please take me home. Those two deserve each other."

Brian never took his arms from her until the servant arrived with her cloak. Then gently he wrapped it about her trembling shoulders and buttoned it. He listened to her halting whispers of what had happened and resisted to urge to throttle the swooning woman resting her head against Morgan Hawke's shoulder. Much of the group that had happened upon the quarrel returned to the festivities in the main hall by the time the servant announced their coach was waiting.

Morgan Hawke watched reluctantly as the couple left. He promised to give their regrets to the King and tell the Admiral and Mrs. Bedlowe that Brian would send the coach back for them. When he was at last left in peace with his shaken fiancée, he turned a cold look of steel on her pale face and spoke harshly.

"Don't ever tempt Shannon too far, Corrinne. I know her well. She is not as adept as you at the games you play, but she has a temper to be reckoned with and a punch to back it up."

"How well I know, darling," Corrinne whispered fearfully, unaware that she had admitted her guilt until disgust showed in the deep blue eyes that charged her unmercifully. Her fingers touched the scratches on her shoulder in defense.

"Shannon did not do that. She may have bloodied your lip or blacked your eye, but fists do not leave long fingernail scratches."

"Just how well do you know my sister, Morgan?" Green eyes narrowed as she took the offensive in desperation. They widened, however, when his expression hardened and she felt the sting of his words.

"Better than I ever knew you." With that, he left her abruptly and joined the other guests.

Chapter Seventeen

The warmth of the fire on the hearth in the sewing parlor was a startling contrast to the cold wind that relentlessly whipped the trees outside Kenton Place. No barges enjoyed the bright afternoon sun on the river, only crafts that provided the livelihood of their pilots braved the choppy water. The light through the blown glass of the large window was sufficient to permit Shannon to see the painfully small stitches she made on the embroidery clearly.

The sharp point of the needle jabbed her finger and she bit her tongue and cut her eyes over at her aunt working serenely in her chair by the fireplace. The woman was smiling as she drew out the length of thread and dipped expertly into the hoop-bound material. Every lady of quality took pride in her needlework, she said. It was a favorite pastime and often women would gather in a group and talk as they sewed their handiwork. Shannon shook her head in aggravation and took a deep breath to renew her effort. She would much rather be riding or working with the gardener, she thought as she shoved the needle in again.

"Milady, you have a visitor," the doorman announced politely.

Shannon glanced up and was surprised to see that the green clad gentleman was speaking to her.

"Mistress Corrinne Devage would like to see you."

"Oh dear!" Aunt Harriet exclaimed, dropping her needlework to her lap in dismay. Brian had informed his aunt and uncle of the confrontation between Corrinne and Shannon and the woman had been quite put out by Corrinne's incriminating performance.

Shannon wondered what her stepsister could be up to as she gladly put aside her hoop and needle and rose from her high-backed chair. She had neither seen nor heard from Morgan Hawke since the night at the Banquet Hall although she had received a note from Lady Elaine expression her regret over the incident and her sincere hope to see Shannon at the Winter Ball.

"Where should I see her?" Shannon asked her aunt.

"Right here is fine, dear. I need to see the cook about supper anyway." Her aunt stopped at the door. "I'll send in tea and some cakes and . . . do take care."

Shannon nodded and instructed the doorman to show her stepsister in. Her hands were clasped nervously as the young woman entered the room and stopped before her. It was apparent from the apprehension in Corrinne's green eyes that she felt the same way. Her lips were trembling as she waited expectantly for Shannon to speak.

"Why do you want to see me?" Shannon asked bluntly, disposing with useless amenities.

Corrinne hesitated nervously.

"For heaven's sake, Corrinne, I am not going to attack you, although you damned well deserve it."

"Shannon, can you ever forgive me? I . . . I have been beside myself since that night." Tears welled in the sea of deep green and she hurriedly opened her purse to search for her embroidered handkerchief. As she dabbed at her eyes, Shannon stood mute and bewildered. "I . . . I was out of my mind with jealousy. So much h . . . has changed since Morgan brought you here, and mother . . ."

"Is that why you came . . . to ask my forgiveness?" Shannon asked warily, unable to believe the sudden change in character. At Corrinne's nod, she motioned for the distraught woman to sit on the settee and she resumed her seat by the window. "Then you have it," she said at last.

Corrinne smiled and closed her eyes in relief. "I have been trying to muster enough courage to face you this whole week. You cannot imagine my horror at my own actions. I have been so cruel to you."

"You have," Shannon agreed. "But I have heard that you have been under a lot of stress these last weeks. Perhaps that is the reason."

"I always wanted a sister . . . really. And now that I have one, I promise I will do my utmost to be worthy of one." Corrinne reached her gloved hand across the table and touched Shannon's. "I have so much to be grateful for."

Shannon looked at the small hand and raised her eyebrow. "Why have you changed your mind? I recall your saying that you hoped it was all a mistake."

The maidservant opened the doors and brought in the tray of tea and cakes Aunt Harriet had promised. Corrinne offered to pour it and Shannon allowed her the privilege, still unsure of the etiquette required. When the servant left, the guest held her cup daintily and spoke.

"You have been more than generous with us. You might have thrown us out had you chosen to, but you did not."

"Your father is mine. Even if I could not tolerate you, I could not do that to him," Shannon replied incredulously.

"He is your father, not mine. He is my stepfather. But no matter. The fears I had of you have certainly been allayed by your kindness. I know now that you would do nothing to hurt me."

Shannon looked out the window in exasperation. She could handle her stepsister when she was hostile, but teary-eyed and full of remorse left her perplexed and uncomfortable. The girl's mother had just died and then Shannon's arrival removed her security. It was certainly understandable that she might react in such a way. Then there was the Lord of Snowden. Corrinne loved Morgan Hawke as much as she did. She had his love first. So much so that she acted irrationally in an effort to keep him.

"We should be the best of friends . . . not enemies."

"We can try," Shannon relented.

"Then you must come to your home. Sterling Court is one of the loveliest homes on the outskirts of the city."

"I don't think I am quite ready for that. Although I would like to see it," Shannon admitted. She was comfortable with the Bedlowes and her aunt would be devastated if she should decide to leave.

"Then come with me for supper this evening. Father would be delighted. He's been waiting for you to show some sign of acceptance toward him. He doesn't want to push himself on you." Corrinne's beseeching look touched Shannon.

"I would like that." Shannon smiled and replaced her tea cup on its saucer. She rose from her chair. "I must tell Aunt Harriet so that she will not plan on me for supper."

"Then I shall be going." Corrinne stood up and

hugged Shannon. "Father will be so surprised," she told Shannon in delight.

Shannon crossed to the door ahead of her stepsister and folded it back as a brown-jacketed arm grabbed her waist and pulled her into the hallway. "Brian!" she squealed, startled by the sudden attack. Her response invoked a similar one from Corrinne who stood behind her with her hand to her chest.

"Damnation, what takes you here?" he exclaimed upon seeing his fair-haired cousin. He released Shannon guiltily.

"Why cousin, how good to see you, too," Corrinne exclaimed looking from Brian to Shannon and smiling at what she saw.

"You have a nerve coming here after that little charade you played at Shannon's expense."

Shannon placed a hand on Brian's arm. "She came to apologize, Brian. It's all settled." She saw her cousin's eyes narrow as he surveyed Corrinne who demurely placed her hand on his other arm. "Shannon and I are going to be the best of friends, cousin. Perhaps we also might reconcile our differences?"

"Corrinne, if there was not a lady present, I would have a most appropriate reply to your suggestion." His biting words hit their mark and for a moment an angry spark flickered in Corrinne's eyes. It faded with a becoming smile.

"Shannon dear, I look forward to seeing you this evening and if you would like, you may bring our rude cousin. He can be charming company when he chooses."

Shannon placed a restraining arm on Brian and then left him behind to show Corrinne to the door. She instructed the manservant to advise her aunt of her change in plans and went to seek her cousin who had disappeared from the hallway. When she found him in the sewing parlor, Brian was pacing the floor impatiently. As she entered the room, he walked up to her and placed his hands on her shoulders to confront her.

"You, madam, are as mad as she is!" he accused.

"I could hardly say no, Brian. She was in such a state . . . and she has been through a lot," Shannon pointed out in Corrinne's defense. "And I want to see Sterling Court. I have been in London for weeks now and have yet to see my real home."

"This is your real home, Shannon," Brian told her, his eyes warm as he gazed at her. "Not some brick building documented by seals and papers, but by love."

"I am just going for dinner . . . not to live there," she explained, pinching his chin playfully. "Are you going out this evening?"

He leaned his forehead against hers and grinned. "Are you propositioning me?"

"Only if you behave yourself. I'll not have you being rude to Corrinne when she is trying so hard to make up for the way she has been," Shannon warned soberly.

"I promise to be nice to Corrinne if she is nice to you."

"Shannon, I've just heard you're not going to be here for supper . . ." Aunt Harriet stopped as she saw the couple. "Brian, I didn't know you were home, dear."

Brian dropped his hands and straightened before he approached his mother and gave her a peck on the cheek. "I am only just here, and will not be here for supper either."

"Are you going out again tonight?"

"Not to the gambling house, Mother," he assured

her. "I'm going to Sterling Court with Shannon to protect her from the fair-haired viper who for some reason has sheathed her fangs and apologized for her dastardly behavior."

Again Shannon explained the reason for Corrinne's visit and her desire to see her family home. Then she excused herself to retire to her room so that she might dress for the occasion.

When Brian assisted her from the coach, lanterns on either side of the large white door lighted the front of the red brick mansion. It was as grand as Kenton Place in size and the windows were like bright eyes staring at her as she stood on the semi-circled steps of her grandfather's home. She regretted that she had not postponed the invitation until she could see the house in the daylight where it would be less imposing.

The doorman announced their arrival when they entered the walnut-paneled hallway with the wide stairway that led to the second floor. The rail and balusters were intricately carved and raised panels ran the length of the rise in symmetrical diagonals. The landing was so large as to be furnished, and a large portrait of a gentleman and lady hung over it crowned by a fan-shaped window that sparkled in the light of a large crystal chandelier.

"Shannon, I am so glad that you have at last come home." Her father emerged from his study. She accepted a hug from him and allowed him to help her with her cloak. As he handed it to the maidservant, he swept his eyes over her and shook his head. "I am still awed each time I see you, child. So if I stare, do not think me rude."

"I understand, Father. I am sometimes struck by

the resemblance myself. If only I could remember her," Shannon sighed.

"You were so young when she was killed." He touched his hand to her cheek, as if trying to be sure that she was real. "We left you asleep covered by her cloak, and sought to hold out against the rogues at the gallery entrance. Dear God, it was a nightmare. He turned abruptly and took his nephew's extended hand. "Brian, forgive my rude manners! I was distracted for the moment. Welcome to Sterling Court."

"I can find that understandable, sir. Your daughter is a lovely distraction for any of us."

"Sir, . . . Father," Shannon corrected herself, "did you know him well?" She nodded toward the portrait.

"Only that he was a stubborn old coot who made your mother miserable. I only keep the picture up there out of respect for the house rather than for him. I could never forgive him for what he did to Jenny." The dark eyes were hard as they appraised the man who would deny him his fortune even in death.

They retired to a parlor decorated in the muted shades of blue with damask drapes and upholstery contrasted with white braid trim. A large oriental carpet covered the oak plank flooring, darkened with the wear of time. Her father served Brian and himself a brandy while he gave Shannon a glass of sherry. By the time they emptied their glasses, Corrinne swept into the room in a gold taffeta gown and apologized for keeping them waiting so long.

She hugged Shannon warmly and extended her hand to Brian. "I see our cousin managed to divert you from your bachelor pursuits to join us, Brian."

"Corrinne, you are lovely as ever," he commented politely as he pressed her hand to his lips. He ignored

296

her remark and glanced at Shannon to be sure she noted that he kept his word.

"Why thank you, Brian!" Her eyes sparkled as she slipped her arm in his. "Father, would you please escort Shannon. Harrington has informed me that dinner is ready."

The long banquet table was set in silver and china bearing the same coat of arms as the crest that hung over the mantel of the fireplace. Shannon was seated opposite Brian while her father and stepsister presided at each end. The conversation was cordial and Shannon found herself enjoying the company more than she had thought. Her father spoke of the family holdings and of the various ways he had expanded them through the years to include other properties such as a summer house in Dover.

"It's a pretty cottage on the sea," Corrinne told Shannon. "But I hate to leave London for too long. It's so far away from everyone."

"Corrinne is ever the social princess," her father teased.

"Father, I adore London. I simply cannot imagine wanting to leave the city for too long!"

"What will you do when you marry Lord Hawke? He's not the sort to be led about by the nose," Brian pointed out. "You'll find your wings clipped, cousin."

Shannon's stomach clenched at the mention of the impending marriage. It was something she would have to adjust to, she told herself unconvincingly.

"It's ironic that my Morgan saved my own sister," Corrinne reflected, cleverly avoiding Brian's directive and changing the subject. "I am sure he had no idea at the time that you would be his sister by marriage."

"I'm sure the thought had not crossed his mind,"

Shannon remarked wryly, putting down her fork as her appetite slipped away.

"I do hope that you and he can reconcile your differences before our marriage. It makes it very difficult when those you love are at odds."

"I will try not to cause you concern, Corrinne, although I fear our differences are irreconcilable." Shannon toyed with the handle of her spoon as she felt all eyes upon her. "Your fiancé as much as killed the man who raised me and the man I had hoped to share my life with. I cannot forgive him for that." It was a lie they would have to accept, she thought as she detected a glimmer of satisfaction in her sister— and Morgan Hawke's lies *had* killed her hope for happiness.

Reprieve came as the servant cleared away the dessert dishes. The men retired to the parlor while Corrinne showed Shannon the ancestral home of the Sterling family. She was clearly proud of the manor in which she had been raised, and for good reason.

The mansion was elegantly decorated, three stories in all. Yet, as beautiful as it was, Shannon felt no warmth to beckon her, only emptiness and depression. It was the Devage home. As Corrinne showed her the portrait done after her mother's and stepfather's wedding, she realized that Sterling Court could never be her home. Her mother had fled the big house and Shannon would not live there. It would forever be the Devages' to do with as they pleased, legalities or no, Shannon decided.

"Mother was so fragile. I fear I shall never get over her death," Corrinne mused aloud. "But Providence has sent in her place a sister. So I am most fortunate after all," she added, taking Shannon's hand and squeezing it affectionately.

When they returned to the parlor where the gentlemen had gathered, Morgan Hawke was among them. Corrinne rushed over to her fiancé and brushed his lips with hers, leaving Shannon standing awkwardly in the doorway.

"Father, why didn't you tell me Morgan was coming?" Corrinne chastised, not bothering to take her eyes from her young man's face.

"Your father did not know it, Corrinne. I have some rather pressing business with him," Hawke explained, looking past her at Shannon.

Shannon inadvertently clutched the folds of her dark blue gown as she turned from him to Brian. "I think it best that we leave, Brian. Your mother will be concerned if we are out too late."

"Don't rush on my account, Shannon. I do not want to drive you away from your home on your first visit," Hawke protested as Brian put aside his glass to rise. "What do you think of Sterling Court?"

"It is more than I expected, my lord." And no more my own than you, she thought miserably.

"Morgan, Shannon and I are going to be the best of friends. Aren't you just delighted?" Corrinne searched his face anxiously for approval.

"Well I am," Jonathan Devage spoke up before Hawke could reply and taking each of the girls by the hand. "I am blessed to have two such lovely daughters."

Hawke could not help but compare the two sisters as they stood side by side. They were as different as night and day. Shannon's dark hair and rosy complexion, almost too healthy for the day's fashion contrasted Corrinne's fair hair and porcelain skin. While Corrinne's eyes sparkled under his attention, Shannon's reflected a myriad of troubled emotions that twisted his soul and made him long to comfort her.

299

When Jonathan Devage showed Shannon and her escort to the door, the polite but familiar way Brian touched her made Hawke more determined to pursue his purpose in visiting at this late hour.

It took a while to convince Corrinne that his visit was purely business. When she finally came to that realization, she sullenly withdrew to her room to leave the men to their conversation, having no interest in the commercial affairs of either of them.

Jonathan Devage poured another brandy for each of them and retired to his chair near the warm hearth. He motioned for Hawke to take the matching chair opposite him and sipped his drink watching the dancing flames intently. Finally, he looked at Hawke and broke the silence.

"I know you are impatient, Morgan. But I fear it is still too soon. You saw how bizarre her reaction was to Shannon at the Banquet Hall." The man sighed tiredly. "I fear for her mental state."

"But what about Shannon?"

"Shannon is Jenny's daughter. I saw that the night she showed up in the Bedlowe parlor in breeches defying us all. If Nick Brennan did anything, he raised a fighter."

Hawke frowned and protested. "Yes, and it is that trait that makes her as unpredictable as Corrinne."

"Give Corrinne until Christmas. Give the girls a chance to know each other . . . become friends."

"I cannot see how that can be, sir!"

"Tell Shannon. Explain to her about Corrinne," Devage implored. "If things are the way you say they are between you, she'll understand."

Hawke snorted. "You do not know your daughter as I do, sir. She has condemned me in her mind and damned me to hell. Each time I try to speak to her . . . to reach her, she manages to rile me in such a way

300

that I . . ." He ran his hands through his dark hair in exasperation. He was unaccustomed to having to seek another man's approval. The great Lord of Snowden twisted in knots over a mere slip of a maid was something he resented and was helpless to prevent.

"I beseech you, Morgan, give her to Christmas. Tell Shannon. Solicit her as an ally. She's a strong girl and Corrinne is so delicate. I implore you."

Hawke shifted uncomfortably under the gaze of the man and it rankled him. He respected Jonathan Devage and felt upon his honor to grant the request. It was the least he could do under the circumstances. "I shall attempt to do so, sir," he relented, knowing as he spoke that his future father-in-law expected the impossible.

"You are doing the honorable thing, Morgan."

Hawke nodded mutely as he finished off the brandy. Honorable yes, and this honor might cost him his love.

Chapter Eighteen

Snowden was more beautiful than Morgan Hawke could possibly have described. It was a two-day ride by coach from London, nestled on the top of one of the rolling hills so richly adorned by checkered forests, fields and pastures. The great hall stood in the center of the gray stone manor and to each side were wings, each built around a courtyard that, under Lady Elaine's supervision, boasted the most artistic arrangements of shrubs and flowers.

"I only wish you could have seen them this summer, Shannon. I have had to cover so many of my plants since the first frosts."

Shannon could imagine the colorful display her hostess spoke of as she looked through the wide window that was part of the gallery separating the great hall from the courtyards. This south wall was almost entirely made up of windows and double doors. The heat of the sun warmed the wide furnished corridor through the glass uncovered in daylight hours by bound groups of draperies on each side of the partitions that would be unfurled on cool nights to seal off the drafts.

"You have a gift, milady, that even the harshness

of winter cannot completely hide," Shannon complimented sincerely. "I think I would love to see it in the
summer."

"You must! I have spent hours there simply trying
to absorb the beauty and tranquillity. When Morgan
was a small boy, it was there that I watched him play.
Of course, my flowers did not flourish quite as well
in those times, trodden by little feet," she explained,
"but my heart did."

The sparkle in Lady Elaine's eyes warmed Shannon and she envied Morgan Hawke for his fortune to
have such a mother. She turned her attention back to
the garden and tried to picture Lord Morgan Hawke
hiding among the giant rows of hedges and darting
through the covered flower beds and smiled at the
image she conjured in her mind. She could see a
small boy in disheveled finery startling his mother
with a play sword as he emerged from the bushes, his
blue eyes shining up at hers in delight.

"I have kept you long enough, dear," Lady Elaine
told her, as the picture in her mind vanished. "We
really should join the others."

There were thirty guests by the time the last arrived
just before supper was served in the great hall. It was
festively decorated with fresh pine and holly tied up
with red ribbons. The centerpiece of each table
consisted of beautifully arranged fruits and pastries
on tiered silver trays. Shannon sat with the Bedlowes
at the head of the line of tables to the right of Lord
Hawke's head table. Lord and Lady Flemington
shared their table and the names of the guests beyond
that Shannon could not seem to grasp although she
recognized their faces as having been at the Banquet
Hall.

When Corrinne appeared on Jonathan Devage's
arm at the last minute, heads could not help but turn.

Her sister had dressed in one of the new gowns she had picked out on a shopping trip they had shared together the week after Shannon's visit to Sterling Court. Mrs. Benson had created a masterpiece in ice blue draped over a darker blue fabric. Corrinne glanced at Shannon seeking her sister's approval. Shannon forced a smile and her sister's face brightened as she proceeded to take her place next to her fiancé.

In the past weeks, Corrinne had gone out of her way to make up for her initial treatment of Shannon so much so that Shannon had begun to feel smothered with sisterly affection that she found hard to return. Her guilt kept her from refusing her sister's invitations and many of the guests present who had witnessed the scene at the Banquet Hall were privy to the change in the girls' relationship as a result.

Shannon fingered the burnished gold fabric of her gown self-consciously. She had only ordered one gown for the Christmas Ball. The rest of her clothing was from the original purchase from Mrs. Benson. They were new enough she explained to her astonished sister, who required a completely new wardrobe for the visit. The white brocade ball gown was more than sufficient to satisfy her modest tastes.

Lady Flemington dominated the conversation with details of her recent illness while the Admiral and Aunt Harriet listened politely to the gray-haired matron. Shannon ate as best she could trying to swallow the delicious pheasant and to smother snickers as a result of Brian's inconspicuous mimicry of his mother's friend. She nearly choked as her cousin groaned lowly and cast a sideways glance to see Lady Flemington watching her in dismay.

"Lady Shannon, are you quite all right?" she

asked, peering from under heavy painted eyelids.

"I nearly strangled," Shannon apologized, "but I am fine now." She took a large swallow of wine to drown her amusement while her cousin watched her with disgusting composure.

"Oh look," one of the guests near the double doors that led into the gallery exclaimed, "it's snowing!"

"I hope this won't cancel out the hunt tomorrow," another guest called out merrily, lifting his glass as he enjoyed the fine spread and company his host provided. "I have a peregrine that is recently manned and broken that I am looking forward to trying in the field."

Shannon briefly met Morgan Hawke's gaze before forcing her attention to her plate as a mutual recollection brought color to her face. She attacked her food with renewed effort and was grateful when the meal was over so that she could avoid the scrutiny of her host.

Most of the women gathered in the ladies' parlor to talk while they worked at their handiwork. The men enoyed after dinner drinks over billiards in the game room. Shannon found herself with Corrinne as the sister insisted that she learn to play bassett. She declined politely, preferring to learn the game by observing her sister and her friends.

Leaving Corrinne engrossed in her game, Shannon found her way through the lighted corridor to the gallery. The scent of the fresh cut greenery adorned the doors and mantels filled the air throughout the manor. Echoes of the men's voices were faint from an adjoining hall as she stepped up to the double doors that opened into the courtyard. Through the glass panes she watched the large white flakes that peppered the night and fell softly to the garden that was just beginning to cover over. Faint lights from the windows illuminated the courtyard and the shining white dusting gave it a fairy-like appearance.

She resisted as long as she could before unbolting the door and lifting the latch. As she slipped through the opening she breathed the cold night air deeply, thrilled as the wet flakes hit her face and melted. The silence was as enchanting as the soft dust that she scooped up with her fingers. Curiously, she touched her tongue to it and let the melted snow trickle down her throat. As she made little designs on the brick walk her fingers protested at the icy cold, and she realized her slippers were becoming soaked.

When she started to rise she felt a cold chunk drop in the neckline of her back and straightened in a jump as she was spun around into a warm embrace. "Brian!" she cried out at the perpetual prankster, as she tried to loosen her dress enough to let it slip through. She wriggled with her forehead against his chest as he tried to help her. When there was nothing left except the damp spot at her waist where it had lodged, she raised her face to his to admonish him.

"Morgan!"

"It's our first snow, Shannon." His gaze was as warm as his arms that tightened about her when she thought to flee. "I will not let you run this time . . . or allow your futile lies to infuriate me."

"Please, Hawke, let me go." Her voice shook, but not from the snow that lay on her dark lashes and crowned her braided hair.

"Shannon, you will listen to me. I cannot let you leave until you hear me out." The pain in his words caused her to meet his eyes where it reflected. "I love you."

"You have no right to say that." Her heart embraced the words anxiously while her mind reminded her of the lies his lips had already spoken.

306

The scent of tobacco and brandy penetrated her senses as she buried her face in his jacket to avoid the temptation to fall victim to him in spite of her previous resolve to lock him out. That was easier to say in the privacy of her room than in his arms. "Do not torture me with your words," she cried miserably.

He pulled her close and wrapped the front of his jacket around her shoulders, kissing the snow from the top of her head. There was no safer, warmer place, and she denied her guilt momentarily just to be there in his embrace. The sweet torment of his lips nibbling at her neck bade her to seek them hungrily. "This is wrong," she protested weakly as their lips met with equal fervor.

Her mind was stumbling futilely as it reasoned with her abandoned passion. She wanted him as much as he hungered for her and his hands roving down her back made her press her body against his and curse the clothes that separated them.

"Shannon," he whispered, "you belong here with me. I will tell Corrinne that . . ."

The name was like a cold wave that froze her blood in remorse. "Corrinne!" she gasped, reeling to her senses at the mention of the sister who had been so devoted to her of late. "Oh God, this cannot be!"

"Shannon, listen to me!" He shook her as she pulled away from him, staring at him in horror. "I love you, not Corrinne!"

"Morgan, I will not stay at Snowden another moment unless you keep your distance. If you have any feeling for me at all, please grant me that." Hysteria mounted as her emotions tore at her unmercifully. "I will walk to London if I have to!" she warned. Her eyes reflected her distress and she began to shiver from the exposure.

"It is only because I love you that I do this," he told

her softly. "But in time I will explain it all to you, Shannon."

"I cannot bear more lies," she shouted, backing toward the door. "I must be done with them no matter how I long to hear them."

She slipped through the door and ran toward the corridor that led to the main stairway. When she realized that he did not try to follow her, she stopped to catch her breath and leaned against a paneled wall. The sound of guests making excuses to retire drifted her way and she climbed the stairway to the second floor. As she made her way to her room, Brian emerged carrying a glass of the liquor.

"Shannon, I've been looking all over the house for you," he chided gently. "I knocked and when I received no answer, I was concerned." He placed his arm on her shoulder and felt the dampness from the melted snow. "Good God, you're cold as ice! Where have you been?"

Shannon was shaking uncontrollably as she attempted to laugh. "It's my first snow and I w . . . went out in it."

"It will be your last, if you don't get into dry clothing. Come on."

Brian glanced over his shoulder as he permitted her to precede him into the room and closed the door. He put his glass down on a table and took charge. Shannon welcomed his cheerful company and undressed behind a beautifully carved dressing screen while he retrieved her gown and robe from the huge wardrobe where the maid had placed her things when they were unpacked. Quite the gentleman, he tossed them over to her and she donned them quickly.

When she emerged, he met her with a blanket and wrapped it about her before leading her to a large chair that stood by the fireplace. The servants had apparently just prepared the room, for the bed was turned back and the fire was going nicely. Shannon was grateful for its warmth and leaned forward so that her braid might dry.

"Here, drink this," Brian ordered, handing her his glass. "I have had quite enough anyway." As Shannon obeyed, he perched on the arm of the chair. "I do hope you do not become ill from this, cousin. It was a risky thing to do . . . at least without a cloak."

Shannon nodded in agreement for different reasons. "You're absolutely right." She should not have ventured too far alone in Morgan's own house.

"Now finish that up, and let's tuck you in," Brian ordered authoritatively.

"Brian, I am not a child," she snickered, amused at his sudden parental nature. She put aside the empty glass and rose to stand with her feet as close to the fire as she dared get. The firelight behind her showed the shadow of her shapely figure through the delicate material of her gown and thin robe.

He took the discarded blanket and wrapped it around her again. "I am all too aware of that fact, cousin," he told her gently as he guided her toward the canopied bed.

She did not take her robe off before climbing onto the high mattress, but kept it on to help her fight the chill. Brian pulled the covers over her and then folded the blanket double to place it over her feet. By the time he finished with his administrations, the blankets were so tightly tucked about her that she could hardly move. She smiled up at him as he surveyed his handiwork.

"I am glad you were here. I think you'll make an excellent father someday."

"Ah!" he exclaimed, glancing at the ceiling uncomfortably. "What I feel for you is not the least bit fatherly, I assure you."

"Well, you already are a wonderful cousin, and I thank you. Goodnight, Brian."

He leaned over her and gave her a peck on the forehead. "Goodnight, dear cousin." He straightened and cocked his ear as if listening. "Now I have to sneak out of here before I am accused of something that I am . . ." He broke off, and started for the door.

His meaning dawned on Shannon and she rose up on her elbow. "Do be careful, Brian."

He opened the door a crack and peeked out cautiously. Then giving her a thumbs up he slipped out into the hallway and closed the door behind him. Shannon rested back on the pillow and pulled the blankets around her neck. If anyone could help her endure this visit it would be her cousin. Brian could make her laugh and be at ease—something that became difficult in the presence of her host.

Shannon was reluctant to rise the following morning. The blankets were warm about her and her pillows surrounded her cozily. It was still overcast as the stirring rays of the morning sun did not try to penetrate the room through the small openings around and between the heavy drawn royal drapes that covered the windows. Out in the hallway she could hear voices of other guests and admitted that she had lazed about long enough.

A brisk knock on the door followed by an inquiry from without announced her aunt and Shannon beckoned her in as she threw back the heavy mantle of covers and braved the cold air. Aunt Harriet was fussing over Shannon's foolishness at going outside and Shannon made it a point to admonish her cousin at first sight for his tattling.

"I hardly think you should consider going out today after taking such a chill," the woman spoke up as she helped Shannon find her slippers. "No sense in tempting pneumonia."

"But I am quite warm now and I do so want to be out in the snow before it goes away," Shannon protested.

The maidservant arrived with fresh wood for the fire and proceeded to rekindle the warming flames as Shannon picked out her riding clothes, including her breeches. Her aunt ordered that hot tea be brought to her room and when the maid returned she served Shannon the refreshment on a small table by the chair next to the fire which was now going briskly. As Shannon sipped it gratefully and listened to her aunt's account of the latest gossip discussed in the sewing parlor, the maid returned again with warm water for the blue and white bowl and pitcher on the washstand near the bed.

Her aunt left her to dress after she promised to join her family for the big breakfast that was now being served in the hall. Shannon donned the heavy blue skirt and jacket over her blouse and breeches and pulled on a new pair of black boots her cousin had bought her as a surprise gift. She carefully pinned her fresh braid in a knot at the back of her neck so that it would not interfere with the matching bonnet she intended to wear later when those of the guests that dared brave the weather left for the hunt.

The men were particularly engrossed in speculation over the prowess of the assorted peregrines they had brought to Snowden when Shannon took her seat next to Brian. She was relieved to see that she was not the only one who had slept late. There were many vacant seats in the hall including that of her sister next to Morgan Hawke, who was attentive to the conversation of his guests and did not notice Shannon's arrival.

Brian was his usual morning self. He was rarely as talkative or amusing as he was later in the day and he concentrated on his food which he put away with relish. At best he would be civil, until the ill effects of the previous night's liquor and late hours wore off.

"Good morning, tattletale," Shannon remarked stiffly, as a servant began to fill her plate with smoked pork, boiled eggs and assorted tempting pastries. "Not so much," she protested politely. The servant nodded and replaced her plate in front of her.

"Did you ever warm up?" Brian asked, ignoring her jibe.

"Of course. I was hard put to part with the warm little niche you made for me," she admitted, taking one of the scones and buttering it. "Could we go outside after we finish here?"

"You mean you didn't get enough last night?"

Shannon's eyes twinkled as she shook her head. "Please! I promise to wear a cloak," she quipped. "Just a little walk."

"Dear cousin, when you look at me that way I could not refuse you anything, no matter how wretched I feel."

After breakfast, Shannon felt as if she would have to walk off the delicious scones and jams that she chased with tea. She dutifully donned her cloak and pulled the hood up over her head while Brian dressed equally warmly. Gloved and booted they carefully made their way down the slippery steps and out onto the plush white carpet that with little exception was untouched by the morning risers.

The landscape was white and glistened when the sun managed to peek through the clouds that grayed the skies above. Blackbirds scurried about from tree to tree hoping to spy a place where the snow had drifted leaving a shallow spot nearby from which they might scratch some food. Whinnies from the stone and wood stables echoed in the air as the horses waited impatiently to either be turned out in the snow-covered pasture or exercised.

They walked around one of the wings of the manor house and observed a neatly rowed orchard at the end of the rolling lawn and in the back Shannon saw the pond that Morgan Hawke had described to her. They walked down to its edge and Brian tapped the icy surface and shook his head as it cracked.

"Still too early," he informed Shannon who had expressed a desire to try to slide on the ice. "But we've loads more snow and freezing weather in store," he consoled. "Ah, I've an idea!"

He bade Shannon wait for him while he went to the stables and spoke with one of the stableboys. She could see the boy nod enthusiastically and disappear within the structure. In a moment he was back with a crudely made vehicle of wood for which Brian gave him a shining copper to borrow.

"I never knew a young lad who hasn't made one of these of some sort."

Shannon stared blankly at it as Brian dropped it on the ground at her feet. "What is it?"

"A sled, dear cousin!" Brian laughed. "All we have to do is walk to the top of that hill near the side of the manor and we can ride it down."

As they made their way up the slope, dragging the sled behind them by a rope tied to its front, Shannon was dubious. It was such a small vehicle of planks on metal runners.

"How do you direct it?" she asked, as Brian helped her tuck her skirt in so that it would not tangle under it.

"You sort of lean with it."

"Are these the reins?" Shannon held up the rope

and tested them with little result.

"No. All you do is basically ride where it takes you. Now hold on and I'll push you."

His cheek touched hers as he leaned over her shoulder and pushed the sled ahead. She glanced to see its cold red color and noticed the mist of his heavy breath as he gave a last shove and released her. The vehicle carried her swiftly and smoothly toward the pond losing its speed as the ground leveled out and coming to a stop yards from the icy water. Shannon squealed to her cousin in delight as she climbed to her feet and grabbed the rope to pull it back up for another ride.

"Your turn," she said breathlessly as she reached him.

He shook his head as she handed him the rope. "No, you go on again."

"But it's fun! You try it," Shannon insisted.

"How adventuresome do you feel?" he asked, grinning mischievously.

"Very!" Shannon answered excitedly. "What are we going to do?"

"You get on first," he ordered. When Shannon obeyed, he tucked in her skirt again and then climbed on the back of the sled. "Scoot up so I have room for my knees."

"This is not going to work," Shannon laughed, drawing her legs up closer to allow him more room.

"Have faith, dear lady!" he teased. "Now I am going to get us going with a push, and then hop on, so hold on tight. I will have to use your shoulders to brace myself."

Shannon held her breath as her cousin's pounding feet sounded behind the moving sled. Her gloved fingers tightened about the side of it and she braced herself as Brian shouted "Now!" and jumped on

314

behind her. Under the added weight the sled gained more momentum and moved faster than ever down the slope. Suddenly the pond seemed to be too much within their path and Shannon cried out in alarm as they passed where she had stopped before.

"Let's go!" Brian shouted, falling to the side and pulling Shannon with him so that they tumbled in a flurry of skirts and cloaks to a stop well away from danger while the sled careened to a stop opposite them.

Shannon lay on top of her cousin for a moment. His laughter shook her and she realized that she had been victim of another prank. She rolled over to glare at the twinkling brown eyes with a flush of indignation. "You devil!" she exclaimed, grabbing a handful of snow and rubbing it in his face.

He surprised her by rolling her off into the snowy bank and before she could recover she was pinned beneath him. "If I am as you charge, then I shall have to act the part, cousin."

He leaned down and started kissing her face repeatedly.

"What are you doing," Shannon gasped, turning her face from him as he continued his playful attack.

"Removing the snow from your lovely face," he replied in a wounded tone.

"Get out of here!" Shannon exclaimed in mock disgust as she threw another handful in his face and twisted under him to unseat him.

She scrambled to her feet and dusted him again as he held up his hands in surrender before charging up the hill toward the manor. She sped faster as she heard him shout in mock anger and start after her. Her skirts hampered her and he was gaining on her as she rounded the corner of the manor and slammed into the Lord of Snowden who caught her as she bounced off him and started to fall backward.

She grabbed his arm to steady herself and saw that he was accompanied by a few of the male guests as she fought for her breath. With as much dignity as she could muster, she shook her snow-dusted cloak and skirts as Brian cleared the corner and straightened under the curious looks cast his way.

"We were playing in the snow!" Shannon blurted out defensively, as Hawke swept over her with his eyes. Her cheeks were hot pink and her lips were the same hue. Pools of royal blue glistened with the reflection of the snow as she watched him expectantly.

"Actually, I was showing Shannon how to sled and she took a tumble down there by the pond," Brian spoke up, trying to cover Shannon's innocently incriminating remark, and pointing to the sled. "We were rushing up to get her dried out before the hunt this afternoon," he added, offering Shannon his arm to accompany him.

"Indeed," Morgan Hawke remarked curtly. "Then you'd best hurry before she freezes from such folly." He wanted to knock the dashing smile off young Bedlowe's face as Shannon familiarly linked arms with her cousin.

"Ah, young love!" One of the guests remarked nostalgically as the couple disappeared around the corner, bringing a general round of amusement from all, save one.

After the noonday meal of cold meats and fresh baked breads, the men gathered at the stables anxious for the hunt. Corrinne, heavily dressed in fur-lined cloak and gloves sat upon a proud mount that danced about the stableyard, impatient to be off while the others organized. Shannon enviously noted her sister's ease as she moved the horse through strict paces before she met the placid gaze of the mount Brian had chosen for her.

There were only two women who accompanied the half-dozen men. Shannon came because Brian expressed her interest in the sport and Hawke indulged her. Corrinne insisted on coming along as a result of her stepsister's presence.

As her cousin lifted her up on the sidesaddle, Shannon caught the cold stare of her host across the stableyard where he sat on a great black beast that matched his mood. On his leather gloved arm was a hooded fowl and the threesome presented an impressive and imposing sight. His horse pawed at the snow-muddied ground and snorted mists of heated breath in the stark air.

"Now she's not Sarah, but she appears to be relatively gentle," Brian assured her with a pat on the hand, diverting her attention.

Shannon took the reins in her gloved hands and held the horse in check while Brian mounted his. The hunt was something she had looked forward to with curiosity. She could hardly imagine the hooded birds that some of the men carried could be so fierce as to attack and kill other birds.

As the last of the guests mounted, Morgan Hawke gave the stallion its rein and led the group away from the stables. Brian stayed behind with Shannon as she maneuvered her bay mare to the rear and plodded along. The master of the hounds fell in behind her with the anxious setters who were trained to find and flush out suitable game for the caged falcons.

The ride to the recently harvested field where only stubble remained of its bountiful crop was uneventful, yet Shannon was exhilarated. There were so many new experiences for her and she reveled in them. There was no well-trodden path as in the park and she felt a certain freedom as she gazed about the boundless expanse of fields and forests where one could ride seemingly forever without repeating the breathtaking snow-dusted scenery.

The company stopped at the edge of the woods. Some of the men dismounted to uncage their birds. There was some quiet conversation as they kept their eyes on the dogs that had been turned loose. Hawke sat straight in the saddle and issued a sharp command to the fidgeting black horse who quieted instantly. Brian left his mount to help one of the hunters with the cage in which he kept his bird of prey and left the reins of his well-trained horse hanging as it began to graze patiently.

"There!"

Hawke saw his brown spotted setter point to a thicket at the same time as his guest. As master of the hunt, he untied the leather thongs that held the big falcon to his arm. Then with a swift and sure movement, he removed the hood. Shannon watched as the bird began to beat its wide wings rapidly, showing the blackish-brown bars on its white underside, and flew in a circle above them. The dog flushed the prey from its hiding place to flight. The speed of the peregrine was amazing as it spied the frantic grouse and swooped down to seize it with the deadly talons. The smaller bird struggled briefly in its final moments before the peregrine brought it to the master on the horse and dropped it at the feet of the servant who held the game sack. A quiet command brought the falcon back to his master's gloved hand.

Hawke carefully replaced the hood on the blue-gray falcon and coaxed it until it was settled enough to hand to his attendant who placed it in a cage. He accepted the congratulations on fine performance of his hunting fowl and took strong refreshment, allowing his fellow guests the field for their own luck.

There was a short period of time before the dogs found another victim for the hunt. The guest who had expressed his desire to try his new bird went through the same motions as his host. There was a loud beating of wings as the peregrine lifted from his arm and Shannon rose in her saddle and leaned forward to admire the wild beauty of the bird when her mount whinnied loudly and jerked beneath her.

The horse's head reared back as it lifted its front hooves off the ground. Shannon cried out in alarm and dropped the reins as she grasped the beast's neck to keep from being thrown backward. The movement caused the animal to shriek in protest and thrash about.

"Whoa, girl!" Brian shouted as he approached the pawing mare cautiously trying to get close enough to seize the reins.

Suddenly the horse bolted forward and Shannon saw Brian knocked to the ground as the mare trampled over him. She screamed his name as she held her desperate grasp in the coarse mane. The horse stampeded across the fields in the direction of the manor carrying its terrified rider. The racing hooves of the black stallion was closing the distance between them.

Shannon tried to reach the reins while holding on to the saddle tightly with her other hand. Her hands slipped on the wet lathered neck of the beast and again she caught a hold in its mane. Her heart froze as she saw the large hedgerow that bordered the outer limit of the stableyard ahead. The mare was going to jump it, she realized as it veered sharply away from the orchard and took the straightest path to the stable.

Frantically, Shannon struggled to unhook her leg from the stirrup of the sidesaddle as the mare snorted in anticipation of the last hurdle between it and its home. Time was running out as she straightened enough to free her leg and threw herself away from the charging horse.

She hit the ground feet first and pitched sideways, her momentum rolling her into the prickly hedge that scratched her face and tore at her jacket. The sky spun dizzily overhead as she tried to pull herself to her feet. She could hear the thunder of hooves and was confused because she knew she was free of her mad horse. Her legs were unsteady and her head ached abominably.

She knocked off her bonnet and felt the back of her head where her braid had come undone. She touched a warm sticky substance and when she looked at her hand it was covered with blood. A wave of nausea threatened to make her ill, but she fought down the bile and looked about to see where the voice that called out her name was coming from.

"Somebody help me!" she cried in bewildered pain. Where were they, she thought desperately.

"Shannon . . . dear God, be all right!"

Arms were about shoulders helping her straighten and her head rolled back as she tried to focus on the blurred face of Morgan Hawke.

"Morgan . . ." she mumbled, falling against him for support. Suddenly a torturous pain ripped at her abdomen and she dropped to her knees gasping as it robbed her of breath. "Morgan," she screamed, her eyes widening in agony, "help me . . . the pain . . . I . . ." Her body screamed with her until it could bear no more and sought the anesthetic of unconsciousness.

Chapter Nineteen

"We had to shoot it, sir." The stablemaster stood before the pale-faced Lord of Snowden and shifted uneasily under the steel blue gaze. "Its leg was broken," he explained, aware that the eyes of everyone in the room were on him.

Morgan Hawke nodded solemnly. It had been hours since he had carried Shannon to the room upstairs where as far as he knew she still lay unconscious; yet, it seemed like days. The blood from the cut on the back of her head still stained the jacket he had not changed, and he could not bring himself to partake in the supper and games that were planned. He had, however, seen that the other guests continued to enjoy their stay and was grateful for the competent staff that kept things going as planned.

"Sir, there was a reason the horse went mad," the servant spoke up hesitantly.

Hawke snapped his attention from the stairway that could be seen from his desk chair back to the stablemaster. "Well speak up man!" he demanded.

"It was the saddle, sir. When we took it off the animal, the poor thing's back was bloody. We found a long tack that had worked its way through the leather to gouge the mare. It's little wonder that she bolted like she did.''

"What exactly are you trying to say, sir?" Hawke's hands clenched the edge of his desk and his jaw was locked so that the muscles bulged. "That it was not an accident?"

"I can't say for sure, sir. I was sure I checked the tack thoroughly for any defects. I suppose I could have missed it.''

The misery on the loyal servant's face bespoke his true feelings. He had long been stablemaster and took great pride in his work. If there were negligence on his part it was obviously unintentional.

"You suppose you could have missed it?" Corrinne exclaimed incredulously. "My sister is possibly dying because of your lack of attention to your duty, sir.''

"Corrinne, let Morgan handle this," her father warned. "There is enough tension as it is without adding to it.''

"Jonathan, perhaps this may be a bit much for Corrinne," Hawke remarked crisply, turning to face his fiancée who stood behind her father's chair. "It has been a long evening and may be longer. I suggest you retire to your room, lest we have to call a doctor for you as well.''

Corrinne stared at him for a moment before she broke into a smile and swept across the floor to his side. "I am so sorry, darling. Of course you are right. I was just so upset . . . the blood . . ." Her voice quivered slightly. "She was like a broken doll!''

Hawke looked over her head at Jonathan Devage as Corrinne embraced him and sobbed into his chest. His eyes beseeched assistance from the man who acknowledged his plea and rose from his seat to attend to his distraught daughter. He could feel no compassion for Corrinne, only disgust at her theatrical behavior. His thoughts and concern was for Shannon.

Jonathan Devage gently coaxed Corrinne away and after they had left the room, Hawke turned back to the stablemaster. "I have no doubt as to your devotion to your work, Derry. It was something that just happened," he consoled stiffly. "I will want to see the saddle as soon as we hear from the doctor. In the meantime, you may go."

As the servant left the room, Admiral Bedlowe rose to cross to the liquor cabinet to help himself to the decanter of brandy displayed with matching glasses. He poured himself a drink and offered one to his son, who sat reclined against his chair back, his head bandaged from where the pain-stricken horse grazed it with a flying hoof as it leapt over him. Brian accepted the drink and stared at it thoughtfully.

"I wonder," he mused aloud, calling attention to himself as he swirled the liquor carefully. "It seems such a coincidence that Shannon nearly met her end that day the wagon almost ran her down and then a tack works its way through the leather to incite a normally calm mount into a mad runaway."

"What motive, Brian?" Hawke questioned, reflecting on the statement.

"Greed?" the young man suggested dubiously. "After all, aren't Corrinne and her father literally at Shannon's mercy?"

"By God, son! Do you realize what you're suggesting?" the Admiral protested. "Why Shannon is more his daughter than Corrinne. Blood runs thicker than water."

"Well what other motive could there be?" Brian exclaimed in frustration.

Morgan Hawke rose to his feet and stalked over to

323

the window restlessly glancing out at the moonlit lawn that glowed white on tree and shrub alike. "None," he answered curtly. "I find it hard to believe that Jonathan Devage would try anything that suspect. For now, we have to accept things as they appear . . . coincidence. However, between the three of us, we must make certain that no more near misses take place. God give us the chance," he added in remorse. "What in heaven's name can that man be doing up there?" His clenched fist hit the window frame with such force that the glass rattled in its panes.

"Morgan." Lady Elaine entered the room with Doctor Lloyd Humphrey following her. She crossed the room to her son and placed a comforting hand on his arm as he turned to face the tired gentleman. "Admiral, would you be so kind as to pour the doctor a drink."

Hawke's mouth went dry as he met the doctor's gaze. "How is Shannon?"

The doctor opened his mouth to speak and then stopped to close the paneled doors behind him. "She is a lucky young woman. There are no broken bones . . ."

"Is she conscious?" Hawke interrupted, in spite of the restraining grasp of his mother's hand.

"Very much so!" the elder man snorted, accepting the brandy and taking a sip. "She has not accepted my diagnosis gracefully at all. In fact, I have been cursed to a fare-thee-well, but . . ." he emphasized, "I insist that she remain in bed at least until the end of the week. I'm not sure then she won't lose the child."

"Child?" Hawke whispered in astonishment. He relaxed his weight against the wall as his legs threatened to give way. He closed his eyes to shut out the others as the word echoed in his brain. Shannon was going to have his child.

"You fornicating bastard!"

Hawke stiffened and pushed his mother behind him as Brian Bedlowe sprang from his chair and charged him furiously. Admiral Bedlowe stepped between them and struggled to hold the red-faced young man who seethed with hostility.

"Brian, there is a lady present!" his father reminded him, shaking him roughly.

"Damn you, Morgan Hawke!" Brian shouted, oblivious to his father. "If she dies aborting your bastard, I swear I will kill you! Do you hear me?"

Hawke ignored the enraged man as he spoke to the doctor. "Dear God, she won't die?" He wished Bedlowe would turn loose his son. He would not lift a finger to defend himself. No pain the angered young man could inflict could hurt him more than what he already felt.

"She's a strong young woman. I think she and the child have a good chance if she remains calm and rested. It's hard to tell what that fall has done," the doctor replied apologetically. "I wish I could tell you more."

"I'm going to see her." Hawke walked determinedly toward the closed doors. He had to touch her . . . to be sure she was all right no matter what she felt about him. He had caused her enough anguish, he thought wretchedly.

"Morgan!" his mother called out in warning.

His path was suddenly blocked by Brian Bedlowe. Blood pounded at the young man's temples and his breath was rapid like a snorting bull about to charge.

"Get out of my way, Bedlowe," he growled through clenched teeth.

"You have no right to see my cousin."

"Out of my way," he repeated ominously.

"Morgan . . . Brian, please!" Lady Elaine implored, backing away as the two men poised for attack.

"You have the morals of a tomcat, with little regard for your innocent victims." Brian spat at his feet.

"What would you know of morality, Bedlowe? I've seen you with your hands on her . . . lusting after her. If you were such a prime sample of morality, why were you leaving her room last night?" Hawke braced himself as he saw Brian's eyes ignite in unsurpassed fury.

"By God, sir. Do you slander her as well?" His voice was filled with rage.

"Never . . . it's your motives I question." Hawke suddenly wanted the young man to make a move. He wanted to seek revenge for the familiarity and laughter he had enjoyed in her company.

"Brian!" his father shouted in an effort to check his son's wild charge.

With the experience of a trained fighter, Morgan Hawke stepped sideways and brought his knee up under Brian's chin as the young man plunged past him. The action halted Brian's momentum enough and Hawke lifted his fists clenched together to crash them down on the stunned man's neck.

"Morgan!"

His mother's voice made him draw his blow short and instead he pushed the back of Brian's head roughly and sent him sprawling face down. As he stared down at the groaning man, the doors to the hallway opened and Jonathan Devage entered the room. Hawke swung his gaze to his shocked future father-in-law who looked from Brian to him speechless.

"This has gone far enough, sir," Hawke declared

firmly. "Your daughter is with my child, and if God will spare her, I swear I shall marry her and be done with this farce . . . honor be damned!"

Jonathan Devage watched as Admiral Bedlowe and the doctor tried to help a half-conscious Brian to the settee where Lady Elaine cleared pillows to make room for him. He shook his head tiredly. "Do what you must, Morgan. I understand."

"I must warn you, Lord Hawke," the doctor called from across the room as he dabbed blood from Brian's mouth, "the lady is not quite herself. I have sedated her as much as I dare."

Hawke heard Jonathan Devage questioning the doctor as he climbed the stairs three at a time and nearly ran down the corridor to the room he had carried Shannon earlier that day. His stomach knotted in anxiety when he reached the door and opened it slowly.

The lamp flickered on the table next to the large bed that seemed to dwarf the small form under the covers. Harriet Bedlowe rose quietly from the chair she had moved to the bedside to keep an eye on her niece and approached him. She informed him that she would be in the next room if he needed her and left him standing frozen to the spot as he tried to muster the courage to face the girl he would have killed for moments before.

As he walked toward the bed, he saw the bandage that held the masses of dark curls tight about the nape of her neck where a stone had cut cruelly. Her cheeks were pale with red scratches and her breasts rose and fell softly under the blankets her aunt had tucked around her. Her eyes were closed when he stooped over her and kissed her gently on the lips.

Her eyelashes fluttered and he could see that she made an effort to hold them open as she stared up at him blankly, as if trying to identify him. Her tongue ran over her lips slowly, trying to moisten them. Morgan looked about for a cloth to help. There were plenty of clean cloths by the bowl and pitcher where the maid had replenished the ones used by her aunt and his mother to bathe and dress her. He dipped the corner of a towel in the fresh water and gently touched it to her lips.

"Thirsty . . ." she sighed, closing her eyes as if to rest.

Upon searching the room without luck for a cup, he carried the pitcher back to the bedside and soaked the corner of the towel. When he put it to her mouth, she parted her lips so that he might wring enough water from it to soothe the dryness from the medication. Her eyes opened again drowsily and the corners of her mouth twitched in an attempted smile.

"Shannon . . ." his voice cracked, and he tried to swallow the blade in his throat.

"I . . . I'm going to have a . . . a baby," she told him as if hardly believing it herself.

"The doctor told me." Hawke wanted to pick her up and cradle her in his arms, but feared it would hurt her. "Are you too upset?" he asked, recalling the doctor's account of her outburst. He held his breath and let it out as she shook her head and stared at the canopy above.

"It's all I'll ever have of Morgan." Her pitiful words pierced him as he realized she did not recognize him.

"Shannon, I . . ."

"Don't tell him! Please . . ." With an effort she placed a hand on his arm and squeezed it weakly.

His mind reeled from the pain in her words as she innocently dealt him the justice for his honor bound deception. "I shan't," he consoled her wretchedly.

She closed her eyes again and let her arm drop to the blanket. "I thought you were hurt," she murmured tiredly.

"I'm fine," he assured her as it struck him that she mistook him for her cousin. She was obviously too drugged to know what was happening. He watched her nod in relief and held a question on the tip of his tongue. Dismissing his guilt and fearing the answer he asked what was he had to know. "Shannon . . . do you love me?"

She managed a sleepy giggle. "You're silly and make me laugh."

"But . . ."

"Brian, I'm so tired." She pulled her arm in under the blanket and snuggled down. "Tuck me in an' lemme sleep," she mumbled into the pillow as she turned her back to him.

Hawke obeyed the sleepy request with tenderness. As he tucked the heavy covers around her, he rested his hand on her flat stomach and wondered that there was a child conceived by their love struggling to survive there. He was not a devout man, nor a humble one. Yet in the privacy of the room he closed his eyes and prayed.

Lady Elaine, Harriet Bedlowe and even Corrinne took shifts around the clock to attend to the bedridden Shannon the next two days. Much to everyone's surprise Shannon's stepsister took the breaking of her engagement to Morgan Hawke fairly well. There had been the tears of betrayal upon finding out that Shannon carried his child, but after a while to herself, Corrinne emerged from her room and accepted her fate with a maturity and strength no one recognized.

Brian treated his host with barely restrained hostility which Morgan Hawke ignored. He understood the young man's hatred of him. Brian's feelings toward Shannon were obvious. He had fallen in love with his cousin. He had been in several times to rest his mother for short spells and spend time with the sleeping girl.

Even though his affairs with the sisters had been straightened out, at least with Corrinne, Hawke still had to deal with Shannon whom the doctor kept heavily sedated in order to keep her in bed. She had recognized him on many of the visits he had made to her room, but could not or would not attempt much more than a few words in conversation.

The night of the ball, Hawke was engaged with the prospect of overseeing his guests. The tables in the great hall were filled with the sumptuous dishes prepared by his cooks and the music was gay as the dancers whirled about the center of the room to the allemande. He sipped Madeira from a crystal goblet idly as he watched the gowned ladies smiling up at their partners wisk by the head table, his mind absorbed with Shannon.

The doctor was extremely pleased with her recovery, and had reduced her medication that morning to permit her to get out of bed and move about the room if she felt up to it. Lady Elaine informed him that she had eaten ravenously at supper, but tired easily and had to lie down to rest afterward.

Most of the guests would be leaving the next day and then he would have the opportunity talk to Shannon. He would explain the circumstances that had kept them apart and propose the marriage, no insist on it. He knew his task would not be an easy one, for there was much damage to undo.

"Sir, does the breaking of betrothal mean that you cannot dance with your future sister-in-law?" Corrinne stood at his side, lovely in silver-white woven silk. Her eyes searched his and she bit her rose colored lips nervously.

"I suppose not," he smiled, rising from his seat and taking her hand in his. "I have my blackguard's reputation to uphold."

There were those among the guests who accepted the turn of events at Snowden without question as friends. The others could not wait to return to London with the saucy details concerning the Lord of Snowden and the pirate wench turned lady. The eyes of many watched him as he led Corrinne to the center of the hall and placed his hand at the small of her back to begin the dance.

"It is very difficult . . . knowing they talk behind your back," Corrinne explained. She glanced about the room with troubled eyes.

"To hell with them!" Hawke swore under his breath.

"That is easier for you to say, Morgan. A man is admired for his . . . intimate exploits. It is Shannon and I who willl suffer most." She saw the flicker of concern in his eyes and continued. "I suffer from being jilted . . . but I realize that I am young and attractive. I still might find a suitable match, although never one I could love as I did you, Morgan." She struggled to hold back the tears that welled in her eyes. "Shannon will suffer the reputation of a harlot, who stole you from me and got with child in the process. In doing so she forced you to marry her."

"I told you that is not true, Corrinne," Hawke warned lowly under his breath.

"I know that, Morgan . . . but the ones you damn

331

to hell do not!"

"The marriage will cease the wagging tongues."

Corrinne smiled as the dance ended. "You have forgotten something, my lord. My sister has not yet accepted your proposal and is not likely to as long as our enamored cousin is about." She dipped low to give him an enticing view of her neckline as she gazed at him. "Excuse me, my lord. I must relieve my aunt for a while, so that she might join the party."

When Corrinne entered her room Shannon was sitting up in the canopied bed. Her aunt had propped up several pillows behind her and she had just changed into a fresh long sleeved lace cuffed and collared gown embroidered with small blue flowers about the yoke. It fastened high at the neck with a matching ribbon woven through the lace in a drawstring effect. Shannon gave her stepsister an approving nod.

"Your gown is lovelier than I pictured. You look like a faerie princess in one of the books Cudge read to me as a child."

"Cudge?" Corrinne raised a thin lined brow as she noted the natural color that was returning to Shannon's cheeks.

"My dear tutor," Shannon explained. "If you can imagine having a tutor in the midst of a den of pirates. He was an ex-clergyman who fell from grace with the Church and the authorities and somehow wound up on Nose' Be as my teacher and local tavernkeeper."

"Good heavens, you have known some colorful characters. How are you feeling?"

"Too feisty for her own good," her aunt Harriet spoke up as she folded the fresh towels the maid had brought and hung them on the washstand. "Watch her or she'll be down there dancing in her nightdress.

332

I shan't be too long."

Shannon accepted a peck on the cheek from her aunt and promised to stay in bed until she returned from eating her supper with the other guests. She frowned as she saw the tired lines on the elder woman's face and decided to tell her when she returned that she was well enough to be left unattended at least during the night.

The past days had been a myriad of dreams and voices. She was grateful when the doctor reduced the bitter liquid she had been forced to take. Although now that she had her wits about her, her cuts and bruises confirmed that she had really jumped from a runaway horse and landed hard in a hedgerow; and the way she had been fussed over since she became fully aware of her confinement, confirmed her dream that she carried Morgan Hawke's child.

Corrinne walked over to the table by her bedside and held her hand to the teapot sitting on a tray with all the accouterments. "It's still warm. Would you like some?"

"Yes, thank you. I have yet to rid my mouth of that awful medicine taste." Shannon made a face to emphasize the point. "In truth, I think the sooner it is out of my system, the better off I'll be."

"Well the doctor would certainly know more than I about that," Corrinne responded matter-of-factly. She poured the tea and placed the lap tray in front of Shannon carefully so as not to spill the cup of tea sitting on it. "I don't suppose you have been told anything about Morgan and I?" Her question was casual as she poured herself a cup as well.

Shannon replaced her cup in the saucer and turned to look at the woman whose voice quivered slightly. "No . . . I've heard nothing except that Brian is all right, and your fiancé is concerned for me." She could not help the sarcasm that tinged her statement.

"He's not my fiancé anymore." Corrinne forced a smile as she faced Shannon. "He's broken the engagement."

"Because of the child?" Shannon whispered. Seeing her stepsister nod, she leaned back against the pillows and winced at the sharp protest of the healing wound she rested on.

Corrinne turned away from her. "Damn!" she swore in a shaky voice. "I vowed that I would not become emotional."

"I am truly sorry, Corrinne." Shannon sighed in remorse. "I did not know that you existed when the child was conceived."

"I do not blame you, sister. I blame Morgan!"

Shannon looked up in surprise at the vehemence in the fair-haired woman's voice and the anger in her eyes as she spun about to face her again. "He has betrayed us both! And now I fear . . ." Her voice broke and tears fell down her contorted face, "I fear we are sisters in more ways than one."

Shannon was stunned as the meaning of her words sank in. "Are you sure?"

Corrinne shook her head. "I only fear the consequences of the night you arrived. I had not seen him for so long and I . . . I could not deny the want he made me feel with his kisses."

Shannon felt sick at the words of her stepsister. No more than hours after she had lain in his arms, he had sought the love of another. While she had cried lonely in her bed, he had been sharing Corrinne's.

"My God, Shannon, are you all right?" Corrinne exclaimed as she saw her draw her legs up and rest her head on her knees weakly. "I'm sorry . . . I shouldn't have said anything."

"Just leave," Shannon moaned. She could stand

no more of her sister's confession.

"Should I send for the doctor? You look horrid."

"Just leave me alone." Shannon forced the words out.

When Corrinne hurried out of the room, she sat up again and breathed deeply to quell the faintness she felt. The tray with the empty tea cup tipped over and tumbled on the rumpled covers as she knocked it out of the way. Slowly so as not to upset her delicate balance of equilibrium she slid off the mattress. The floor was cold to her bare feet as she made her way to the wardrobe to search for her clothes. She could not stay another moment in his house.

Her head ached as she slipped her tattered blue skirt over her nightdress and fastened it. It was as muddied as the jacket and breeches which she managed to pull on tediously, resting as she made her progress. Her stomach knotted and another wave of nausea overcame her. She staggered in her bare feet to the washbowl and splashed the water in her face. Her hair fell forward and dipped in the bowl and she brushed it back irritably.

She had to find her boots, she thought as she looked down at her cold feet. She walked back to the wardrobe and began to throw her things on the floor as she searched in vain. They had to be here, she thought, holding her head to keep the blood from bursting from her temples and looking around the room. She crossed to the huge dresser that matched the bed and pulled the drawers out. With the exception of spare linens there was nothing in them. She leaned on the top and gazed at the reflection of the room behind her. Near the head of the bed on the floor, she saw a black toe peeking out from under the dust ruffle.

She got on her knees and paused to halt the room

from moving before she reached under and retrieved one boot. Sitting on the floor and bracing her back with the side rail of the bed, she shoved her foot into it. The other one was farther under the bed. With a concentrated effort she stretched out on her stomach and crawled under to get it. By the time she had it on, she was wet with perspiration and winded.

She resisted the urge to fall back on the mattress and rest. Her aunt would be back soon and there wasn't much time. She picked through the pile of clothes on the floor and found her heavy cloak. As she fastened it about her shoulders, she made her way to the window and opened the shutter.

The way to the stables was clear. With the merriment downstairs, she might manage to slip down the back stairwell that led to the wing of the manor that housed the staff. The question in the back of her mind demanding to know where she was going, was smothered by the simple urge to flee the clutches of the Lord of Snowden. Someone would help her, she assured the doubtful voice.

The corridor was empty as she used the wall for support and made her way to the servants' stairs. Her hands clutched the rail to keep her from falling forward on the stone steps that dropped to the first floor pantries. Halfway down she sank to a step and lay back on the sharp edges of those she had passed. Tears of frustration sprang to her eyes as she realized she lacked the strength to go on.

"Damned medicine," she sniffed, wiping her nose on her sleeve. The stone on the step was cool as she turned and laid her cheek on it. She closed her eyes just for a minute and remained there.

She felt herself being lifted from the hard cold surface and embraced the warmth as Morgan Hawke carried her back to her room. When she opened her eyes and saw who it was that set her down so gently on the bed, she was not surprised nor dismayed. It was his house.

"I cannot fight you here," she admitted tiredly as he slipped the jacket off her shoulders ignoring the surprised looks of his mother and Harriet Bedlowe who had come to him in a panic when she discovered her niece missing. At the same time a servant had come to him and informed him that Lady Shannon had been found sleeping in the servants' stairwell.

"Ladies, I would appreciate some privacy with my future wife," he called over his shoulder in a tone that denied any challenge.

Shannon hardly noticed as the two women left. She leaned against his chest as he pulled her up to unfasten her skirt and dropped back against the pillows so that he could lift her enough to slip it down over her hips and legs. He reached up under her nightgown and removed her breeches as well as her boots as they came off roughly together. She watched him try to separate them awkwardly. There was little expression in her voice when she spoke.

"I am not your future wife."

He glanced at her and threw the tangled garment aside. "I thought you were too tired to fight."

"I was just warning you. You will not have me or the baby."

"Where were you going?" he asked, refusing to engage in a confrontation that might upset her.

"Away."

"You couldn't have made it to London, you know."

"I couldn't make it to the stable," she admitted. "I hate this!" She turned her face away as the frustrated tears emerged again.

Hawke pulled her into his arms and she did not

resist. "I do too, Shannon. I want you and our child well. Promise me you won't try to run away again." She did not answer him. She would not lie as he had. "What do you want me to do to keep you from running away? Tell me, Shannon." He lifted her chin so that her face met his.

"Let me leave when I'm well enough to go."

She closed her eyes as he nodded solemnly and lowered his lips to hers. The most heavenly feeling in the world would be to spend the night in his arms that held her and forget his lies, to feel his consoling kisses on her head as he comforted her, to lie with her head on his chest and let the sound of his heartbeat lull her into the slumber she fought in order to savor his kiss.

When he lifted his lips from hers and lowered her back against the pillows, she studied him through half-lidded eyes. She had never seen such strong emotion in his face. It was neither anger nor hunger, but it urged her to reach out to him. She commanded her hand to touch his face, but it felt too weighty to move. He was so far away. She felt the covers being tucked about her and heard the clink of the saucer and teacup as he removed it and the tray from her bed. Don't leave, she cried out silently as she felt him brush her forehead with his lips once more. Exhaustion silenced her thoughts with sleep and she did not hear him settle into the chair next to the bed or feel his eyes on her as her body sought the rest it needed.

Chapter Twenty

Shannon gazed out the window at the readied coach below in the stable yard. Across the fields beyond were scattered remnants of the snowfall and it added to her depression. She was doing what she had wanted since the night Morgan had kissed her and held her in the snowy courtyard. She was leaving Snowden.

The lord of the manor had changed since that evening. He no longer tortured her with his unsettling attentions other than to bestow an affectionate peck on the forehead from time to time, such as one one would give a child. What little conversation he held with her was trivial, avoiding the mysterious emotions that showed in his eyes. So many times he had started to speak and then stopped as if he thought better of it; and she was glad. The fewer his lies, the easier it would be to pursue her plan.

In the hours she had spent confined in her room by the doctor, she had had time to think. When she returned to London she would contact her solicitors about purchasing a house away from all those whose lives she had changed so innocently. There she could have her child and raise it on a modest pension from her grandfather's estate. The bulk of the money would remain in the hands of her father and stepsister to do with as they pleased. It would be the least she could do after ruining Corrinne's plans to marry the Lord of Snowden; and if she disappeared with the illegitimate child, there might well be a chance that he would reconsider the marriage.

Her disappearance would accomplish something else that had troubled her deeply. It would perhaps save the Bedlowes the public embarrassment her unwed condition would indubitably bring. They were too dear to her to cause any further humiliation.

"Shannon dear," Harriet Bedlowe called to her from the open doorway, "we are almost ready."

"I'll get my cloak," she answered, dismissing her thoughts and rising from the windowseat. "You go ahead, Aunt Harriet. I'll be right down," she promised, as the servants entered the room to pick up her bags. "I just want to finish with my hair."

She gazed at her reflection as she wound the braid in a crown around the back of her head and pinned it securely. The color had come back to her cheeks in the week she had been confined, but her eyes reflected the strain.

As she made her way down the main staircase, she could hear the voices of her family in the front palor as they thanked their host and hostess for the extended hospitality. Shannon hesitated for a moment and passed the half-closed parlor doors. With a compulsion that she did not understand, she found her way to the courtyard.

Snow still crusted a few of the shrubs as the morning sun peeked over the high walls that protected it. Shannon could see the running droplets of water that ran off the tiled roof and fell around the edges of the enclosure to splash in the small gully they had made. She slipped through one of the glass paneled doors and stepped on the slush-covered brick patterned walk.

There was a wrought iron bench at the intersection of the walks and Shannon found her way to it. Of all the beautifully landscaped properties and elegantly furnished rooms, this was her favorite place. Even in the cold winter air, it was warm. She could see why Lady Elaine spent so much time here. Her eyes were glazed as she silently said farewell to the manor.

"Your family is waiting." Morgan Hawke stood solemnly beside the bench and watched her as she rose.

"I like this garden, Morgan . . . maybe because it reminds me of home and Marie," she admitted. "I suspect she knows," Shannon added thoughtfully.

"About what?"

Shannon smiled. "The baby." Marie had known about so much. She had known that Morgan Hawke was the only man she would ever love, but she had not foreseen Corrinne.

"Stay here, Shannon. Everything here is yours for the taking." He stood tall above her, his hands at his side, but his eyes touched her warmly.

Shannon rubbed her arms roughly as if to remove the unseen hands and looked away. "I cannot, Morgan. Too much has happened."

"I did not ask you to marry me on the *Sea Lady* because I was engaged to Corrinne."

"I do not want to hear this!" Shannon exclaimed as she started past him, but he grabbed her arm and held it firmly.

"Just hear me out, for God's sake, Shannon!" His eyes implored her so that she stopped trying to pull away. "I intended to break the engagement as soon as we reached London. However, when we arrived, Corrinne's mother had just passed away and your father asked me to wait until she was better able to handle things. He feared for her health."

"And that is why you waited until now to tell me?" she asked bitterly.

"Damn it, Shannon, I tried!" he blurted out impatiently. "But you were so busy seeing London on your dashing cousin's arm, that you could not seem to find time to see me . . . and when you did . . ." he added, raising his voice to cut her off, "you came out with a few lies of your own!"

Shannon looked away guiltily as she spoke. "Is that all there is to your story?"

He took a deep breath and let it out slowly. "Yes."

Shannon avoided his disturbing appraisal and pulled on the fingers of her gloves nervously. She hardly expected him to admit to his intimacy with her sister. After all it would tarnish his projected image as a knight in shining armor with only the highest of motives. God willing, her child would never know this man with the silver tongue.

"I shall think about what you have said, my lord. Good day, sir."

Shannon ignored the water that ran over the rim of her slippers as she walked through a low spot on the walk toward the door.

"Shannon, you leave and I may not come after you." His words were low and even, not a threat but a statement. "As much as I want you and our child, I will not beg."

She stiffened as she opened the door. His reflection in the glass showed him standing emotionless behind her. She could not stay, she told herself to deny the longing to run back to him. Each time he held her or kissed her she would think of him sharing Corrinne's bed.

"I should hope not, my lord," she replied coolly. "That would only serve to lower the base opinion

I already have of you."

Shannon hurried down the corridor to the main hallway where Brian and his mother waited for her with Lady Elaine. Admiral Bedlowe had departed from Snowden a few days earlier with the other guests to return to his duties in London, leaving Shannon and his wife to the care of his son. Lady Elaine smiled at her warmly and hugged her.

"I shall miss you, Shannon. While I regret your unfortunate accident, I was glad to get the opportunity to know you better from our little talks together."

"I do not know how I could ever repay you, milady," Shannon answered with emotion that carried over from her encounter in the courtyard. Her eyes glistened, and she blinked them irritably.

The gracious lady took a lace handkerchief from her pocket and dabbed at Shannon's cheeks. "An expectant mother is allowed to be emotional, dear. You hold onto this." She put her arm about Shannon's shoulders comfortingly. "And please come back to Snowden."

"Th . . . thank you, milady."

"Well now, ladies, I think our horses are anxious to be moving and we had best be in the coach when they do," Brian suggested lightly. "Shannon?" He offered her his arm gallantly.

"Oh dear, you should give your regards to Morgan," her aunt exclaimed, looking about for the Lord of Snowden in the empty hallway.

"I already have," Shannon assured her, forcing a smile, "but you may give my regards again, if you wish, Lady Elaine. You both have been wonderful."

She wanted to leave desperately now. When Brian helped her into the coach and spread the blanket over her lap, she looked anxiously at the doorway where their hostess stood. She knew that she would not see the handsome face of the one she loved appear. He had warned her of that. Her heart sank in despair as her mind sighed in relief when the coach pulled off. As it moved out of the tree-lined circle that graced the front lawn of Snowden, Shannon leaned her head against her cousin's shoulder and closed her eyes to hide her tears.

The coach had a difficult journey to the inn at Pulcherchurch. The roads were extremely soft with the mud formed from the recent snowfall. Several times the vehicle slid sideways and the horses struggled to right it. Their hooves made heavy sucking sounds as they pulled them out of the muck. Once the coachman had to climb down and submerge himself in mud to his knees to lead them out. The many delays caused it to be nearly dark as they rode the final mile to the Whithorn House.

Shannon was not as tired as she was hungry. It had been hours since they stopped at Barkway for their noonday meal of meat pie and hot bread and she had long since eaten the spare rolls Aunt Harriet had insisted that they bring along. Her stomach growled angrily as she stared out at the seemingly endless forest that hovered over the muddy road.

Her Aunt Harriet sat across from her and toyed with the edge of the sampler she had been working on until it became too dark to see the neat stitches she made with such care. Her aunt was distraught over the conditions of the roads and remarked more than once that they should have remained in Barkway or even stayed at Snowden another day.

Brian reassured his mother until he could think of nothing else to say. He kept Shannon amused with a deck of cards he carried in his coat. His mother clucked her tongue in disapproval but he managed to bring a matronly smile to her face with a roguish wink. After a while even Aunt Harriet was watching the confounding tricks with interest. As the sun started its downward path in the west, he tucked the deck back in his coat and leaned against the side of the rocking coach to nap. Shannon took her lap blanket and tucked it around his shoulders and teasingly wrapped a corner of it around his head in the fashion of a hooded cloak.

When the coach stopped and the driver shouted angrily, Shannon did not pay much attention. It had been happening all day. She heard him leap down as her aunt made a disgusted sound and rolled her eyes toward the ceiling. Curiously Shannon pulled aside the blind and tried to see what was happening, when the door opened with a violent jerk. She instinctively shoved her body back against the seat of the coach. The coach brightened in dim lantern light and an arm reached inside with a pistol pointed at Brian.

Without thinking she kicked at the pistol. Her aunt screamed bringing Brian up from his sleep with a start. The gun fired harmlessly into the door on the opposite side of the coach and someone cursed as it dropped at Shannon's feet. Suddenly Brian, blanket and all, leapt across her and plunged through the open door at the surprised gunman.

"That ain't no flittin' laidee!"

Shannon looked out the coach door to see another man on horseback aiming his pistol at the two men wrestling in the mud. He was cursing as he tried to pick out which of the fighters was his partner and which his victim. Their coachman stood helplessly at the end of a pistol of another robber.

"We do not have any money to speak of and you're welcome to whatever we have," Shannon called out to the horseman in an effort to save anyone from coming to harm.

"Now we's gonna do that anyways, Laidee Shannon."

"Get back in the coach!" Brian shouted as he dealt the man beneath him a silencing blow.

A shot rang out splintering the wood beside Shannon and she pulled back in. Those people knew who she was, she thought wildly as she shoved her crying aunt down on the seat. Another shot splintered in the side of the coach and Shannon heard Brian swearing from under them.

"Hand me my cane out the other side!"

Shannon found the cane in the darkness and dropped it out the door away from the robbers. She saw Brian's hand grab it and pull it under.

The man on the horse was riding around to the dark side of the vehicle as he reloaded his pistol. Shannon could see Brian's shadow cast in the dropped lantern near the unconscious robber and realized that he was a perfect target.

"Do you have a weapon, Aunt Harriet?"

"W . . . What?"

"Do you have anything I might use as a weapon?"

"No . . ."

"Stay down on the floor!" Shannon warned the trembling woman.

"What are you going to do?"

Shannon ignored the question as she glanced back out at the lantern. The man who held their coachman hostage had moved him around the front of the horses in order to keep an eye on his comrade and calm the nervous animals. It was the chance she needed and she dropped to the ground lightly.

She felt her feet sink in the mud and lost one of her slippers as she scrambled over to the unconscious robber and seized the overturned lantern. Quickly she blew it out, and lay down beside the still body as the man with their coachman called out to her angrily. There was a soft thud followed by the sound of something heavy falling near the horses that were whinnying loudly at the front of the coach. She held her breath as she heard his footsteps coming for her.

"Ferget 'im, the laidy's out 'ere!" he called to the horseman.

There was a flash as the powder exploded in the man's pistol and the unconscious body next to her jerked violently. She cried out and buried as close to the now still body.

"Shannon!"

Brian attempted to crawl toward her, but another shot ricocheted off the wheel and suddenly he gasped out in pain and fell back under the coach.

"Brian!" she screamed, straining to see her cousin in the darkness.

"I got 'im, mate!" the footed gunman called out to his companion on the other side of the vehicle. "It's just us 'n the laidies now."

As she started to move toward the couch to her cousin she inadvertently touched the wet fabric of the dead man's clothes and she felt the shape of a leather sheath. Desperately she moved her fingers up to the hilt of a large hunting knife. They closed about it and drew it quickly. At the sound of the rider coming back around the coach, she huddled again and waited in the darkness.

The man on foot stopped a few yards from her to reload his pistol. From the swift and sure way he moved, she knew he was not unaccustomed to the use of the weapon. Shannon contemplated rushing him, but decided against it. Her best chance was to surprise him and there was no way to move speedily through the mud at him. At the sound of the horse's hooves plunging in the mud she cringed. She was caught between the two of them.

She held her breath as the robber started toward her again, his pistol primed. She could hear a low chuckle emerge from his chest and shivered involuntarily. He meant to kill her. His gun was extended menacingly as he approached. Behind her she heard the horseman as he cleared the rear of the coach and spied them.

"Now ain't this an unexpected pleasure," he laughed. "Christ, I'm gonna shut that cryin' hag in the coach up," he exclaimed irritably, nudging his horse toward the open door.

"The hell you are!"

The horse reared frantically as Brian sprang out from under the coach and swung his cane, knocking the off-balance man from his seat to the wet ground. Shannon seized the chance the distraction provided and swung widely at the startled gunman's hand, slashing his wrist viciously so that he dropped the gun. As he cursed and grabbed his bloodied wrist, she lunged at him driving the knife upward between his ribs. He gave a strangled cry and fell beside his comrade.

The grunts of the fighting men beside the coach drew her attention away from the gruesome sight. She picked up the weapon her would-be assassin had dropped and struggled over to where Brian rolled about with the horseman. She saw the man strike Brian with his fist driving her cousin back in the mud. With a sudden calm that surprised her, she stood squarely behind him and held the pistol to his head. At the sound of the hammer being pulled back and touch of the metal barrel behind his ear, he froze.

"Move away very slowly, you mud-grubbing cur, or I'll blow your damned brains out." She did not recognize her cool voice as she spoke.

The man held up his hands slowly and pulled himself to his feet.

"Brian, are you all right?" she asked breathlessly.

"Yes, quite," came the strained reply as her cousin struggled to his feet. He swayed a bit and steadied himself against the side of the coach. "Mother, we're all right!" he called inside the coach to the sobbing woman. "Shannon has everything under control here," he added, with a hint of admiration in his voice.

"Whadda you gonna do now, laidee?" the prisoner asked apprehensively.

Shannon looked at Brian for help. Her hand had started to shake desperately and she felt nauseous as the gun slipped in the sticky wetness of the blood of the man she had knifed earlier. Sensing her distress, Brian took the gun. Shannon backed against the side of the coach and started to sink to the ground. Her cousin reached out to catch her with his free hand and the opportunity was seized immediately by their prisoner who kicked at the gun sending it to the ground near Shannon, and started off into the dense woods.

Brian retrieved the gun quickly and aimed it at the retreating figure disappearing in the trees, but held his fire. "Damnation!" he swore as he lowered its sights. "T'would be a waste of powder."

"Sir . . ."

Brian started and swung the barrel around to the front of the coach. He dropped his hands as their coachman staggered toward them. "Dear God, Charles, how badly are you hurt?"

"A blow on the temple, sir. Bloody painful, but I'm spared a blade or a bullet," the servant replied with forced bravado.

"See to mother, please," Brian instructed as he bent down in front of Shannon. "Shannon?"

"I'm fine . . ." Her voice trembled as much as her body from the ordeal. It was ridiculous, she chastised herself, that she could remain so cool in the midst of the chaos and now acted like a frightened child.

Brian carefully released the hammer and shoved

the gun in his belt. He reached down and pulled her to her feet. When he released his hands he wiped his own on his pants.

"It's his blood," Shannon told him, choking on her words.

"Ah, Shannon," he whispered pulling her to him tightly.

"I killed him, Brian," she mumbled as the shock began to set in.

"I know, love. He would have killed you if you hadn't."

His words were reassuring and she hugged him, seeking the strength of his embrace. "Do you think that man that ran will come back?"

"We're not going to take the chance. Charles . . ." he called over her head to the coachman, "are you up to driving on to the inn?"

"Indeed so, sir. I have no intention of tempting the scum to have at us again."

Charles climbed down from the coach and Brian lifted Shannon up to the step. Suddenly he cried out and nearly lost his hold on her.

"Brian, you're hurt, aren't you?" Shannon exclaimed, turning as her feet landed on the floor of the vehicle. She started back out again.

"No, no!" he protested, holding up his hand to stop her. "I'm just nicked, I think."

Shannon would have seen to her cousin immediately, but the news that he had been wounded was more than her aunt could bear. Harriet Bedlowe slumped down against the carriage seat with a low moan. Shannon caught her aunt and managed to swing her legs up on the carriage seat so that she reclined against the side of the carriage. She found her aunt's lap robe on the floor and spread it over her, as Brian climbed in.

"She's fainted, I think," Shannon told him, as he

leaned over his mother worriedly.

"Small wonder, poor dear." He touched the side of his mother's face as she stirred.

"Brian . . ." she moaned, clutching his hand grateful to see him.

"I'm fine, mother. You can see for yourself."

"Oh, thank God!" the woman whimpered.

"Now you just lie there until we get to the inn. Everything is quite all right for the moment," he assured her, as he withdrew his hand and dropped back against the seat opposite her.

Charles called a warning to the passengers that they were about to move on and Brian tugged at Shannon's skirt to pull her down beside him. Shannon made sure his mother was secure before turning her attention to her cousin. He shook his head as she started to open his coat to see to his wound.

"Later," he whispered. "I think the bleeding's stopped anyway. Now let's huddle together. Your lap robe's out there somewhere, muddy and useless, and we're in the same condition."

"And both my shoes are lost," Shannon added, shivering as he slid over and put his arms around her so that their bodies shared their warmth.

The lights of the inn were a welcome sight. Charles saw to the horses while Brian and Shannon helped Harriet Bedlowe out of the coach. The woman was truly shaken, and as soon as Brian made the arrangements for their rooms, he and Shannon took her straight to bed. While Shannon helped her change into her nightdress, Brian secured some food and a bottle of brandy. After a small roll filled with cheese slices and a healthy portion of the liquor, Aunt Harriet settled in.

"Now you go to your room and get decent so that I can see to your shoulder," Shannon ordered lowly.

She did not want to disturb her aunt. "I'm going to change into some clean clothes, and I'll be right with you."

The dead man's blood did not show on her dark red dress, but she knew it was there and it made her shiver with revulsion as she stepped out of it. She ducked under the low slant of the ceiling and reached in her bag for another garment to wear. The cornflower blue day dress was terribly wrinkled, but after washing away the bulk of the mud from her arms and legs, she donned it and put on another pair of slippers, her others having been lost in the muck during the skirmish.

She had already eaten with Aunt Harriet, but she helped herself to another roll to satisfy the nagging hunger she had nearly forgotten in all the excitement and to another glass of brandy to help offset the terrible chill she felt. A small stove sat in the corner of the room on the inside wall and she walked over to place her feet on the footrest of it. By the time she finished the last of her brandy, she decided to see if Brian was ready to have his wound dressed.

The hall was narrow and lined with doors on both sides. Brian's room was next to hers and Aunt Harriet's and when she knocked on the door lightly, there was no answer. She frowned and looked about the dimly lit hallway as if to reorient herself. She was about to knock again, having decided that she had the right door, when she heard footsteps on the stairs and saw her cousin climbing them tiredly.

"I thought you were supposed to be undressing!" she remarked in surprise as he reached her.

"Cousin please!" he exclaimed, glancing about the abandoned hall. "One might get the wrong idea."

"Brian, are you sure you're wounded?" Shannon remarked wryly as he opened the door to let her in before him.

There was a small lamp on the table by the single bed that was snugged in the corner. On the wall that divided their rooms was another small stove that most likely shared the same chimney and it put off a cozy heat that drew Shannon to it as Brian stripped off his coat and tossed it on a small ladder-back chair. She heard him catch his breath and turned to see him pulling his shirt away from the blood crusted patch on his shoulder.

She quickly rushed over to help him and winced with him as she gently pulled his shirt off his shoulders.

"I reported the attack to the innkeeper. He says he'll take care of contacting the authorities," Brian told her as she reached around him to finish removing his shirt and her cheek touched the skin of his chest. "This is really quite wonderful!"

"Brian, will you please be serious," Shannon admonished as she rolled it up and threw it on the floor near his bag. "Now go lie on the bed. You're bleeding and you need to be cleaned up."

He raised his eyebrows and dropped them as she shot him a warning look. The strain of the evening was beginning to catch up with her and she wanted to go straight to bed as soon as she was sure Brian was all right. As he stretched out on the mattress, his feet hanging over the end of the cot, she poured water from the pitcher into the washbasin on the crudely made washstand and dipped one of the fresh towels she found folded on the shelf above it.

Shannon gently began to wash away the dried blood to reveal an ugly gash near his collar bone. It was deep but not so much as to lead her think there was still a piece of the ball in it. He was lucky it had grazed him and not struck head on. She was glad even so, that her Aunt Harriet had been persuaded that he had only been scratched. The dear woman was in no shape to see this.

"There's a bottle in my coat. I could use some of it right now," her cousin mentioned, watching her intently as she administered to the wound.

"Brian, must you drink every night?" she chastised as she wrung out the towel in the water.

"No, cousin, not every night. But this one, definitely. Besides, I got it so that you could use it to clean out the wound."

"Oh!" Shannon exclaimed in embarrassment. "I'm sorry . . . I'm a bit edgy. I never thought . . ."

He put a finger to her lips to silence her. "One glass for you, one for me, and the rest can be liberally poured all over my body. I've always fancied a bath in brandy," he teased.

Shannon laughed as she retrieved the bottle and found a mug. She searched his pockets for another in vain.

Seeing her dilemma, he spoke up. "You take the mug, I'll take the bottle."

Shannon poured her cup full and placed it on the table. She handed Brian the bottle to help himself while she tore some bandages out of one of his spare shirts she found in his traveling bag. When he relinquished the liquor, she carefully poured it over the wound and closed her eyes as her cousin gasped and clenched his teeth.

She applied the bandages and secured them by wrapping a large bandage all the way around his body and tying it. As he sat up to help her, his breath was warm on her neck and it made her uncomfortable. She pushed him gently but firmly back against his pillow.

"You need to get the mud out of your hair, cousin. It's really quite a fright to look at," she teased, ignoring the way his brown eyes appraised her.

"Maybe tomorrow morning you can wash it if you get a good night's rest."

"You are one of the most amazing women I've ever had the pleasure to know, Shannon." He took her hand and squeezed it affectionately. "An expectant mother knife fighting in the mud one minute and the next, an intoxicatingly beautiful nurse . . . or a laughing nymph rolling in the snow. Which of you intrigues me the most, I cannot say."

"Brian . . ."

"You once said I would make a good father. Well I would do my damnedest to be one for your child if you'd have me." He searched her face earnestly for her reaction.

She could not help the tears that came to her eyes as she was touched by his sincerity. She truly loved her cousin in a platonic way.

"That is the most unselfish thing I think I have ever heard, Brian, and I love you for it. But not in the way a woman should love a mate," she added hurriedly as he started to rise. "I told you once my heart was taken. I cannot give it again. Oh, damn!" she cried, turning away from him and holding her head in her hands.

"Shannon, please don't cry," he whispered, rising up on one arm and placing the other about her shoulders. "I care too much for you to see you suffer so. I watched you sleep when you were confined. You cried then, too, love."

Shannon wiped her eyes with the skirt of her dress. "I've had much to deal with of late that has brought me to these tears . . . But I will overcome it all," she sniffed raggedly as she made to rise.

"No, no . . . don't go into mother's room in this state or I'll have two hysterical women on my hands!" He swung his legs around until he sat beside her. "Stay here for a while. Talk to me, if you will.

Come on, now," he coaxed.

It was easy to lean back against the wall where the cot butted to it and lean on his good shoulder. Somehow the words just came out. She loved Morgan Hawke, but could not have him for his deceit. She might have overlooked his not telling her about Corrinne, but she could not forgive his unfaithfulness on the very night they returned.

"And that was why you tried to run away from us?" He rolled his eyes to the slanted ceiling incredulously.

"Silly wasn't it?" She smiled sadly.

"Yes, it was," he answered shortly. "The bitch! I thought she was taking everything too well. She just has to get her claws in."

"Brian, Corrinne had every reason to be upset."

"If you want to run away, I can help you," he offered, ignoring the defense of her stepsister.

"Brian, I can't . . ."

"I am going to Italy to study architecture."

Shannon looked at her cousin in surprise. "Well that's wonderful!" she exclaimed. "But how will you manage?" She knew the Admiral would not finance the schooling. There had been many a heated debate over it.

"I am not as destitute as my father thinks," he answered bitterly. "I have made a few investments with my winnings at the gambling house that have paid off quite well and will continue to do so."

"Why haven't you told your father? It would show him you're not the ne'er-do-well he accuses you of being." Shannon bit her lip, as she realized how the reminder hurt him. "I'm so sorry, Brian." She pulled his face to her shoulder and patted him on the head. "I would not hurt you for the world."

"Cousin, you expect too much." He drew his face away and admired hers as it pinkened becomingly. "If you insist on treating me as a lap dog, then I shall oblige."

"What are you doing?" Shannon asked as he struggled to his feet.

"Getting you your drink, and I, the pitiful remains of my bottle."

"I really should go," she protested, starting to rise.

"Sit!" he commanded, with a surreptitious wink. "We have much to discuss, and we both need this."

Shannon obeyed and took her glass obligingly. Brian stretched out on the bed and put his head on her lap.

"Now you may pat me on the head all you wish and should you spill your drink, make sure it's right over here," he instructed solemnly, pointing to his mouth.

She giggled and shook her head at his folly. "What am I to do with you?"

"Go to Italy with me. Now, now . . ." he shushed, putting his finger to her lips again. "We are both outcasts of sorts and if we face exile, let it be together!" He raised the bottle in toast and tried to drink it from his supine position.

Shannon patted him on the back when he sat up quickly to keep from choking. "It won't work, Brian," she warned him, taking a healthy sip from her own glass.

"I should have known better," he admitted, between fits of coughing. He reached for his pillow and put it on her lap before lying back down. "This will work much better. Here let me fill you up again."

Shannon handed him her glass, and shook her head. "I meant my going to Italy with you. I could not have you taking care of me and my child and ruin your chances of finding a love of your own."

"Ah, but I might improve my chances of winning your heart away from the scoundrel who has abused it so. I may be a gentleman, cousin, but I am also a man. And I have a certain charm about me that would inevitably bring you to me given half the chance," he teased.

"I do not want to talk about this anymore, Brian. It is because I care for you that I will not go. Now let it be, and tell me what your plans are for study and later."

"Without you?" he asked mischievously.

"Without me," she confirmed. Shannon was relaxed as he spoke and when she finished her drink, she allowed him to refill her glass again. He settled back down and continued to divulge his intentions to become an architect. He hoped to return to London eventually to work with Christopher Wren, his mentor in the field.

His plan was well thought out and as she listened she was certain that his father would be proud of him. Not only was he going to finance his studies himself, but he aspired to work with one of London's architectural geniuses; and Shannon was certain that he could do it. As much as he loved to drink and make merry, Brian did have a serious side when it came to his field of interest.

Her glass was refilled again and his words seemed to fade into a drone as she stared blankly at the flickering lamp on the table. She knew it was late and that she should be joining her aunt, but it was so comfortable on the cot. Her eyelids fluttered before closing and she slumped to the side while Brian talked on until he too gave in to the sluggish effects of the liquor.

It was nearly dawn when Shannon roused. There was a commotion going on in the hall that dragged her from her slumber. She stared drowsily around the room that was dimly illuminated by the last throes of the moon. Soft snoring brought her attention to her cousin who slept wrapped around his pillow with his head still in her lap. The empty brandy bottle lay at his side, but it was not the sight of it, but the dull ache in her head that reminded her of her own excessive consumption.

A woman's cry from the hallway caused her to start. Brian stirred and mumbled before stretching out in a wide sprawl that covered the bed. Shannon shook him as she heard footsteps in the hall. Suddenly, there was loud banging on the door.

"Bedlowe, open up!" came a thunderous demand from the hall.

"Brian!" Shannon shook him again more roughly. He groaned, as he let the pillow fall to the floor.

"Damn it, Shannon, watch my shoulder!"

Shannon thought the whole wall would cave in as the door burst open, splintering the latch. She screamed as Brian rolled onto the floor. He growled as he assumed a crouched position and charged the intruder. She heard a surprised grunt as the men tumbled into the hall.

"Stop it, stop it!"

At the familiar sound of her aunt's voice, Shannon rose to her feet. She grabbed the empty bottle and rushed into the hall, prepared to help her cousin who was now pinned to the plank floor. The intruder shook him violently and Brian grimaced at the infliction of pain on his wound. Shannon raised the bottle to smash it on the assailant's head and was astonished as he spun and caught her wrist, twisting her arm until she came to her knees and dropped her weapon.

"You!" she gasped as she recognized Morgan Hawke. Her attention turned to the steel fingers that crushed her wrist. "You're hurting me!" she accused in angered shock.

"Bastard!" Brian's fist shot up and jolted Hawke as

it made contact with his jaw. He shifted his weight and threw the man off.

The Lord of Snowden rolled to his feet and crouched waiting for him to make his move. "Well, there is your missing niece, Harriet," he remarked bitterly.

"Missing?" Shannon looked at her aunt in confusion.

"Lord Hawke arrived first thing this morning. He left Snowden as soon as he heard of the attempted robbery and rode all night to get here," her aunt explained, stepping in front of her panting son. "When he knocked on my door, I answered and then realized your bed had not been slept in. I'm afraid I panicked," she apologized, her face reddening as she grasped the situation. "Oh dear!"

"No, Aunt Harriet. It's not what it seems!" Shannon protested. She turned suddenly to Hawke again. "How did you know?"

"I sent word to him," Brian spoke up as he rose and brushed off his breeches. "I never dreamed the bloody fool would come here!"

"Obviously," came the sarcastic reply from Hawke.

"Brian, your shoulder!" Harriet Bedlowe cried out in alarm as fresh blood spotted the clean bandage Shannon had put on it earlier. "You said it was a scratch," she admonished indignantly.

"We didn't want you to worry, Aunt Harriet. So I cleaned it and bandaged it last night," Shannon explained.

"And it took all night for your ministrations," Hawke snorted indignantly.

"Damn you bastard, you have no right to speak to her that way!" Brian cursed, pushing past his mother.

"No, Brian," Shannon warned, jumping in front of him and seizing his arm determinedly. "Don't hurt yourself. It's not worth it. Please . . ." she beseeched, ignoring the fury directed at her through steel blue eyes.

Harriet Bedlowe took her son's other arm and between them, she and Shannon led him back into his room. His mother took the other bandage off and instructed Shannon to fetch a nightdress from her traveling bag to make fresh bandages. Shannon hurried out of the room and passed Morgan in the hall. She kept her eyes straight ahead as she entered her room and started to search for the garment her aunt described. She became aware that Hawke had moved behind her, but she concentrated on her task.

When she found it, she struggled to her feet, suddenly very drained. Her nerves were on edge as she moved toward the door and stopped before him where he blocked her path.

"Please move, Morgan," she asked tiredly. "I do not think I can stand much more."

"Oh, I doubt that. Any more than your condition is so delicate. Hell, you can still fight like the wildcat you are." His hands grasped her arms painfully. "And you have the morals of one as well."

Shannon looked up at him and he recognized the angry flash of blue with some satisfaction. "Do not try me, sir. I am in no humor to take much more."

"Then call your gallant protector . . . or should I say seducer," he added, narrowing his penetrating gaze as he did so.

"I have yet to find someone to replace you, sir," Shannon retorted tartly, immediately regretting her impetuous response as she saw the change in his expression.

He kicked the door shut behind him and seized her again roughly. "Then I shall claim all rights as both."

Shannon kicked at him viciously as he pinned her

361

arms to her side in his embrace. She knew her foot made contact, but it did not seem to faze him as he traced the line of her neck to the back of her ear with his tongue. She dared not call to Brian, certain that one or both of the men she cared for might get hurt.

"Confirm what you said, my love," Hawke taunted, blowing in her ear.

"Bastard!" she gasped as he lowered his kisses to her bodice and teased through the thin material with his teeth.

She was rapidly losing her will to reject his touch Sensing her weakening, he freed a hand to cup her breast and manipulated it until her knees gave way and she fell against the strong band of muscle that held her.

"Haven't you done enough to me?" she moaned, pressing against him so that his hand was caught between them.

"Kiss me, Shannon," he commanded softly, knowing his battle was nearly won.

"I hate you for this, Morgan," she whispered as she gave in to the rising passion he inflamed in her.

Her lips were soft on his and tasted of the sweet brandy. They started slowly, sensually, before her hands snaked up his neck and pulled his head to hers. She sought his mouth hungrily, starved for the passion they had shared—the passion only he could inspire in her. She was his and no other's.

This was what he demanded of her, yet deep inside she rebelled. If he would reduce her to this glorious humiliation then she would retaliate. There would be little he would do with her aunt and cousin in the next room. Deliberately, she began to caress his neck with her fingertips. They teased his spine as they trailed down it and stopped at his trim waistline. As he returned her kisses, she reached for the front of his breeches, stroking tentatively at first and then more arduously as she felt his response. It pleased her when she heard him catch his breath and he crushed her to him with a low moan. Neither of them heard her aunt until she knocked again.

"Shannon, did you find the gown?" she called from the hallway.

Shannon backed away from Morgan and tried to catch her breath as her eyes locked with his. "How does it feel, Morgan, to ache for something you cannot have?" she hissed lowly before raising her voice to answer her aunt. "Yes, Aunt Harriet. Coming!" She stooped to pick up the nightdress she had dropped. Her heart pounded in her chest as she warily stepped around him.

"This is not done, Shannon."

"No, Morgan, it is not. I still have your child to bear and raise. It will be years before I am truly done with you.'

"Is that what you really want?"

Shannon felt as if he saw through her and she could not bring herself to answer. Instead she turned to leave.

"If you are determined to go on without me, Shannon, then for God's sake, be careful. The murderers are likely to try again."

She looked back over her shoulder and nodded mutely. It was difficult to move as the steel blue eyes looked down on her and she knew she would never be done with him as long as she drew breath.

"Shannon!" Aunt Harriet called impatiently from the other side of the door.

"Right here, Aunt Harriet," Shannon replied as she slipped through the entry. She handed her aunt the gown. Morgan's voice followed her through the doorway and the finality of his parting words struck her numb with pain.

"Goodbye, Shannon."

Chapter Twenty-One

The holidays were a busy time for the Bedlowe family. The desk was covered with invitations to dinners and dances. Like the manor at Snowden, the servants decorated Kenton Place with fresh greenery on the mantels, windowsills, staircases, and doorways. Mistletoe hung from the grand chandeliers in the main hall. Aunt Harriet had a flair for putting the right touch to each of the arrangements, and Shannon, unaccustomed to this form of celebration, was overcome with awe at the transformation of the home.

The dining room table fascinated her with the tiered silver trays of fruits and pastries colorfully displayed. She could not imagine disturbing the arrangement to try one of the tempting delicacies the cooks had prepared under her aunt's careful supervision.

Shannon had kept to herself as much as possible since their return to Kenton Place. The ordeal near the inn had left her shaken and drained. While her aunt and cousin encouraged her to accept some of the gracious invitations, she had pleaded exhaustion and remained at home. She knew that London's social circles were well aware of her condition and she simply did not want to face the condescending looks and overbearing sympathies.

Even Aunt Harriet was more reserved in her treatment of her since the night she innocently spent in Brian's room. Although Brian assured her that his mother understood the circumstances, Shannon still sensed a difference in the woman. Whenever she and Brian were together, her aunt was not far away and Shannon was uncomfortable under her curious scrutiny. It was hard to blame her though, for it had been an incriminating scene.

Jonathan Devage and Corrinne had visited on Christmas Day to share the traditional feast of roast boar chased with muscatel to help digest the strong meat. There had been so much food, Shannon could hardly finish a small sampling from each dish. Corrinne and Aunt Harriet took turns at the harpsichord while everyone stood around and sang festive songs. Although Shannon struggled with the unfamiliar melodies, she could not help but enjoy the warmth of the fellowship.

In the weeks that followed the holiday, Shannon neither saw nor heard from the Lord of Snowden. It seemed the finality of his words was indeed real and while she should have been relieved, she was distraught. The tender moments they shared haunted her night and day and the child growing within her served only to keep the recollections fresh. The thought to overlook his deception played on her mind more than once, but the fact that her sister might also carry his child quickly brought its dismissal.

When Shannon received notice from her solicitor that the papers handing her estate over to her father and stepsister were prepared and ready for signature, she asked Brian to take her to the man's office. Her cousin was curious but held his questions, absorbed with the prospect of taking her out of the house for the first time since their return from Snowden. She had also arranged to meet her sister at the Tabard. After they spent the afternoon at the Frost Fair that Brian had told her so much about, she was to join her father and Corrinne for supper while Brian went on to the gambling house. While her cousin was not thrilled at spending the afternoon with her stepsister, he humored Shannon and went along with her plan.

The meeting with the solicitor did not take long. The man was well prepared and presented the papers to Shannon, explaining each one briefly. Shannon signed her name where the man indicated, ignoring his disapproving look, and tucked the papers in her purse to have her father and stepsister sign them at dinner that evening. The business being done, she then turned her attentions to the promise of an interesting afternoon with her entertaining cousin.

The Tabard was crowded with patrons that sought refuge from the cold weather outside. Corrinne had only arrived moments before when they joined her at the stretcher-based table and ordered the body-warming refreshments. She chattered excitedly about the fair and the hope to have her name imprinted on paper with the day and the year.

"Shannon, you must have yours done, too!" her sister told her emphatically. "It's quite the thing!"

"I hear they've set up a sort of Wooden O right on the ice," Brian mentioned, appreciating the wonder on Shannon's face. "We'll take in the games if you two are up to the chill."

"I am," Shannon exclaimed with genuine enthusiasm. "I cannot wait to see such a grand fair . . . and on the ice at that!"

Just south of the Bridge, she saw the fair when their coach made its way down a makeshift ramp onto the iced-over river. There was a large assembly of tents arranged in such a manner as to form streets between them. Within them, were miniature shops like those on London's busy streets furnished and well inventoried with all sorts of commodities. Delicious smells rose from the smoke that filled the air—the baked goods and roasted meats were actually being cooked in the tents over stoves heated with wood and sea coal.

Shannon carefully walked on the snow-covered ice in the boots Brian had instructed her to wear and insisted on checking in each tent. She was amazed at the crowds that braved the cold to take part in or simply enjoy the winter carnival.

"Look," she exclaimed, grabbing Brian's arm and pointing in astonishment at a half-dozen men pulling a small boat with its sail hoisted to catch the afternoon breeze. Another dozen or so men pushed at the sides of the vessel that was loaded with goods to sell at the market.

"I'd say that is sailing at its worst," her cousin replied with a chuckle.

The small printing press was set up in a heated tent and Shannon did not mind the wait. The craftsman took a sixpence from her and her sister and proceeded to carefully set their names in type. He chose characters from a large chest that displayed them all and lined them up neatly on the press. Shannon watched the procedure with curiosity and when he presented her a small slip of paper with her name and the date, the twenty-first of January in the year of 1683, she tucked it in her bag delightedly.

"I think we should go back to that little shop where that old woman was selling assorted items for

367

babies, Shannon. I am sure Aunt Harriet is already busy making things for my prospective . . . whatever, but I have heard one can never have enough clothing for the nasty little things."

Shannon colored at the reminder of her condition and she self-consciously flattened her cloak against her stomach to be sure it did not show.

"No one can see a thing," Brian assured her realizing her discomfort. His breath clouded in the cold air and was warm on her nearly frozen ear.

"Well, it would take us out of the chill for a moment," Shannon relented. "And I have to admit, my hand is not nearly as expert with a needle as I need it to be."

Corrinne laughed and hurried ahead of them while Brian held Shannon's arm and followed. Shannon wondered if Corrinne had dealt with the fact that she herself might have one of those nasty little things as she called them. Somehow Shannon could not picture her selfish sister with a child.

When they left the woman's tent, Shannon had purchased a beautifully embroidered nightdress and a cotton blanket that had the same design on its border. It had been difficult to find the lighter garments and the woman's indignation was satisfied only when Shannon explained that she would not need them until summer.

"Now I know that this is extremely ill-mannered, dear ladies, but in view of the extreme cold, I took the liberty of purchasing this small bottle of brandy. I could be persuaded to share it, but alas, we have no Venetian glasses," Brian bemoaned in mock dismay.

"How clever of you, cousin," Corrinne remarked, glancing about to see if she was being observed. "I would love a sip. Without it, I fear we shall never make it through a game."

To Shannon's astonishment, her sister wiped the top of the uncorked bottle with her gloved hand and took a healthy swallow. As it made its way down her throat, she handed the bottle to Shannon. Shannon followed her sister's example and as they made their way toward a large circle of people she could feel it begin to take the edge off the chill that made her feet and hands ache.

There were all classes of spectators to watch the huge mastiffs attempt to fight and kill a large thick-coated bear. The bear's hind legs were tied and it swatted angrily at the dogs who threatened it. Its deadly claws lashed out at one of the hounds who dared too close and ripped the yelping animal's side open. Shannon closed her eyes in revulsion as its blood stained the white snow crimson.

"Are you all right?" Brian asked as he felt her lean against him.

"Why are they doing that?" Shannon asked in disbelief.

"To see which will win, silly!" Corrinne told her in a condescending tone. "Everyone knows the dogs will eventually wear the bear down."

"But it's tied!" Shannon objected.

"That's because it's so big, sister. It would run away if they didn't tie it and then what would amuse us?"

Shannon turned back to the spectacle in time to see one of the dogs leap at the bear and sink its teeth in the howling animal's neck. Before the bear could rip it away another dog latched onto its neck from the other side. The bear furiously knocked both hounds bleeding to death to the icy surface, but two more resumed the torment. The bear was beginning to bleed profusely around the leather collar that encircled its neck and the crowd roared in approval.

Her mind made an involuntary association with the gruesome scene and she suddenly saw Nick Brennan's body lying on the deck of the *Plunderer*, the splintered decking protruding from his blood-soaked chest. She shook her head to clear the image away, but her father's eyes would not release her from their death stare. The noise of the crowd became the thunder of the explosion that sent her reeling across her father's body at Morgan Hawke. Then came the blessed darkness that followed.

"Out of my way!"

Shannon heard Brian's voice and light seemed to penetrate her retreat. Her body seemed to float, yet she could feel his arms under her as he carried her. Corrinne was calling for a coach in the background. When her head cleared, she tried to sit up in her cousin's arms and grabbed at his scarfed neck as he nearly lost his grip on her.

"Whoa there!" Brian exclaimed, shifting his arms to accommodate her change in position. "You're back with us!"

Shannon was confused as he set her down on shaky legs and helped her into the coach her sister had acquired.

"Are you all right, sister?" Corrinne asked, peering at her closely.

Shannon nodded her head and rested back against the seat as Brian climbed in beside her. There had been so much blood, she recalled, shuddering involuntarily, and the noise . . .

"You just called for father, papa actually, and went down in a heap! We feared for the child!" Corrinne told her.

"If I had known the spectacle would have upset you, Shannon, I would never have suggested you see it," Brian apologized. His face was a mirror of

370

concern, as he ignored Corrinne's presence and put his arm about her.

"I feel sometimes as if I am going mad," Shannon said slowly. "I saw the blood and suddenly I saw my father dying . . . I don't know what happened." She shook her head as if to clear it. The pallor on her face alarmed her companions.

"I think we should take you to Kenton Place right now. Forget your plans to dine with your father," Brian spoke up.

Shannon stiffened. "No! I must . . . I mean I want to have supper with my family tonight. I have only been to Sterling Court once."

"Are you sure you are up to it?" Corrinne asked. "I mean, I am sure Father will understand. Your condition causes these sort of things, I've heard."

"I will be fine. I have witnessed a living nightmare and the gruesome scene reminded me of it. I feel ridiculous enough as it is without changing all our plans. Now please, let's go on to Sterling Court and then Brian may leave to pursue one of his favorite pastimes." Shannon winked at her cousin in a forced attempt to tease.

In truth she felt horrid. She wondered if carrying a child could really cause such unstable emotions. Her stomach churned as the coach made its way toward Sterling Court, and her hands, engulfed in the fur muff Brian had given her for Christmas, shook. She wanted to snuggle against her cousin and feel safe under his protection, but dared not seek his attention for fear of misleading him to think it was more than it was. Surrounded by family, she never had felt so alone.

Brian left her reluctantly at Sterling Court. Corrinne ordered hot tea for Shannon and then went upstairs to change her clothes for supper. Shannon sat in the ladies parlor where a servant had just put fresh logs on the fire and warmed herself. Her feet began to thaw and she wriggled her toes as she held them as close to the flames as she dared without singeing the woolen stockings she had worn under the boots that sat on the hearth drying out.

The portrait of her father and stepmother that hung over the mantel caught her eye and she studied it. The resemblance between Corrinne and her fair mother was evident. The mother was heavier than her slender daughter, but they shared the same coloring and delicate features. As Shannon studied her father, she frowned. There was nothing in the dark eyes and black hair that reminded her of herself. The picture left her feeling as unattached as the polite relationship that had developed since her arrival in London. She was more her mother's daughter . . . and Nick Brennan's.

She closed her eyes and rested her head against the high back of the French damask-upholstered chair. How she missed him. She wondered what he would think of her now. Although she had not married, she carried his grandchild. Her baby would never know the strong bounce of his knee and the loud yet gentle laugh. It saddened her.

In the background she heard Jonathan Devage arrive. He greeted the doorman and his footsteps clicked on the polished floors as he made his way to the gentleman's parlor across the hall. As he closed the paneled doors she realized that he was not alone and she caught her breath as she recognized the voice of the Lord of Snowden. She thought she detected another gentleman's presence, but the closed doors muted the conversation so that it was not clearly audible.

Corrinne startled her when she entered the room

dressed in a full skirt with a slashed jacket over a lace-collared blouse. "I thought I heard father come in," she remarked, glancing back across the hall to the closed doors. "Does he have company?"

"Morgan Hawke," Shannon informed her suspiciously. "You wouldn't know about this, would you, sister?"

"Indeed not, but I am delighted." Before Shannon could say another word, Corrinne rushed across the hall and burst through the closed doors. "Morgan, how delightfully unexpected! Shannon told me you were here."

"Shannon?" Came the surprised response, that caused Shannon to jump to her feet and close the parlor doors quietly.

It was all ruined now. She had hoped to talk to her father and stepsister privately. She dropped back in her chair and seized her boots in frustration. As she pulled them on, the door opened and Corrinne proudly led the gentlemen into the room. She concentrated on her task until a familiar voice made her look up in delighted surprise.

"Well now, it's been awhile since ye left us on the *Sea Lady* a homeless lass, and look at ye now."

"Michael!" Shannon let her foot down and stood awkwardly, trying to force it the rest of the way into the boot, before running over to the big Irishman and hugging him. "I am so glad to see you!" she told him earnestly. "What are you doing in London . . . I thought the *Sea Lady* was sailing to the Indies."

"I've been in Glasgow watchin' them Scotties build our new ship. A fine one she'll be when we bring 'er down this spring . . . that is if the river ever thaws," he laughed, his blue eyes twinkling.

"I ran into these two gentlemen at a tavern down near the office and shared a glass of Madeira before

373

inviting them here for supper. Lord Hawke has recommended this Scottish shipbuilder and Mr. Finney was good enough to tell me more about the man," Jonathan Devage explained, taking Shannon's hand and giving her a peck on the cheek as a greeting. "I hope you do not mind, Shannon."

"Of course not," Shannon answered quickly. If sharing a meal with Morgan Hawke meant a chance to visit with her old friend, she would make the sacrifice. Perhaps she would have time later to talk with her father and Corrinne.

"Father, could I see you for a moment?" Corrinne asked coquettishly, as she drew her father out into the hallway.

Morgan Hawke took Shannon's hand and raised it politely to his lips. "Knowing your feelings, I would decline this invitation now, but I can see you are pleased to see Finney."

"You are right, Morgan. Please stay." She gave him a genuine smile that faded when she overheard her stepsister's barely concealed whisper from the hall.

"How could you invite that common seaman here?"

Shannon's face colored in embarrassment at her sister's rude words and faced Finney to apologize. Before she could say a word, the first mate winked at her and leaned over to whisper lowly, "I don't like her worth a damn either."

"Oh, Michael," Shannon said taking his hand and squeezing it warmly. "I am sorry."

When Jonathan Devage reappeared, he too showed his dismay at his daughter's ill manners and asked the gentlemen to join him for another drink, while Corrinne saw to the final dinner arrangements. Shannon excused herself to go help her sister. She found Corrinne fuming in the dining room where he was having the steward put additional china and crystal settings on for the unexpected guests.

"I think you should apologize to Michael, Corinne. We all could hear you!" Shannon exclaimed heatedly. "It was very rude and very embarrassing."

Corrinne tossed a linen napkin on the table defiantly. "I will not! Why Morgan ever accepted that crude man for a friend is beyond me. I detest him and I don't care if he did hear me."

"He is my friend, too!" Shannon informed her.

"Well, I could expect no less considering the class of vermin you were raised with."

"Well maybe if you had grown up in the same situation you might have learned something about manners and consideration for the feelings of others!"

"Madame, should we serve dinner now? The cook is ready." The steward stood uncomfortably in the doorway and waited for a reply.

Shannon held her lips in a firm line as Corrinne ignored her comment and in a biting voice ordered the manservant to announce dinner. Shannon sat between Michael Finney and her father, while Corrinne abandoned her customary seat at the end of the table to sit next to her ex-fiancé. Green eyes flashed across the table at Shannon as the woman lifted her glass.

"Morgan, this is a new wine we have just received from Italy. I know you are drinking the Madeira but would you like to taste mine?" she asked in a kittenish voice.

"No thank you Corrinne. I do not mix liquors."

"Oh, just a taste, silly!" She dipped her fingertip in the red wine and wiped it across his lips causing him to stiffen irritably.

"So tell me more about this Macleod," Jonathan Devage spoke up in an effort to divert attention from his daughter.

Morgan Hawke took his napkin and dabbed it at his mouth before speaking. "He's fair as far as the price he charges goes. And as I said earlier, he trained under the tradesman who built ships for my father for years. I do not see how you can go wrong in ordering one from him."

"Unless you're in a hurry," Finney pointed out. "When ye're as good as he is, people seek ye out to do their work. He's a busy man running two crews as it is."

"How long do you think it will take," Devage asked, "before he might start on a ship for me?"

"Shannon fainted at the Frost Fair today."

Shannon dropped her silver fork so that it clattered against the blue patterened china plate.

"We were absolutely panicked," Corrinne informed the men who turned concerned faces toward Shannon who began to color in horror at her sister's revelation. "I found an empty coach and Brian literally carried her to it."

"Did you send for a doctor?" Jonathan Devage asked Shannon.

Shannon answered curtly and glared at her sister as she spoke. "There was no need. I was merely sickened by the sight of vicious dogs tearing at a tied-up bear. The blood reminded me of too much that I have tried to forget. I was fine when I got away from there and am fine now," she added, hoping to dissuade further comment on her health. "I think I should like to see a ship being built. I've heard it looks like a giant skeleton of wood." She hoped to redirect the conversation back to its original course.

"Aye, that it does . . . and it makes ye appreciate the men that build 'em too," Finney agreed.

"I think it was your condition," Corrinne injected,

refusing to drop the subject. "I've heard that when women are pregnant, they cry a lot and have fainting spells."

"Corrinne, that is quite enough. You are obviously making your sister uncomfortable," Jonathan Devage snapped angrily.

Tears sprang to Corrinne's eyes as she looked at her father with a hurt expression. "I only thought that you would be concerned and would want to know. You know how fond I am of her." She turned to Shannon. "I am so sorry if I have made you uncomfortable, sister. Truly I am."

Shannon wanted to shrink under the table. She knew her sister was deliberately trying to embarrass her because she had chastised her for insulting Michael Finney and she had certainly accomplished her goal. She ought to leave her penniless, Shannon thought as she met the tear-filled eyes. Corrinne was a spoiled and selfish girl who acted more like a spiteful child at times than the beautiful woman she was. Suddenly Shannon pitied her. Child was correct. She had been catered to so much that she knew no better than to expect to have her way all the time. She had not faced many of the hardships of life that made one grow up fast.

Shannon could not bring herself to forgive her sister, but she tried to bring the subject around to the Glasgow shipyard once more. It was readily accepted by the others who were as uncomfortable as she was. Finney described in detail how Macleod went about his trade and both Hawke and her father were intent on his words. Corrinne picked at her food and occasionally cast a glance sideways at her handsome dinner partner.

Throughout the meal, Morgan Hawke paid no more attention to her sister than he did to Shannon.

That he and Finney were there on business was clear. After the meal, he and the first mate excused themselves from the usual after dinner cordials, insisting that they had previous plans. When Hawke bade her goodbye, he merely gave her another polite touch of his lips to her hand. His eyes as they met hers were distant and aloof. Finney, however embraced her warmly, and promised to visit her at Kenton Place before he left London to return to the shipyard in Scotland.

Corrinne pouted as she plopped down on the gold on white settee in the parlor and pushed her untouched glass of wine aside. Shannon ignored her sister's bad humor and proceeded with the real purpose of her visit. She did not have much time. Brian had promised to pick her up after the dinner hour. When her father entered the ladies parlor with his brandy, Shannon took the papers from her purse and presented them to him.

"Please read these over carefully, father," she told him nervously. "I really want this and I will not be talked out of it."

Shannon sat straight in the chair by the hearth opposite his and waited while her father scanned the papers. She studied the designs on the imported Turkish rug that complimented the French damask upholstery and prepared her argument mentally.

"Shannon, I cannot permit this! You obviously are not thinking clearly, and no wonder with what you have been through." Her father folded the papers and handed them to her.

Shannon shook her head firmly, refusing to take them. "Please sign them. I do not need, nor want, my grandfather's estate. I cannot help the way I feel, but I do not belong here . . . you and Corrinne do."

"But the business . . ."

"Is yours. You have run it successfully all these years. I see no reason to change that. I have made provisions for all I need," she assured him.

"You're giving away your inheritance?" Corrinne exclaimed incredulously as she caught on.

Shannon nodded. Her sister jumped up from her seat and perched on the arm of her father's chair, reading the documents over his shoulder.

"Well, since you're marrying Lord Hawke, I suppose you can afford to be generous. When is the wedding? I thought you two might have given some indication tonight," she asked pitifully.

Shannon took a deep breath and let it out slowly. It was difficult to tell her father that she was not going to marry the father of her child. She was certain of the disgrace it would bring both to her immediate family as well as the Bedlowes. "I am not marrying Lord Hawke. I am leaving London and will not return . . . at least for a long while."

As accomplished as she was at masking her feelings, Corrinne failed to hide her satisfaction while her father registered shock.

"I do not understand, Shannon. Is that why you have retained ownership of the cottage outside of Dover?"

"You're going to live at that little place?" Corrinne gasped. "But it's a summer retreat!"

"I do not need much room for myself and the baby. I hope to hire a woman to help me with the house. That is all I will require," Shannon informed them.

"Why will you not marry Lord Hawke? You once had a . . . some sort of feeling toward him," her father stammered at a loss for the proper words.

"That is gone forever, sir. Too much has happened to rekindle that relationship."

"Not because I asked him to give Corrinne some

time after her mother's death before breaking the engagement, I hope?"

"Father, how could you!" Corrinne jumped to her feet. "You mean he wanted to break our betrothal before he knew Shannon was going to have his child?"

Shannon could see that her sister was visibly shaken and sympathized with her in view of the way the man they both loved and trusted had taken her with the same deceit.

"But he said he loved me and missed me," Corrinne moaned miserably.

"We only wanted to protect you, dear. It's been a damned quandary for all of us," Devage remarked in exasperation.

"It need not be anymore. I cannot stay in London for obvious reasons. I will not have Morgan Hawke. Perhaps Corrinne might use her charm to win him back with me and the child out of the way."

"What of the Bedlowes?"

"No one but the three of us must know. Especially Brian and Morgan," Shannon insisted.

"Have you bewitched every man in London?" Corrinne sputtered indignantly. "Brian fairly fawns over you. When you fainted, I thought he was going to run you home on foot!"

"Corrinne!"

The girl settled back on the arm of the chair at her father's warning, but her eyes glared at Shannon.

"I will not allow you to simply sneak off in the night. I insist on taking you to Dover myself if that is your final decision and you will not change your mind," her father stated firmly.

Shannon smiled gratefully at the offer. "Thank you, father. I have to admit, that the prospect is a bit frightening, especially with someone out there who wants me dead for whatever reason. If I leave, perhaps they will give up their murderous plans for me."

"Then I shall go, too," Corrinne announced. She continued before either Shannon or her father could object. "In spite of our differences, sister, I feel it is the least I can do. After all, you are leaving us everything." Particularly Morgan, her look told Shannon.

The knock on the front door announced Brian's arrival. Shannon rose from her chair and spoke hurriedly before he was shown in.

"Please, not a word to anyone. Let me know when you will be ready to take me."

"Next Monday I have to go to Dover on business. I deal with merchants there regularly," her father explained. "I will take you then, but you must make the arrangements to meet me."

"I'll send a message with the details as soon as I work them out," Shannon promised, somewhat taken back at the suddenness of his cooperation. "Thank you . . . both of you."

Brian was in a jovial mood when the doorman showed him into the parlor. He had apparently had good luck at the dice and plenty of beer to celebrate it with. His hair was tousled wildly and his cheeks, nose, and ears were red from the cold. Her father offered him another drink and he accepted readily to Shannon's dismay. She was more than ready to leave her sister's company.

Corrinne, however, became the gracious hostess. Shannon could not believe the switch of personalities and began to understand why her father was so concerned for her emotional state. Brian finished his cordial quickly, while the doorman fetched Shannon's cloak and by the time she put it on, he was ready to escort her home.

As the coach was pulling out of the drive, Brian slid over next to her and put his arm about her. "Did you have a pleasant visit?" he asked, his face so close to hers that when Shannon turned to answer, their cheeks brushed. She drew back startled and he chuckled. "Didn't you know I was here?"

"Are you drunk?" Shannon asked warily.

He put his forehead to hers, still amused. "Possibly. Although I can still walk. I thought I presented myself rather well when I picked you up."

"Brian, your parents are going to have a fit when they see you. How are you ever going to convince them that you are responsible enough to go to Italy?" Shannon asked in exasperation.

"I will be sober in time to go to Italy!"

Shannon laughed in spite of herself. "You adorable fool! What am I to do with you?"

"Love me."

"Brian . . ."

He silenced her with a kiss. His weight pressed her into the corner of the coach. Shannon pushed at his chest but could not move him away. Her teeth were clenched refusing to let his tongue penetrate her mouth, and when he raised his head, she turned away from him.

"Stop it, Brian. You don't mean this," she told him.

"Shannon, I want you and your baby," he whispered hoarsely. "I cannot go on playing the gay cousin without a care. I care . . . very deeply for you."

"I told you, Brian . . ." Shannon started, but his lips closed over her mouth hungrily. She pulled her head away and he began to caress her neck with his tongue. "Brian, I don't want to hurt you!" she warned, trying to twist away from his attentions. He reached inside her cloak and felt for her bosom within the folds. "Brian!" she gasped, freeing one of her hands and striking him hard with her fist. His head jerked to the side. "Get your hands off of me this instant," she demanded as he rubbed his jaw and stared at her bewildered. "Get away from me!" She pushed him back against the opposite side of the vehicle.

He sprawled on the seat and drew up his hands about his shoulders, his eyes watching her in the dim light from the lantern that hung outside their coach. "Is this far enough, cousin?" The pain in his voice touched her. "What is it? My father thinks more highly of Morgan Hawke than he does his own son . . . And you love the man in spite of the way he has deceived you!" he accused. "I would do anything for you, Shannon."

"Brian, please . . . you are such a wonderful young man. Any girl would love you."

"I don't want any girl. I want you. Damn it, Shannon, I could take you by force if I just wanted your body. I have had any number of opportunities to have dishonored you . . . you're so damned trusting! But I didn't, Shannon. I have not sought to deceive you ever, yet you reject my love for that of a proven liar."

"You have been so good to me, Brian. I am so fond of you for your friendship." Shannon reached out and took his hand. "I feel so guilty for letting you think that I could be any more than your cousin." She sniffed back the tears. "I am so sorry."

"Just let me kiss you, Shannon. I promise I will do no more."

"Brian, it is wrong . . ."

"I love you and you are fond of me. What can be wrong about an innocent kiss?"

He had moved over to her again. His eyes begged her as much as the misery in his voice. She had taken his friendship. A kiss was harmless enough payment for that. Shannon closed her eyes and relaxed her guard.

Brian's arms were strong and comforting as they embraced her and pulled her to him. His body was warm and his lips caressed hers as though savoring them. The scent of beer was heavy on his labored breath. She knew she was safe in spite of his earlier loss of control. This was her protector—her knight of laughter and security. Her response astonished them both. They were each desolate for different reasons and the comfort of each other's arms was too much for either to turn away.

When the lights of Kenton Place came into view and the coach stopped in front of the pillared steps, Brian backed away from Shannon and touched her cheek tenderly, wiping away a stray tear. As the coachman climbed down from his cold perch, her cousin took her hand and brushed his lips across it softly, never taking his gaze from her. "You will always have my deepest love and respect, milady," he whispered, as the coachman opened the door for them to exit.

Chapter Twenty-Two

Monday was a dreary day. The sky threatened freezing rain and the streets of London were less crowded than usual as the coach Shannon asked her father to send carried her to Sterling Court. Her uncle had left early that morning for his office and Aunt Harriet had gone to visit the ailing Lady Flemington. When Shannon left Kenton Place, her cousin had still not risen, having spent most of the night out with his friends.

The doorman gave her a questioning glance as she had her trunk brought downstairs and loaded on the coach. She briefly explained that she was going to have the lock repaired and would be out shopping most of the day. He seemed to accept her explanation with little suspicion. If all went well, her family would not take her absence seriously until that evening. By then she would be out of the city.

When she reached Sterling Court, her father had her trunk tied on the Devage coach which was already loaded with the baggage he and Corrinne were taking on the trip. Shannon went inside to warm up near the fire for the last time in a while and shared some hot chocolate with her stepsister. The servants placed footwarmers in the coach and after the passengers were settled in, handed them the heavy lap robes for the long, cold ride ahead.

Corrinne chatted gaily about an upcoming Winter Ball to be given at Whitehall and about the gown she was having made especially for the occasion. Shannon listened idly as she watched the skyline of red tiled roofs and sharp steeples grow smaller behind them. The sooty clouds from the coal fires hovered above the city, dark against the lighter gray sky. Soon there was nothing but the rolling brown hills and green forests behind them and the same stretched ahead between them and the chalky lands of southern England.

Jonathan Devage kept to himself, absorbed in the papers that he had brought along in a leather pouch. From what Shannon could see of the neatly lettered pages on her father's lap, they were bills of laden. She was comforted by his presence in the coach and the fact that the Devage coachman was armed. Her father had assured her that they would take no chances with booted shrews or highwaymen. She gathered that her safety was not the only reason for the weapons, for her father also carried another case with money to complete his business with the Dover merchants.

The coach ride was rough. The muddy ruts in the narrow road had frozen and the wheels bounced from one track to another unmercifully jolting the passengers. The cold weather soon led Shannon and Corrinne to huddle as close together as they could under the heavy blankets. Corrinne was starting to complain, so that when they reached the inn on the first leg of their journey, Shannon was grateful to get away from her overbearing sister for a while.

After a good hot supper of roast lamb and hot rye rolls, Shannon retired to the small room next to her sister's upstairs. There was a small stove in it like the one at Pulcherchurch that heated the room cozily. The mattress was hard, but the linens were clean and she had no trouble sleeping at all, unlike the restless night she had spent before.

When they left the inn at Rochester, Shannon was refreshed, but somewhat sore from the rough jostling that continued the rest of the way to Dover. The busy port rested on the shore of the English Channel. Large chalky cliffs loomed over it and the sight in the dead of the harsh winter was as chilling as the whipping winds that lashed in from the water.

Her father had sent word a few days earlier that they would be arriving. Shannon was relieved to find out that a young woman kept the house when the family was not there. She had been instructed to have the rooms upstairs made ready and that Shannon would be staying on indefinitely. It was Shannon's hope that she might talk the young woman into sharing the house instead of living in the small servants' kitchen in the back that Corrinne said she lived in.

Shannon's first view of the house, perched high on a plateau that overlooked the town, was a welcome one. It was a story and a half structure with small dormers in the front and back. The roof shingles were blackened and grayed from the weather and the stone walls with the small leaded glass casements were overgrown with vines of ivy. There were stone chimneys on each end and both invited the weary travelers with smoke that promised warm fires within.

The girl named Molly opened the plank door as the coach stopped in front of the low stone fence that enclosed the yard. It had started to drizzle and the wind blew the icy droplets in Shannon's face as the coachman opened the door to help them out. Shannon clutched her cloak about her tightly and ran up the worn path to the open door, followed by her father and stepsister.

Molly took their wet wraps and hung them on a rack of wooden pegs that was mounted on the back of the door. The three travelers gathered about the blazing fire in the large hearth and warmed their hands and nearly numb feet. The servant moved about quietly and it seemed they had been there no time at all when she announced that there were warm buns and hot coffee on the table behind them.

As Shannon ate the delicious buns and enjoyed the coffee that burned her tongue, she watched Molly stirring a tempting smelling dish in a pot over the fire. The girl was not much older than herself, she thought, and she definitely would be company on the dreary days of winter.

"Molly, now that we are thawed sufficiently enough to speak, I would like to introduce you to my daughter, Shannon," Jonathan Devage called out to the girl as she put the lid back on the simmering pot.

Molly walked over to Shannon and offered her a work-roughened hand with a beaming smile that was as warm as the fire she tended. "Pleased to meet you, Mistress Shannon, although I must admit, I'm a little confused. I've known your family for the past five years and have never heard your name mentioned."

"It is a long story, Molly," Shannon told the girl, shaking her hand. "But I am so glad to know that you will be here. In truth, I am hoping that you might consider moving in here with me."

The girl's face registered surprise. "In the main house?"

"Shannon, she is a servant!" Corrinne objected.

Shannon looked at Molly who reddened at the insult and ignored her sister's outburst. "I hope that we will be friends . . . not just a mistress and her servant."

Molly nodded at Shannon slowly, sensing the sincerity in the girl that her stepsister lacked. "I would be honored, miss," she answered, with a short dip of a curtsy. "Would you like to see your house?"

Shannon pushed the small bench that she sat on away from the table and rose with a smile. "Of course I would. I am sure you've made it as warm and welcome as you have this kitchen."

There was another large room that had a fire going in its stone hearth as well. It was furnished with a dark blue upholstered settee and two rocking chairs with woven seats that graced either side of the fireplace. A winding set of steps were revealed behind a door to one side of it that led to a long narrow bedroom upstairs. Molly led the way with a lighted candle into the next room that had another set of steps that led back down to the kitchen where her father and Corrinne still drank their coffee.

"Not exactly Sterling Court, is it, Shannon?" Corrinne remarked sarcastically, eyeing her sister for a reaction.

"I like it," Shannon replied genuinely. "It reminds me a little of our house on Nose' Be, except for the cold," she added, rubbing her arms briskly.

"Excuse me, miss, but I was thinking . . ." Molly began.

"Go on, Molly," Shannon encouraged.

"Well the rooms upstairs don't have a fireplace or a stove. The one that used to be there was never replaced because the house was used in the summer only. I was thinking, perhaps we'd best bring the mattresses down from the upstairs rooms until you can make some other arrangements."

"I cannot believe this!" Corrinne exclaimed indignantly. "Father, we simply cannot sleep on the floors. I'll catch my death!"

Jonathan Devage rubbed his chin thoughtfully. "I hadn't thought of this before," he admitted. "Maybe we should go on to the inn. We could stay down at the inn near the outskirts of the port city," he suggested. "There's still time to reach it before dark."

"I'm sure we can manage nicely here, father," Shannon assured him. "It's a sort of adventure."

"Well you can stay and have your adventure, I prefer the inn!" Corrinne announced rising to her feet. "And you know how badly your back hurts, father!"

Jonathan Devage looked from his dark-haired daughter to his fair one. His discomfort was obvious, not wanting to disappoint either.

"Perhaps it would be best if you and Corrinne did go to the inn," Shannon proposed in an effort to relieve the situation. "If Molly would agree to stay here with me, I would prefer to stay. This is my home and I must get used to this cold if I am to last."

"I do not like leaving you alone on your first night away from home, Shannon," her father protested.

"I'll be glad to stay with the mistress, sir," Molly offered.

"There, it's settled then. Molly and I can set up camp near the fire and get to know each other and you two can be comfortable. I don't want anyone put out because of me," Shannon told them firmly. "So please do not feel obligated. You can come back tomorrow."

"Well maybe I can acquire a stove for you as well while I'm in town," her father suggested.

"Or two, perhaps. I have the funds to pay for

them," Shannon added quickly. "Molly will need one for her room, too."

As soon as her father and Corrinne left for the inn, Molly and Shannon busied themselves with moving two mattresses and accompanying linens downstairs. They laid them out in the parlor near the hearth and piled heavy quilts on top of them. When the edges were tucked neatly under them, Molly started to open Shannon's trunk to unpack it.

"I can do that, Molly. I am not helpless and you have prepared the house so well for my coming that there is little else to do," Shannon told the young woman.

"Well, if we both work at it, Miss . . ."

"Shannon, please. If we are to be friends, let's do away with titles," Shannon insisted. She held out her hand to seal the agreement and Molly accepted with a smile.

"You're not at all like your sister," Molly told her as she unfolded one of the gowns Shannon had brought along. She had left the beautiful ball gowns at the Bedlowes' since her prospects of attending a ball in her future role as mother were dim.

"Thank you, Molly." Shannon laughed, smacking her face gently in a reprimand for her smart comment. "I know I shouldn't say such things, but Corrinne can be such a . . . spoiled child," she finished, choosing the sweeter of the two names that sprang to her mind.

"You are too kind . . . Shannon," Molly remarked meaningfully.

Shannon studied the brown-haired girl curiously. "Your speech . . . it's very proper for a servant and your carriage speaks of a higher station. I don't mean to pry, but . . ."

Molly hung the gold gown up on a peg behind the

391

door that separated the kitchen from the parlor. "This house used to be mine . . . my father's actually. When he was . . . when he died, I was left penniless. I had to sell it to pay off his debts. Your father bought it and was gracious enough to let me stay on and care for the place. The wages are good enough," Molly mused aloud. "And I am home."

Shannon nodded in understanding. At least Molly was home. She sympathized with the girl. "I lost my father also . . . My adopted father or . . ." She frowned at her confused words. "The man that raised me was killed. He died in my arms." Shannon paused, seeing the interest spark in the wide brown eyes that reminded her of Lillianne. She hung the last of her gowns on the door and then turned to her new friend. "I'll tell you all about it over supper. Whatever is in that pot is driving me mad, it smells so good!"

Molly had planned for Jonathan and Corrinne Devage as well, so the meal of stewed rabbit and vegetables was more than ample. Shannon was glad that Molly was such a good cook and told the girl that she must teach her more about the arts of cooking, explaining that Marie had not taught her as much as she would like to know. The cooking on Nose' Be was also very different.

Molly listened with fascination as Shannon revealed her past. She could not believe that Shannon had actually been raised and trained to fight like a pirate. Shannon playfully picked up a wood-handled carving knife and balanced it in her hand, testing its weight. She threw it with a fluid motion, easily hitting her mark—a large circular swirl in the facing of the plank door.

"My God!" Molly gasped, looking at her companion with renewed admiration. "Do you hunt?"

Shannon laughed and shook her head. "Although

I have set a few box traps and caught guineas on the island. They knock themselves out for me and all I have to do is pick them up."

"Go on!" Molly snickered in disbelief.

"It's true," Shannon protested. "We make a circle of clay into the shape of a dish, with the rock itself as the bottom. There's lots of clay and rock where I come from," she explained. "Then we put some grain in the center and hide until the guineas find it. They peck so hard they knock themselves out, I swear. Cudge says it's because their brain is so close to their bills."

"Well English guineas are smarter than that," Molly retorted, still doubtful as to whether or not Shannon teased her.

"So tell me about you now. This was your home, so your father was a farmer?"

Molly nodded. "A good man. We had a few servants to help on the farm. But then the smugglers came."

"Smugglers?" Shannon echoed in surprise.

"Yes. They're not around for a while and then they show up again. They hide out in the caves in the cliffs. Our house was over one of their tunnels and papa discovered them."

"They killed him then," Shannon surmised.

"No, worse," Molly told her. "They made it look as if he were involved with them. They hid some of the goods in the cellar and tipped off the sheriff." Molly's eyes clouded. "They hung my father in disgrace and you know the rest."

"Do they bother you? I mean, are they still around here?" Shannon asked, suddenly uneasy.

"I usually hide when they are about. They'll show up drinking at the local tavern. One of the maid-servants there is a friend of mine. She sends me word when they arrive and I go visit an aunt in Rye,"

Molly explained.

"Are there locks on all the windows?" Shannon asked, glancing at the heavy bolt mounted on the door.

"I've frightened you, haven't I?" Molly questioned in dismay.

Shannon smiled sheepishly. "A little. But I have something that will help us, if we should need help, that is."

Shannon rose from the smooth wooden bench and crossed the slab floor to go into the other room. When she returned, she carried two pistols and a kit. She had felt guilty taking Brian's weapons, but had left the small pouch with her jewels for payment and a brief letter of explanation. With the recent attempts on her life, he would surely understand.

"Do you know how to shoot as well?" Molly asked, backing away from the guns Shannon put on the table before her.

"I am not as good with the pistol as with the blade, but I am fair," Shannon admitted. "Do you know how to load them?"

"I have helped father before with his musket," Molly told her uneasily. "I do not like guns."

"Well, I have no aunt to visit . . . that I can visit that is, and I'll not be run off by some thieving scum who fancies my home," Shannon snorted indignantly. "I'll teach you to use these if you're game."

"Here?" Molly asked incredulously, glancing at the door frame where the carving knife still hung.

Shannon laughed. "Of course not. Outside, where we can set up some sort of target. Meanwhile," she sighed, "I'll feel better knowing they are loaded . . . You see, Molly, someone has been trying to kill me. I don't know why, but they are." She saw the color drain from Molly's face. "I think, however, that they are still in London waiting for me to leave my aunt's home. So we should be safe here," she reassured the girl.

Shannon went through the steps of loading the pistol slowly for Molly so that the girl might catch on. Although she didn't like the idea, Molly paid attention and copied Shannon's motions with the second gun. When they had finished and Shannon was satisfied with Molly's work, she put the weapons on the mantel over the fireplace.

It was extremely cold when Shannon helped Molly bring in more wood for the fires. They piled the coals in the kitchen hearth and let the fire die down a bit, while they rekindled the fire in the parlor where they prepared for bed. Water from the rain barrel had to be heated to wash with, and it did not take long for either girl to don her nightdress and snuggle down in the covers.

"Shannon . . ." Molly called out across the flickering light of the hearth. She heard Shannon mumble an acknowledgment and continued. "I couldn't help but notice the small nightdress and blanket in your trunk. Are you . . ."

"Yes, I'm going to have a child this summer," Shannon informed her softly. "It was another reason to leave London."

"Because of the disgrace to your family?"

"Partly," Shannon answered. "But you know, Molly," she said rising up on one arm and staring at her friend, "I am looking forward to it. I hope it looks just like Morgan."

"Morgan . . . that's a strong romantic name."

"Don't say anything to Corrinne about the baby or its father, please," Shannon asked suddenly. "Promise?"

"Promise," Molly affirmed, wondering at the connection. "Was he handsome, this Morgan?"

Shannon's eyes glazed and she dropped back on

her pillow. "Yes."

"And you loved him?"

"Yes."

"Is he dead?"

"No . . . he is very much alive in my heart and in my child." Shannon's voice caught in a soft sob, and Molly ceased her questions.

She felt sorry for her new mistress. She had gone from a pirate wench to a lady. She had all the money she needed. Yet she sought refuge from it here in the country, removed from her family. She liked this independent girl with the penetrating blue eyes and warm smile. She had no doubt that after surviving all that had befallen her mistress in the recent year, Shannon would still triumph over the pain that gently wracked her body with sobs that she tried to smother in her pillow.

The small tavern near the frozen docks at Billingsgate was nearly empty. The tavernkeeper observed the last of his serving wenches cleaning the empty tin cups from the tables. In the corner, one of the wealthier captains that patronized his establishment finished the last of the four bottles of Irish whiskey. The man slapped his first mate heartily on the back and laughed as a once fair mort whispered in his ear. He shook his head and pointed to the sandy-haired mate. The prostitute motioned for a younger girl, who stood quietly near the door and watched with wide eyes as her more experienced companion worked at soliciting her patrons for their evening entertainment. A dell most likely, the tavernkeeper thought to himself in disgust—just a matter of time before the soft face under the soot became as harsh as that of her sister of the street.

The tavernkeeper noted that he was not the only

one who watched the game the doxie played. At the end of the bar, a stocky looking fellow, bearded, with a hat pulled low on his face watched them. From his dress, he looked to be a ruffler. It was odd though, that he had been there all evening and paid with good coin for his beer. From the way his leather pouch bulged as he withdrew his payment, he lacked no funds at the moment. Yet, he could well be sizing up the tall dark-haired captain and his mate for a robbery once out in the streets, the tavernkeeper decided.

"'ere now, luv, if I'm too much woman fer ye, me niece would be glad to warm yer bed. She's 'ardly used a'tall," the doxie cooed, sticking her tongue into Morgan Hawke's ear.

He jerked his head away sharply as she shrilled with laughter. "'e's a fine specimen now, Mary. Come sit in 'is lap and show 'im 'ow a young arse feels."

"That won't be necessary, madame," Hawke told the woman, holding his aching head from the quick movement. It had been hours since he and Finney had eaten their supper—and four bottles ago.

"Now you sit right 'here, darlin'. Ain't no need of us leavin' these two lonely men on a cold night like this," the woman instructed the girl, who wriggled into Hawke's lap, ignoring his protest. "I was always taken by the big burly types like you, luv," she added, turning to the first mate.

"Well now, sit right down here," Michael Finney told her patting his knee. "Ain't no need to be disrespectful to these lovely ladies, cap'n. I never was one to leave a woman in need."

"What they need is your purse, Michael," Hawke reminded him as he seized the small wrist of the young girl who had tried to snake her hand around his waist to his pocket.

"Aow, sir. You're 'urtin' me ye are!" the girl exclaimed, rolling large blue eys up at Hawke. "I was only goin' to scratch yer back, maybe tickle ye a bit." She reached up and touched the three-day growth of beard on Morgan's face.

Hawke's eyes narrowed as he met the wide-eyed stare through stray wisps of dirty dark hair. "Damn it, get out of here!" he ordered, standing so that the girl dropped unceremoniously to the floor. "Take this and go, both of you!" He reached in his pocket and tossed out two gold coins on the floor.

The young girl scrambled and seized the coins greedily. She bit them with her teeth as she had seen her older partner do. "Real enough, sweet," she told the astonished woman in Finney's lap. "It's early to bed for us tonight."

The woman jumped to her feet and leaned over, kissing Hawke full on the mouth. "You're a real generous gentleman, sir. Let's be off, darlin'," she said to the girl on the floor.

As the doxie and the dell made their way to the street, Finney snorted and checked the last bottle for another drink. "Damn, lad. An empty bed and an empty bottle! What right did ye have runnin' off mine!"

Hawke pushed his bench away from the table and eyed his first mate. "I saved you from waking up to an empty bed and empty pockets."

"Since when has that made a difference to ye? I recall many a time that it didn't!" Finney reminded him.

"I've had enough of blue-eyed women to last me a lifetime. To hell with her!" Hawke cursed, raising the empty bottle and staring in disappointment at its lack of content. "Madame, another bottle for me and my irate friend here. It seems I'm doomed to spend the balance of the evening with him and I'd as soon improve his humor!"

"Why don't ye just go get her and be done with it?"

Hawke looked at the first mate in surprise. "Why? She can find the damned bottle by herself. It's right where she got the rest of these!" he told Finney, knocking the bottles off the table so that they clattered on the floor, miraculously failing to break.

"Shannon, ye drunken sot!" Finney explained in frustration.

Hawke put his head between his hands and rested his elbows on the table. "To hell with her! I rode all night, terrified that she and the child might have come to harm and what do I find?"

"I know, I know," Finney replied, raising his eyes to the ceiling. "But like ye said before, ye know she was innocent."

Hawke slammed his fist on the table. "But tonight she's tucked away in Kenton Place conveniently for him to work his way into her bed . . . the smiling sonovabitch!"

"Then let her stay there till the laughing sonovabitch as ye call 'im, does win her over," Finney snorted indignantly. "Let him father your child."

"She won't have me, Finney. I apologized for not telling her about Corrinne, I broke the betrothal, I asked her to marry me and she still won't have me. She's pigheaded and stubborn and damn her if she can't have one bit of understanding. The Lord of Snowden will not beg!"

"Now look who's pigheaded. Drinkin' yourself into a stupor is much more dignified to be sure than beggin' the sweet thing to forgive you and marry ye." Finney's sarcasm went without answer for both men became aware at the same time of the bearded man who stood at their table holding out the bottle Hawke had ordered.

"Damn me, if the wenches don't get uglier by the

minute!" Finney remarked, his hand reaching slowly for the knife he wore strapped to his leg inside his boots.

"I offered to help the poor wench so that she might get home earlier this damnably cold night," the intruder replied, uncorking the bottle and putting it on the table in front of them.

Hawke squinted as he studied the face nearly hidden under the brim of the hat. The stranger's voice was familiar, yet he could not place it. "Do we know you, friend?"

"I'd say that you did. You saw fit to enjoy the comforts of my tavern till you led His Majesty's marines in and destroyed it all."

"Cudgins," Hawke replied evenly. "Henry Cudgins."

"What brings ye to London, sir? If it's revenge ye're lookin' for, ye're a fool I didn't take ye be back there on that island," Finney told the man, ready to move if he showed any indication of violence.

"Shannon," Cudgins answered shortly. "I need to find Shannon."

"You mean Lady Shannon Devage of Sterling Court," Hawke corrected sarcastically. He poured himself a mug of the whiskey and motioned for Cudgins to join them.

"Then she found out," Cudgins sighed, dropping down on the bench beside Finney. "You can put away your knife, mate. I've no bad feelings toward either of you. You did what you had to do and with good reason."

Finney released his grip on the hilt of the knife and accepted the mug Hawke shoved toward him. "We were all surprised at the lass's identity . . . especially her father and sister."

"Her father is dead," Cudge told them firmly. "Brennan told me he was run through and shot.

They fed the sharks with her parents before they burned the ship to the waterline and it sank."

"Well, Jonathan Devage survived," Hawke informed the man. "He was thrown over by the explosion of the ship's magazine. He was wounded, but he survived. Another ship picked him up the following day . . . found him floating on a piece of wreckage."

"That is not Shannon's father, Hawke. That is a fast-talking swindler who took the letters Brennan removed from the cabin where he found Shannon. He bragged about how he was going to London and claim the fortune he'd read about in the papers. Shannon's mother's letters gave him enough information to assume the identity of a man who was not known to her family. Anyone with a bit of polish could have pulled it off, myself included. But this man Hicks, had the same general looks as Shannon's real father, poor soul."

"Dear God man, are you sure of this?" Hawke asked, the effects of the whiskey wearing off rapidly.

It would explain the attempts on her life, he thought. Brian had made an extremely intuitive guess that had seemed preposterous at the time.

"I have taken great risk in coming here, but I owe Shannon that much. I was afraid the bloke might still be around and I knew if her identity was discovered, he would want her out of his way."

"You're a good man, sir," Michael Finney told him, raising his mug in salute.

"We'd best tell the Bedlowes immediately," Hawke decided, rising from the bench unsteadily.

"Ye show up at this hour in your condition and they'll likely not believe ye. Best wait till mornin'," Finney advised, taking his friend's arm and pulling him back down.

"Someone has tried to kill her at least once and we

suspect two other attempts," Hawke told Cudgins, giving the logic in Finney's reasoning.

He proceeded to tell the man about the wagon that had almost run her down and the runaway horse with the tack sticking through the saddle. When he gave him the account of the last outright attempt, Cudgins smiled and Hawke raised a questioning brow at the man.

"I see London hasn't changed my girl too much," he chuckled. "Killed one of the robbers with their own knife! Damn there's no other like her!" he announced proudly. "She's Nick Brennan's daughter all right."

"Would you know this Hicks, if you saw him?" Hawke asked, his concern for Shannon's safety growing.

"Aye, I'd know him," Cudgins affirmed.

"Would you testify in the courts against him?"

"For Shannon, I would."

"Then, sir, you shall have no need to worry for your own neck. I will ask the King for a pardon for you . . . although in truth, all I know that you have done is run a tavern where pirates frequented," Hawke pointed out.

"I would appreciate anything you could do in that respect, Captain. While I am not destitute, I've saved every cent I've earned those years on Nose' Be," he explained, "I would like to spend my remaining years in peace in the England that has always been my true home."

"Well, if the Lord of Snowden here can't arrange that, he better go back to captainin' his men and give up lordin'!" Finney remarked, finishing off his whiskey. "Damned fine liquor!"

"You sly fox!" Cudgins accused Hawke good-naturedly. "I had you figured for nobility. Told

402

Shannon so that day she sneaked up to see a real noble for herself. She was always the curious one . . . about books, or knowledge of any kind. Anxious to learn. As she grew older and read more, she was more than I could handle . . . or Nick either. Taking her away from there was best for her," he told Hawke appreciatively. "If she's in London's socially elite, she's where she was born to be."

"Finney, first thing in the morning, you and Cudgins go to the authorities and report this. I'll go to Kenton Place and tell the Bedlowes and Shannon."

"I thought you said she was at Sterling Court," Cudgins remarked.

"She is staying with her aunt and uncle. Her sister did not take well to the fact that she had a new relative . . . and Shannon did not accept her father or Corrinne readily either," Hawke explained.

By the time the bottle was finished, the serving woman had put out all the lights except the one that hung on the wall behind their table. Hawke invited Cudgins to spend the night at his London apartment along with Michael Finney. It took a while to find a coach for hire at the wee hour of the morning. As it carried them toward the fashionable part of the city where the Lord of Snowden resided while conducting business in his shipping firm, Hawke's mind dwelled on the girl who had denied him her love and his child. Her long dark hair and blue eyes haunted him and made him ache with a desire that only she in her innocent and beguiling way could satisfy.

His fists clenched in determination. Tomorrow he would speak to Shannon again. If she would not listen to reason, then he would take her to Snowden against her will, propriety be damned. He would not allow her to escape again, until she admitted to the love that bound them in the chains of tender passion.

Chapter Twenty-Three

Morgan Hawke squinted at the early morning sun through the window of his coach. It was a welcome change from the past few days of drizzling rain. With the harshness of the winter, he and Finney had been studying the maps of alternative ports where his company ships might put in. They had needed to find the shortest and best routes over land to London as well. The evenings presented quiet times in the idle taverns near the docks, the bulk of the patrons being sailors whose ships could not make it to London.

As the coach pulled up in front of Kenton Place, Hawke turned his thoughts to more pressing matters. He stepped lightly out of the vehicle and motioned for his coachman that he might be a while. Finney and Cudgins, both with aching heads, had gone on to the sheriff and delivered his message to the King about the fraudulent Devage. He felt remarkably well himself, considering the awesome amount of whiskey he had consumed with his companions. A hearty breakfast and fresh clothing had helped. He rubbed the stubble on his chin and admonished himself for not taking the time to shave.

He had barely touched the front door with his fist when it was yanked open by a haggard-looking Brian Bedlowe. Before he recovered from his shock, Bedlowe seized the lapels of his jacket and hauled him inside.

"Where the hell is she?" the young man demanded, throwing Hawke against the wall.

Hawke locked his hands around the younger man's wrists and threw them away from him, scowling as he did so. "Don't ever try anything like that again, Bedlowe," he warned. "What's the matter with you?"

"Shannon is gone."

Hawke looked past Brian at a grim-faced Edward Bedlowe who stood in the entrance to the gentlemen's parlor. He inhaled deeply to quell the sinking feeling in his abdomen. "When?" he asked somberly.

"You didn't take her then?" Brian asked, his voice revealing a surprising disappointment.

"Of course not!" Hawke snapped.

"Come inside, Morgan," the admiral told him. "We might as well be comfortable. Perhaps between us we might figure it out."

Brian stood aside and motioned for Hawke to precede him into the room. There was a tray of hot coffee on the table. The admiral poured a cup and offered it to him.

"I apologize for my behavior," Brian spoke up, dropping into a chair with a groan. "I have been all over London, and ridden most of yesterday and last night to Snowden and back. I cannot imagine where she has gone!"

"Why would you think she went to Snowden?"

"Well her father and Corrinne are not at home. Besides them, who else does she know?" Brian asked in exasperation. He closed his eyes and shook his head. "She took my pistols, thank God."

Hawke hardly noticed the coffee scalding his tongue as he watched Brian. "When exactly did she leave?"

"Monday morning. She took her trunk and told our doorman that she was going to have the lock fixed and do some shopping," Brian told him, straightening up in the chair. "I nearly panicked when I found out she'd gone out alone. I searched all the shops she frequented. No one had seen her. When that failed, I went to Sterling Court, thinking Corrinne and she might have planned something together, but the servants said that Devage and his daughter left on a business trip and would not be back for a week or so."

"I suspect he'll be devastated when he finds Shannon missing again after all these years," the admiral remarked.

Hawke put his coffee down and looked from the older to the younger Bedlowe. "I doubt it seriously," he said. "I have a witness from Nose' Be that can identify Jonathan Devage as a fraud."

Brian jumped to his feet. "Then Shannon has to be with him. I knew it!" he exclaimed, running his hand through his uncombed hair. "The servants were so damned evasive, as if they'd been instructed not to give out any information."

"Have you notified the authorities?"

"That is the first thing we did when she did not come home the night before last as she had said she would," Edward Bedlowe answered. "You are certain about Devage?"

"My man knows him as a swindler named Hicks. He took Jenny Devage's letters and used them to inherit the Sterling estate," Hawke explained, rising to his feet. "I think we had better go back to Sterling

406

Court and find out where Devage went. I agree with Brian. Shannon must be with them."

"I'll send for our coach," the admiral offered.

"Mine's waiting," Hawke informed him. "We'll use it."

The admiral turned to his son who pushed himself out of the chair. He noted the circles under Brian's eyes and sympathized with the agony his son had felt the last twenty-four hours. He had seen Brian's infatuation with the girl growing each day, but held his tongue. He knew it would do no good to advise him to forget her, that she was committed to Morgan Hawke. He had known there was something strong between the Lord of Snowden and his niece since they had dined with him on his ship at the Horn.

"Perhaps you should rest, son. You've done more than your share to find Shannon."

"With all due respect, sir, I cannot," Brian answered in a tone that bespoke his determination.

"I expect Finney and Cudgins to arrive here shortly. They were to meet me here as soon as they notified the sheriff. Someone needs to fill them in on what has happened and have them meet us with fresh horses at Sterling Court," Hawke suggested. He was impatient to be moving.

The father and son exchanged looks and it was the admiral who relented graciously. He could no more dissuade his son now than before, he realized. "You two go on, I'll arrange for the mounts and meet your first mate and this pirate."

"Not a pirate, sir . . . a tavernkeeper," Hawke corrected. "He is the one who tutored Shannon . . . another father of sorts." He waited while Brian pulled on his heavy jacket and gloves.

There was an uncomfortable silence in the coach as they made their way through the crowded streets. It seemed at each intersection there was a traffic blockage. Hawke opened the door of the coach and motioned for the driver to take another route as an overturned peddler's cart brought the vehicles ahead to a halt.

"Damnation!" he cursed, throwing himself back against the seat. "Two days . . . God, she could be anywhere!" His palms were sweating in spite of the cold and he wiped them on his legs. The effects of the liquor he had thought to have eluded made his mouth dry and he moistened his lips and bit them. He became aware of the intent study of the young man sitting across from him and returned the stare obstinately.

"Do you love her?"

"That is none of your business, Bedlowe," Hawke replied evenly.

"It is, sir, because I do . . . and I would never treat her the way you have," Brian accused.

"I have explained to Shannon why I did not break the betrothal, I owe you no explanation."

"I must be out of my mind for telling you this, but I believe you really do care about her. You're white as a ghost." When he received no comment, he went on. "I would do anything for Shannon . . . give her up if it would make her happy. She would have forgiven you for not breaking the betrothal because of Devage's request . . ."

"How the hell do you know all this?"

"Because Shannon needed someone to talk to and I was there," Brian snapped, beginning to lose his own patience. "The night you came barging into my room with that holier-than-thou attitude, she confided in me. It's no wonder the poor thing tried to run away from you."

Hawke stiffened. "I thought it was the medication

. . . that she was delirious."

"She had just found out that her sister also carried your child . . . and for that, Lord Hawke, she may never forgive you," Brian added with disdain.

The surprise was evident on Hawke's face. "Where did she get a foolish notion like that?" as if he didn't already know. He recalled the way Corrinne had smiled and reminded him that Shannon might not accept him. She had certainly made sure of it. It was no wonder Shannon had acted so rashly and tried to run away and then been so unreasonable when he tried to explain the late breaking of the engagement. "The lying bitch," he growled, absorbed in his thoughts.

"So you're not the father of Corrinne's child?"

"If I am, sir, she should have had it while I was in Nose' Be," Hawke retorted angrily. "And if she is with child, it is not mine."

"I was afraid of that," Brian sighed, looking out the window of the coach. "Then, God help us, when we find her I'd suggest you straighten that matter out and then maybe she'll go with you to Snowden and stay put!"

Hawke detected a slight tremor in Brian's voice and pretended not to notice. That he cared for Shannon was evident. He owed this young man his future happiness if, as he said, they found her. The coach turned in the drive of the red brick manor. Hawke reached out his hand to Bedlowe.

"Thank you, Brian. You have been far nobler than I, I fear," he admitted.

Brian accepted his hand and shook it. "So help me, if you hurt her again, I will see that you never get another chance."

The doorman answered their knock promptly. He informed them as he had Brian that the Devages had left London on business and would be returning the following week. The man did not seem to know exactly where they had gone, nor was he aware that Shannon had accompanied them, until Hawke turned to Brian and questioned him for the servant's benefit.

"How do you think His Majesty will treat this innocent man who seeks to protect a known fraud and potential murderer?"

"I'd say he'd likely get the Tyburn tippet, if we don't see justice done now ourselves."

The thin-haired man stared wide-eyed at the Lord of Snowden. "What is it you mean, sir? A fraud and a murderer?" His voice trembled in fear and he cried out as Hawke lifted him by the lapels.

"Where did they go with Shannon, man? I've not the time nor inclination to explain a thing, except to promise you, if she is hurt because you have held up justice, you will pay dearly."

"Dear God, sir, I beg you, I only followed Master Devage's orders. They've taken her to Dover. But she went willingly, sir!" the man added in confusion.

"A full day's ride at best," Brian commented.

"We'll wait here for your father and our mounts. Send for some hot coffee and then we'll have more words with you, sir," Hawke instructed the servant as he put him squarely on his feet again. "We'd appreciate your cooperation."

The servant joined them in Devage's parlor and took the seat Hawke motioned for him to take. He shifted uneasily under the steel blue gaze and started when the Lord of Snowden spoke.

"Tell me, why were they going to Dover," Hawke snapped.

"I wouldn't know . . ."

"Damn it, man, do you take us for fools? Servants

410

listen to our conversations. Now tell me what you heard!" he demanded again.

"Mistress Shannon signed over her inheritance to them. They . . . they were very pleased," the man stammered.

"Why did they go to Dover?" Brian prompted.

"To help Mistress Shannon settle in their summer house there. I believe she was very unhappy here in the city."

Hawke spoke as Brian glanced his way. "I know the place. I've been there."

"If they've taken her there under that pretense, they may not rush into any rash action . . . and their motive is removed. They have the inheritance."

"Let's hope so," Hawke replied.

The admiral's group arrived within the hour with the horses. The older gentleman, not being an avid horseman, promised to follow in his coach. The sheriff had sent a letter to be presented the authorities in Dover to gather support. At the inn in Rochester they would need to trade their mounts and press on. Hawke tucked the letter inside his jacket. Upon donning a heavy traveling cloak, he mounted a reddish brown steed and swung its head about, waiting for Brian, Michael Finney and Henry Cudgins to join him. As he led the way to the outskirts of the city his thoughts tumbled to one end. He had to find Shannon and he prayed that she would be unharmed.

The rocky landscape did not look quite so drab in the crisp morning air as it had the day Shannon arrived in the misting rain. The frost was beginning to melt under the late morning sun's assault. Gulls flew overhead in wide circles and chased away any of

411

the blackbirds that tried to scavenge the fallow fields for food. Their calls were familiar to the girl. She could not recall having seen any over the city, the city more given to pigeons.

Molly had risen before her that morning and fixed a staple breakfast of porridge and cream, compliments of the cow the young woman kept in the makeshift shed in the back of the yard. The cream was thick and foamy and Shannon thoroughly enjoyed her first breakfast in her new home.

After they had cleaned up the dishes, Shannon decided to walk to the cliff's edge and peer over the port below at the channel she had sailed months before. The wind made whitecaps in the water and the chalky rocks appeared to have been stained with the same color. From her vantage she could see trails among the rocks, steep and treacherous. Even though the sun had thawed the icy frost, the rock surfaces were still too slippery to trust, so she decided to head back toward the house. Molly was going to move some of her things today and she wanted to be sure to help.

Shannon observed the smoke from the kitchen fireplace curling its way upward against the blue sky. It appeared as though the weather would be clear. Perhaps she would be able to lie on the floor tonight and watch the moon through the casement window in the parlor. It was something she had enjoyed on Nose' Be, stirring from time to time to check its westwardly progress. By all rights, it should be nearly full, she thought, as she picked her way through the stubbled field leading to the house.

A messenger had come up from the village earlier that morning and delivered a message from her father. He would be tied up with business until later that afternoon and Corrinne had taken a bit of a chill and would not be coming until he brought her. It was their hope to join her and Molly for supper and then return to the inn. He promised in a footnote to look for a stove to put in the upstairs room and assured her that he would find at least one before he returned to London.

As Shannon rounded the corner of the house she saw a petticoat and a pair of woolen stockings bound in a ball on the stone walk. Molly must have already started her move, the girl mused, stooping to pick up the dropped items. The kitchen door was ajar when Shannon reached it. She pushed it open and called out to Molly as she stepped inside.

"Molly, I found some of your things out on the walk!" she called, frowning when she did not see Molly in the kitchen.

The door to the parlor was closed, so Shannon shut the outside entry and made sure the latch caught. The wind had already blown it open on her once that morning when she had carelessly slung it to. She pushed down on the thumb latch to the adjoining room, and shoved the door open.

"Molly, I . . ."

Shannon froze at the sight of her friend bound and gagged in a chair near the dying fire. Without thinking, she rushed over to her, missing the frightened look directed behind her.

"What hap . . ."

Shannon did not finish her question. The blow on the back of her head was sharp and painful. She could feel herself falling, but could not catch herself. The room swirled above her and she strained to see Molly, who seemed to move with the room. Then she could not see or feel at all.

When she opened her eyes again, there was still nothing but darkness. Her body was stiff from lying stretched face down on the damp rock surface. As she tried to move, her cheek scraped the abrasive floor. It was so cold that the cut burned her. Her arms would not free themselves, and as her feeling returned, she realized that her wrists were bound in front of her and her weight held them down.

The ache in her head pierced her brain as she rolled over clumsily and sat up. Her head hit the rock wall behind her and she whimpered. A wave of nausea rose to the back of her throat and the darkness began to move around her. She pressed her face up against the cold wall and fought to maintain consciousness.

When it stilled, her mind began to slowly put things together. Whoever had hit her over the head, had taken her to a cave. She wondered how long she had been unconscious and how far this cave might be from her house. If she could get away, maybe she could get back there. Voices drifted her way from her right. She strained to see through the darkness and detected the faintest glimmer in the distance.

Her captors must be between her and the exit from this place, she surmised. She glanced to her left at the pitch blackness. If there was another way out, she'd be hard-pressed to find it without a light; but she could do very little until she rid herself of the ropes that had cut off her circulation so that her hands and fingers felt numb.

She felt around in the darkness for an edge to work the rope across. Her hand closed around a large stone, but its bumpy surface was not sufficient to cut through the jute and she discarded it. As she fumbled blindly, her thoughts turned to Molly. She hoped her abductors had done no more than leave the poor servant as Shannon had last seen her. Shannon stiffened as the picture of her maidservant lying somewhere in the darkness came to her mind. She had been unconscious, perhaps Molly was here with her. Shannon listened carefully, but only the voices of men in the distance came to her.

"Molly . . ." she whispered softly. No answer.

Giving up, she returned to her search for something to break through the bindings. She smiled as she felt a rough edge of a rock that stuck up from the floor of the cave. It had apparently been broken off by the activity of the men in the other end of the cavern, for the sides were smooth. Shannon began to rub the rope determinedly across the sharp surface. It was a tedious and demanding task, considering the pounding swelling in the back of her head.

The rope slackened and Shannon was able to turn her wrists within the bonds. She flexed her fingers as the blood rushed into them and seemed to prick them with several tiny invisible needles. She began to rub the bindings again with renewed effort. When one of the wraps of jute broke through, her wrist jammed into the rock and she caught her breath, pulling it away and holding it to her breast as she winced with the pain. As it subsided, she tried pulling at the rope and it gave. She tried harder until it was loose enough for her hands to slip out free.

Her triumph was short-lived. Her stone prison seemed to suddenly flood with light as two men made their way back toward her. The stockier of them held a lantern above his stocking capped head and both peered at the spot where they had left her. Shannon resisted the urge to spring up and run. It would be foolhardy to plunge deeper in the cave without a light. If she could just bide her time, perhaps her father would arrive, if he had not already, and send for help.

"Well now, lookie here, mate. Dickie said she was a tough one," the heavyset man spoke up upon finding her with his eyes.

"She 'minds me of a angel. I always was weak for a pretty face," the shorter one remarked, reaching out and touching her cheek with his rough hand.

Shannon threw his hand away causing him to leap back in surprise. "Don't touch me!" she spat, flashing angry blue eyes at him.

"Sweet Jesus, she's free!" he exclaimed, reaching to his waist for his pistol. He drew it and leveled it at Shannon's breast. His hand shook and he steadied it with his other one. "Now you just calm down, missy. I wasn't meanin' to hurt ye."

"Watch 'er, Al! Ye know what Dickie said about 'er," his comrade warned, touching his free hand to the pistol tucked in his waist.

"Set the lantern down and go get another length of rope. We'd best tie 'er up again."

A cry of dismay escaped Shannon's lips and she dropped to her knees miserably. "Please don't!" she begged, carefully watching their reaction. "My wrists are bloody and I'm nearly numb with cold." Her chin trembled as she held out her hands so that they could see the damage done.

The man with the pistol glanced at the other man and then fixed his attention on Shannon again. "Promise me ye won't try anything, missy, and me 'n Mort 'ere might consider lettin' ye warm up by the fire."

"I promise," Shannon whispered tremulously, widening her eyes at her armed captor.

"I don't like it, Al," the other man snapped, not taking his eyes from Shannon.

"One quick move from 'er, Mort 'n I'll blow 'er away an' deprive Dickie the honor. Do ye understand that, missy."

Shannon shook her head to let him know she

416

understood his intention. As he motioned that she walk ahead of him, she moved toward the light in the distance. The name he mentioned did not ring familiar in her memory; but whoever it was obviously intended to kill her.

The center of the cave was a large room that had been furnished with rough tables made out of barrels as pedestals with plank tops. A fire burned in the center of the room and the smoke drifted upward. Although she could not see an opening, Shannon guessed that there was one above it from the apparent draft. It still did not ventilate the room sufficiently and her eyes watered as she took the seat they pointed out near the fire.

She extended her hands over the smoldering coals and looked at her captors who sat across from her. The stocky man Mort eyed her suspiciously and kept his hand near the butt of his pistol. Al, however, tucked his weapon back in his breeches, and smiled at her showing staggered yellow teeth.

"Ain't that better, missy?" he asked with an all too familiar gleam in the eyes that peered at her from under thick eyebrows.

"Yes, thank you, sir," Shannon answered returning his smile. "Who is Dickie and why does he intend to kill me?" Her frightened look was not completely an act.

"Dickie's an uprightman turned smuggler," Al told her. Upon seeing the confused look on her face, he explained. "The leader of a band of robbers, missy. Now he's leadin' us smugglers."

Shannon frowned. "But what does he want with me?" she asked innocently.

Mort laughed loudly and startled her. "Cause ye killed 'is brother, Will. Knifed 'im clean, ye did."

Shannon's shoulders sagged and the blood drained

from her face. They had found her. Dickie was the robber who had run away into the woods the night near the inn at Pulcherchurch. "I thought he was going to kill me," she said lowly, putting her face in her hands.

"Like as not, 'e was," snickered Al. "'e just 'adn't figgered on coming up on a pirate instead of a laidee. Let 'is guard down 'e did."

"When will he be here?" Shannon asked, fighting the fear that pressed her toward panic.

"Sundown, like as not . . . had some bus'ness to attend to. But when 'e comes back, 'e intends to cut ye slow and kill ye with a blade like ye did Will," Mort informed her, delighting in the horror that filled her eyes.

"Oh my God . . ." Shannon whispered hoarsely. Tears sprang to her eyes and she turned her head away from the men. She trembled as much from fear as the cold dampness.

She was not surprised when Al moved next to her and put his arm over her shoulder. "There now, missy. Me 'n Mort can't stop Dickie. What 'e says goes . . . but maybe if you're good to us, we can make it quick for ye. Maybe shoot ye clean in the 'eart as you're tryin' to escape?"

Shannon turned to the man and took his hand. "Let me escape . . . please. Tell this Dickie that I fell off the cliff. He'll never know. My body could wash out to sea."

Mort snorted incredulously. "And we'd best just throw ourselves off . . ."

"Hush, Mort!" Al cut in. He gave the man a sly wink that Shannon pretended to miss. "Maybe we kin figger a way . . . if'n she's nice enough."

"And you'll let me go?" Shannon asked naively. She shivered involuntarily as he touched her cheek

418

and trailed his rough finger down her throat to the clasp of her cloak.

"Free as a bird," the kidnapper lied. He leaned over and kissed her on the mouth. His breath was sour and Shannon tried to hide her revulsion. His hand sought the entry to her cloak through the heavy woolen folds.

Shannon grabbed his hand and pulled away. She raised her eyes to his suggestively and touched her lips to his hand. "Could we go back there," she asked quietly, darting her eyes to where she had been left tied, "away from prying eyes?"

"I don't like this, Al," Mort protested as Al rose and drew Shannon to her feet.

"For gawd sake, Mort. Just sit 'ere with your gun. If she did try anything foolish, she'd have to get past you!" Al burst out in exasperation with his partner. Then he grinned. "Ye'll 'ave your turn and I'll keep watch, fair enough?"

Mort looked from his partner to Shannon and then nodded mutely. "Search 'er."

"What?" Shannon exclaimed in astonishment.

"Check 'n see that she ain't got no knife strapped to 'er leg."

Al made a disgruntled noise. "I'll find that out soon enough," he objected.

Mort jumped to his feet. "If you don't, I will!" he announced determinedly.

Shannon endured the search in silence. Their hands ran up and down her legs and inside her cloak, squeezing her bosom painfully. When Mort was satisfied that she was unarmed, he motioned for Al to take her back in the cavern. The shorter man put his arm tightly about her waist and led her into the darkness of her prison.

Her hands were shaking as she dropped to her

knees and pretended to spread her cloak into a makeshift bed. The man called Al worked at the laces of his breeches anxiously, incensed with the lust from his fondling search. Her hair fell in her face as she felt about in the dark for the stone she had found earlier, but Al was down beside her before she located it.

He grabbed her roughly and kissed her on the lips again. His lips were wet and smeared down the hollow of her throat while his arms locked about her waist and pulled her so tightly to him that she could feel his hardness. He pressed her back against the hard bed and started to fumble with the laces of her bodice. His rapid breath was putrid. Shannon feigned a moan of pleasure as he pulled her dress open and rubbed her breasts roughly. She stretched her hands over her head and searched furtively for the stone. He made crude snorting noises as he buried his face in her exposed bosom, oblivious to the fact that she tensed when her fingers latched on to the elusive rock. When she struck him, he grunted in surprise and fell on her pinning her beneath his limp body.

Shannon rolled him off and struggled to her feet. Her mouth was dry as she swallowed the bile that rose in her throat. She pulled her camisole up over her naked breast and fastened it as best she could. Al's pistol lay still loaded near the discarded pants. Shannon took the gun and leaned against the wall. In a matter of time, Mort would come looking for them.

She started when the figure at her feet began to stir. Quickly, she grabbed the rock and struck Al on the head again. He made a loud groan and dropped his head banging it against the rock floor. Mort's inquiry from the front of the cave made Shannon flatten against the wall. She could see the lantern light move away from the fire as he made his way toward them.

"Al, you all right?" the stocky man called out warily.

Shannon held her breath. She had to get past him.

"Damn it, Al, stop yer ruttin' an' answer me!" he cursed, holding the light up and peering at the dim shadows where Shannon waited.

Shannon carefully pulled the hammer back on the pistol and aimed it with both hands. He had to get closer, she thought wildly, unsure of her aim. She mustered her strength and made a noise of pleasure. "Don't stop!" she gasped loudly. She let out her breath slowly as she heard Mort chuckle and move closer. A few more steps and he would be able to see Al's unconscious form.

His exclamation at the sight of his partner was smothered by the explosion of the pistol in Shannon's hands. Mort screamed and dropped the lantern. The light rolled toward Shannon down the incline. In its reflection she could see Mort drawn up in a ball holding his leg. He swore vulgarly and reached for his pistol. As the shot smashed against the rock above her head, Shannon dropped to the floor.

She scrambled to her feet again and prepared to rush past the wounded man, when he pulled a knife from his boot. Its long blade shone in the flickering light and Shannon froze. The passage was narrow. There was no way to get around him. She looked back over her shoulder at the seemingly unending darkness. If there was another way out, he could not follow her, she reasoned. Making her decision, she seized the lantern and started away from the wounded man. As she reached a turn in the passage, she tucked the discharged pistol in her sash, and glanced back once more.

Mort's curses became fainter as she went deeper

into the cavern. The path was a natural one and she could only hope that it might lead to the outside. Perhaps it would empty out at one of the trails she had observed cut in the side of the cliff. Wherever it led, she noted, it was descending. There was a fork ahead of her when she heard a pistol explosion that spurred her on. She arbitrarily chose the right path. Faint shouts announced the arrival of the smugglers' leader and her intended murderer.

They were following, she thought desperately as she plunged ahead, nearly tripping over a broken crate that had been abandoned there. There had to be a way out, she thought, encouraged by other bits of debris, remains of a smuggler's goods. Her dresss caught and tore on a jagged edge of rock. She snatched it loose and as she glanced back, she saw a flickering light in the distance that she had just traveled. A cry of dismay escaped her throat and she hurried ahead frantically. Suddenly it struck her that if she put out her lamp they would not know which passage she had taken. She took a good look ahead to map out her path. Then reluctantly, she opened the back of the lantern and blew out the flame.

Chapter Twenty-Four

Their horses were lathered with sweat by the time Morgan Hawke and his company reached the cottage. The setting sun provided a brilliant backdrop for the sharp-pitched dormered roof. Hawke's blood chilled as he noticed the lack of smoke coming from the chimneys. No lights burned within, its casement windows reflecting only the crimson of the sunset. His horse had not fully stopped when he leapt to the freezing ground. He heard Brian on his heels as he raced up the stone walk.

The open doorway slowed him down with caution. He reached inside his cloak and withdrew two of the pistols Finney and Cudgins brought them. With one in each hand, he kicked open the door so that it beat against the wall behind it. He listened keenly and his eyes searched the dim kitchen. He glanced at Brian, who had armed himself as well, and shook his head.

He stepped inside and looked around the empty room. The coals in the hearth were dying from lack of tending. He reached over and picked up a piece of women's clothing that had been dropped in the floor as Brian motioned for him to step away from the door that led to the parlor. They both remained motionless as they detected a slight scraping sound. Brian flattened himself against the wall, his pistol cocked as Hawke reached for the latch. His thumb pressed down on it and he kicked it in simultaneously. Brian charged in the room and checked his aim at the sight of the feminine figure bound to an overturned chair.

"Shannon!" he exclaimed, rushing over to the moaning girl.

He put his gun on the floor and between him and Hawke, managed to upright the bound victim. The fading sunlight cast its weak rays through the distorted glass on the tear-stained face that did not belong to Shannon. Large brown eyes stared at him in terror and fresh tears welled in them. Hawke worked at the bonds that held her hands behind her back while Brian untied the kerchief that had been used to gag her.

"Don't be frightened, miss. We're here to help," he assured the shaking girl as he fumbled with the tight knot.

When the gag came loose, the girl moved her jaw around and moistened her lips before speaking. "I'm not Shannon," she whimpered. "They took her."

"Who took her? Devage?" Hawke demanded, as the knot gave way and her hands were freed.

The girl began to sob hysterically. Her speech was incoherent. Hawke grabbed her roughly by the shoulders and shook her. "Damn it, girl, who took Shannon?"

"For God's sake, Hawke, give her a chance. It's hard to tell what she's been through herself," Brian protested.

The girl pulled away from Hawke and threw herself at Brian for protection. She clung to him, nearly shaking him with her convulsive sobs. Brian gently stroked her soft brown hair as Hawke threw up his hands in frustration.

"There now, miss . . . what did you say her name was?" he asked the perturbed dark-haired man.

"Molly, Devage's servant," Hawke answered with forced patience.

"Now Molly," Brian said in a coaxing tone, "Shannon is in real danger. You must control yourself enough to tell us what happened." He patted her on the back. "Come on now, please tell us."

He led Molly over to the settee and sat down beside her, holding her trembling hand. Molly gasped, trying to stop the ragged breaths that made her speech impossible. Before she could speak, Michael Finney and Henry Cudgins charged into the room, pistols drawn. She screamed and buried her face in Brian's chest.

"It's all right. They're friends!" Brian reassured her. "Now tell us what happened."

"They t . . . tied me up . . . I was m . . . moving my things like Sh . . . Shannon told me to do," Molly stammered, her eyes fixed on Brian's face.

"What about Shannon?" Hawke asked, trying to keep his tone even.

"She came in the house . . . sh . . . she didn't see them. They hid behind the door and h . . . hit her on the head when she came through. I . . . I don't know whether they killed her or not." Molly's voice rose in hysteria and she succumbed to her tears again.

"Molly . . . Molly, please . . ." Brian implored, taking her in his arms. "Did you know who they were?"

Molly nodded and responded haltingly. "Sm . . . smugglers by the look of them."

"Did they say where they were going . . . any hint at all?" Hawke asked desperately, fighting the sinking feeling of doom that chilled his soul.

"N . . . no." Molly whimpered. Suddenly she looked up at Hawke. "But it must be the caves!"

"Cudgins, take this to the sheriff," Hawke instructed, handing him the letter from the High Sheriff of London. "Tell him we need all the men he can muster . . . guards, laymen . . . I don't give a damn."

"Right, sir!" Cudgins tucked away his pistol and disappeared through the doorway.

"The rest of us can start searching as best we can until they get here."

Hawke clenched his teeth. The muscles in his jaw twitched. He had never felt so helpless. The whole area was catacombed with caverns. That he might find one girl was nearly an impossibility.

Molly pushed away from Brian and crossed over to the anguished man. "You're Morgan," she said flatly. She now knew why Shannon did not want her to say anything to Corrinne as she recognized the Lord of Snowden, Corrinne's fiancé. She put her hand on his arm. "I . . . I think I might know where to start looking."

Hawke stared at her blankly as she turned and started to pull the makeshift bed across the floor. To the men's surprise, when she rolled back the worn Turkish carpet, a trap door was revealed.

"This was our cellar," she explained. "The smugglers tunneled through from the caves below. They've used this house from time to time." At the puzzled expression of the men, she went on. "I leave when they're about. I'm terrified of them. They brought my father to the gallows unjustly because he would not work with them."

426

Hawke sprang into action and lifted the iron rung to open the hidden door. A wooden ladder led down to pitch darkness below. "Have you a lantern?"

Molly nodded and disappeared in the kitchen. She came back with two small candle lamps. "Will these do?" she asked.

Finney took them and lighted the candles from the fire he had been building with the kindling in the box on the hearth. After he carefully placed them back in the tin shells, he placed them on the floor by the opening. "It ain't much to see with, but they'll have to do. No wonder Devage bought this place. He could associate with his own kind."

"Oh, Master Devage isn't with those vermin!" Molly corrected the Irishman. "He and his daughter are in town. They were to come here for supper with Shannon and me tonight. Anytime as a matter of fact. He'll be frantic!" Molly exclaimed in dismay.

The men exchanged bewildered looks. Hawke took a deep breath and let it out slowly. "If that's the case, one of us had better stay here."

He and Finney both looked at Brian. Brian nodded reluctantly. Hawke and Finney were both more experienced in fighting the caliber that had abducted Shannon. He halfway smiled as Hawke gave him an appreciative look and disappeared down the ladder. Finney handed down the lanterns and followed him.

Molly started to light the lamps and Brian went outside to the wood pile to get more fuel for the fires. When the fire in the kitchen was blazing, he sat at the table and sipped the hot coffee Molly had made. In a short time the chill that had made Molly wrap her woolen shawl about her shoulders was gone. He watched her move quietly about the kitchen, preparing a meat pie from some leftover stew. Her hands still shook as she rolled out the heavy crust.

427

"I'm glad you stayed, sir," Molly told him, grunting slightly as she forced the tough dough flat on the table. "I don't think I shall ever stay here again."

Brian raised a curious brow. "What will you do then?"

"I'll go live with my aunt in Rye. She's given me refuge from the scoundrels before," Molly explained with a forced smile. Her chin trembled as she took out her nervous energy on the biscuit crust.

"Do you really want it that thin?" Brian teased, reaching over and putting his finger through the place she had gouged with the wooden roller.

Molly gave a small cry of frustration and ran into the parlor abandoning her culinary attempts. Brian pushed away from the table and started to follow her when he spotted a corked bottle on the shelf of the corner cupboard. He checked its content and was satisfied that it was about a quarter full of a homemade fruit liquor of some sort. Upon finding a tin mug, he carried them both into the room where Molly sat crying quietly.

He sat down beside her on the settee and poured some of the sweet wine into the cup. "Now you drink some of this, Molly. It'll help to calm your nerves," he promised. He placed the bottle on the floor at his feet and coaxed the distraught girl to take the cup.

"I . . . I'm worried for Shannon. What could she have done to those men?" Molly sniffed She took a sip of the wine and shuddered. "I don't drink spirits, sir." She handed him back the cup. "Thank you just the same."

"This is for medicinal purposes, Molly. Now I insist you finish this small cupful. You've been through a terrible ordeal." Brian's mind went with Molly's as he wondered where Shannon was and what she must be going through.

"You care for her, too. I can see it."

Brian handed her the cup again and forced her fingers around it. "I do, Molly. My cousin is very dear to me. Now drink!" he ordered. "And I will finish your biscuits." He stood up and took her hand. It was so small in his. "If you wish some amusement to distract you, come watch."

Molly laughed. Her voice was light and soft and her eyes sparkled through her drying tears.

"That is much better," Brian told her, picking up the wine bottle. "To the kitchen . . ." He grinned and motioned for her to precede him.

The stew Molly had left over the edge of the fire was bubbling slowly with irregular plopping noises. The room was much warmer and Brian stripped off his outer jacket and tossed it on a bench next to Molly who sipped the wine and watched him curiously. He stirred the pot to keep the food from sticking and went back to the uneven dough sheet. He rolled it up in a large ball and when he had worked it to his satisfaction, he pinched off small sections of it and flattened them in the palms of his hands.

"Instead of a pie, why not just boil them in the gravy . . . dumplings of a nature," Brian suggested. Without waiting approval, he grabbed a handful of the dumpling balls and dropped them in the bubbling gravy. When they were all in, he turned and smiled at Molly. "Now all we have to do is wait for our guests!" He met Molly's look and his smile faded as his thoughts merged with hers.

The sound of horses approaching distracted him and he crossed to the window. In the light of the full moon he could see a coach drawing up at the end of the walk. He drew back and peered through a crack at the edge of the curtain. He motioned for Molly to go into the parlor and took a seat at the table facing the door. His pistols lay drawn in his lap under the table.

When no one answered the repeated knock on the door, Jonathan Devage opened it and stepped inside ahead of his daughter. He stopped short at the sight of Brian. He was surprised, but he showed no sign of dismay. Instead, he smiled at the young man in greeting and motioned Corrinne in out of the cold.

"I see you have found us out!" Devage remarked good-naturedly as he helped Corrinne out of her wrap.

"Indeed so, sir," Brian answered. He nodded to Corrinne who eyed him curiously.

"Why cousin, what a delightful surprise. Perhaps you can convince Shannon of the folly of this." Corrinne glanced at the closed parlor door. "Is she in there?" Without waiting for his reply, she crossed to the door and opened it. "Shannon . . . ! Why, Molly, where is . . . My God!" Corrinne backed against the wall and paled. "Father, those men have been here!" Her voice shook and real fear showed in her green eyes.

Devage looked at Brian. "What the hell is going on here?" he demanded, his good humor vanishing. "Where is Shannon?"

Brian hid his bewilderment at the man's genuine surprise. "I was going to ask you the same thing, Hicks."

"They've taken Shannon, sir!" Molly burst out as she appeared in the doorway.

Devage did not pay any attention to Molly or Corrinne who rushed over to him and put her hand on his arm. His eyes were locked with Brian's.

"Father, do something!" Corrinne exclaimed, tugging at his heavy coat. "They could kill her!"

Before anyone realized what was happening,

Devage upended the table sending Brian sprawling backward off his bench. One of the pistols fired and splintered the table top from below. Brian scrambled to retrieve the other gun. He grasped the handle and aimed it, but held his fire as Devage seized Corrinne by the neck and pulled her in front of him.

"Would you shoot a woman, Bedlowe?" he demanded above Corrinne's loud protest.

Brian was aware that his adversary's other hand was reaching for a weapon within his cloak but dared not risk a shot with Corrinne squirming in front of his target. The ugly barrel of the gun appeared around her tiny waist.

"Now if you are a true gentleman, sir, put your pistol down slowly," Devage ordered, assuming the upper hand.

"Father, what are you doing?" Corrinne gasped, half-strangled by his arm pressing against her throat.

"Surviving, Corrinne," he informed her curtly, watching young Bedlowe put his pistol aside.

"Your father is a fraud, Corrinne," Brian explained to the girl who had paled so much that he was certain she would swoon. "The real Jonathan Devage died with his wife in the pirate attack."

"No! Father, please . . ."

"Tell her, Devage. Tell her that you're a murderous swindler who saw a golden opportunity and took it!" Brian growled angrily. "Tell her that you conspired to kill Shannon."

Devage grimaced as he saw the horror on Corrinne's face. "I did, but I am not responsible for this. She gave us everything. What reason was there to pursue her death?"

Brian saw his attention waiver and dove for the gun. He pulled it up to fire when Devage's pistol reported thunderously. He heard the women screaming as the ball tore into his shoulder and knocked him back against the small hutch behind him. Dishes clattered to the floor, breaking around him. He saw Devage thrust his daughter to the floor and hesitate to make sure his shot had hit its mark. Painfully, Brian raised his gun and squeezed the trigger. The recoil jerked his shoulder unmercifully and his fading vision saw Devage disappear from the splintered-faced doorway and he realized his shot had missed before blacking out.

The water that trickled down the wall of the black cavern was starting to freeze. Her fingers could hardly bend anymore. Shannon huddled low and held her breath as the men with the lanterns passed the crates that sandwiched her against the icy stone wall. She had pulled some of the straw packing over her in an effort to fight the numbing cold that beckoned her to sleep.

She had lost track of time. All she knew was that if the man called Dickie and his companions found her, it meant certain death. When she discovered the stack of crates, she squeezed behind them and made the nest of straw. The men had passed her several times, but their numbers were so many that she dared not leave her seclusion. They seemed to be everywhere.

She let out a trembling sigh of relief as the light faded leaving her in total darkness again. Surely her father would know she was missing by now, she thought, trying to find a reason to keep going. Or perhaps the men might give up their search. She wondered if she had the strength left to find her way out of this cold hell.

She bit her lip as she heard a rustling noise in the

straw in the crate and fought the knowledge of its source. Suddenly something light dropped in her lap. She gasped and shoved it away frantically. It was warm and furry to her touch and she whimpered in an attempt not to cry outright. Decisively, she pulled herself to her feet. She was about to slide out from her niche when she saw lights coming her way and she dropped back down to the straw.

"Where the hell is the bloody bastard?"

"He's down 'ere somewhere, sir. We been lookin' in groups fer nigh on three hours."

"If I get my hands on him, I slit his throat. I need that girl alive!" The familiar voice made a grunting sound. "Dickie is a fool. She was out of the way. He should have left well enough alone."

"I tried to tell 'im so, Mr. Hicks, but ye know how strong in the 'ead, 'e kin be."

"I'm going back up. When you find him, tell him I want the girl alive. They've found out I'm not Jonathan Devage and she is my passage to France. They'd not try to stop me if I had her as hostage. Now is that clear, Smoot?"

"Aye, sir. Find 'er and keep 'er alive. I'll tell 'im."

As the lantern disappeared, Shannon's mind struggled from its astonishment. It seemed there was more than one kind of rat in these caves. She could not help the tinge of disappointment that lingered in her turmoil of emotions. Both her parents were really dead, killed by the man she had loved as a father—the man that raised her to fight, to be a survivor. By God, they would not get away with this.

She eased out of the small hiding place and held her cry as her furry companion ran across her foot. Again she started down the incline. If the smugglers stored their goods in here, they certainly would not have carried them from the height of the cave.

Perhaps there was an access to the rocky shore farther down.

Her progress was painstakingly slow. The rocky floor bruised her knees until she was forced to stand and feel her way with outstretched toes. She now realized what it must be like to be blind. She feared reaching the edge of a crevice and plunging to her death. The walking brought the ache of the cold back to her feet and hands again. She began to lose the sluggishness her straw bed had induced. It occurred to her that if it had not been for her furry companion, she may have lain there and frozen.

She rubbed her sleeved arms. Her dress was a heavy woolen weave, but she missed her cloak. At this rate, she still might freeze. It would just take longer. She caught her toe on a jagged piece of rock and fell forward, crying out as the fall knocked her breath away. She lay still for a moment and mentally checked to see if she had been seriously hurt. The only casualty was a torn sleeve at her elbow where she had scraped the hard path.

There was a dim light cast from around the corner of the passage where she lay. Someone would find her if she could not find another cover. She glanced around at the dark walls as she pulled herself to her feet. As her hand trailed down the side that rounded where the light was her arm gave way to the empty space that promised her refuge. She felt with her foot as well and finding firm rock, slipped into the narrow crevice. Her aching fingers protested as she locked them around the barrel of her empty pistol and held the wooden handle up in a club-like fashion.

Shannon's face pressed against the icy wall as the man turned the corner. His giant shadow was cast against the wall opposite her. To her relief he was alone. This was the opportunity she needed. If she could render him unconscious, she might arm herself and have light to expedite her escape. She hardly dared to breathe as he walked in a stooped position past her. Gathering her courage, she slid out of the niche and raised her pistol above his head.

"Watch it!" came warning whisper from behind her, making her hesitate too long. Her intended victim swung about and knocked the plunging cudgel out of her hand with a sharp blow on her wrist. Before she could react, someone grabbed her arms and held them so that she could not protect herself from the man who leaped at her. She started to curse them when his hand clamped over her mouth, pushing her head against the hard chest of his comrade.

"Shannon, it's Morgan," came a hushed whisper. "Now be quiet!"

Shannon stood motionless. She had to be hallucinating, she thought as she felt the man behind her relax his hold. She narrowed her eyes in the flickering candlelight at the rough-shaven face. It was only when they met the steel blue gaze that seemed to envelop her entire being that she believed him.

"Morgan . . ." she whispered, throwing her arms about his neck. Tears streamed down her face as she kissed the stubble on his face. His arms engulfed her wrapping his cloak about her as well. She clung to his warmth. She breathed the warm air through the heavy wool, and whispered as she returned her face to his. "I thought I'd never see you again."

"I feared the same," he answered, lowering his lips to hers and holding her as if he thought she might vanish.

Suddenly she pulled away. Her eyes sparkled as she

spoke. "Morgan, Jonathan Devage is not my father! He's in with these smugglers and Dickie is trying to kill me for knifing his brother. They weren't robbers, they were hired to kill me by my father . . . who is really a man named Hicks. But now he wants to use me to escape." She failed to notice the upturned corner of his mouth as he glanced at his first mate. "We have to get help and stop these rogues. There's too many for the three of us," she finished breathlessly.

"Damned right and they're all around us," Michael Finney snorted, looking around warily.

Shannon turned away from Hawke and hugged the big Irishman. "Oh Michael, I'm happy to see you, too!" she told him excitedly.

Finney winked at her mischievously. "And I'm glad to see ye, too. Now," he exclaimed quietly, "since we're all so glad to see each other, let's be movin'. I ain't goin' to be glad to see no damned smuggler."

"We're taking you home, Shannon."

Shannon looked back at Hawke. "But what about help?"

He removed his cloak and fastened it about her small shoulders. "I've sent for help. I have one little task to perform and then I'll join you. Finney, take her on ahead to the fork. Wait for me there if you can." He double checked the pistols that were strapped to his chest and picked up the lantern. He needed to insure that they would not be followed.

"Morgan . . ." Shannon hesitated as she saw the determined look on his face and knew she could not dissuade him. She did not want him to leave her again. She stepped up and kissed him affectionately. "Be careful, please."

He touched her face in a caress that made her want

436

to cling to him and beg him to stay with them. "I promise," he answered solemnly.

She watched until the light of his lantern disappeared. Finney held out his outstretched hand and she took it gratefully. It seemed her strength was giving out on her as she struggled to keep up with the long strides of the Irishman. When they reached the fork Hawke had mentioned, Shannon dropped to the floor and sat back against the wall. Morgan's cloak was warm and comforted her in the dampness.

Finney stooped over and started to rub her feet glancing up at her as she winced. He lightened his touch and continued as Shannon relaxed. The warmth and gentle masage made her eyelids heavy. She fought to keep her eyes on the passage they had just come through for the tall figure of the man she loved. Whatever he had done no longer mattered, she could not live without him.

When Hawke did appear, Shannon tried to pull herself to her feet, but her legs would not obey her mental commands. As he lifted her in his arms, she nestled her head against his chest. There was a strong smell of wood smoke in his clothing, but Shannon was too exhausted to question it. She was in his arms and that was all that mattered. She must have dozed, for when she opened her eyes, Hawke dropped her gently to her feet and pointed to a small hole in the ceiling of the cave where faint rays of light filtered down on them.

He hoisted Finney up through the opening and then handed her up to the Irishman who pulled her onto a dirt floor. As Finney hauled Morgan Hawke up beside him, Shannon saw a wooden ladder and could hardly believe her eyes as she recognized the blue settee in her parlor above the trap door. Finney preceded them up the ladder and swore, apparently disturbed at what he saw.

"What happened, lass?" Shannon heard him inquire.

As Hawke helped Shannon up the ladder, she saw Molly leaning over her cousin, wiping his forehead gently. Brian was deathly pale and his breathing was labored. His eyes were shut and fear seized Shannon as she found the strength to bound up the last few steps and go to her cousin.

"Brian!" Her voice choked on his name. She raised questioning eyes at Molly.

"Master Devage shot him. He took the ball in the shoulder. I got it out with a carving knife, but he's bled terribly." Molly forgot her concern for her patient as she leaned across him and hugged Shannon. "My God, you're all right!" she exclaimed.

"I'll go for a doctor," Finney offered, backing away from the group.

Hawke nodded and turned back to Molly, trying to ignore the pang of jealousy he felt as Shannon leaned over and kissed her cousin on the cheek.

"Devage escaped?" he asked, as Finney exited the room.

"Aye. He used Corrinne as a shield. Master Brian couldn't shoot him with her in the way. She's in a terrible state . . . in there." Molly nodded her head toward the kitchen.

"He was in the caves, Hawke,' Shannon spoke up, as she caressed her cousin's cheek. "That's how I knew he was not my real father. I heard him."

"Damnation!" Hawke swore, running his hand through his hair in frustration.

A groan from the unconscious man on the floor drew everyone's attention. Shannon smiled when her cousin's eyes fluttered open. He took a shaky breath and mumbled lowly. "You're safe."

Shannon nodded, her eyes misting.

"Everybody else all right?"

"Everyone but you," she whispered, brushing a lock of brown hair out of his face.

He laughed shortly and winced. "I stay here at the house and I'm the only one who gets shot!"

Shannon laughed with him and shook her head. "Are you ever serious?"

"Of course! I'm very serious about my nurse." Shannon was pleasantly surprised when he reached for Molly's hand and squeezed it. "She's kind of handy with a knife in her own way."

Shannon smiled at Molly, who blushed becomingly. "Then I shall leave him to you, Molly."

She was embarrassed when Morgan had to help her up. Her knees ached terribly from the abuse they'd received on the rock floor of the caverns. He carried her to the settee and deposited her gently. As he laid her back against the small pillows Shannon recalled Molly's mentioning of her sister. She was so tired, yet she could not rest until she saw to the poor soul that had suddenly lost everything.

"Morgan, I need to see Corrinne," she murmured tiredly.

"So do I," he told her. "But what I have to say can wait." His eyes rested on the untied laces of her bodice exposed in the parting folds of his cloak. Her camisole had slipped down provocatively.

Shannon glanced down and quickly rearranged the bodice. Now that she could see what she was doing, she could fix it. When she looked up, she answered the question he could not bring himself to ask. "They didn't hurt me. I . . . I bashed his head in with a rock. That's how I escaped,' she explained, seeing the relief come over his face.

He helped her up again and held her tightly to him

439

for a moment before releasing her to check on Corrinne. When they entered the kitchen, Corrinne sat quietly on a bench by the fire. Her pale face was red from crying and she held her arms folded across her chest, rocking back and forth. She did not notice them.

Shannon started across the room when the plank door burst open and a bearded man came in unannounced. He blew his warm breath on his hands and rubbed them together. When Hawke made no move to stop him, Shannon looked at him closer, recognizing the stocky tavernkeeper from Nose' Be.

"Cudge!" she cried as she rushed over to him and hugged him tightly.

Cudge's laugh was loud as he picked up the light girl and swung her around. "My goodness, you are a sight for these aging eyes. I thought we'd lost you in the fire."

"Fire?" Shannon asked.

He looked past her at Hawke. "Caught Devage and the lot of them. It seems some of their wares caught fire. There was only one way out of the cave. Right where myself and the sheriff waited with twenty or so men. Where's Finney and Bedlowe?"

"Devage shot Brian. Finney's gone to get a doctor," Hawke answered, glancing curiously at the blond woman who did not acknowledge their presence.

"Serious?" Cudgins asked.

"Shoulder wound."

"Hmm. His father's with the sheriff now. Maybe I should go tell him," the stocky man offered.

Hawke protested. "I can go. You've just come in out of the damnable cold."

"I insist. You take care of this little urchin," he teased, shaking Shannon's head with his heavy hand.

440

"I'll take care of her!" came a seething offer from nearby.

Shannon turned to see Corrinne standing by the hearth, her slender silhouette outlined by the flames behind her. Her sister glared at her with a hatred that frightened her as much as the barrel of the pistol leveled at her. Corrinne had apparently taken one of the guns Shannon had left on the mantel.

"You have ruined everything Shannon Brennan . . . or whoever you are!" she spat in rage. "You took my fiancé, you took my fortune, and now you've taken my father. I hate you!"

"Corrinne . . ." Hawke called out, walking slowly toward her. He froze when she pulled the hammer back on the pistol.

"Don't come any closer!" she cried hysterically. "I'll kill her and your damned baby!" Her breathing was rapid as she spoke. "You'll never see the whelp that has separated us. You can marry me and I'll give you a child if that is what you want."

Shannon looked at Corrinne incredulously. "You're not with child now?" she asked.

"I can give you one, Morgan," Corrinne begged, averting her eyes from Shannon. "I'm not weak like my mother. I could have a manor full of children if you would father them."

"But you're not with child now because I have not shared your bed since I returned, have I, Corrinne?" Hawke baited.

Corrinne shook her head and lowered her voice in a growl. "Not since she came. I have wanted you, Morgan. I want Snowden."

"You lying bitch!"

Shannon sprang across the short space between them and grabbed at the pistol before anyone could stop her. She twisted Corrinne's wrist until the woman dropped the gun harmlessly to the floor. Corrinne raked her nails at Shannon's face but Shannon turned to the side and brought her elbow up under her sister's chin, sending her backward onto the hearth. In an instant Shannon was on top of her. She yelped as Corrinne locked her fingers in the long dark hair and pulled unmercifully.

"Let go, damn you!" Shannon cursed, swinging her fist and striking the rouged cheek of the squirming woman under her.

Corrinne screamed hysterically and let go, drawing her hand to her face where the enraged girl had hit her. Shannon could feel herself being lifted off the sobbing woman and her own angry tears streamed down her face. Because of her she had nearly given up all that was dear to her and nearly met her end as well. Morgan Hawke handed Shannon to Henry Cudgins and bent over to help Corrinne up. She watched in disbelief as Corrinne clung to Morgan and he tried to quiet her, whispering gently.

Reason deserted Shannon for a moment. It was like the scene at the Banquet Hall. Corrinne had started the fight, yet he had taken her side. He had not broken the betrothal because Corrinne was weak. And now it was Corrinne he comforted when the crazed woman had tried to kill her, Shannon thought incredulously.

She backed away from Henry Cudgins who watched her as she turned and walked into the parlor. Molly looked at her anxiously, still holding Brian's hand while he somehow managed to sleep as she opened the door to the side of the hearth and started up the steps. She was tired of being strong. She needed to be alone to think. The strain of her recent experiences left her physically and emotionally drained. She barely made it under the covers of one of

442

the made-up beds before she collapsed in exhaustion and tears.

She did not hear Morgan climb the steps nor the click of his booted heels as he crossed the moonlit room to the small cot where she rested. His weight made the mattress sag as he sat down beside her and stroked her tangled hair that spread over her shoulders and back. She lay on her stomach, her face buried in the pillow.

"Shannon . . ." he called gently, leaning over and brushing his lips across the back of her neck.

"Wh . . . what?" she mumbled in the pillow, refusing to give up its cold solace.

"Come here, my love," he coaxed, trying to turn her to take her in his arms.

Shannon drew her arms about the pillow tightly and burrowed deeper. "G . . . go back to Cor . . . Corrinne," she sobbed miserably. "I . . . I don't n . . . need you."

"The woman is insane, Shannon. We've had to bind her so that she won't hurt herself or anyone else," Hawke explained patiently, trying to pry the pillow away. "Shannon, come here to me," he implored, at a loss for what to do to convince this strong-willed girl that he loved her. "Shannon, I need you."

His pained words reached her and she raised her head, afraid to believe her ears.

"If I have to, I will get down on my knees and beg," he said stiffly, "but I love you and I need you. I nearly drank myself into oblivion when you left me at Pulcherchurch. I almost went berserk when I found you had disappeared and I must have died a hundred times searching that cave, afraid I'd not find you and terrified that I would find your body. Shannon . . ."

Shannon released the pillow and rose up on her

arm. Her cold fingers pressed against his warm lips, ending his confession. She rolled against the wall and made room on the cot for him, pulling the covers back in invitation.

"Morgan," she said timidly, "I'm cold."

In one movement, she was in his arms. His body, warm and hard, pressed against her as he pulled the covers over them, boots and all. She raised her face to his and felt the rough brush of his beard as he lowered his mouth on hers tentatively, as if he feared she would change her mind. Her heart burst with joy and her blood warmed under his sensuous assault. When he lifted his head and peered down at her, she caressed the stubble on his cheek and whispered to him.

"I never could deceive you in your arms, Morgan, nor could I ever deny you. I need you just as much and I have never stopped loving you."

This time it was her lips that sought the hollow of his throat and moved up to his own. She would always belong to him, body and soul. She was as much his as she was Brennan's daughter.

Epilogue

Snowden seemed to blossom as brightly as the summer wild flowers that grew in abundance in the waving green fields on the estate. Servants that worked the land glanced up at the stone manor, majestic in its setting. Word had spread quickly that the midwife had been sent for the beautiful wife of the Lord of Snowden. There was friendly betting on whether or not the day would present Snowden with a future lord, but all wished the happy couple well.

Shannon reclined against the large pillows of the massive four poster bed in the master suite. The pain had been intense but short-lived. There had been no time to send for the doctor, so one of the local midwives had come quickly. The heavyset woman arrived just in time for the birth of Snowden's future lord. Now she concentrated on preparing for the current lord to visit his wife and new son.

When Shannon had dropped to the wrought iron seat in the courtyard with her first intense contraction, Lady Elaine who was working in the flower beds hurried to call her son. Morgan left his ledgers in his study and nearly ran down one of the servants to get to Shannon while his mother sent for the midwife. The last she had seen of her apprehensive husband was when the bustling woman who immediately assumed control of the situation ran him out of their bedroom.

"Would ye like a mirror, milady, to see if I've combed your hair to suit ye?" the woman asked, admiring the pretty girl in the bed whose face glowed in spite of the tortuous pain she had endured earlier.

Shannon shook her head. "I'm sure it's fine. I feel so pampered. You've already bathed me and dressed me in this beautiful lace gown."

"Well when you're an angel, ye can't help but look like one," the kind woman remarked. "Look at the color in her cheeks. She looks like she just come in from a walk in the gardens instead of birthin' a babe."

"With such a lovely mother and handsome father, my grandson cannot help but be the most beautiful baby ever born," Lady Elaine commented, picking up the newborn infant. She crossed the room and handed Shannon her son.

For the first time Shannon held the product of her love for Morgan. She stared at the squirming baby in awe. He was perfectly formed with miniature features. He had thick black hair that her mother-in-law had brushed up in a little curled tuft, soft as down. Shannon touched his cheek with the back of her fingers and his eyes opened. He immediately turned his face toward her fingers and tried to suckle them. When there was no result, a loud wail rose from the small puckered mouth and Shannon glanced at her mother-in-law panic-stricken.

"What's wrong with him?" she asked, trying to hand the baby back to Lady Elaine.

Her mother-in-law laughed and pushed the child back to his mother gently. "I cannot feed him. That is up to you."

"Just open up yer gown, milady. Put yer breast to his cheek. He'll know what to do," the midwife chuckled.

She leaned over and helped Shannon open the white laced gown Lady Elaine had made her for this special occasion. The tiny satin ribbons hung to the side as she revealed a bare breast to the baby. When it touched the baby's cheek, the infant whipped its small head around and made a loud sucking noise as his puckered mouth closed over the dark areola. It was a strange sensation and a warmth filled the girl that brought tears to her eyes as she watched the tiny fingers opening and closing as the baby boy nursed.

"May I come in now?"

Morgan's voice sounded impatient on the other side of the door. The women in the room glanced at Shannon and she nodded. When the Lord of Snowden was at last permitted in, they exited quietly to leave the new parents to their privacy. Shannon smiled at her husband who stood near the door and stared at her and his son in wonder.

"You can come closer, Morgan."

"Are you all right?" the man asked, still motionless.

"I'm fine," Shannon replied, her eyes misting. "Now come see your son."

Morgan approached the bed and leaned over, supporting his weight on the carved walnut headboard. His blue eyes studied his son and he reached down and just touched the tip of his finger to the fine black hair.

"Scrawny, isn't he?" he said awkwardly, drawing his hand away.

Shannon chuckled and the sudden movement startled their son. He drew his head away from her breast and howled. Shannon cooed softly and the baby returned to his feeding, sucking noisily.

"Well he won't stay scrawny if he eats like this all the time," she murmured, smothering her amusement so as not to startle the infant again.

"I'm jealous already."

Shannon blushed as his eyes rested on her breast. "Morgan!" she chided gently.

"I love you, Shannon," he said. He leaned over and kissed her tenderly. When he lifted his head, he stared at his son. "I have a name I hope you will consider for our son."

"What is that?" she asked. She had assumed it would be named after the late Lord of Snowden.

"Nicholas." He was pleased as his wife's eyes brightened to a blue that rivaled the summer sky.

"I think that is just . . . wonderful," Shannon whispered, touched by the thoughtfulness of the man she had married. A picture of a laughing giant of a man with flaming red hair came to her mind as she looked back down at their son. "Nick," she whispered softly. "Nicholas, it shall be, my lord."